The Devil to Pay

The Devil to Pay

Gene J. Parola

Rod — Thanks for your many kindnesses through the years — Gene 1/1 2001

Writers Club Press
San Jose New York Lincoln Shanghai

The Devil to Pay

Writers Club Press
an imprint of iUniverse, Inc.

For information address:
iUniverse, Inc.
5220 S. 16th St., Suite 200
Lincoln, NE 68512
www.iuniverse.com

ISBN: 0-595-20653-0

Printed in the United States of America

Dedication

This work is dedicated to my first mate, my help mate and my soul mate, with whom I've partnered for many years in projects domestic, professional, nautical and spiritual. Thank you, Shirley.

Gene

Epigraph

'The devil to pay and only half a bucket of pitch' was the original expression. This is understood when it is known that the 'devil' was the longest and most difficult seam to pay and was found near the garboard strake; hence, 'between the devil and the deep blue sea.' 'Pay' is from the French word 'poix' meaning 'pitch', hence 'to pitch the seams'.

Leland P. Lovett, Lt.Cdr.,USN,
Naval Customs, Tradition and Usage
U.S. Naval Institute, Annapolis, MD, 1939

'The devil to pay and only half a bucket of pitch' symbolically describes the imbalanced situation of sailors ever since man first pitted his puny strength against the overwhelming might of sea and wind. Often only his will to live, his tenacity—and a little luck allowed him to survive and confront these elements again. Such seasoning builds a sailor's courage and confidence to confront any of the far lesser threats of a man-made kind ashore.

GJP

Contents

Chapter One

Matt did not lead an uninteresting life, but it had certainly never been this interesting. Until yesterday, he had not seen an automatic weapon up close. But now, in less than one normally tranquil, tropical night, his life had been threatened by two.

She stared at him over the muzzle of the Uzi and as he raised his hands, the last remnant of the torn shirt fell away and he stood naked before her.

Once I had thought to begin this report there. My editor had approved that lead when it was a Sunday feature piece. But before it got to print, the several smelly aspects that made up the larger hard news story caused everything to be safely snuffed out. With no explanation.

Sven, the delivery captain, had called it incident number two in his testimony before the Coast Guard Board of Inquiry. But it was actually number four as it related to GULL's delivery. And that series of events, however harrowing and terminal, paled almost to insignificance when placed in the larger context.

And that context began to make sense in the 1963 meeting at the Chinese restaurant on I Street in D.C. But I have only Carlos' story about that parley. The official records of both sides are, of course, silent about it. No surprise there. And Carlos has never surfaced since the shooting in the wee hours of that pivotal Miami night.

Leda's discovery is not the best place to begin also because Matt would never have been confronted by the Uzis except for errors and chance. Had the giant not mistaken her for his actual target, the cruiser would not have been a derelict and fair game for scavengers. And if not for Diego's single wild shot, Sven would never have risked stopping at the derelict.

Leda's entry into the affair, while dramatic and early, is not so significant as the pivotal role she played later, at what one Agency report referred to as the "Biscayne Incident".

As for the other women, Flash and the party girl, they are not starters either, for they flip into the deck—cards being shuffled—space and time separating them. And there they stay until all are dealt in the single hand played in the dark lower deck of the burning casino ship. That one was a trump card, impacts GULL'S story only after the fact and she had no effect on the final moonlit confrontation in the Gulf Stream months later.

And Sybil was the wildest of cards.

Sven was bound, he felt, to relate to the CGBOI only what he, the Captain, had seen and heard, so he hadn't counted the incident that occurred in the morning before he and Matt arrived at GULL's anchorage. In separate interviews with me both men started with the next one.

GULL

The engine noise had long since made conversation impossible and the vibration plus the heat from the tropical sun had lulled Matt into a drowsy haze. He hadn't been sure what had aroused him, the pilot's rapping on the side window or Sven leaning over him to squint against the glare of the sun speckled sea below. At first Matt saw only the glare, but then the pilot made a wide banking turn and as the plane came between the sun and the sea, he saw the white cabin cruiser, 55 or 60 feet long, lying partially submerged in a small cove.

Suddenly all the sensations of flight intensified as the plane dropped down to skim breathtakingly close astern of the sunken boat.

"GAVIOTA," Sven shouted as they passed the gleaming lettering on the transom. Matt had no chance to respond for the roaring engine was straining now to regain altitude.

"Did you see anyone?" the pilot shouted as he leveled off.

"Not on deck," Matt yelled back.

"Most likely anyone still on that barge would be on deck. She's listin' ta almost 45 degrees," Sven observed.

The pilot completed another turn and now began a long shallow descent, this time rumbling past the length of the boat, 20 or 30 feet off her starboard side and hardly more than that above the water. At the last minute he pulled up sharply over the mildly sloping beach and the low scrub growth that passed for trees on the small Bahamian cay.

GAVIOTA rested on the bottom, listing sharply to port in 7 or 8 feet of water at her stern, her high bow thrust awkwardly out of the rapidly shoaling water of the cove. Her anchor line was still stretched taut against the pull of the elevated bow.

"Ain't nobody on her, Pete," Sven shouted to the pilot. "Couldn't stand up with her listin' that bad. Woulda gone ashore. Anyway, they'd aheard us the first pass we made and woulda come topside if they was lookin' fer help."

Pete, trying to raise Nassau on the radio, seemed to sense the finality of Sven's evaluation and having regained altitude, set his course for Elbow Cay.

"Somethin's funny," Sven muttered in Matt's ear. "Can't put my finger on it, but somethin' ain't right about that boat."

Sven enjoyed that special dispensation that nature has bestowed on the male half of the race. He languished in that temporal matinee of robust middle agelessness; maintaining a physical virility under a great mane of wild blonde hair that had only lately surrendered its edges to the inevitable gray. But the shaggy black brows asserted his Mother's Italian genetic contribution.

Sven had spent his entire life around boats. In the early years he sailed as cabin boy with his Down East, Maine grandfather on one of the last square riggers; as a young adult, the captain of a wealthy man's yacht; his middle years since, primarily as a surveyor and as a specialist for the various Maritime museums around the country, one of which always needed his counsel on some aspect of the rapidly disappearing world of sailing ships.

In between these bouts with the suit and tie world, he did what he liked best to do—deliver sailing yachts from one place to another. While he spent much of the time grousing about the poor seamanship displayed by most pleasure boaters, he privately enjoyed the task of preparing a craft for a long distance voyage and took great satisfaction in knowing that when the boat was safely delivered it would be in better shape than when he came aboard.

"Nassau says no *Mayday* report received." Pete yelled. "How long do you figure she's been there, Sven?"

"Hard ta tell fer sure." Sven paused to think. "Not much seagull crap on her yet and very little build-up of sand on the windward side of her hull. Maybe she's been there two or three tides, not mor'n three though."

Sven's powers of observation fascinated Matt. They were so subconscious, yet so keen. The plane had swooped past the derelict twice at high speed by any measure, and Sven's all encompassing gaze had amassed enough data to fill several typewritten pages if anyone wanted or needed to know that much.

The two men were an unlikely pair, the Down Easter who lived off a depth and breadth of life experience and Matt, the computer type, whose experience was largely theoretical.

They had teamed up quite by accident on a delivery five years before and Matt had been such an eager pupil that Sven had called upon him with increasing regularity when he needed a delivery crew. The label 'computer whiz' allowed Matt to enjoy a very flexible work schedule and since his fledgling business had grown large enough to support a manager, he thought little of taking two weeks off to help Sven run a boat down the Intracoastal Waterway or even longer with a little notice.

Matt's trim athletic build and his dark good looks were also in contrast with the blond Viking quality of his older colleague. The two men, like many teams, found strength in their opposing characteristics.

Matt had made a habit of sharpening his own critical eye on each trip he made with Sven. As his powers of observation and analysis had improved, it had become a game between the men to attempt to figure out as much about a boat owner as possible from the way he kept and operated his craft. The effort had paid off for Matt in more ways than one. He now found himself applying his sharpened abilities to his entire world of experience.

"I'll report GAVIOTA to the Island police and ask around among my insurance company friends," Pete broke in again.

"Ayeah," Sven observed, "ya oughta get a few bucks finders fee."

"That's you down there," Pete responded, pointing beyond the window to the right, and he began a slow, banking turn.

Matt got first sight of the boat they had come for as she appeared in the transparent rectangle for a moment. She lay in a shallow cove created by the two arms of the narrow angular island that, along with several others, was called Elbow Cay. He mentally reviewed the fact sheet that Sven had sent him in the letter inquiring about his availability. Boat name: GULL; 40' on the water line, 60' overall, cutter rig, with a bowsprit, wooden hull, (a modified Herreschoff design), diesel power, latest electronics.... The list went on and at the bottom: Location: Elbow Cay, 24 degrees, 08 minutes North Latitude, 78 degrees, 25 minutes West Longitude, Bahamas Islands. Destination: No Name Port, Key Biscay, Florida.

"S'funny," Sven remarked.

"What?" Matt asked, straining to see.

"Look at her."

Pete, having flown a little beyond the island, banked again and began a long low return glide past the anchored boat in order to search the shallow water for coral heads.

The plane flashed past; the anchored boat flashed accordingly in and out of view. Matt leaned across the narrow aisle as the plane leveled, then banked to start the landing approach. His pulse had suddenly quickened. Elements of the scene below were contradictory and as he straightened up in his seat he became aware of the 'gaze'.

Sven, instead of looking out of the window, studied Matt's furrowed face and waited—a small smile playing at the corner of his mouth.

"One?" he said.

"No awning," replied the younger man.

"Two?" Sven barked.

"She's anchored perpendicular to the tide flow. She's straining both her anchors in this ebb."

"Three?"

"The dink is fouled under the stern anchor line."

"Four?"

"Companion way hatch closed and boarded."

"Meaning?"

"No one aboard, unless he's got an air conditioner."

"Five?"

"But the dink is tied astern, so how could he have gone ashore?"

"Swam!" Sven declared and shouted, "Five?" again.

"No tracks on the beach below the high water mark and darn few above it that are fresh. OK so he got tired of waiting for us and left in another boat."

"Looks that way," Sven agreed, as the plane taxied past the tethered dinghy. But Matt knew that he was not happy with the deduction.

Pete stepped deftly to the starboard pontoon, released the anchor from its mount and cast it off. The plane, having just lost its forward motion, began to drift aft in the 2 to 3 knot tidal current as Pete payed out anchor line. He snubbed the line, stopping the plane before it could foul GULL's stern anchor rode.

Sven poised on the port pontoon, a boat hook in his hand. "Damn fool thing to do," he growled as he stretched to reach the lashing on the dinghy's cover. "Gimmie a hand here, will ya?" he asked as Matt slipped out of the plane. "When I pull it free of that rode, it'll want to drift with the tide. Get a hand on it if ya can."

The dinghy cover was expensive. Two flexible bows, one fore and one aft, held the cover in a gentle curve to insure rain runoff. The tide had caught the small boat under, and perpendicular to the anchor line and raised it up so that the line compressed the cover between the two bows. The higher it rose on the tide, the tighter it had been caught.

With first a push and then a pull, Sven disengaged the pretty little wooden boat from its trap and muscled it, stern to tide, in Matt's direction.

"When ya get the cover loose, take the end of the lashin' an' tie it to the pontoon strut. We'll dump our gear in an' retrieve it later when we're aboard," he ordered. "I'll get yer bag and bed roll."

The dinghy's painter was long enough for the little boat to have swung free beyond the anchor line, but it was tied up short to the larger boat. A flood of puzzling new questions preoccupied Matt as he fumbled at the lashings with one hand and held the boat against the tide with the other.

Many knowledgeable yachtsmen anchored fore and aft in these waters when the channel was too narrow for the boat to swing on her hook. Another common practice was to drop two anchors an appropriate distance apart in line with the tidal flow, then lead both rodes forward so that the boat changed direction with the tide, but remained virtually in the same spot.

Only a dolt would anchor perpendicular to the flow, however, Matt thought heatedly.

"And why cover a beautiful cedar dink in this heat?" he asked aloud as Sven approached.

"To keep the rain out."

"And keep the fungus alive and well inside. Hold this will you? This guy couldn't even tie a square knot. Look at this mess."

The narrow pontoon allowed no room for Sven to deposit the armload of sleeping bags, so he squatted, compressing them between his torso and thighs, thus freeing his hand to hold the dinghy.

"I thought you said this guy was a sailor?" Matt muttered.

"Don't know this new fella. This Ramariez. He just came aboard a few months ago."

"Finally." Matt lifted the edge of the boat cover, pulling to slack the line all around, and then he peered into the shadowy depths. Suddenly he stopped and looked at Sven. "Does Pete know Ramirez?"

"Yeah, why?"

"Better call him. I need an identification more than an introduction."

* * *

And so it had begun—even before they had gotten aboard GULL.

Pete had somehow known how to handle things and after a lengthy exchange on the radio with the police in Nassau, he went on about his business. Sven and Matt sat in the sweltering sun for two hours, unable to do anything in preparation for their departure except to immediately weigh the offending stern anchor and stow it on the foredeck. Then they waited for the police helicopter to arrive. Finally it did.

"And how long will you be at Dinner Key, Mr. Olafson?" The Bahamian policeman was very precise; a replica, he was sure, of his predecessor, Major Barnes. Barnes, a relic of the English presence, had not gone with the flag. When the Union Jack came down in Nassau for the last time and was sent home to Parliament, a few white colonials who had been good at making black friends had managed to stay. Barnes had been one—respected for his efficiency and even-handedness in enforcing the white man's law.

But he was gone now too—replaced by Inspector Brown.

"Just long enough to cash th' man's check, Inspector, an' visit a few friends who live aboard there," Sven replied as he eyed the too-polished, too-young police official who stood rather absurdly in GULL's cockpit consulting his too-lengthy notes.

"Then back to Boston?"

"Dorchester, just outside of Boston."

"Ah, yes. And Matthew Blair." Matt winced at the sound of his full name but looked steadily at the posing youth before him. Sitting in a pool of sweat, he studied the cocky young official whose milky blackness was in mild contrast to his pressed, white uniform. A descendent of an escaped slave girl and an English shop owner, Inspector Brown had graduated from the PoliceAcademy in London. Now at age 24 with a purchased rank and an inflated sense of self importance, he stood in GULL's cockpit wasting the last crucial hours of the day that had been slipping away ever since the ghastly face of the dead Ramirez had first appeared in the boat bottom.

"I may have to fly back to Boston without Sven. Since we lost today, we'll be delayed in getting back," Matt concluded.

Inspector Brown had stood with them in the sun soaked cockpit for two hours, listening, asking questions and taking notes. Even when he went below to poke gingerly into the messy piles of groceries and spare parts that littered the cabin sole, no trace of perspiration dared wilt his collar nor dampen his armpits.

"But we may contact you again. The investigation is not closed. Three days, at most to Florida, Captain?" He continued, not waiting for Sven to reply, "We shall talk again then."

He pocketed the notebook and stepping deftly up onto the cockpit seat and over the teak splash board, he straddled the lifeline a moment then jumped primly into the inflatable. The small boat reacted badly and he abruptly sat down on the thwart. And just as abruptly the coxswain cranked the outboard to life and the boat sped away toward the waiting helicopter—the inspector sitting, knees primly together, almost comically erect in the bow.

"About damn time," growled Sven.

The end of English influence in the islands had done nothing, in Sven's opinion, to improve the speed of minor minions in the Civil Service. In fact, it now took noticeably more time, if one were white, to transact any sort of business—a circumstance that tended to enrage Sven. His narrow conception of economics and his memories of the prevailing poverty of these same islanders, made him very impatient with the new Bahamians who appeared to bite the tourist hand that fed them, particularly the yachtsman tourist. And it was Sven's streak of Yankee stubbornness that made him choose to meet GULL at Elbow Cay—to avoid a Nassau Customs agent who had insulted him years ago.

"Wasted the whole damn day. It'll take till dark now just ta clear a path ta a berth."

The statement was only a small exaggeration. They had arrived just after two p.m. and two hours had passed before Inspector Brown arrived. Now another two hours had been lost to the inquiry. And the boat below deck was a jumbled mess.

According to the prior arrangements, GULL was to be ready to sail upon their arrival. Ramirez was to have been flown back to Nassau by their pilot and they were to have put to sea immediately. Sven had agreed to such an arrangement only because he had moved this particular boat several times before and knew it and the owner well. The yacht was well found, well maintained and sailed regularly. Ramirez, a Cuban refugee, could not enter the U.S. but had been hired full time so that when the yacht was in the islands, it would have a resident crew and would not be left unattended when the owner and his guests had to hasten back home to mundane commitments on short notice. Another Cuban immigrant maintained the boat in Florida but never sailed with her because of his young family.

The two men stood in the cockpit squinting down the companionway hatch.

GULL's cockpit was flanked by two seats seven feet long and a cross seat aft of the helm completed a horseshoe shape which was closed at the forward end by a raised bridge deck running in a gentle hump athwart ship. This bridge deck was some ten inches higher than the cockpit seats where it met them at each forward end. The companionway, shuttered by two small folding doors, opened off the bridge deck at the center, its steep steps covered by a sliding hatch cover of narrow, matched planks of finely fitted teak. A few feet forward was the first of two transparent, hinged hatches that gave light and air to the large main saloon below. At about mid-ship, the mast jutted through the teak planking of the cabin top and a Fiberglas deck box nestled aft of it under the gooseneck fastener of the high boom.

The forward hatch and the chocks for the dinghy spotted the foredeck. A roller furled genny, anchored to the butt of the bow sprit and functioning as a staysail was teamed with a roller furled jib at the tip of the sprit.

Sven spoke first. "No use putting up the awnin' now. Sun'll shine right under it. Let's get a coupla wind scoops in the hatches though. Mebby it'll cool it enough for us ta work."

The men had moved forward to the commodious deck box just aft the mast and had begun to unlatch the top when the last throb of the police chopper faded, panting away toward Nassau.

Suddenly a quiet tropical evening was in the offing and a serenity descended on the anchorage that only a sailor knows. Both men straightened a moment as if to retune dulled senses. Subconsciously, they each scanned the horizon, cast a weather eye to the sky, then bent again to the locker and the series of tasks at hand.

Soon, two nylon scoops were gulping the fresh breeze, funneling it into the steaming bowels of the yacht where the men stood staring uncertainly at the chaos before them.

GULL was a beautifully built boat. Her mahogany joinery gleamed in the late light pouring in horizontally through the portholes. Matt stood to the left of the ladder in front of the chart table which nestled aft beneath the bridge deck. Above the table a short row of books—light lists, island pilots, almanacs—shared a shelf with a VHF radio, a wind speed indicator, a combination depth-finder/anchor alarm and a compact stereo system. At a point directly aft of the ladder, the transparent lid of a circuit breaker box glowed with red pilot lights. Along the port quarter a settee, with a deep, richly upholstered seat and a high back, was strewn with books, sound tapes, magazines and odds and ends which had been pulled from the rail-protected shelf running the length of the main cabin above it. Amidships portside, finely crafted mahogany locker doors stood agape, the contents disheveled or dumped on the sole in front of them.

On the starboard side, a pilot berth was tucked into the space beneath the bridge deck and starboard cockpit seats. Its mattress, pillow and linen had been piled at the shadowy aft end in order to gain access to a locker underneath. Engine spare parts from that space were strewn about—some with split plastic bags allowing the grease coated contents to defy quick remedy.

Forward of the berth, a U-shaped settee semi-surrounded a fine teak dinette table, one-half of its hinged top folded over the other half, and piled high with the contents of lockers that formed the settee back rests. The shelf above had again been emptied onto the disarray of settee cushions. A section of the banister-like rail of finely turned spindles had been ripped from the shelf and it hung perilously from one shattered end by a single gleaming brass screw

Beyond that, the galley—its gimbaled stove tilted under the imbalanced load of utensils and packaged food—suffered the same abuse in every respect as its neighboring areas. Foil wrapped packets had been removed from the freezer built into the back of the forward curve of the dinette settee. They sat defrosting on the flat surface above it. The galley sink and cupboards were backed up against a short bulkhead running down the centerline forming a narrow companionway with the lockers to port. Beyond, a door closed off the forward compartment. Inside it, to starboard was the head, opposite, a hanging locker to port. The V-berths were commodious but the space between them at the door was the only place in the boat without full headroom. The most forward of the transparent hatch covers opened there onto the foredeck and it was through that, and over the piles of spillage round-about, that they had hung one of the wind scoops.

"Look on the navigation table there an' see if ya can find a stores log, Matt."

"Got it," he replied after a short shuffle. He opened the small spiral binder and quickly scanned the lists of supplies and spare parts.

"Jesus, it'll take a week to stow all this again." Matt leafed through page after careful page, each locker identified by name or location and a list of items stored therein.

"Don't need no log ta see that," Sven growled. "Them piles a-crap do that just fine. See if what's piled next to a locker is what's supposed to be in there. If the piles are dependable that a-way, then go down the list an cross off anythin' that's broke open. Put the open stuff inta one a-them black garbage bags from the galley. If the pile is still too big to stow quick, cross off anythin' *we* don't need and pitch it too."

Matt heard the emphasis on 'we' and after filling several large bags with spilled cartons, he deftly stroked out the Stroganoff in boil bags,

Instant Rice Pilaf, and Keech-in-a-Kan. The lockers readily accommodated the remaining cans of baked beans, beef hash, soup and other 'instant' foods of Sven's definition.

The spare engine and rigging parts were not so simply dealt with.

By the time the heavy trash bags were rowed ashore and their contents buried amid the scrub growth, the pale light of a waning moon flecked the water with silver. An hour later, after a hearty dinner of soup, chunks of cheese and crackers, the two exhausted men sank onto the cockpit cushions. The wind, in seeming sympathy, began to soften and die too.

"Just as well we ain't ready.... This wind is gonna lay fer sure."

"Maybe it'll come back stronger in the morning if it gets a little rest." Matt smiled at his own humor. "If it doesn't, we can motor for a while."

"Not 'til we get the engine a runnin' we won't"

"What's wrong with the engine?"

"Ya think they got what they was a lookin' fer," Sven asked instead.

"They must have. They left."

"Then why'd they button this thing up tighter than a spinsters thighs? Why not just take the prize and go. Why go to all the trouble? Why not just dump the body?" He waited a few minutes, then went on, "If they didn't want him a floatin' about, why not take him with them 'till they got inta deep water."

"What are you saying?"

"Well, if I didn't find what I was a-lookin' fer I'd lock things up and come back better prepared. After all that trouble and them a killin' a man, don't you think they'd wanna take a longer, closer look for whatever it is?

"Tell ya what I think. I think they was a gonna take her in somewhere so's they could spend some time."

"What? And they couldn't get the engine started?"

"Yep."

Matt glanced down at the key protruding from the ignition switch. Impulsively, he turned it and hit the starter button. The starter solenoid did not even click.

"Ya see!" It was a statement, not a question. "Think about it."

"OK What do we know?" Matt leaned forward and peered quizzically at his older friend who had finally removed his canvas hat, allowing wisps of a mane of sweaty hair to blow dry in the last gentle sighs of breeze.

"Number one: This boat was ready to sail. Pete dropped off th' owner an his cronies in Miami yesterday. Number two: Ramariez stayed here, waitin'. Number three: Somebody a lookin' fer something came aboard, killed him, then ransacked the boat."

"Wait a minute," Matt countered. "How about ransacked the boat, then killed him?"

"What's th' difference?"

"I think they ransacked the boat first."

Matt had opened the cockpit seat behind the helm giving access to the lazarette. An English-made outboard motor hung from brackets on each side. The back of the ignition panel and a taped bundle of wires clung to the forward wall . He pulled on each wire until he separated out the disconnected end of a red one.

"They didn't find what they were looking for and decided to take the boat away, but Ramirez had pulled the ignition wire to keep them from moving her. When he wouldn't tell them what he had done or how to fix it, they got mad and killed him." He touched the wire to a terminal, hit the button, and the starter growled momentarily.

"Anybody who knew anything about boats could have found the loose wire, maybe. But not just anybody. Especially if they were depending on an experienced crew."

Matt fished his rigging knife out of his pocket and using the blunt end of the blade as a screwdriver, secured the wire to the terminal. He punched the button to check and the engine responded. He turned the key and the lagoon was silent again. But before the thoughtful Sven could speak the VHF cracked into life with a call to GULL. It was Pete in Nassau.

"Medical Examiner says Ramirez was killed sometime about 11 a.m.," came the report. "Looks like he was pistol whipped, then thrown over the side. He had salt water in his lungs."

"Like hell," Sven growled.

"Something interesting on that cruiser, too," Pete continued. "No report on her loss, but she left Walker Cay two days ago in the a.m. After having fished out of there a couple of days, the owner was met by his wife; she flew in on a private charter—buddy of mine from Nam outa Miami. He said her name was Leda Malone. Dock master at Walker said the guy signed his credit card slip Eddie Malone."

"Yeah, yeah," Sven thumbed the transmit button and broke in. "So get ta the interesting part."

"Dock master at Walker said the day before yesterday, Saturday, a big Cuban—and he stressed that the guy was big, about seven feet, was snooping around asking about a boat named GULL. When he happened to see Malone leave, he stopped mid-sentence, ran to his boat and started yelling '*gaviota*' into his radio. Then it seems he almost had a fit when he couldn't get someone to fly him out. He finally got back on his boat and took off." Pete paused, then, "I think I saw a Spanish-English dictionary on the navigator's shelf when I was aboard today. Why don't you look and see what '*gaviota*' means in English? I gotta go. Call me when you get under way."

"We ain't a-goin' nowhere 'till mornin'. We just got the stores off the cabin sole. I wanna take a good look at this rig in the daylight before we so much as heave the anchor."

"OK. Keep in touch."

"'Bout this GAVIOTA thing. Did you get a position on her when we was there today?"

"Yeah. She's at…just a minute…she's about 20-25 miles north-northeast of you. Almost a oh-three-oh or three-five magnetic from you." Pete paused, waiting for Sven to come back. Then, "You going over for a look at her?" The radio crackled again as he waited.

"Naw. Naw, she's outa the way. I gotta sail about a three-twenty-five or thirty. I'll call ya in the morning when we're under way. Out."

Pete, whose livelihood depended on such things, signed off properly and again the lagoon was silent. Sven, who had drawn the microphone from over the navigation table to his perch on the bridge deck, stretched to reach the hook to replace it and Matt asked for the dictionary.

"Don't need it. Back in the late fifties a bunch a smooth-talkin' Miami real estate types tried to get their hooks inta a bunch a smooth talkin' Cubans who was gettin' out of Havana with some of their dough ahead a Castro. They was a-gonna build this great big condo in Coconut Grove—one of the first in them days. Seems the Cubans was smoother talking than the Miami boys and they left the locals with real red faces. What made it worse, the Cubans insisted on naming the place *Las Gaviotas*."

"Damn, you're as bad as Pete. So what the hell is the point of all this?"

"*Gaviota* is Spanish for gull. The Miami boys was gulled outa their money and every morning they had to look at the building with their shame name written all over it."

"So, two boats named GULL." Matt ran down the implications: "A big Cuban inquisitive about the whereabouts of a boat named GULL seems surprised when he realizes that there may have been a misunderstanding by translating '*gaviota*' to 'gull'. He takes off in pursuit of GAVIOTA. Both boats fall to bad luck within a few hours of one another." He paused a moment. "You think that's what happened to the cruiser? The big Cuban got to it?"

"Real possible," Sven nodded. "The guy who owns this boat ain't a marina rat. He likes to be at sea. I'd guess that he didn't make port again, once he cleared entry in Bimini, 'till he had ta hop ashore in

Nassau yesterday. Anybody looking to find this boat at a dock would have ta do what the Cuban did: wear hisself out—hell, there ain't no cays north of Walker—and then he'd settle for anythin' that might save a chewin' out by his boss."

"Even to boarding the wrong boat?"

"Somebody smarter than me once said, desprit men do desprit things." He reflected a moment then, "So they ransacked GAVIOTA, didn't find anythin', then found GULL and they know this has ta be the one where it's at." Then he finished thoughtfully, "Whatever it is."

"How'd they find GULL?

"I don't know. This is way off the beaten track. They

musta had a lookout in a small boat lurking around Nassau in case it showed up there too."

"What makes you so sure it was a small boat?"

"Well, I think that if they had a big one it would have been doing what the Cuban was doing—out checking harbors. When Ramirez left Nassau right away, it radioed the big boat and then followed GULL here." He paused a moment, then went on. "Wherever the big boat was, it was too far away ta get here soon and so this morning the guys in the little boat boarded her." He paused, then went on. "If it had a-been a big one, they'd a towed her off somewhere."

"And when they didn't find what they were looking for, they tossed Ramirez overboard."

"Naw. He drowned, if the M.E. says he did, but he wasn't never all the way in the water. Them polly parrot threads he was wearin' would a showed a dunking."

"Polyester doesn't shrink."

"Naw, but it supports a layer of pure salt crystals when the water dries—takes a broom to brush 'em off. If the body hadn't been naked when the M.E. got it, or if somebody had thought to take a careful look at them clothes, they'd a seen salt on the surface of his pants. You could tell how much of him had been in the water by the line of crystals just below the belt all the way around his body."

"I'm missing something here," Matt said. How could he drown standing in water that didn't reach his waist?"

"Naw, ya don't understand. Th' salt crystals wuz above the line. He was dunked, head first. His pant legs never got wet."

"Maybe he wouldn't tell them what they wanted to know and they over-did it trying to persuade him," Matt reasoned. Then added thoughtfully, "At least that explains why they killed him."

"Makes as much sense as the rest," Sven shrugged. He had backed down the companionway as he listened and now he boosted the bound sleeping bags up to his young friend.

"How do you see the rest of it?" Matt asked, running his fingers through his dark, curly hair. His longish hair was the last vestige of a period of student days and college faculty life. His cropped curls were a sop to the business world he now owed his livelihood to—but they were not very short. He pursed his lips, smelling the faint aroma of the soup he had not completely washed from his full mustache, but he was too tired and it was too hot below to make another trip to the head.

Sven was silent as he loosed the ties and spread his bag on the starboard cockpit cushion. Matt began to remove his deck shoes while he waited. "Gets iffy after that," Sven finally ventured. "Let's say Ramirez did loosen the ignition wire. Don't say much for the bad guys if they couldn't find a problem like that."

"Not if they're lubbers. And I think that's the key here. These guys don't know a damn thing about boats. They tried to sink GAVIOTA in water too shallow to fill her, they cover a wooden dink…."

"Reason enough for that." interjected Sven. He now lay full length on his back, squinting through the accumulated facts at the stars above him.

"Right, but why'd they leave him? Hide him?"

"Because they planned ta come back with a boat big enough ta tow GULL somewhere so they could dismantle her—piece by piece, if necessary. And they didn't want him floatin' around, attractin' attention while they was gone."

"So," Matt began in summary, "you think it was a stakeout that found her late yesterday after the owner flew out, then jumped Ramirez when it got light enough to see this morning."

"Yeah, Ramirez probably stayed in port just long enough to top up his tanks, so th' stakeout had ta follow him here."

By now Matt had also reclined, and seeking some clarity, had begun to isolate the navigation stars. There was order in their location and juxtaposition and that order was reassuring right now. The wavelets lapped the waterline and somewhere a fish broke the surface with a muted splash. When he finally spoke, his voice had a quieter tone.

"Did you notice the stand of mangrove on the opposite side of the island when we flew in?"

Sven allowed as how he had.

"Let's assume that Ramirez was smart enough not to let his tormentors know he was expecting us. Let's say they were done with their preliminary search and were waiting for the larger boat to come. The tide turns, Ramirez is dead. Why do they leave?"

"Because mebbe he was dumber than that. Mebbe he told 'em what time we was to come. Ta scare 'em off. But they didn't scare, they just went off ta meet the big boat—warn it not ta come yet and ta hide when it got here."

"And they were hidden in the mangroves when we flew in and we couldn't see them."

"Yeah, they didn't expect that the first thing we'd do was uncork that dink. Certainly not while Pete was still here."

"Damn good thing we called the cops when we did, or they'd have been down on us as soon as Pete left."

"Damn good thing we found Ramirez when we did. If they was a-watchin' from somewhere, they knew right then it was over. We'd call the cops. I'm sure they took off then. They had no way of monitorin' the frequencies Pete uses, but they knew he'd call the cops right away and they had no way of knowin' where a police patrol might be. So I suspect they got out of here pretty fast, sos to be far enough away when the cops did arrive, by sea or sky, that they wouldn't be connected to this cay."

"I didn't hear any motor."

"Naw, with the high spine of the island between us and us not lookin' to hear anything special, we mighta heard it and didn't notice it."

Matt lay down again. "Yeah, they were probably long gone by the time Little Napoleon's chopper showed up."

It was quiet a while, then Matt said, "So they met the big boat…."

"…or radioed it and it stayed away," Sven finished.

Silence lay heavy on the lagoon again. The fish leapt. Somewhere on the island a nocturnal insect ventured a tentative staccato call. The wavelets lapped the water line.

"What if…," Matt started. "What if they were so sure this was the right boat and wanted it so badly for a thorough inspection, that they'd risk being seen by the cops from the air and they'd stay hidden in the mangroves all afternoon…waiting for the bigger boat, stay until it was dark..?" Matt looked over at Sven.

Sven began to snore softly.

Chapter Two

I depend heavily on these transcripts and find them reliable in that the interviews were held separately and all the stories match. I'm fortunate that all of them, even the untutored, Diego, are perceptive people—and very articulate.

In every case the happenings were still fresh enough in their memories to assure accuracy and yet after-the-fact enough so that the overburden of emotion, tension and fear, would no longer tend to inflate the experience. Nonetheless each man sat on the edge of his chair as he told of the first night aboard GULL.

Sven, with a touch of his seldom heard dry humor, dubbed their opponents:

THE BAD GUYS

It was one of the few areas on which the two men had failed to come to a meeting of the minds.

Sven refused to accept the possibility that a computer could be anything like a human brain and Matt refused to allow him to refuse.

Matt pointed out how the machine consulted a program list of items, chose one or many and then took an action according to the chosen list. He had compared that operation with the human brain automatically consulting a check list of subconsciously recorded conditions before proceeding to a decision or an action.

Sven allowed as how his decisions were consciously made and Freud and Jung and the rest, particularly the computer types, could be damned.

Sven's subconscious forgave him, however, and went on, even as now while his conscious self slept, recording the multitude of sounds, vibrations and conductions that combine to form a psycho-sensory environment. And in its self-important way, it tirelessly reviewed the repetitive data entries, waiting, it almost seemed, to justify its existence.

Sven moved his head slightly. Somewhere within a curtain was partially drawn and fractionally his brain told him all was not the same as it had been. The synapses leapt and the conclusions called for more awareness and the awareness sought further data: The regular, gentle response of the hull to the water and the recurrent cycle of strain and slack on the anchor line had been disturbed.

There it was again…a very slight change in the series of events.

And then there was the new sound. So soft, yet different from the water line's incessant gossip, the rub of the rudder gudgeon, the almost inaudible flutter of the wind indicator, the flashlight rocking in the navigator's drawer…. It matched something on file…heard countless times.

The milliseconds raced by: Now the subconscious railed at this tardy, heavy-lidded school boy. Would he never learn? Wake fool, before it is too late!

SQUEAK OF AN OARLOCK!

Sven sat bolt upright on the cushion, his eyes straining in the darkness. He saw no distinct figure, only the massive body that blotted out the stars as it leapt the port lifeline, stepped squarely on Matt's broad back and bulldozed Sven to the cockpit cushion again. The man lay on him like a dead-weight, trapping his arms against his torso and making any struggle useless.

Suddenly there was a bright light, then the deck gave, heaved and gave again to new arrivals. Three on board, Sven's mind raced: we're outnumbered.

Then the ludicrousness of the thought was brought home to him, for the huge man suddenly stood up in the cockpit. Clasping one of Sven's wrists in each of his vise-like hands, he snapped the older man erect and stretched his arms full length overhead. Sven was astounded. His assailant's head was a foot above his own fully extended 6'4" frame.

The man from Walker Cay.

The light shifted from Sven to Matt who still sat, both hands gripping the splash board bordering the cockpit— attempting to suck air into his collapsed lungs. Small stars of light punctuated his vision whether his eyes were open or not. The unmistakable nudge of a gun barrel probed his rigid spine as if selecting a place to do some awful mischief.

The hand-held spotlight was suddenly flicked from spot to flood focus by someone still on the other boat. Sven's hands were released and he was forced again into a sitting position.

The third man, pudgy and short-legged, stepped over Matt's white knuckled hands to the bridge deck and addressed the cockpit congregation.

"I have only a little time left," the pudgy man began in a heavy Cuban accent. "Precious time was wasted on someone who knew nothing today. He told my associate here," the fat man indicated the huge one, "that the delivery crew might know. You are the delivery crew, are you not?" He paused to look at each man expectantly.

Matt still hadn't the breath to speak, but Sven returned the man's beady gaze and replied, "Ayeah, we're the delivery crew. What is it we're suppost ta know?"

"Hah. Do not be a funny man. If you are to deliver it, you must know where it is. Yes?"

"We're to deliver the yacht," blurted Matt and having found his voice, he released the splash board only to have the gun muzzle assert itself.

Not knowing whether the gun-bearer disapproved of his joining in the conversations or of losing sight of his captive's hands, Matt decided to find out by again grasping the splash board. But the action brought no decrease in the muzzle's pressure.

"The yacht! Of course the yacht. But the canister too. I am a busy man and an impatient one, for I have a superior who is even busier and more impatient than I."

"I dunno nothin' about no canister," Sven began, "and I ain't interested in what the owner's got aboard. My contract says ta deliver the boat. There ain't no fine print about what's on her."

"Don't try to make a fool." The man's voice took on an ugly tone. "Ramirez told them today that he knew nothing. But, when you came, he said…you were specialist," he hissed.

Matt shifted to look at Sven on the opposite seat. The gun barrel bruised his flesh and he turned back.

"Yeah, that's right. He kept the boat up and crewed when the owner was in the islands. But he didn't have no U.S. visa and couldn't get one, so the owner hired us to come and get the boat and deliver it to Florida. I've done it four or five times."

"No lie! You specialists. You sent here to get canister," he shouted, his face contorted in the glare of the harsh light.

Matt feared his anger, for the madder he became, the poorer became his English, an indication that he was not a nimble thinker. If his frustration became too great for the slow mind to control, the gun might do more than bruise.

"Here, look at this," Matt said, not moving. Then slowly he lifted one hand from the board and drew a business card from his T-shirt pocket where he had placed it that afternoon in preparation for the arrival of Inspector Brown. "It's the name of the company."

He leaned forward to hand the card and the muzzle ground cruelly into the meaty muscle next to his spine.

The fat little man, almost panting now in his anger, stepped down onto Sven's cushion and reached across for the card.

"Sven's company's name is 'Yacht Specialists'. Read it for yourself. That's what Ramirez meant. Our specialty is delivering yachts anywhere in the world. Ramirez was...."

"*Que es¿*" the man demanded, stepping closer to Sven and handing the card to the Goliath-like figure. Holding the card at arm's length, the giant read the card in a loud bass that Matt felt sure could fill a stadium.

Sven tensed. This was the first opportunity for a break. The giant was momentarily distracted; the fat man had the spotlight in his eyes. But Sven could not see Matt, for the giant's bulk, belt buckle at eye level, blocked the way. The glare of the light made it impossible to see how many, other than the light bearer, there were still on the other boat and how they were armed, if they were. Submitting to the reality, he turned back to the translation, but it was over and the rapid Spanish rattled back and forth. The fat man's temper flared again and many 'stupeeds' populated his outburst.

The bossman was now screeching instructions to the gunman who abandoned Matt and moved to the bridge deck and grunted in reply. Then in a no less high pitch, but slow enough for Sven to understand, he ordered someone to call '*la casa*' on the radio.

A voice behind the light muttered call letters and repeated them when there was no response. He tried again a third time. Then the giant explained the trouble. Sven surmised that the short antenna on the hand-held was too low to broadcast over the high spine of the island. The bigger boat could not be summoned.

New instructions came from the boss.

Suddenly the big man turned and snatched Sven's left arm, pulling him erect.

"Kneel," he commanded, forcing Sven to the cockpit cushion. From somewhere he produced a spool of wide surgical tape and in seconds had bound Sven's hands behind him and them to his ankles. Just as swiftly, he did the same to Matt, the gun bearer relaxed on the bridge deck.

The fat man, struggling amid his oaths, panted his way over the lifeline and into the other boat. The light wavered as the passenger was helped aboard, but a *basso profundo* growl brought it hastily back to bear on the final touches of Matt's bindings.

GULL rolled to port as the huge man stepped from the cockpit to rail and it rebounded accordingly when he stepped to the other boat.

The light was doused and Sven caught a glimpse of the other boat for the first time. The only crew was the coxswain and he now held a portable VHF radio in one hand and the dark spotlight in the other. The boat was one of the inflatables made popular by the documentary film crews, reacting badly to the sudden added weight on one side. So nearly as he could see, it was not more than 10 or 12 feet long. Had this been the boat that had found GULL and followed her to Elbow Cay? Sven wondered. It must have been. The larger boat, hidden on the other side of the Island had brought Fatso. It was too noisy to allow for a surprise boarding, so he came out tonight in the small boat thinking he might be able to wrap up the whole thing if he caught the 'delivery' crew and they would surrender the canister.

The huge outboard motor sprang to life.

The guard bellowed one last question or request and the fat man screeched a reply. Then the boat was on its way, wrapped in a cloud of oil-fouled exhaust that characterizes the outboard engine.

Sven scowled in disgust, for even in his current distress, he had time to curse a favorite enemy: "Damn stinkpot."

He stared after the boat as it plowed its way across the moon-dappled sea, the drone of the motor receding slowly as the craft struggled with its load toward the mouth of the cove.

The two 'specialists' knelt uncomfortably on their respective cushions facing the gunman, whom they could see for the first time.

He was a short, thin, wiry man, swarthy of complexion, wearing a white shirt open at the throat. A small crucifix hanging from a gold chain around his neck reflected a beam from the moon which was now low on the western horizon. His white linen sport coat hung loosely from his narrow shoulders and the cuffs of his light slacks were rolled up revealing the tops of a pair of silky socks that disappeared into expensive loafers.

Sven peered at his too neat mustache and the carefully tousled dark curls and decided that here was a man who spent too much time looking at himself in the mirror.

"So what's the deal?" Sven asked.

The guard raised the gun, then carelessly cradled the barrel in the crook of his left arm. Sven knew little about guns, but he was pretty sure the stubby automatic weapon was not of American manufacture.

"No deal."

Matt was not sure by the short reply whether the man's English was poor or if the two words were a shortcut, no-frills sentence.

"So what the hell? You gonna leave us kneeling here all night?"

"They will be back before all night," the man said simply. And, suddenly, as if to punctuate his reply, the two were tumbled off balance. The wake from the departing craft surged under the larger boat, lifting her gently and nudging her slightly toward shore.

The anchor alarm shrieked. The startled guard leapt away from the open companionway as if jabbed by the piercing electronic noise.

"Damn," Sven swore.

"We're going to go aground and it's ebb tide." Matt's remarks were primarily intended for the guard. The situation was too obvious for a seaman to have spoken aloud about it. Sven had set the dial on the alarm to sound when the water below the keel fell to six feet. There was no danger to the boat as she lay. The dying of the wind meant that only the ebb tide was pulling the yacht away from the beach. The wake of the departing boat had pushed GULL over a shallow spot and the alarm did what it was supposed to do.

GULL was in far greater danger of being towed away and dismantled in a search for the mysterious canister. Somehow her crew had to take advantage of the situation as it presented itself. The guard was spooked. Matt was sure that in the strange world of water and boats, the nervousness could be turned to their advantage. The notion was immediately strengthened by the chiming of the ships clock, adding to the uncanny feeling that the boat was a thing unto itself, that it had come alive, and was demanding that steps be taken to keep her out of trouble.

"That's eleven now," Sven said, "It'll be dead low in a half-hour."

"Turn it off," screeched the gunman, with growing signs of irritation. The alarm had been designed to increase in pitch and volume if not promptly turned off and the sound had now begun to unnerve even Matt, who was accustomed to the whines and bleats of the electronics industry.

The men lay on their sides facing one another just as they had fallen when the wake rocked them from their knees.

"And how do you expect me to do that? A little help here pal. One or the other of us has to be cut free."

Matt studied the frightened man's face in the bright moonlight. "You'll catch hell from Fatso if anything else goes wrong with this job. Tell him what will happen to this wooden hull if we ground on that hard packed sand bottom, Boss."

"Open a seam more'n like," Sven growled. "And if she goes inshore much she'll trip on her keel, lay right down on her side and the incoming tide'll fill her full," he continued in as offhand a manner as he could muster while almost shouting.

"Wait-a minute! Watta you doing? We got to save her." the Cuban shouted above the rising din.

"How we gonna do that? The tide's ebbin' fast." Sven shook his shaggy head in mock despair.

"Hey, like this morning. The guy took the other anchor out in the little boat and we pulled on it." He waved the gun in the direction of the bow where the anchor again lay in its chocks.

So one mystery was solved. The second anchor set athwart of the tide stream had been used to kedge off the shore. When Ramirez had purposely disabled the engine, the kedging job was the only way to keep the wind or tide from carrying her ashore. After the boat was safe, the assailants had been eager to return to their first concern and had left the anchor out.

"Maybe too late for that," Matt mused, shaking his head.

"Well we gotta hurry," the Cuban insisted, flicking a worried look in the direction of his departed comrades.

"Now, I don't wanna start no hard feelin's, but I just don't think you're gonna be able to get that anchor out by yerself in time ta do no good."

An almost invisible shudder shook the linen-clad shoulders and the wiry little man began a search of his pockets. The gun had been leveled again with the first shriek of the alarm and now it steadied on Sven as the guard advanced toward the nearest set of bound wrists. Fumbling a small gold plated pen knife from a pocket he opened it with his teeth. A moment later Sven was rubbing circulation back into his hands. He swung his still taped feet to the cockpit floor when it became obvious that his captor was not rattled enough to carelessly cut him completely free.

"Hurry it up. That racket ees giving me a headache." The hint of a Cuban accent escaped with the shouted words and the menacing gun barrel waved encouragingly toward the open hatch.

Sven stalled for time. His mind raced but no plan would form. He'd have to take it as it came. He again swung his bound feet up onto the cockpit cushion, facing aft, then raised himself with his hands to a sitting position on the slightly higher bridge deck. Pivoting again on his buttocks, he lifted his feet to the same level. Then reaching out for the hatch combing, he hoisted himself high enough to swing his feet into the opening. His hands still remained on the combing but one of his bound heels had found footing on the steep run of steps that led to the cabin sole. At once he felt the sharp jab of the gun muzzle just below his neck.

"Now lookie here, sonny," began the provoked Sven. But he was silenced by the tense snarl of the Cuban.

"Shut up! What the hell you tink I am? Turn off dees noise! You keep you hands where I can see." The nervousness had been replaced by calculated calm. Sven's mind raced for a way to unnerve the man again while keeping his trigger finger steady.

"OK, I gotta turn around on the ladder and let myself down with my hands. I'll do it real slow."

He was as good as his word and when he stood at the bottom, the naked snout of the weapon copied at eye level even the most subtle movement of Sven's head as he squinted to pierce the dark of the cabin.

"The alarm switch is behind this ladder," he shouted. "I gotta lean in there at arm's length ta reach it." He looked at his captor for approval, then keeping his left hand in sight on the top step, he ducked his head behind the ladder and pivoted slightly in an attempt to provide the smallest target possible.

Squinting from behind the steps, he measured the distance between the advancing muzzle and his left hand. At five inches, he snapped off the offending noise and the muzzle sagged, telegraphing the holder's relief. Instantly Sven thumbed the spreader light switch and the entire deck was bathed in bright light from halfway up the mast. But before the startled Cuban could react, Sven had the gun barrel in hand, and pulled it and its bearer through the hatch onto the cabin sole. Unable to separate his feet, he closed his knees instead and knelt forcefully in the smaller man's groin. A single shot blazed over his shoulder, then the fingers turned to jelly and the gun had a new owner.

Sven pushed the gun muzzle into the soft underside of the man's chin and snarled: "Move an' ya get yer tonsils out real cheap, and fast. Where'd yer friends go?"

The Cuban's body convulsed and he vomited on the fine teak of the cabin sole. Sven searched the limp figure and found a .32 caliber Beretta tucked into his waistband. Stuffing the handgun into his own belt, he rummaged in the jacket pockets for the pen knife, stood up and threw it out the open hatch. He then pulled his rigging knife from his pocket by its lanyard, snapped it open and cut the tape from his ankles. The Cuban, curled now into a fetal position, retched again before being snatched to his feet by the offended Sven.

"Now ya'll hafta clean that up," he said softly.

"Will you please get the hell up here," Matt yelled.

Instinctively, Sven straightened. It sounded through the water like the whine of a sine wave. The Cuban had heard it too and the sound had considerably stiffened his rubbery knees, but before he could lay foot to the ladder, Sven's sizable fist crashed into the side of his head and he skittered over the dinette table into an unconscious heap on the settee beyond.

"Damn it, what's going on down there? Those bastards heard the anchor alarm; they're coming back. Get the hell up here and untie me."

The whine of the outboard's propeller transmitted through the water had given Sven no indication of its proximity, but if Matt had heard the surface noise, then there was no time to lose. He bounded up the ladder, his open rigging knife in hand.

"Stay put," Sven ordered, deftly cutting the twisted tape at Matt's wrists and ankles. "Soon's they get into shoutin' distance, tell 'em we've sprung a leak and to hurry." Matt remained kneeling and grasped one ankle in order to maintain the appearance of being bound.

"Here's something to use on the cox'n." Sven pressed the Beretta into Matt's other hand, then whirled and bounded toward the mast. "Get him on the first shot. Yer gonna be too busy ta fix mistakes." He was pulling himself up the lower portion of the mast in order to reach the rungs screwed at intervals into the varnished spruce farther up.

Despite the fact that the gun metal had been nourished on the body heat of two sweating men, it felt cold in Matt's hand. He had rarely ever fired a gun and had never pointed one toward another human being. Suddenly the sweat ran from every pore and as it cascaded down over his brow into his eyes, he struggled mightily against the urge to wipe it away with his hand. He squinted into the glare the spreader lights cast on the water, but could not see if the inflatable had appeared at the cove's entrance or not. He flung a hasty glance forward. Sven, the Cuban's gun slung across his back, climbed frantically up the mast in an effort to reach the spreaders before their visitors came into view, gambling that the high spine of the island and its scrub growth would mask the sailboat from any observer sitting so low in the water.

The aluminum rungs screwed to the sides of the mast were quite far apart, so each step up carried him quickly closer to the darkness above the spreader lights and the comparative safety it offered, as well as the meager platform of the spreaders themselves.

Gaining his objective and squinting to hasten the adjustment of his eyes, he searched the lagoon's surface for the craft whose sound now pervaded the entire area. Quickly he squirmed around to the opposite side, placing the mast between himself and the oncoming boat. Then planting each foot firmly on top of the starboard spreader, he again fished out his rigging knife. The lanyard that secured the knife to his belt at the right hip was plaited from four strands of cotton cord and was long enough to reach the length of Sven's arm extended above his head. Passing the knife around the mast above one of the rungs, he sucked in his stomach and pushed the closed knife up between his belt and the faded waistband of his dungarees on his left hip. Thus the lanyard became a crude safety belt. Then he stole a look down at the deck for the first time. Sven was not afraid of heights, but he was glad of the margin of safety the lanyard would provide when the arrival of the boarding party would make a carnival ride of his perch. He decided to leave the gun slung over his shoulder until the giant and the fat man boarded so that he could hold on with both hands as the mast cut its wide arc back and fourth. If he dropped the gun, he immediately changed from being the most lethal player in this game to being a sitting duck.

His eyes were slowly becoming accustomed to the dark and he suddenly realized that in the mad minutes since the departure of their assailants, the moon had gone down. Beyond the bright pool of light in which the yacht sat, the night was black.

Below, Matt arched his back and again wiped his sweat streaked face on the already soaked shoulder of the T-shirt. Then he stole one last glance, checking the mast, but the glare of the lights was impenetrable. Fearful of shouting, he returned to his task, reassured by the knowledge that Sven had never let him down before.

Writer, actor, director. "Renaissance man," Matt croaked aloud. He quickly put aside thoughts of killing anyone, deciding that the circumstances, when presented, might provide an alternative. If worse came to worst, at least it would not be premeditated. But the rest had to be scripted.

Now: words they'll understand, events that are logical, an attitude of agitation that will prompt haste for fear they'll lose their prize. Enough haste and fear and they'll become careless. The element of surprise will be the clincher. He hoped.

Circulation had returned to his hands but the kneeling pulled the denim cut-offs tight around his upper thighs and his feet tingled. He would desperately need to stand up soon. And walk and run and fight probably, and his legs and feet needed blood to do that. But he dared not lie down on his side, for now, some almost imperceptible difference in the sound of the approaching motor told Matt that the inflatable had finally rounded the point and entered the cove again. He was on-stage; the curtain was up and the lights were on!

Matt pivoted around so that he faced the oncoming boat squarely. His toes hung off the edge of the cushion and he leaned forward so that the muzzle of the Beretta emerged from between his ankles. He felt for the safety, having clicked it on earlier during his hasty examination of the weapon. He needed to be ready now.

An awful thought struck him. He had released the clip to count the number of rounds, then snapped it back, but he had failed to check if there was one in the chamber. Now he had to know. He could afford no additional disadvantage. He leaned further forward and pulled back on the slide.

Matt was sure that the proximity of the occupants to the inflatable's motor prevented them from hearing the noise, but to his ears and his psyche, the sound grated and reverberated at an awful volume.

The cartridge sprang from the chamber and rattled across the cockpit. "Damn," he swore. "I hope I won't need that one." He released the slide.

The hammer of the dependable little pistol was cocked. Matt was as ready as he could be.

Sven had also sensed the boat's entry into the lagoon and he strained against the darkness for the first glimpse. It came as a dim reflection of the spreader lights on the white froth of the bow wake. The motor was almost wide open, forcing the bow up into the air. Water curled away from the tubular hull of the over-loaded craft in a live lace-work of froth and phosphorescence.

His mind raced. What to do? He could kill them all with one burst of gunfire. But then, he *couldn't* do that either. Capture them? Then what? The temptation to unsling the gun washed over Sven with the first glimpse of this impending danger, but he fought it off and concentrated instead on presenting as little of himself for view around the mast as possible. Matt's yell froze him in rapt attention.

"Hurry up! She's sinking!" Matt had straightened himself as much as he dared and still keep the illusion of his bindings. A Spanish shout was answered by a higher whine from the outboard, but with little increase of speed.

"We need help, bad." Matt screamed. "Have you got a pump aboard?" He was pretty sure that only a few words were penetrating the outboard's noise barrier but he was equally sure that the feeling of urgency was being transmitted.

"The big hose on the engine intake split," he bellowed.

Then someone on the smaller craft began to think.

"Too soon," Matt muttered. "Maybe I blew it."

The throttle was cut way back and in the ensuing silence the great bass voice demanded, "Where is Diego?"

Just the sound of the man was enough to make Matt shiver, but he bellowed back: "He and Sven are trying to get the pump running. We're taking on water fast." He paused as the Spanish rattled back and forth, then rushed on: "The big hose on the engine intake split. We're taking on a couple of hundred gallons a minute." Again he paused for effect. "The incoming tide's going to wash her up on the beach. You got a pump aboard?"

Suddenly he was drowned out as the throttle was pushed forward and the boat again bounded toward GULL.

Matt braced himself. It would not do to go toppling over on his side this time. He had to stage-manage this next scene with care.

In his haste the coxswain waited too long to cut his power and he also failed to turn soon enough, so the inflated tubular bow hit GULL's topsides with some impact, compressed, and attempted to spring away again, but the long arm of the giant had seized the yacht's life line and he gave the illusion of pulling its tonnage through the water to him.

Matt bellowed immediately when the engine noise subsided enough for him to be heard. "They're below, forward. They have to take up the floorboards to get to the seacock. Hurry!"

The giant muttered hasty Spanish to the fat, little man then leapt aboard. The bow of the inflatable, held only by the coxswain in the stern, sprang away from GULL's side amid much Spanish profanity from the fat man. The action produced two things Matt had hoped for. The giant went back to help his boss aboard and the coxswain put his automatic weapon on the seat and used both hands to steady the craft against the yacht's side. Both boats were rolling badly now with the sudden shifts of large amounts of weight from one to the other.

Matt leaned back and then forward and back again, trying to remain vertical, if not steady. Finally the fat one was aboard, and GULL listed sharply under the combined weight of three on her port side. The big man released his charge and arrived in one step at the main hatch. He knelt on the bridge deck and ducking his head, attempted to pierce the darkness inside. But the sharp contrast to the brightly lit whiteness of the cabin top made it impossible for him to see.

Matt yelled again, "They're up forward, past the head. Hurry, they need help."

By now the fat man stood astride one of the giant's legs and was attempting to peer past his shoulder into the dark cabin.

Matt looked at the coxswain. He was coming aboard GULL, a painter in his hand.

The fat man leaned over and yelled Diego's name into the darkness.

The coxswain had been holding the boats together with both hands. Now he retrieved his submachine gun and laid it on the deck inside the toe rail and bent over to tie the line to a cleat on the splash board. Matt raised the Beretta and brought it down with all his might at the base of the man's skull. The Cuban grunted and pitched silently forward onto the side deck.

"Have you got a pump aboard? A big pump?" Matt yelled again, struggling to keep the rising tension from his voice.

The fat man yelled Diego's name again and pressed further forward over the bigger man's shoulder.

Matt, reaching out to the binnacle for support, slid off the cushion and stood upright in the cockpit. He could not feel his feet. He pitched forward on the cushion again and crawled in what seemed like slow motion toward the bridge deck.

"They're forward," he yelled again."They're trying to get the floor boards up. The seacock's under the floorboards!"

The fat man called Diego's name again.

The giant started to turn toward Matt.

The fat man was in the way.

Matt was at the bridge deck but his knees wouldn't work.

The giant turned the other way.

And released the combing with one hand.

Matt, reaching with both hands, grabbed the fat man's pant cuffs and pulling with all his might, catapulted him into the off-balance giant. The falling body should have gone over the giant's shoulder and pitched into the dark cabin, but instead it clung to the massive head and dragged the teetering giant headlong into the void too.

With one last supreme effort, Matt stood up, grasped the still-protruding feet and, pushing and falling, forced them completely into the companionway. Then, kneeling on the bridge deck, he deftly closed the two small hinged doors and pulled the sliding hatch shut. Before the bellowing hulk could untangle himself, Matt had folded down the bronze hasp to tightly latch the opening.

"I got 'em," he bellowed. And he fell backward into the cockpit, gasping for breath. "Could of used some help, ya know," he shouted as he scowled into the glare at the spreaders.

The hatch cover bucked twice on its bronze slides before Matt could level the Beretta and fire toward the louvered doors. The sharp report of its discharge was probably more forceful than his shout and the little mahogany that the .32 slug had managed to splinter.

"Get down, stay away from the companionway. Sven is in the rigging with Diego's gun. Show your head at any one of the hatches and you're a dead man."

The flurry of belligerent Spanish was stilled by a short staccato burst from Sven's perch. He had peppered the inflatable and several hisses, audible to the captives, announced its rapid passing.

Matt straightened up. The feeling was returning to his feet. He stepped to the life line and rescued the other automatic weapon from the deck as the heavy motor began to drag the stern of the inflatable under water.

Almost as an afterthought, he rolled the still unconscious coxswain off onto the sinking boat and shoved it into deeper water.

As he strode forward, blood and strength returning to his legs, he unsnapped the lines from the wind scoop amidships, stuffed it down the hatch and slammed the cover closed. Sven having stepped from the mast, collapsed the forward chute and stowed it likewise.

"Where the hell were you?" Matt muttered.

"Watchin' you. Didn't wanta distract 'em. You were doing fine." Then he turned to Matt and nodded toward the helm. Matt leapt to the cockpit and thumbed the engine alive. Slowly he inched the boat forward as Sven took in the anchor line. When the line was vertical, the bow immediately above the hook, he backed down and in two or three deft pulls, Sven had the clanking monster on the deck, Seconds later it was in its chocks and secure.

Sven strode aft and stood just forward of the main hatch, Diego's gun in hand.

By now the yacht was in deep water, still backing and, at a signal from Sven, Matt kicked the shift lever to neutral.

"Awright," Sven barked. "We're gonna open the main hatch now. We want you out one at a time. Hands on yer head. Fatso first."

Matt strode to the bridge deck, puzzlement rife on his face. "What are you doing?"

"Com'on," Sven urged. "I'll explain later. We ain't got much time."

Matt leaned forward, gun in hand, and lifted the hasp. Sven waited until he had returned to the helm, then stepped down and slid the hatch cover open.

The pudgy man emerged tentatively from the darkness, squinting against the bright light. Opening the small doors before him, he stepped gingerly out onto the bridge deck and stood blinking uncertainly in the glare.

"Awright, Diego next," Sven bawled as he stepped forward, planted his foot squarely in the small of the fat man's back and propelled him into the knee-high lifeline. Flipping neatly into the water, the man bobbed up immediately amid much sputtering and protests about his inability to swim.

"Where's Diego?" the basso voice inquired from the darkness. It hadn't occurred to Sven that Diego was still unconscious. Then he recalled the crumpled figure's journey across the table top and his disappearance onto the settee beyond.

After being told of his diminutive friend's hiding place, the giant piled Diego's inert form unceremoniously onto the bridge deck, then slowly mounted the steps himself.

His appearance was the cue for the fat man to begin screeching again. With hardly a glance at the gun-wielding Matt and not looking at Sven at all, the giant methodically unscrambled Diego's limbs, grasped the two ankles, stepped to the rail and dunked the floppy figure head first into the sea.

"Answer yer question?" Sven asked the thunder-struck Matt.

But there was no time to reply, for the limp figure was alive and flailing. The giant released him, paused to see where he would surface, stepped back and dived neatly over the life line.

Matt pulled the lever into reverse and spun the helm. As the yacht fell away from the group, the relieved crew watched as Diego swam and the giant towed the furious fat man toward the beach.

Suddenly they were upon the wreckage of the inflatable, the folding plywood floorboards of which had trapped an air-pocket sufficiently large to support the wide-eyed coxswain who still clung, white knuckled, to the side. His struggle caused the rusty hinge of the floorboards to squeak again in mimicry of an oarlock…the sound that had awakened Sven a scant half-hour earlier as the giant had stood up to reach for GULL's lifeline.

"The big guy is busy right now," Matt yelled, "but give him a yell later. Maybe he'll swim out and get ya."

With that, the yacht slipped past and Matt pressed the throttle farther. The great diesel throbbed and GULL turned her back on the worst day of her life.

Sven slipped below, killed the spreader lights and replaced them with running lights. Then, thinking better of it, he snapped them off again. He stowed the two wind scoops that had been thrust below and secured a few loose items that had been used to prepare their meal.

Matt, meanwhile, set the course he had heard Sven

quote to Pete earlier. He listened, and felt the boat under him. The pre-cruise checkout would have to wait. Like it or not, they were under way. He scanned the horizon for traffic and the skies for clouds. The engine gauges all hovered at their prescribed points but Matt wondered at the accuracy of the fuel gauge which read only 3/4 full. He was sure Ramirez would have topped up the tank before leaving Nassau.

Sven appeared on the bridge deck and Matt realized that the two men had lived through a harrowing experience, something out of a 'B' movie, yet with both of their lives at stake and they had exchanged only four sentences.

"We should have kept 'em locked up and run into Nassau," Matt ventured, still puzzled by his mentor's decision.

"I thought about it," Sven grunted. "But it was too risky. If they have a bigger boat on the other side waiting, they'd attack as soon as these guys failed ta show. Besides, he's too big ta contain very long… something was bound ta go wrong with three of 'em down there together."

"Better get on the horn to Nassau and tell them to get a chopper out here. It'll take those guys 'till dawn to traipse through the brush and mangrove swamp to their big boat."

"Can't do it," Sven said.

"What?"

“Can’t do it. Only damn round Diego was able ta fire and it had to hit the radio. Thing’s stone dead.”

“Then we’d better head for Nassau ourselves. When they get to the boat at dawn they’ll come after us.”

“They’ll call ahead and have us intercepted. We can’t get ta Nassau from here in the time it takes for them ta cross that island.”

“Then they’ll come after us anyway. What’ll we do?

We can’t outrun ‘em.”

“Yeah, yer right about that.” Sven muttered.

“We’re about to be sitting ducks again.” Matt blurted in frustration.

“But, we’re a lot smarter than them,” the older man counseled.

* * *

Trauma burrows into the subconscious. For some, the immediate aftermath may be more terrible than the incident itself, because during the engagement there is no time to think of the danger or its deadly aftermath.

For others it’s shrugged off with only a fleeting thought to the luck of a blow, the error of an opponent, and finally to the good fortune of having survived.

For Matt the former was the case and for Sven, who had lived a more adventuresome existence, it was the latter.

Sven had backed the throttle and kicked the shift to neutral. The engine vibration subsided, and only then did he realize how tired he was and how much the steady throb of the diesel had contributed to it. Any engine noise was an invasion of Sven’s inner space and the four hour run under power would have tired him under the best of circumstances. In light of the night’s acrobatics, both emotional and physical, the steady incursion had made the promise of silence in the new anchorage a matter of anxious anticipation.

"Heave," he shouted when GULL's forward motion ceased. Stepping on the shift lever, he gently nudged the throttle. Matt, at the bow with three fathoms of nylon line in one hand and the small, 'lunch', anchor in the other, leaned over the side and dropped them both. The additional rode, flaked down along the deck, rippled over the side as GULL backed away. Deftly Matt snubbed the line just past the brightly colored 9 fathom mark and GULL hesitated, then stopped as the hook dug into the sand bottom. He finished securing the line and Sven gunned the engine momentarily, setting the anchor.

Then it was quiet.

The two met at the bridge deck. "It'll be light in an hour," Sven began, "and hot as hell an hour later. I'm gonna open these hatches and then sack out under the forward wind scoop. I'll hand it up to ya if ya'll rig it fer me." With that he coaxed his tired body up to the bridge deck and let himself down into the now cool darkness of the cabin below.

Matt squinted across the short stretch of dark water at GAVIOTA's ghostly form in the pre-dawn darkness. As he rigged the wind scoop, he speculated again on the chances of the new plan's success. By deciding to run for GAVIOTA, Sven had hoped to board the derelict and either find her radio working or find one that could be removed to GULL and made to work. They could then report their boarding to Nassau and, even if the marauders were monitoring, perhaps the police could keep them at bay long enough for GULL to escape across the Stream to Florida. Matt had been skeptical about finding working electronics on a derelict and about several other aspects of that plan but had been unable to offer a better one.

"Anyway," Sven had finally argued, "if they ain't no radio, maybe we'll be lucky enough ta get there when Inspector Brown arrives ta check out Pete's report on GAVIOTA." Both men had smiled in the darkness at the dubious quality of the luck that would bring another encounter with Brown.

The quirky predawn breeze engorged the tubular wind scoop then abandoned it, the effect of a wanton siren, promising, but failing to fulfill.

After tinkering with the scoop's rigging to little avail, Matt turned his attention to the ever-brightening shape of GAVIOTA. The rim of the horizon was now aglow with the promise of the new day. In the improved light it was apparent that with a high tide under her, GAVIOTA had sufficient buoyancy on the starboard side to cause her list to worsen considerably. Perhaps an unhappy combination of an empty fuel tank and an empty water tank on the same side-who knew? She still lay aground on her port side, creating a terrible cant to her deck.

The thought of an empty water tank reminded Matt that last night's sweat still clung to his aching body. He had taken the first wheel watch on the trip, standing for two hours peering alternately at the red-lit compass card and at a waning star for guidance. He then took his turn in the rigging, peering into the black water ahead, helping to pick a way through the coral in a place where no wise yachtsman sailed at night.

Now all the accumulated tension and fatigue rose up in him and he yearned for a long, hot shower to purge it all. Such luxury on a sailboat the size of their charge was rare, but the thought of the much greater capacity of the power boat's tanks tickled his fancy. If her radio is going to work, he thought, why not be equally optimistic about a shower.

But he'd have to wait for the tide to ebb, for GAVIOTA's skewed decks were too dangerous to negotiate. Until then, a skinny dip would have to do.

In a moment he had stripped the still damp T-shirt from his back and kicking off his deck shoes, he peeled off the frayed cutoffs and stood for a naked moment in the wanton embrace of the temperamental breeze. Then he dived cleanly, shallowly, into the dark water.

Tracers of miniature phosphorescent sea life outlined, emphasized and otherwise registered his every move as he deftly stroked away from GULL.

Whatever the limitation of a saltwater bath, the combination of the cooling water and the thorough stretching of the muscles so recently tensed and constrained, gave new life to his tired body and while subconsciously acknowledging the folly of swimming alone at night in these warm seas, he swam on.

Then like the magnet that it was, GAVIOTA drew Matt toward the troubled cruiser's stern. He remembered a swimming platform low on the transom, designed to be almost awash under normal conditions. Now the slatted mahogany was submerged on the port side and thrust up into the air on the other. He approached cautiously, feeling for barnacle growth. Finding none, he drew himself up on the high end and sat for a moment. Shaking the water from his ears, he snorted to clear it from his nose, producing a mild cough in the process.

His legs dangled off into the phosphorescence-flecked water. Nature in all her infinite glory, he thought, staring into the sparkling stew around his ankles.

Then….

The sound had an almost ethereal quality and it drew him to his feet at once. Clinging to the top and side of the transom, he listened.

It came again—a mix of a cry and a shout.

A child?

Again.

He pressed his ear to the cold mahogany of the transom.

It came from inside.

He reached for the stainless tube of the stern rail and was suddenly reminded of his nakedness as he straddled the top bar and kicked himself over and down onto the canted sun deck.

It came again. This time a word singled itself out: "Here".

He strode forward and cautiously entered the dark saloon. Groping, he found a light switch whose snap activated a row of concealed fixtures around the ceiling. Matt was mildly surprised. The battery bank must be high enough to prevent wetting when the tide surges into the holed engine room, he thought.

The light revealed a cabin full of expensively upholstered settees and chairs fastened against the crazy angle of the canted deck,

Forward on the starboard side a tastefully carved sign over a doorway cautioned "Watch Your Head" and a set of steps led to the staterooms below.

"Where are you?" Matt called. The sobbing reply came from the dark lower level where he knew there must be substantial water covering the deck. Taking a large flashlight from its recharging bracket on the wall, he gingerly entered the stairwell. He found it to be a spiral that deposited him exactly seven feet below where he had entered above.

No water covered the three foot wide corridor deck. The passageway ran aft along the starboard hull which was pierced by a row of large portholes through which the brightening day waged war with the murk within.

A door on his right was open, held there firmly by debris originating from within the stateroom. Soggy mattresses and smashed drawers were everywhere. Papers and photos floated in the water, the top surface of which scribed a diagonal line from the bottom of an open closet door to the overhead on the port side.

Matt's flashlight probed the corners. Disheveled clothing hung along with empty hangers in the small closet that ran half the length of the bulkhead that separated this cabin from the one immediately aft.

But there was no one there.

He rushed on down the passageway to the door to the aft cabin. It was closed. Soon he knew why. Something resisted his push, but not his shove.

The scene was little different, except for less debris. This was probably the guest cabin and there were fewer personal belongings in the drawers and lockers. The same accordion fold doors hung agape on the small closet in this room as well.

But the cabin held no one.

"Where," he called again, leaning in the doorway against the wearying list of the deck.

"The other room. The closet," the small voice sobbed.

Matt hurried back and as he climbed over the soggy mattress he was aware again of his nakedness. Snatching a shirt, which hung from the door knob, and wearing it apron like, sleeves tied in the back, he waded to the closet and threw open the remaining door.

There was no one there.

"Where the hell are you?" he cried out in frustration.

Now the voice was steadier, calmer and much closer: "Here, in the wall at the side of the closet. A secret compartment."

Matt stood frozen. The fairy tale quality of the statement was in sharp contrast to the brutality represented by the strewn wreckage.

"You must open the door to the left half of the closet and close the door to the right half." The voice had a studied calm. "Then lift the closed door by its knob and slide it to the left." The voice was completely under control.

Matt did as he was instructed, pushing against the gravity of the list. The end of the wall of the closet where it was hinged to the louvered door slid a half inch to the left, releasing a tall, narrow, spring-loaded panel which slowly opened against the press of the shallow water.

The compartment was barely twelve inches wide and twice that deep. A space between the end of each of the stateroom closets. It was occupied by a young woman standing in profile in order to fit.

She held an Uzi submachine gun.

Chapter Three

She had not been eager to talk to me. It required a hurried and hushed long distance call on her cell phone, which she took out onto the balcony of her small office in downtown Miami.

When Matt had reassured her that he regarded me as legitimate, she returned to her desk where I sat waiting—but the misgivings did not totally leave her eyes until we were well into the interview. My questions quickly convinced her of the depth of my knowledge of the entire affair and much about her role.

Some, she assumed that I had garnered in my talks with Sven and Matt, but she was noticeably unnerved at the Agency report on the 'Biscayne Incident'. Perhaps it was because, for all that had happened on GULL at sea, it was at the gala party at Key Biscayne that she had first come to really fear for her life.

BAD GIRL?

Matt did not lead an uninteresting life, but it certainly had never been this interesting. Never before yesterday had he seen a real automatic weapon up close. But now, in less than one normally tranquil, tropical night, his life had been threatened by two.

He caught a glimpse of himself in the mirror on one of the closet doors, it's skewed angle a commentary on the absurd image it threw back. Involuntarily he had dropped the light and raised his hands above his salt encrusted hair. He stood, awkwardly leaning against the cant of the deck, the soggy shirt hanging limply from his hips.

Then it fell off.

She fell too. Her eyes glazed, then her knees buckled and she pitched forward into his arms. The Uzi clattered to the deck and slid harmlessly into the water. Matt took a necessary step into the situation and, hands under her arms, lifted her. Then, hugging her to him, he backed out of the cabin, dragging her limp feet over the soggy piles.

In the passageway there was more light and he became aware of her red hair and the faintest whiff of perfume. By the time he got to the top of the spiral steps she had begun to stir in his arms. Crossing to the port settee, he gingerly stretched her out full length. Then crouching, he took off her shoes and automatically loosened the belt of her jeans. He was working on the top button of the waistband when her eye lids fluttered. Shifting to her head, he removed a cushion from under it and placed it under her feet instead. He then picked up her wrist to check her pulse. She was awake now, confused and growing fearful.

"You're O K," he said reassuringly. "Unbutton your waistband. It'll improve your circulation." She looked at him a long moment. "Red Cross first-aid. Lesson one."

It was obvious that she wore no bra under the cotton shirt, the tails of which were tied together across a flat, freckled, sun-browned midriff.

"How long you been in there?"

"I don't know. What day is this?" The tension that betrayed itself in the high pitch of the first sentence was suppressed in the delivery of the second.

"It's Tuesday—about 5 a.m. Tuesday."

"It happened Sunday. Late in the afternoon." Her voice broke and she suddenly sat up, throwing her feet over the elevated edge of the settee, allowing her head to loll back against the cushion.

Matt had been able to hide his nudity by crouching beside the settee. Now, thinking she was about to stand up, he straightened, turned quickly to a chair near the door, sat down and hastily crossed his naked legs.

"Don't talk about it," he suggested. "Just rest for a moment before I take you out to breakfast." Then suddenly, "My god, you must be famished. Is there any food handy? She didn't answer immediately. She just sat still. Then it occurred to him. She may be a stranger to GAVIOTA too.

"Water." She uttered the single word assuming an immediate understanding.

What a dunderhead, Matt thought. Of course, she must be dehydrated. He stood, casting about for the galley.

"On the flying bridge. There's a small fridge opposite the controls. There should be bottled water, cheese, yogurt and milk in there."

Whatever apprehension she may have had about this stranger who had suddenly appeared, seemed gone. Perhaps the vulnerability created by his nudity had helped to dispel any threat. Whirling quickly to the door he let himself out onto the sun deck. To his right, near the portside, a chrome ladder led to the cabin top.

In the growing light of the balmy dawn, Leda Malone leaned forward on the skewed seat and through the large after port light, she studied her rescuer in as much detail as the eight rung ladder allowed.

Matt gained the top deck and strode toward the open control station. The sun, just now clearing the horizon, stabbed horizontal shafts under the Bimini top. The small camp refrigerator had been installed for the helmsman's convenience. Coral heads made the top deck the favored location for the operation of a craft in these waters and it took only a short time in the tropical heat to work up a thirst. The obligatory cans of beer had to be pushed aside to reveal the more substantial items he sought. He decided on the starboard ladder for the descent. It deposited him on the main deck again, just forward of the sliding door to the main control station.

Having found no radio on the flying bridge, he was sure he'd find one here. He pushed the door forward with his elbow and looked in. There it was, within easy reach of the chrome helm, the microphone torn from its connection and tossed upon a pair of swim fins crowded together at the port end of the dash board. Above these hung a pair of swim trunks and a diving mask. Pausing only long enough to don the trunks—they were for a man of considerably more girth than Matt—he gathered up the food again and started aft via the inside connecting companionway: controls to galley to saloon.

Leda was still perched on the edge of the settee. She accepted the bottle of water, drank half before she stopped to breathe, then finished it before attacking the first container of fruit-laced yogurt. She eagerly squeezed the contents into her mouth while Matt opened the package and broke off several bite size pieces of cheese. After a hearty pull at the juice carton and another cup of yogurt, she seemed ready to talk.

"Thanks. How did you know I was here?"

"I didn't." Hesitantly at first and then with growing conviction that she had a right to know, he quickly outlined the events of the last day and night, then looked expectantly at her. "Your turn, Mrs. Malone."

"I'm afraid your pilot friend was in error on that item." She stood up awkwardly and walked up hill to the starboard port light. "I'm not Malone's wife. I'm his daughter." She paused, then turning toward him, she visibly shuddered. "They took him away." She paused. "We had just finished supper. Dad had caught a dorado that afternoon and we'd anchored early to have a leisurely meal and ease into the evening. We'd seen the trawler—an island boat, maybe thirty feet—twice earlier in the afternoon, but hadn't paid much attention to it. But it passed astern when it entered the anchorage and there was considerable discussion among the men on her. I was below, but I heard one say 'gaviota'"

Abruptly she turned again, arms folded, hands clasping each bicep—almost as if she were hugging herself in comfort against the memory. "Can we get off this damn boat? Please?"

"Oh God. I'm sorry!" he blurted. "Look, I swam over. I'll go back and bring the dink. You get your stuff…."

"I'll swim too. We can come back later. I've got to get off this boat." With that, she strode out onto the sun deck. Matt caught his breath as she pulled off the tight jeans and stepped to the rail in shirt and very brief briefs. In a single fluid motion she slipped between the chrome bars of the stern rail, poised on the high end of the swim platform just long enough to take a deep breath, then dived neatly into the dawn-dappled sea.

By the time Matt had done likewise, Leda was half way to GULL, stroking evenly, cleanly and with a purpose born of the ordeal she was leaving behind.

Sven stood red eyed at the companionway hatch, having awakened the moment the first hand had grasped the bob stay for support. Finding Matt's cut-offs on the deck and GAVIOTA's saloon lights ablaze, he was not surprised to see his young friend clamber aboard over the bow sprit. He was about to complain about being awakened when Leda, her wet shirt clinging, was helped aboard.

"This is Sven," a panting Matt stated. "Leda Malone. Daughter of…."

"Eddie Malone." Sven finished. "Where's he?

"Kidnapped." Matt said, leading their guest into the cockpit where she stood amid a growing pool of sea water. Sven ducked below for a towel, returned immediately and handed it to the dripping figure.

"I'll put some water on fer coffee," he said, disappearing down the ladder.

Half an hour later, breakfast behind them, the three sat in the growing heat as Leda finished her story.

"Somehow Dad had sensed trouble. He was afraid I'd be raped if they boarded, so at first he told me to stay out of sight. Then when it was certain that they'd board, he sent me to the gun compartment. With the growing number of boat disappearances, Dad had decided to arm himself. Through some old army buddies, he had acquired the Uzi and he brought the more conventional stuff from home. But some countries don't react well to automatic weapons, so he had the secret compartment built to hide them." She paused and Matt described the gym locker size accommodation.

"Handy." Sven acknowledged, for he too had misgivings these days with drug runners and other opportunists who regarded the unarmed pleasure boat as easy prey.

"I had trouble getting the locker open. I'd done it only once before and by the time I got the Uzi and found a clip, I could tell that at least four were aboard. I thought it would be better to bide my time. Maybe, if they thought he was alone they'd drop their guard after a while and I'd be able to do something.

"I got a good look at the guys who stayed on the trawler. They were too interested in what was goin on on deck to notice me at the port hole. They all looked Cuban!"

On her note of surprise, Matt and Sven exchanged glances.

"It looked like they were after something special. I've heard tales of other boardings where the boat was immediately ransacked for anything of value. But I could hear them quizzing my father about something. Then he got mad and I heard him shout 'I don't know anything about any damned canister.' That's the last thing I heard him say. They must have hit him then, because the next thing I knew they were carrying him aboard the trawler.

"I was about to do something dumb when I realized that there were still more of them than me and they had spread out over the boat and were tearing her apart. They were going to find me any minute. So I got into the locker and held the door closed with my finger tips. There's no release on the inside, so I didn't dare close it. I pulled the corner together enough to look normal at a casual glance—hoping that's all the closet would get. But they took everything out and in slamming the doors open, the joint closed and I was trapped." Her voice trailed off.

The two men studied her as she huddled on the cockpit seat, her knees drawn up under her chin, mentally reliving the terrible moment in the darkness when she realized what had happened to her. Then she looked up at the faces watching her and she straightened body, countenance and voice.

"At first I was too scared to think of the long-term. The present danger was what I had to deal with. I had to stay quiet. I thought I'd break out later, when they were gone. Then, when they finally were gone—it must have been after dark—the terror started. The fake end wall of the closet that looked so thin was top-grade marine plywood and the place was too cramped to point the gun at the latch. I found the lever in the dark and moved it to single shot and fired one round, but it went no where near the latch and the smell in the trapped space almost made me vomit. And there wasn't room to back off and thrust against the door." Her voice was a mere whisper. "Every few minutes I realized a new depth of danger and I grew more and more sick at my stomach. Suddenly I realized that the boat had begun to list and then water began to seep in under the door. I screamed until I was hoarse, then she grounded at the stern and the water stopped rising...."

Sven stood up quickly as if to overcome the claustrophobic scene and free his body from the trap his mind presented.

"I'm goin' over and have a look," he said, striding toward the stern where the dinghy bobbed busily at the end of its towing painter. "Why doncha rig th' awnin'. I'm gonna try to fix that radio." He had drawn the dinghy up along the quarter. "Didja see a tool box anywhere over there?" he asked Matt.

"Just aft the wheel house on the main deck there's a generator compartment. I just glanced in, but I thought I saw a tool box in there secured to the bulkhead, port side." He had already risen to go for the awning and was looking to Leda to give him a hand. She sat with her eyes closed, then spoke: "There's a soldering gun in the locker in the wheel house."

Sven nodded and pushed off. Matt could tell that he was impressed. Even in her present state she knew that a soldering gun could be the most useful tool to repair a radio.

By the time the awning was rigged, the sun was almost high enough for it to work. But the small square did not yet shade the cockpit. As Leda reached high up on the port half of the split back stay to lash the last tie, the wind blew at the towel she wore for a skirt and Matt felt a rush of blood as the inside of her thigh flashed in and out of view. Her shirt had dried, but the image of her as he had helped her aboard was still sharp in his memory. She finished the tie and turned in time to see his too measured look.

"I know you ragbaggers are pretty stingy with fresh water, but I'd really like to wash the salt out of my hair. You can top up your tanks with what's left on GAVIOTA." With that she brushed past him toward the companionway hatch.

"The towels are in the locker next to the sink in the head," he offered, following her as far as the bridge deck.

"Any shampoo?" she asked as she descended into the cabin.

"I'll get it," he said, perhaps too eagerly, as he followed. The door to the forward compartment was closed and as he paused he could hear her pumping the small sink full of water. In a moment he had found his ditty bag and produced the small vial of shampoo.

"Save me a little," he said, rapping on the door. It opened a crack and he handed her the vial. The towel had been pressed into even greater service, for now it was wrapped around just under her arms. He was sure that it hardly overlapped on the side, yet he saw no flesh as he marveled at the small corner tab that had been tucked under in order to hold it closed and up. The door closed and he made his way up the ladder, pausing half way up to examine the damage the bullet had done to the mahogany the night before. He reached for his rigging knife and realized that he was still wearing Eddie Malone's oversize swimming trunks. He opened a nearby drawer and removed a sharp steak knife. He had cleaned the splintered wood from the rim of the hole where the slug was still lodged and had begun to remove the most dangerous slivers from the shattered louver when he heard the door open behind him.

"How about a rinse? It's pretty cramped in there. Could you pour a pan of water over my head while I stand at the galley sink? She stood with a sauce pan she had taken from the rack and was busily pumping it full of water. She had thrown a second towel over her shoulder and as she passed the filled pan to him she positioned it in preparation to dry the short mop of red hair. She leaned over the sink and he poured the water, sparingly at first, then more generously as he saw that the single pan would do the complete job. He replaced the pan in its rack as she vigorously rubbed her hair this way and that. Then with a sudden stoop, she flipped the towel into a turban that hid every wisp of hair. It also pulled her brows up at the ends so that her features took on a strangely Oriental quality.

The two stood quite close together.

The clean smell of her filled his nostrils and she looked up at him quizzically. Then, taking his head in both hands she kissed him—at first gently, then with more than a little hunger.

"Aren't we pushing this a little," he said, while the blood rush contradicted his logic.

"Maybe," she said huskily. "But I've just spent a lot of hours thinking how short my life suddenly appeared to be. There were many missed opportunities that came to mind, many things that I put off or avoided for one reason or another until a later time. But now I've come to understand that there may not be enough time later. There are things I didn't say to my father. There are people I failed to thank for making contributions to my life. 'Later' may be too late. For example, you just saved my life. Perhaps the depth of that reality hasn't penetrated yet. But it has made a deep and immediate impact on me. A simple 'thank you' hardly seems enough. And later—well, 'laters' may be difficult to come by.

Matt processed this mass of information and went the next step of assuring himself that Sven's curiosity would keep him aboard GAVIOTA for a sufficiently long time. Then Leda's fingers found the draw string on the borrowed trunks. They sagged, snagged on an obstruction, then slipped and fell to the floor. Leda paused to look at the changing scene she had revealed and while thus occupied, Matt flicked the small corner of the towel so that it joined the trunks on the sole.

He drew her to him and as their tongues mingled he wondered how they would keep their liaison from the very observant Sven. But he didn't wonder long, for Leda's fingers were being very distracting.

*　　*　　*

It was Leda, in her open, frank way that told me of their intimacy—along with much of how she had changed her thinking and her life as a result of her entrapment. That and the trauma later aboard INSHALLA might have shattered the feeling of personal safety in one less thoughtful.

She had had barely enough time to don her shirt and the borrowed cutoffs and re-wrap the towel around her still damp hair, when Matt heard the splash of Sven's oars returning to GULL. He was still scrambling into clean cutoffs when Leda climbed to the deck and waited to take the dinghy painter. By the time he joined them in the cockpit, Matt had summoned some control of his countenance, but Sven, by some sixth sense, knew all.

They sat in the cockpit, Matt and Leda on one side and Sven behind the helm. They occupied all of the small rhomboid of shade the awning had begun to provide. The breeze had freshened to the degree that the water's surface rippled and perspiration evaporated if it resulted from minimum effort, but the breeze was not yet a sailing wind.

"So far as you know, this is th' only radio he had aboard?" Sven asked, holding up the unit Matt had seen in the wheel house.

"Yes, he had talked lately of picking up a hand-held job, but hadn't gotten around to it," Leda replied.

"Well, I'm not enough of an electronics man to repair th' mike cable and ours ain't compatible with this unit. This will receive, but we can't get a message out. I'm gonna jury-rig an installation for this in place of the one Diego shot up. Then…" he paused and looked at Matt," we'd better settle on some things." With that he turned to Leda.

"I'm real sorry about yer dad. I ain't sure what we can do about it right now. We're in sort of a jam, as I guess Matt probably told ya. We ain't likely to outrun anybody in a power boat that wants ta catch us."

"Can't we make a dash for Nassau?" she asked, looking at Matt.

"We have to assume that our visitors last night had a larger boat on the other side of the island. They'd have covered a try at Nassau by calling ahead and having someone come out to meet us. They probably started hunting us the minute they got back to the boat. They must also know that something is wrong with our radio or we'd have called the cops. Now that it's light it's only a matter of time before they find us." Matt had looked her directly in the eye as he spoke, but when Sven was momentarily distracted, she winked, and it was suddenly hard for Matt to concentrate. Glancing at Sven, he continued. "If they heard you tell Pete last night that we had to sail a 350 or 355 and if they took off in that direction at dawn…."

"And if they can do ten knots," Leda put in, "and they figure you for two and a half or three in the dark dodging coral heads, they'd look to overtake you…a half hour ago."

Sven turned and smiled approvingly at Leda. "And whadda they do then," he asked.

"It won't take too long to check out whatever craft are in the area, maybe another half hour," she went on confidently.

"And then?" Sven prompted.

"They'll check with their Nassau welcoming committee, then go to the next most likely possibility."

Leda Malone had become one of the crew. Her experience on the boat with her father and her innate good sense had begun to dispel the early misgivings Sven had had about having a passenger along. Especially a female one. Matt was also ready to accept her on the new level, despite the wink.

"Where else do they think you might go?" she asked.

"Well, the 350-355 course was a short cut. Instead of going due north to Chub Cay and turning west into the alley, we would have come out into the alley west of Chub. But we couldn't do that in the dark. Besides, we decided to check out GAVIOTA instead. And it's on a course almost due north, directly toward Chub."

"Which is the next most logical route to have taken," she finished for him. "So they'll come looking here next." She frowned a moment then asked, "Which way will they be coming from?"

"Waal, it's a little hard to say," Sven began, "depends on how much water they draw and how good their navigator is and a buncha other things. If they took off on a 350 degree course and gave themselves a margin for possibly miscalculatin' our speed, they'd be off to the northwest of us. Now we came almost due north at about twice the speed they were counting on 'cause we had deep water soon's we got out of Elbow Cove. Depending on how far north they got 'fore they gave up is one factor, how far north they think we got is another. If they got as far as the alley and then went due east, they could come out north of us."

"And be between us and Chub?" Leda asked.

Sven looked at the intent young woman and nodded. "It's possible. If it was me, that's what I'd wanna do. Come out on top to be sure of an intercept and then work back south till we show up." Deciding to prepare her for the worst, he went on.

"Fatso was runnin' out of time last night. Now that they know what GULL looks like, cost won't be no object."

"Is there any chance that they would come here? Would they connect you to GAVIOTA in any way?" Leda asked. There was a flicker of relief in her face as the two men shook their heads, but it was short-lived when Matt added: "What Sven is suggesting is that they'll probably soon take to the air if the intercept fails. Right?"

"Right. That's why I think we oughta try to make it to Chub as soon as we can. And I think we can make it. I ain't got much faith in their navigatin'. I think we can beat 'em to Chub 'cause they'll miscalculate. Then by the time they get a plane in the air it won't make any difference."

"So we get to Chub safely," Leda was turning the thing over in her mind. "You think they'll give up the chase just because you've reported both incidents to the police? Granted, we'll be safe, but from your experience last night and ours on Sunday, they want something pretty bad. I'm not sure they're going to cave in."

"Naw, but one thing atta time. We can decide step two after step one."

"What's to decide? You're not going to try to

go on, are you?"

The cockpit fell silent.

"We're at the north end of the Joulters now," Leda said. "Isn't there any place near here we can put in and find a phone or radio?"

"Well, there was a couple of places we passed on the west coast of Andros but I wasn't about to try them channels at night. Anyway, I was countin' on gettin' to a radio here. Guess we could back-track, but we'd lose another day, total, foolin' around."

"Sven, we've got to report what happened on GAVIOTA. My dad's been kidnapped or maybe killed. They've got to start an investigation as soon as possible."

Matt came to his friend's rescue. "We've been speculating based on what we might do. They might have done something entirely different. If we double back we could run right into their arms. Also there is no guarantee that they are as far north as we think; they could overtake us if we started back south."

A cloud of worry began to darken Leda's brow. She studied Sven's weathered face intently.

"I got a contract ta deliver this man's boat ta Miami. I ain't never broke a contract," Sven said softly.

The cockpit was silent again. Matt looked at his friend thoughtfully for a time, then asked, "What will they do if we do beat them to Chub?"

"Waal, they'll have someone there pretty quick to keep an eye on us. Then, if it was me ramrodin' this thing, I'd send a boat to patrol the Alley in case we decided not to stop there and tried for home."

"Let me run this down," Leda interjected. "The nearest, safest east-west crossing of the bank is from Chub Cay to Bimini—the Alley as you call it. You draw too much water to risk any other route?"

"Even if we could get through, the channels are so narrow that we couldn't maneuver if they caught us. Bad enough in the Alley. Besides, there's a slight set ta the north and it drops off ta two or two an a half fathoms. It'll be hard not to set thata way some, an' ya always wanna set toward deeper water when ya can."

"Would they dare to try to board you in the Alley? Isn't there a lot of traffic? Wouldn't they risk being seen?"

"Waal, there's a might of traffic all right, but there's always a lull that would give 'em enough time ta board, if their boat was big and maneuverable enough."

"If we don't beat them to Chub, do you think they would try to board us in the daylight?"

"Waal," Sven mused, "they're getting pretty desperate. If they caught us late in the day and they knew we couldn't make Chub or some other port, they'd wait till dark. But they know we got weapons now, so they'll have ta take some precautions."

"They want this boat, though. They want to take it somewhere so they can tear it apart if they have to, to find what they're looking for. That means they're not likely to sink us."

"Not in deep water. If they caught us here, at anchor, they might," Matt ventured. "In real shallow water they could still pretty much tear her apart, if it was an isolated place and they had the time. Like they did with GAVIOTA."

"Do you think we could fight them off if they tried to board us?"

"Waal, if we go in there," Sven nodded at GAVIOTA, "and get that arsenal of yer dad's, and with what we got from them last night, we could rattle around pretty good 'till the ammo runs out. We only got a clip and a half for our souvenirs. What did your dad carry for the Uzi?"

"Two clips and about 500 extra rounds in the locker. It uses them up real fast."

Sven nodded his understanding, "How about the shotgun?"

"A lot—six or seven boxes. We used to shoot skeet off the stern. I'd say about the same for the 30.06 and the .45 pistol. The Winchester's got a scope on it."

"You know how to use all of 'em?

"All but the Uzi. We'd shoot sharks with the Winchester and Dad checked me out on the .45 just as a matter of course. He always said people who didn't know now to handle a gun were more dangerous than the gun itself."

"Did you take them out of the locker?" Matt asked.

"Naw, the brackets holdin 'em were up off the deck and dry, so I just put 'em back." He paused then added, "Damn small place."

Leda shuddered and suddenly stood up. "Well, let's get them all. I've got to go over for some clothes. We'd better get going. I've held you up too long already." She looked quizzically at Sven, "Step one, right?" Then she strode toward the cleat where the dinghy was tethered.

"Well, maybe we should consider one more thing." Matt said. But before he could continue, Leda retied the line and scampered back to the cockpit, fear enlarging her eyes.

Both men heard it then, the first faint throb of the

engine in the distance.

"It's a Island boat," Sven decided, squinting at the blunt bow and the low cabin. "Mebby some one heard about the stranded boat."

"Coming to strip her, probably," Matt offered, not wanting to consider the more fearful alternative.

"It looks just like the one that boarded us!" Leda exclaimed, peering out from behind Matt.

"Could be th' guys from last night," Sven grudgingly admitted. "Best we not take any chances."

"Get below and keep your head down," Matt ordered, pushing Leda toward the companionway. He planted himself between her and the oncoming boat, watching her descend, then following as soon as she had disappeared.

From the navigation table he snatched Diego's pistol.

"It's loaded and the safety is on," he said, pointing to the lever as he did so. "Take it forward and lock the door. If they board and get past us…." He stopped and crossed the cabin. Lifting the settee seat, he pulled out the two submachine guns. Crossing back he looked into the frightened face of the woman he had only begun to know.

"Check the clip. I think you've got eight rounds. If they get past us and crash the door…. This could be nothing. But, if it's something bad, you… you might keep the last round for yourself."

He felt immediately stupid for the melodramatic quality of the statement. A new measure of the reality of his suddenly changed life. He kissed her quickly and herded her through the door.

"Stay away from the porthole if shooting starts. This hull is planked with two inch thick cedar. It will stop most small caliber stuff. Unless they open up with a heavy machine gun, most slugs won't penetrate.

The cabin is thinner wood. Keep your head down. Lock the door," he said and turned to the companionway steps where he stopped and turned to look back. "I said lock, damn it." The barrel bolt snapped home in reply and he turned to find Sven sitting on the bridge deck.

"Don't let 'em see the weapons." he said. "Hang mine here." He motioned to the hook holding a binocular case just inside the louvered door. "It's an easy reach. Why don't you go up forward, so you can shoot out the fore hatch if we have to. It'll make it a little harder on 'em." His eyes had not left the small patch of white hull since he had first located it far astern.

The channel, narrow and perhaps 4 or 5 miles long, ran almost due north and he could see little of the boat except its blunt bow and the bow wave that it pushed ahead of it.

"Quick," he suddenly barked at Matt. "Put your gun on the V-berth forward, climb out that hatch and get the rode in." With that, he leapt aft to the helm and thumbed the engine alive before the startled Matt could move.

"Come on, we're gonna nuzzle up close enough to GAVIOTA sos we only have one flank to defend."

Leda unlocked the door and Matt squeezed past, lay the gun down and pulled himself up through the open hatch.

The small harbor, shaped like a tear drop at the end of the long channel, would allow too little room for a running skirmish, Sven thought. But, if they could keep their tormentors to the starboard side and if they made a good enough show of it, maybe they had a chance.

"Clear," Matt shouted and Sven nudged the throttle. GULL eased forward. It was risky business. The tide had turned at about 6:00 and now the water rushed off the flat tabletops, spilling busily into the ocean depths. As the tide had raced out of the channel, GULL had swung about so that she was no longer parallel and astern of GAVIOTA. The crippled cruiser now lay at a right angle, astern and slightly off GULL's port quarter about 40 feet away. Sven spun the helm to port after a few minutes and brought the cutter up parallel with her partner again. Then when the anchor was set, Matt payed out rode as she swung to the tide, and carefully she was allowed to inch closer and closer to the derelict until finally she lay perpendicular to GAVIOTA's starboard side. The space between the two craft was too narrow and the water shoaled rapidly enough to discourage passage between them. Now the cruiser shielded them from the view of the oncoming boat. Sven shut down the engine and Matt dove into the forward hatch pulling the detached wind chute with him and lowering the hinged cover so that he had only a narrow, horizontal v-shape to peer out of.

The engine noise was louder by this time and Sven moved to the companionway and lowered himself onto the last step, waiting for the visitor to emerge from around the stern of GAVIOTA.

The approaching engine was throttled back and the drone became softer.

A frigate bird suddenly squawked on the beach behind Matt and he banged his head on the hatch cover in nervous reaction.

Now there was no noise at all.

Suddenly, Sven's stomach knotted. His mind raced. Had he screwed up? Were they putting men on GAVIOTA? GULL would be caught in a cross fire....

The rust-stained bow appeared...a hundred or so feet off the stern of GAVIOTA, ghosting along at just enough above idle to overcome the tide race. She was about thirty feet long, a converted island trawler. A skinny youth lounged at the light machine gun on the fore deck while a mustached man, dark glasses pushed up on his forehead, peered at GULL through binoculars from the safety of the deck house.

Chapter Four

"Ahoy! Bahamian Marine Police! Standby for our approach! Prepare to present your documents!" The shout came from a middle aged policeman who's khaki uniform was wrinkled and sweat streaked.

Crews aboard ships and boats form very insular societies, the likes of which, we who live on land, can only begin to imagine. They are vaguely, but more intensely, like those of very small villages or island populations. They are tightly circumscribed by geography and small numbers of people—who come to know one another well. Often too well. As with these groups, any new comer is regarded with a mix of excitement and caution. A priest or a cop generates both and ratchets up expectations considerably.

Mr.'Stache

"So, the only thing you touched was the radio, which you took to your boat?"

The Inspector mopped his flushed face with an already sodden handkerchief as he squinted again at GULL's crew. The three men stood in the partial shade on GAVIOTA's sharply canted sun deck.

"Yes, while Sven disconnected the radio, I looked her over to see that no one was still aboard—injured or asleep. Looks like someone ransacked her. Stuff all over the place."

"There are many poor people here who would look upon this boat just as you have. As a rich abandoned prize to be claimed as salvage. They just don't know the law." The Inspector's eyes were gentle and bloodshot and tired.

"Ayeah," Sven nodded, "but they'd a took everythin' worth anythin'. This looks like...well, like someone was lookin' for somethin' special."

"My friend," the Inspector's voice was quiet with a trace of a soft Devonshire accent, four generations removed. "I have been aboard seven boats in the past year that have shown signs of violence and were empty and abandoned. Some were blood streaked, some neat and orderly. They each had a story. The drug traffic has visited two deaths on our islands, Captain Olafson, that of the dead dead and that of the living dead. Today is my lucky day. There is evidence of neither here."

He closed the small notebook and stowed it in his shirt pocket. "I will notify the U.S. Coast Guard of the boat's name and her documentation number. If the name on the scattered papers proves to be that of the owner, and he is...missing, then we will open a full scale investigation." Clapping his sweat-stained cap back on his head, he strode to the rail and signaled to have the patrol boat approach. "As for the other business, I wish you would return to Elbow Cay with me."

"We just can't," Matt replied. "We lost half a day yesterday and last night. We're behind schedule."

"But, you think we'll find footprints above the high-water mark? And perhaps the wreckage of an inflatable? Anything else?" The Inspector paused, then: "The footprints of four men—one very large. These will lead into the underbrush and on the opposite side of the island we will find a mangrove thicket where the larger boat was hidden?"

Both men nodded in response.

"Have a good trip." He turned to watch the old island 'copton' jockey the patrol boat near GAVIOTA's stern. At the right moment, the two boats only half a fathom apart, the Inspector threw his leg over the stern rail, poised a moment on the canted swim platform, then with a hand from the younger, mustached officer, stepped aboard his command. The captain reversed the engine, spun the helm and in a cloud of diesel exhaust, waved good-by to GULL's gasping crew.

Sven returned the wave and then scrambled into the dinghy where Matt already stood by at the oars.

"Do you think he'll investigate?" Matt asked.

"Oh, yeah," Sven replied. "He's an old time islander. But that don't mean anythin' will be done even if they find somethin'. Apparently no blood was shed. No need ta make a fuss."

"Well, he really sat up and took notice when we said the Elbow Cay crew were Cubans. You notice that?"

Upon their arrival aboard GULL the men found Leda standing at the bottom of the companionway ladder, binoculars resting on the combing, as she studied the departing patrol with silent intensity.

"He's one of them," she declared flatly as she returned the glasses to their peg near the ladder.

"Who?" Matt asked.

"Just a damn minute," Sven yelled, hastily cinching the painter knot.

Sven did not anger easily; however the events and behavior of their guest during the past two hours had stretched his patience and now it snapped.

"What th' hell's goin' on here?" He fixed Leda with a terrible shaggy browed gaze. "Why'd you hide from th' cops? Now, I ain't never had too much good to say about 'em, but I never had nothin' ta fear from 'em either. Lyin' ta 'em comes pretty hard to me. I hope you got a good reason ta put me in this kinda position." He stopped, waiting for a reply.

Leda did not come on deck. Instead she stood away from the bottom of the steps and answered from the shadows of the cabin interior.

"There wasn't time to explain," she began. "I was watching the patrol from the porthole as it approached and I'm sure that one of the men on the bridge was also on the trawler that took my dad. I just panicked. If I had reported what happened, then he'd know I was a witness."

"That's why she told me to fake it," Matt interjected.

"Well, I'd appreciate a little more notice next time," Sven growled, his ire subsiding as he pondered this new information.

"That's why I suggested we claim GAVIOTA as a salvage prize. That way we could protect Leda's interest without anyone knowing she's here," Matt continued.

"Ayeah, but we couldn't report the kidnapping. That's at least as important as telling 'em about last night."

"But, they'll at least begin an investigation based on the abandoned boat. There are enough signs of foul play, even if the Inspector didn't want to admit it, to treat it seriously. Your explanation of the way she was holed left no doubt that she was scuttled. It was no accidental grounding."

"While he was aboard GULL he wanted you to go to Nassau or something?" Leda ventured. "I couldn't hear very well. What was that all about?" she asked.

"He said I had to go there to file a salvage claim. But I told him Pete was getting the paperwork together there and I talked him into accepting a statement signed and dated by Sven and me and witnessed by him. He said he'd pass it along to the proper authorities, but he couldn't guarantee anything."

"I thought he was going to come below one time.... When he was about to leave and he leaned way over the combing to look down inside. I barely got the door closed in time. Do you think he believed you?" she finished quickly.

"Hard to tell. He's an experienced cop," Matt replied. "Masks his feelings pretty well."

"On everythin' 'cept drugs. On that he let his feelin's run pretty high."

"Do you think your salvage claim will stand up?" Leda had begun to realize, now that the immediacy of her trauma was past, that GAVIOTA meant more to her than she first cared to admit.

"Well, I don't think there's any doubt that we're the first to find her. Pete has already contacted the insurance clearing house to try to find out who she belongs to and which company covers her. He'll back our claim that we found her yesterday. Besides, if anyone else had been here, they'd have stripped her of anything they could sell. Trouble is, it don't do much good to have a claim if you can't be there to protect it from the next guy that comes along. Especially if he's got a crow bar with him."

"Is that what will happen to her? The locals will strip her?" Leda finally climbed the ladder to the deck. She had watched the departing patrol until it turned out of the channel and disappeared behind the end of the last of the huge stone islets that sheltered one side of the anchorage.

"Yeah, then the word will spread and someone smart will patch her enough to tow her somewhere so they can play cat and mouse with the insurance company," Matt explained. "It's a wonder she's not been found sooner."

"I gotta hand it ta the cops." Sven said, "Pete reported it late yesterday after he got back to Nassau and they had a boat out here early this morning. Not many thins get such prompt attention. Makes ya wonder."

Matt returned to Leda's concern. "The Inspector promised to call Pete and tell him what happened to us and to ask him to send someone out in a fast boat to guard our interests. The insurance company will probably reimburse us for our trouble. We can make some arrangements for her salvage when we get to Chub."

Leda appeared somewhat satisfied but then asked: "What does this report to the police about the boarding last night do to our safety now. Won't the Cubans still be looking for us and wanting GULL in small pieces?"

"Oh, yeah. That hasn't changed. They'll just have to be a little bit more careful now. I was hoping the Inspector was going toward Chub and we'd have an escort, but he got a call on the way here about something reported to the south, so he has to go down there to investigate. He said he'd call Chub later this evening to see if we get there all right."

"Th' down side," Sven interjected, "is that if th' cop is one of th' bad guys, he can pinpoint our position for th' chase boat. And I'm sure he's got some way of gettin' th' info ta 'em."

"Well, then, we'd better get a move on. I've got to go over there and get some of my things. I won't take long."

"I looked very carefully for your purse or anything that would reveal that you had been on the boat, but either the kidnapers took the purse or they threw it overboard."

"I took it with me to the gun locker. It should still be hanging in there on one of the brackets."

"They apparently took the document too. We all looked thoroughly and couldn't find it. I finally found a credit card receipt where your dad had bought fuel. The attendant had written down the documentation number. The Coast Guard will be able to find his address from the doc file. They'll notify the police. Where does he live?"

"Coral Gables."

"Where'd he keep the boat?"

"Dinner Key Marina. He lives alone, but he has several women friends that live in the same apartment complex. They'll find one of them if they ask around.

"Do any of them know how ta reach you," Sven asked.

"I don't think so… Oh, you mean out here?"

"Does anyone know that you were with your dad on the boat?" Matt persisted.

"My landlady. But I don't follow. What are you suggesting?"

"Well," Sven put in, "you're goin' ta show up in Miami in a couple of days, if we're lucky enough ta get you ta Chub, after having been aboard the boat from which your father disappeared."

"Our not reporting the whole story here will create a ton of suspicion in the mind of any cop worth his badge," Matt concluded.

"I'll tell the whole story at Chub."

"What'll ya tell 'em about how ya escaped? If they choose not ta believe ya, and us, for that matter, we become accessories after the fact."

"What are you talking about?" Leda cried. "We haven't done anything."

"Do you stand to inherit any substantial amount of money from your father? Wait a minute, don't answer. Just think a minute. Did the two of you get along? Anybody hear you have an argument lately? Any of these women friends of his jealous of you or have any reason to cast a shadow on your relationship with your dad?" Matt paused a moment, then went on. "A cop with any imagination at all could come up with enough of a motive to make all of our lives pretty miserable for a long time."

Leda was silent.

"Are ya sure about the cop on the patrol boat?" Sven asked, studying her worried countenance.

"Are you sure my dad is dead?"

The two men looked at each other. Finally Matt responded. "No, we're not. But he doesn't have anything they want now and he has seen the faces of a lot of people who won't want to be remembered. He would be a liability and they don't need to tie up people and places holding prisoners."

Leda was near to tears when he finished. A new flicker of fear jabbed at her heart, but she was too shaken to confirm it. Did they think she had done away with her father, waited until she heard someone coming and then locked herself in the locker knowing she'd be rescued?

"Are ya sure about the cop?" Sven asked again. "Which one was he?"

"The one with the mustache. He stayed in the pilot house all the time. He couldn't keep his eyes off GULL. He still had the binoculars on us when they turned out of the channel just now." She had been sitting on the bridge deck, her knees drawn up against her chest. Now she suddenly stood up and snatched the pistol from her belt, revealing a great red impression of the gun where it had been pressed against her stomach.

"When GAVIOTA was boarded he was on the trawler. I saw him from the porthole. He did the same thing as he did today. The others came aboard, but he stayed and shouted commands and questions. Of course, he wasn't in uniform then." As she turned to go below she released the clip from the gun. "May I keep this?" she asked. "I'm going to find Mr. 'Stache and I want to be prepared when I do."

As she disappeared down the steps, Matt could hear her clearing the round from the chamber and replacing it in the clip.

He had relaxed an hour ago. Finally the police knew of their troubles and he could hope that if an all points bulletin was issued or even if the incident was just discussed on the radio, it would discourage the container hunters. Now with a corrupt cop, or worse, maybe more than one, there was a chance of no protection at all. The knot in his stomach tightened again. Without this latest information, he had allowed a false sense of security to set in.

What else did they not know?

Sven looked at his pale young friend and surmising his thoughts, clucked, "There's one good thing about it. We know what one more of 'em looks like. It's easier ta fight back when ya know who ta hit."

"So where does 'Stache fit?" Matt asked. "He doesn't look much like the 'superior' that Fatso referred to."

Sven was slow to reply. "In this game looks can be more than deceivin'. But…. Fatso seems ta be middle management, and Brutus, a capo that runs a string of enforcers like Diego. 'Stache could be Mr. Big, running things, but not getting involved—hiding in the cop corps with a low rank, attracting little attention to hisself and using police information ta pull off his deals safely."

"What kind of deals is he up to? That's the question.

And what's in the canister? Is the canister the deal or is it profit from the deal that got lost, strayed or stolen?"

"Wrong and who cares," piped up Leda, climbing out of the cabin applying sun screen to her nose. "'Stache was taking orders from someone on the trawler that evening. Someone I never saw. 'Stache isn't the head cheese. And who cares if the canister is the deal or the dregs of one. Whatever it is, we can't help them get it, we're just in the way of their finding it. They're sure that it's not on GAVIOTA, but they won't rest until they've done to GULL what they did to her."

"Over my dead body," Sven growled.

"If you're trying to be funny, you're not," Matt shot back. "But the reality is that it's looking more and more like a possibility. Times three."

"Well, I ain't abandonin' no boat I contracted ta deliver, canister or no canister. I can understand ya not wantin' ta have anythin' ta do with GAVIOTA after what ya went through on her. And I hope your dad would…will understand. But that's your boat. This one don't belong to me. I got no right ta abandon her." He stopped suddenly. "Besides," he finished softly, "where would we go?"

"Well, I guess Leda's point is that, no matter whose boat it is, can we justify risking our lives, three of them, to meet the contract?"

"Do you think the owner would hold you to it if he knew the danger?" she asked.

"Ya still didn't answer my question. Where do we go?"

"I vote for Chub Cay," Leda volunteered. "We can leave the boat there. They'll watch it. We can fly back to Miami and the owner can make other arrangements. You've already made personal contributions beyond the call of duty. Besides, if the canister is contraband why should we risk our lives to commit a crime."

"What makes ya so sure there is a canister? And what makes ya so sure it's on GULL? Just because *they're* sure don't mean anything. They was sure when they boarded GAVIOTA remember." The older man stood and strode forward in an effort to vent the frustration he felt in trying to explain his loyalty to the boat and its owner.

Matt looked at Leda and she shrugged. He felt guilty. Was he being fair to Sven? After all, he had made a deal to deliver the yacht to Florida. Maybe he could compromise: take Leda to Chub and fly her out, then if he and Sven could come up with a workable plan, he'd stay with GULL to Miami.

Forward, Sven fiddled with the knot on the awning in deep thought. Maybe he could put in at Chub, put 'em both on a plane to Miami. By then he'd have a plan and he'd either single hand her home or pick up a crew at Chub. There was always someone hanging around Chub looking for a free ride somewhere.

Leda saw the look on Sven's face and the guilt on Matt's. Not a good plan to come between such close friends, she thought. They'll both hate me for it.

"Hey, I don't have a vote here," she said loudly. "You guys have a contract to honor. I appreciate what you've already done for me. Just get me to Chub and you do what you have to do." She paused, then, "I'm a big girl. I'll get a bird to Miami and when you get there we'll all meet over a drink and laugh about this."

But her light-heartedness did nothing to change the grim countenances of her new friends so she tried again. "Look, when we get to Chub we'll tell the cops the truth…almost. That after the patrol left this morning you went back aboard GAVIOTA one last time and you found me yelling in the compartment. I'll swear out a complaint or whatever I have to do and you guys go on about your business."

"They'll want to know why you didn't yell when the cops were aboard." Matt reminded.

"Hey, I was passed out. Didn't hear a thing until you two came back."

* * *

By the time the anchor was stowed, Sven's glance skyward told him it was near noon. After their scavenger trip to GAVIOTA Leda had cut chunks of cheese and now she broke open a box of saltines and began to pass the chunky sandwiches to Matt at the helm, and to Sven who pored over the navigation chart on the starboard seat.

"Five hours, at best," he growled, dropping the chart to the cushion and moving forward to con them out of the narrow channel.

It was good to be under way again, even if under power, but doubt clouded Sven's mind. GULL sailed with a divided crew and a fretful Captain. Three's always a problem, he thought. And when one is a woman among two men, the problem always reduces down to trouble. Well, a short passage and a brief farewell and it would be over. Matt would come along again on another delivery at another time and the disappointment would have healed and been forgotten.

Matt glanced up from the compass in time to see Leda avert her gaze. She again sat on the bridge deck, her feet pulled up beside her, favoring the tiny patch of shade that the awning bounced around the cockpit as GULL picked her way toward the sea. What the hell had happened? Matt asked himself. One minute we were all friends—all of us in the same …boat—and in a few seconds we were testy, and he feared, more than slightly distrustful of one another. He kicked himself for so readily siding with Leda, if for no other reason than that it made him look like a lovesick kid. But, more important, he had abandoned his friend. Worse yet, he had betrayed himself. He had not given any real thought to alternatives. 'The quicksand', Sven had clucked a hundred times. 'Think of alternatives or make 'em. Don't just stand there sinkin' deeper and deeper.' But Matt sank deeper into his own thoughts as GULL approached the right angle turn that would take her through the cut and into the deep water.

Suddenly Sven yelled from the foredeck and Matt, assuming he had seen a coral head, quickly backed down. But Sven was yelling something else: "Turn back! Turn back!"

CHAPTR FIVE

'In the land of the blind, the one-eyed man is King.'

THE MASQUERADE

This time they had anchored just past GAVIOTA's stern and payed out enough rode so that the two boats were again only a few feet apart. When properly fendered, GULL was pulled within arm's reach of the power yacht's listing stern and tied off.

Then the work began.

GAVIOTA's abundant stores were soon sorted and selectively transported to GULL. Time was even taken to prepare a hearty meal, for Leda's chunky cheese sandwiches would not sustain them for the strenuous labor in the offing.

Then Sven's brainstorm began to take shape.

GULL, like many long distance cruising sail boats had two long spinnaker poles stored on the forward bow sides of the mast itself. These poles, always used individually, held one lower corner of the huge triangular, parachute-like sail, away from the boat so that it would stay full of wind. GULL's poles were 25 feet long, made of solid spruce and tapered into a bronze fitting at each end. While the two men unshipped and removed the fittings from one end of a pole, Leda lay on her stomach under the life line, attaching a two inch wide stripe of red sail repair tape to the top of the hull just below the toe rail.

When she had finished, Matt helped her remove the teak stern board into which the boat's name and home port was carved. The operation took some care to avoid fouling the two brackets and steering harness for the outboard motors stowed in the lazarette. As they lifted the board away from the transom, they revealed the same information painted directly on the gleaming white planking, as was required by the Coast Guard for U.S. Documented vessels. Leda's deft paintbrush changed GULL to GIRL. Then she added 'OF' in the oval between the name and the home port, as Matt and Sven cut the fitting off a long wooden handled boat hook and created spreaders for the mizzen mast taking shape over her head.

By the time she finished cutting and applying large red sail tape letters to the hull on each quarter, the men had mounted the salvaged radar dome from GAVIOTA to the improvised mizzen mast and were ready to run the cable. It was led down one of the two scoop ventilators on the afterdeck. The other had been removed and it was into that fitting that the base of the new 'mast' had been stepped. Upper and lower shrouds, only strong enough to support the bogus stick and the dome, were led down to the toe rail where extra turnbuckles had been rigged. Then the 'boom', with its fake, furled sail attached, was mounted, extending aft over the transom.

The cutter, GULL had become the yawl, GIRL OF MIAMI. The large red letters on her quarters made the name plain and hopefully easy to see from a distance.

Now Matt and Leda returned to GAVIOTA to launch the outboard powered boat that served as its dinghy. The boat, FAST FUN, hung in davits from the crazily listing starboard quarter. The powerful engine, almost too large for the boat, had been chosen so that several water skiers could be towed at the same time. Matt debated about removing it before trying to lower the boat, a task that would require considerable care and some muscle to keep the smaller boat from scraping the sides of GAVIOTA as it descended.

"There's no need to stop at Chub now, is there?" Leda asked. "We can go directly to Bimini and make a police report at the same time we clear immigration."

Matt was thoughtful as he released the safety catch on the set of falls. "Seems that way. Unless Sven has strong feelings otherwise."

Leda punched the 'PULSE' button on the winch control and the boat dropped a few inches and stopped.

"Looks like I'll have to get in and fend off all the way down," Matt remarked, climbing into the slightly swinging boat. "Stay on 'pulse' and let's take it in small doses." Leda responded and FAST FUN lurched downward. When their heads were at the same level, Matt leaned out of the boat and kissed her.

"This is a hell of a place to try to start a relationship," he said, "but in the last twenty-four hours I've come close—and so have you—to never having another one again. If this little masquerade doesn't work, I…we may still not live to have one."

He kissed her again. "In any case, I think you should fly home from the first place we stop. We'll still have to cross the stream and who knows what can happen."

Leda didn't answer. She punched the pulse button again and watched thoughtfully as Matt descended slowly, in short jerks, pushing powerfully against the side of the cruiser. Finally, when it was in the water he brought the boat around to the stern, there to be loaded with an assortment of paints, thinners, rags, bottles, spare gasoline cans and an auxiliary outboard fuel tank.

The electric starter spun the huge outboard to life and the couple circled to the stern of GULL where they gathered her dinghy that a scant twenty-four hours before had given up the body of Ramariez. Now, it held only GULL's small green sunshade, which had been replaced by the larger blue one from GAVIOTA, and some rolls of two inch wide, blue sail repair tape.

A few minutes later the entire inventory of both craft were spread out under the green sunshade on the sand of the nearby small cay.

"I'm a pretty independent type, Matt," Leda began as she selected a paint can and set to prying off its top. "I haven't been deeply involved with a man in almost five years. I fell in love with a Viet Nam vet my last year of college. He was pretty screwed up and I was dumb enough to think that I could help him put his life together again. We tried for four years and got as far as we were able to go. In the end I had nothing to show for it. When Jack and I started falling apart, my dad came to my rescue."

She indicated that Matt should help her invert the dinghy so that she could use the bright red paint that she had been studiously stirring as she spoke.

"Dad ran a string of garden centers in half dozen cities in Florida. I didn't have any business training. I had majored in foreign languages, student government and theatrical productions, in ascending order of priorities. But Dad helped me open a small flower shop in the lobby of a friend's hotel. He was convinced that a lot more people would buy flowers if somebody made it easy for them. He thought they could be marketed as impulse purchases. He was right and now I've got eight mini shops in hotels in Miami Beach.

"They keep me pretty busy running between them and week-ends are the busiest. Dad had to brow beat me to come with him last week and I wouldn't have if he hadn't sent the private plane after me. He said one of the important things about management was knowing when not to manage."

"So, do you like being in business for yourself?"

"There's only one attraction. I'm my own boss. I don't make enough money to justify the time commitments. But dad said I'd learn to work smarter and not so hard." She paused thoughtfully.

"There's a lot of things I want to do and it's so much easier when I don't have to consider the rights and feelings of others."

"How many of those things can you do in the next few hours? Those guys have to pass by here at almost any time now, Sven is guessing about how far north they may have gone. 'Stache, as you call him, will have found a way to let them know that we are here and I think we'll be damn lucky if we get all this stuff done before they show for a look see. If we do get it done and we have any luck, they'll take a quick look and move on, not recognizing us —thinking that we left just after the patrol did and MIAMI GIRL is the new tenant of the anchorage."

"GIRL OF MIAMI," Leda corrected.

"Now don't get me wrong," he continued, nodding in acknowledgment, "Sven's plan has a lot of merit, but if they get close enough to recognize either of us, all the paint and re-rigging in the world won't help."

"What are you saying?"

"Maybe we should still put into Chub and get you out of here before these guys get desperate. If they know we were here, this close to Chub, and they suddenly can't find GULL, or what looks like GULL, they'll start taking a very close look at every boat between here and Miami. Odds are they'll find us again."

Leda stopped working, the red paint dribbled from her brush onto the finished portion of the dinghy bottom. "Then don't go," she said simply. "Get us to Chub and leave GULL there."

"He'll go alone if I don't."

"Why? That's nuts!"

"Sven's sorta old fashioned and stubborn as hell. He

has a contract to deliver this boat and he takes that responsibility very seriously. And he's stubborn enough to try and buck anybody or anything that will get in the way."

"You're frightening me, Matt."

"I'm sorry. You look around us at the sea, the sky—how

peaceful it is, and you can misjudge the danger we're in."

"Look, if you're trying to talk me into a little tumble with you behind those bushes, you're working too hard at it and you'll have to wait till I've finished and cleaned the paint off my hands..."

"Christ...," he retorted.

"But, if you've got some positive suggestion about how to get us out of this, I wish to hell you'd hurry up with it." She returned to the unfinished paint job.

"I want to put into Chub and call Pete to personally fly you back to Miami. You've come to mean a lot to me in this short time," he said awkwardly.

"And what if Sven disagrees?" she asked, avoiding his gaze and the larger issue he raised.

"I'll talk him into it. I don't think he wants the extra responsibility of having you along anyway."

"And can you also talk him into leaving GULL at Chub and breaking the contract?"

"Probably not."

"And you'll go with him if he goes?"

Matt paused a moment before he replied. "I can't let him risk it alone."

"Then I'll go too."

"What? Why, for crying-out-loud?"

"Because those guys have my dad."

"What, and you're going to capture them when they come alongside? Come on!"

"No. You two have beaten them once. At Elbow, you guys came back from a complete surprise to a complete rout. I don't think they're so tough. You can beat them again. But you need me."

She paused a moment for effect then pushed on: "I think Sven's plan is great. There's only one thing. You need to have a different crew on GIRL OF MIAMI. A woman at the helm is the finishing touch to the masquerade. GULL had an all male crew." She completed the last stroke of the paint brush, stepped back to look at the job, dabbed at a place where the old paint shone through, then dropped the brush into a corned beef can half-full of paint thinner.

Matt was silent a moment as he digested this new thought, then he asked, "So how does that get your father back or even punish these guys for snatching him?"

"My father has powerful friends in Miami. They can, 'take care of things' in the Bahamas." She made quote mark finger signs and went on. "But after the bad guys are caught, I need you two to be alive to be witnesses in court. And if Sven is too hard-headed to think straight and you are too good a pal to let a buddy down, then you both need all the help you can get." She paused, but before he could reply she put the paint can down and extending her hands, began to stalk him. "Besides that, I like a guy who wears cutoffs with great red hand prints on his butt." And she proceeded to make him match the description, all the while stifling his protests with ever more aggressive kisses.

They lay on the remnant of the bunk sheet that Matt had ripped his rag fuses from. The awning had been rearranged to shade the small hollow behind the screen of low scrub growth.

"So why didn't you marry her?" Why did other women become subjects of post coital discussions, Leda wondered. She sorted her scanty briefs from the pile of clothing that had been hastily removed and raising her buttocks, she pulled them on—all the while brushing the sand clear of their final destination.

"Oh, Flash wasn't the marrying kind, I don't think." He opened one eye and watched as a freckled breast disappeared under the hem of her t-shirt. "That's why I first nicknamed her Flash." He sat up and fumbled for his own briefs. "She only came to class whenever she wanted to. No more than one or two times the first month of the semester. Then one day I was lecturing on the difference between John Stuart Mill's 'greatest good for the greatest number' and Kant's 'decision based on principle'.

For some reason this was the first thing that I had said that had arrested her attention. She and two or three others loitered after class, asking questions, arguing points of view and giving examples of why one or the other argument was better."

Matt stood up, brushed away the sand as best he could, donned the briefs and the newly decorated cut-offs. "We all retired to the local campus watering hole at her suggestion that she buy us a beer. It was my first inkling that she might be well-to-do. The next 'flash', aside from the fact that she started to attend class regularly, was her question about how she might donate some money to a scholarship fund for philosophy majors."

"Was that before or after she seduced you?"

"Oh, after. But I'm not sure that it was my masterful performance in bed. I think it might have been the abject poverty of one of the guys that was in that inquisitive group at the pub. She may have been screwing him too by then. She was generous with more than her money."

The dinghy paint was still tacky, but they began to load FAST FUN with the other stuff.

"We'd been together pretty steadily for several months and when Spring break came she tried to get me to go to Jamaica with her but I was trying to complete an article for publication and I refused to go. My explanation that my academic career depended on little things like that didn't cut much ice with her. At any rate we got into a discussion about what it took to get ahead in academia and she was very cynical about it all. She said she'd fix it for me."

"She'd *fix* it for you?"

"Yeah. And damn if she didn't. After the break she dragged in this pale-faced guy that she introduced as her accountant and asked how she could establish an endowed chair in philosophy in my name."

"Could she do that?"

"Sure. All it took was 5 million of her dollars."

"You mean her daddy's dollars."

"No. She was descended from old New England money all right. But I took it that her father was the black sheep of the family. Her uncle had expanded the family's business empire by building on turn-of-the-century wealth and attempted to shelter as much as possible in trusts for all his siblings' kids. She was older than the average student and she had come into her trust fund several years before. She and the pale-face had apparently made a lot of good investments and I feel relatively sure that those 5 mills were her earnings."

"So how was this to solve your problem? Or her problem of not having willy-nilly access to your body."

"Well, it didn't immediately. You see, the faculty objected to a chair being named after a nobody and particularly a non-tenured nobody. So they suggested that it be called by another name, but she insisted it had to be in "Dr. Matt's" name. I told her it was an absurd thing to insist on. She wouldn't budge. The board of governors were lusting after the money and the faculty was standing on principle. I urged the board to refuse the money. And I bloodied the nose of the faculty member who said his dick was bigger than mine and with my permission he might be able to get us 10 million.

"The dean pulled strings, knowing which side *his* bread was buttered on, and I was given tenure—thus removing one hurdle. The board ignored the faculty's protest and I was *persona non grata* among my colleagues. Upshot: The college got the money and I resigned. Flash was ticked off at my decision and disappeared."

"End of story!"

"Oh no."

Damn, thought Leda. Why *do* other women become subject matter for post coital discussions?

They decided to leave the dink to dry and Matt cranked up the big outboard.

"That's why she is Flash. She kept reappearing like a fish that rises from the depths, flashing a silvery side to the sun and then darting away before she could fall to anyone's bait. She was waiting for me on the lawn outside a classroom in Florida that next winter. I had enrolled in a computer programming course. I had had it with academia and I wanted a whole new career. Logic had always been my strong suit and the essence of programming is logic. It was as if the whole fiasco in the spring hadn't happened. We took up where we had left off. She paid for trips to every computer convention in the world. It was a hot new profession and developing rapidly at that time and people were creating stuff so fast that you couldn't take it all in if you had to read about it. And there weren't the 'zines that there are now.

"It wasn't long before I probably knew more about the field than anybody needed to know. I was spending all my time assimilating with no time to apply the information. It wasn't necessary—unless I wanted to be a theorist, and I wasn't about to go the academic route again. I had tons more expertise than most companies were prepared to pay for in those days. But I soon had a reputation for getting a system up and running fast and training people to keep it running. The jobs rolled in and I was working too hard and Flash darted off into her world of money and leisure again where I never felt comfortable."

The paint and supplies were returned to GAVIOTA and Matt carefully arranged his home-made pyrotechnics on FAST FUN as Leda prodded the rest of the story out of him.

"Did she come back again?"

"Oh, yeah, two or three times. And I'm convinced that it was for the strangest of reasons. She was far short of being an intellectual but she remained fascinated with the Mill/Kant decision-making contrast. I could never fathom what motivated this interest, but each time, within a day after she'd surface, there would be questions about these theories. The interesting thing was her struggle to accept what's called the '*prima-facie* obligation'".

"The wha-a-at?"

"Well, she was a bit of a purist. At first she embraced Mill's idea that you always make the moral decision based on the consequences that provided the greatest good for the greatest number. That seemed easy. Then she recognized the difficulty of calculating long term consequence and she opted for Kant's idea of always making the decision based on a widely accepted religious, political or social principle."

"Like?"

"Well—, like we ostensibly reject torture to obtain a criminal's confession. That's a principle of our cultural/political correctness. And most of us would like to say that we subscribe to that principle. But lately the '*prima facie* obligation' has allowed us to deviate when we can't always strictly adhere to the principle."

"I don't follow."

"Well, in the extreme case: The kidnapped infant is in danger of dying where it's been hidden by the kidnapper, who's been caught but refuses to tell where the child is. As time passes and the child's doom draws nearer, it may be OK to break the kidnapper's thumb if that would induce him to reveal the hiding place. That's the *prima facie* obligation."

"Hardly earth shaking."

"True. But in another context it might be. Situation: Verified ongoing ethnic cleansing of a minority within the borders of a belligerent country. Effective, preventive, outside interference would trigger World War III. *Prima facie* allows outsiders to substitute vilification for action. That's the part that Flash objected to. It allowed someone to escape a moral responsibility, she said. She called it the 'weasel option'. For all her materialistic behavior, she had a strong inner integrity. And it seemed to have regular confrontations with things going on in the other part of her life—the one that I never entered and that she never explained."

"And which she returned to regularly."

"Oh, yeah. Each time when I became too busy to run off with her someplace to play for a few days. That's how my business finally got organized and I hired the first manager. She showed up one Friday morning with tickets to Cancun for the week-end and I couldn't get away. Then she showed up on Monday morning with this chain-smoking older guy in tow who had just been down-sized out of a management position and was afraid he'd never be hired anywhere again. He was really glad to have a job and he was really what I needed. I still don't know where she found him. When I ask him about it, he just smiles mysteriously through his pall of cigarette smoke. I keep giving him raises and he keeps making more money for me. I hope I can retire before the cigarettes kill him."

"So now you have all this free time."

"Yeah, more or less."

"And so you and Flash can get away regularly now." Leda suddenly detected a little envy, a little—could it be resentment—in her tone. But she lightened up immediately with, "Must be nice. Time and money can make lots of things possible." She smiled down at Matt as she helped him tie FAST FUN along GULL's starboard quarter.

"No, that's the other thing about this whole damned affair. She was just as apt to take off as she had been before. Then three years ago she said she was going to spend a week with her dad—her mother had been dead a long time—on St. Lucie. I haven't heard from her since. She rarely stayed away more than six months at a time, so I don't know what the deal is. I tried to find her for about a year through our few mutual acquaintances. I even turned Smokey, my manager, loose on the chase. He spent the better part of a month on it. I finally filed a missing person report on her, but the cop looked pityingly at me as he reviewed the history part of the report—wondering how a stupid bastard like me could have survived the evolutionary process, I think."

"So where *are* you in this thing now?"

"Oh, *out* of this thing." He paused a moment. "I really didn't know how much she had meant to me until I finally realized that she wouldn't be coming back. But I also realized that we both, rather consciously, had kept the relationship loose—as if we knew that we would finally disengage. Still, the first year after she left was a hard one for me. An occasional delivery job with Sven helped take my mind off things and now I think I've fully recovered. I rarely think of her any more. The last two years have been a pretty sedate period."

Leda readjusted the second fender between the two boats, then reached down and grabbed the hand he offered and helped him up and over the lifeline. Why did she feel so relieved?

* * *

Sven pushed the throttle forward and spun the wheel. The huge outboard roared and FAST FUN's almost flat-bottomed bow came out of the water into an immediate plane. He skimmed along at a right angle to GULL's beam, then turned to parallel her track and throttled back matching her speed.

He had convinced his crew that the chasers were far to the north in the alley or they would have overtaken them by now. So, thinking that if he were wrong they probably wouldn't recognize GULL now anyway, it was just as well to use up some of the daylight. GULL would be even harder to spot in the dark. They had cat-napped while the dinghy's new paint dried and had not cleared the tear drop harbor and turned north until late in the afternoon.

The water was deep now and the course obvious, so Sven had taken the time to appraise the job they had done. Was GULL indeed hidden behind the paint and hasty rigging of a second mast? He looked critically at her from half a mile away… as if he were the approaching pursuers, craning to recognize their quarry.

The newly painted dinghy, turned upside down in her chocks on the foredeck changed the profile somewhat. The larger and different colored awning and the two outboard engines now hanging from their transom mounts were definitely different. The 'mizzen mast' would not stand close inspection by a sailor, but Sven was willing to bet that the ignorance of his adversaries was sufficient that a mast was a mast was a mast. The radar dome looked quite at home on the fake spreaders. Many cruisers mounted them there and its eyes in the coming darkness would give Sven a level of confidence that he could not measure. It had been one of the concluding factors as his plan had occurred to him on the first exit of the harbor.

If he could drop her at Chub...should he drop her at Chub? That part of the plan had not yet become clear. This aspect kept intruding on the fine tuning of the rest of the ploy.

The wide red stripe below the toe rail on the hull and the new name on her quarters gave a gaudy quality to GULL that Sven didn't like, but it was different and that's what counted. She'd be towing the redecorated FAST FUN too. Matt and the girl...woman had redone the maker's logo and speed stripes in blue tape also. All in all GULL should merit a relatively short look before her pursuers would plough past, sure that their prize was still ahead of them somewhere.

Only the bowsprit caused Sven some minor concern. Few modern boats had them and if the chasers came to suspect that their quarry might have attempted camouflage, the first component to look for would be the one impossible to hide and of which there were only a few. Sven put it into the possible, but not probable category. He would depend again on his conviction that his opponents were basically sailboat ignorant.

He pushed the throttle forward again and watched the log needle hurtle into orbit, finally hovering at 42 knots. The boat was difficult to control at this speed and Matt would have to practice with it as soon as possible. If the plan worked, that would be plenty fast enough and he would not have to keep up that speed for very long. Sven eased back the throttle and turned in a wide arc to port. Now well ahead of GULL, he crossed her course, passed her on the port side for a quick inspection, then rumbled up to her quarter where Leda waited to take the painter.

But he told her not to tie off and after he had attached a length of line to the painter, he payed the boat out astern so that it rode, bow up, 30 feet in GULL's wake.

The wind had stiffened in the late afternoon and now there may have been 12 knots of breeze off their port bow. It promised an almost perfect compass course to Chub Cay, if it held. A few minutes later, the sunshade doused, the mainsail up and the ginny and jib a-fly, Matt killed the engine. GULL heeled to the wind and an inner peace flooded into the tension-racked bodies of her crew.

They had two hours of daylight and another three under the moon before Chub Cay. GULL slipped through the water, the gentle 'schuss' of her bow wave punctuating her progress with gentle sighs of contentment. Her crew sat silently in the cockpit, the heat of the dying sun offset by the caress of the wind. Soon the sun would set and it would be almost cool.

It was time to firm up some things.

Sven and Matt both spoke at once. Matt, still at the helm, deferred to his friend.

"Seems to me, the first thing is: do we stop at Chub? I feel purty sure them guys are in the alley west of there and will work back east ta that point. I expect that they got someone there already lookin' out fer us. Might not be one of their men. Could be a dock hand, the manager, anybody, thinking he's doing a favor for a couple of cruisers trying ta rendezvous.

"Now if they get there before we do, they'll check with their guy to see if we made port yet. They might go in ta take a look for themselves, or they might come on without stoppin'"

"And" Matt inserted, "if we could slip past them in the dark, it would be safe for us to pull into Chub later and make a full report to the police in the morning. And get Leda on Pete's plane to Miami," he pressed.

"No," she said, her tone revealing that the argument was already an old one. "You can't wait in Chub long enough to raise Pete—he may not even be available—and then wait for him to fly there and pick me up. For that matter I could call the jockey that brought me out the other day."

"But…, "Matt started to say.

"But," she went on, "that's not the real issue." She turned to Sven and putting one foot up on the cockpit cushion, she leaned an elbow on the raised knee and said with exaggerated seriousness: "You need me on this caper."

Sven smiled for the first time in a lot of hours and realized the growing warmth that had been building toward her.

"If they get to Chub before we do they'll think they're ahead of us and they'll come back looking in every possible anchorage." She looked at Sven for confirmation. He nodded. "And wherever or whenever they cross us," she swung back to Matt, "you need me on the helm. They won't be looking for a woman. They've seen both of you guys close up and if they recognize either one of you, all we've done today will be for nothing." She flushed with excitement.

"Well, that's a pretty good idea you got," Sven launched in, "but we can use it without you, really. We can get up the kid here." Now he had a gleam in his eye as he looked at Matt. "Put him in a towel for a skirt and one of your brassieres up top, a straw hat and sun glasses and…"

"I don't have any brassieres," she said flatly and went on while Sven climbed out of the generation chasm.

"And I'm frankly afraid that if I get off at Chub and report to the police, they'll hold me there. And since we don't know which cops are the good cops, I don't want to talk to any cops 'till I get to Miami."

Neither man spoke as each assimilated and weighed the ramifications of this new tack. She went on. "Is it necessary to stop at Chub for anything if I don't get off there?"

The row of jerry cans lashed to the stern rail held gasoline for the three outboards. Their own diesel tanks were hardly diminished by the several hours of motoring. Food was plentiful, if plain. Only the luxuries of ice and a new radio beckoned them ashore and the siren call for the latter was relatively loud in Sven's ears.

"I don't like this," Matt finally said.

"What?" Leda asked.

"We're getting too tired to think and we don't have enough information to make good decisions even if we weren't. We're going on guesses and assumptions. We only *think* that there was a larger boat hidden at Elbow. We are *assuming* that it is the same boat that boarded GAVIOTA. We are *hoping* that that's the only large boat they have. We're..."

"*Chub Cay, Chub Cay, Chub Cay, this is MOTHER'S FUR COAT, Whiskey, Yankee, Bravo, Two Thousand.*" The volume on the radio had not been turned down when the engine was stilled and the message was heard clearly in the cockpit. "*This is Chub Club,*" answered a very British sounding voice. "*Go ahead, MOTHER.*" No one in the islands bothered with FCC niceties. The conversation continued on the emergency channel.

"*Any sign of GULL yet? Over.*"

"*Sorry? Gull? I've only just come on. 'Fraid I'm not up on Gull. Can you prompt me a bit?*"

Leda hurried down the ladder to adjust the volume.

There was a hint of exasperation in MOTHER'S voice when he came back. "*We're to rendezvous with our friends on GULL at Chub. Their radio's bad and we can't raise them. We called earlier to have your dock master look out for them and tell them we'll be a little late.*"

"*Oh, right! Here's the bloody note. It's one of those sticky sorts. Came unstuck actually. Yes, well, according to this she hadn't showed at half-past—that's uh... twenty minutes ago. I'll check the DM, he's having a bite in the dining room. Do stand by.*"

The silence hung heavy aboard GULL, until suddenly Leda shouted: "MOTHER'S FUR COAT! They were tied up at West End when we stopped there Saturday night. She's a sport fisherman about 55 feet. She had a tuna tower on her and a bunch of very drunk people."

Sven had decided that the bloke at Chub must be the bartender who had been pressed into service to answer the radio while the dock master ate his dinner. Sven knew the DM. He was a Brit too, a blue water sailor who had come ashore almost ten years ago to do a stint as DM on Walker Cay while his wife had a baby. As often happens, one thing had led to another and they had never gone to sea again. Sven shook his head suddenly. An old and painful memory had pushed into his already crowded mind. No time for that now, he chided himself.

"*'Allo, MOTHER, Mr. Dock says no sign of GULL. Can I give them a new message if they show? Over.*"

"*Uh, no,*" the hesitant reply came back. "*We're about a half hour west. We'll be there soon. No need….MOTHER out.*"

"*Uh. Well. Right then. Chub out,*" the bartender said, his British sensitivities apparently bruised by this lack of civility. The transmission stopped as suddenly as it had begun and the gentle crackle of dead air sizzled on.

"What was that all about?" Matt called from the distance of the helm.

"Well, I was right about that," Sven swore. "He's in the alley, west and coming back toward Chub."

"But what's this guy got to do with the Cubans and the trawler and the cops?" cried Leda in frustration. "He's speaking perfect English."

"We don't know," Matt said. "This proves what I was saying a while ago." He turned the helm sharply to port to counter a sudden gust that heeled GULL over enough so that Leda had to grab the ladder for support. Slowly she climbed onto the bridge deck, where Sven lay in wait.

"Tell me everything you can remember about MOTHER'S FUR COAT. Boy, how many times have I heard that one before. Must be a dozen boats with that name. Where's her hail port?"

"I'm trying to remember. It was some place in Virginia. Some place I never heard of. Something about a river."

"Oh, that's a lot of help. There's about 50 rivers in Virginia," Matt said tiredly. The strain had begun to show on all of them. The ordeal of the night before for the men and the captivity of Leda had only been slightly eased by the short naps they had stolen while the paint dried on the dinghy.

"No, it wasn't the name of a river. It was something about a river."

"Deltaville." It came as a statement, not a question. Sven was sure of it. Leda's look and confirming nod invited him to go on. "'Bout an hour's drive from Foggy Bottom on the Chesapeake Bay. 'Bout a dozen marinas there. Most of 'em filled with boats owned by bureaucrats from DC."

"You think that's the key? The head cheese is a politico pulling the strings so these Cubans dance down here?" She asked the question half in puzzlement, half in revelation. "That might explain why they're looking for this boat. Didn't you say the owner was a Washington big wig?" she continued, looking at Matt.

"Yeah, he's a lobbyist. Reps several big corporations that sell almost exclusively to the government," Matt replied.

"All military stuff," Sven injected. "Support stuff, mostly. No arms." He shook his head.

"Sven, this breeze is freshening. I think we could roll in that ginny some. Maybe even douse the jib. It would make it easier for me to hold for Chub and be more comfortable too. And I could use some relief here. I'm really beginning to sag. If you'll take it for a couple of hours, I'll spell you again before we get to Chub."

Sven nodded and still in deep thought, uncleated the ginny sheet and reeled in several feet of the large sail. Immediately GULL righted herself somewhat and the strain on the entire rig was reduced. Thoughtfully, he tied off the sheet again, reeled in the jib completely and made a slight adjustment to the main, then went silently to the helm.

The sun, a great burning ball hanging low in the sky,

sent shafts of the dying day across the port rail. Sven skimmed the horizon with a practiced eye, pausing a moment to study a white power boat several miles astern. The considerable hull above the water proclaimed her modern design. Leda, not being able to make such a quick distinction between the shape of this hull and that of a traditional trawler she dreaded to see, snatched the binoculars to her eyes to study the rapidly gaining boat.

The radio came alive again. "*Chub Cay, Chub Cay*," the voice called. "*This is MOTHERS FUR COAT, Whiskey, Yankee, Bravo, two thousand.*" There was no mistaking that this was a different voice. The rounded drawl of Virginia pervaded the entire speech pattern.

"*Righto. Chub, here. Go ahead MOTHER.*"

"*Yo, Chub. This is Bubba Winfrey. A few minutes ago while we were eatin' dinner, my captain monitored a call to ya-all using our name and call letters. Now, ah know the FCC ain't operative out here, but it gives me some heartburn thinkin' ah might be given undue credit for utterance or deed done in ma good name.*

"*Now if the party's still listenin' in, ah'll forgive a duplication of boat names, but it grieves me sore that ya-all used ma call letters. Now, lord knows ah'd rather it'd be somethin' more like 'Brave Rebel Bourbon', but it ain't. But it* is *mine. And ah'd be real thankful if the offendin' party would cease and desist.*" He paused a moment. "*Now, if it's any hep: we are 'bout an hour south of Chub and we been on this track all afternoon. We've seen nary a boat going north 'cept the yawl just ahead of us. Can't make out her name, but she's got a red dink on her foredeck and she's towin' a runabout. Looks like she's trimmed in red…oh, yeah, I see her quarter boards now. Let's see….GIRL OF MIAMI it sez.*" He paused. "*Sorry. Your friends are probably up ahead there gettin' in pretty close by now.*" The pause again. "*Purty evenin', ain't it? This is MOTHER'S FUR COAT, dubia, wah, bee, two kay. And ah'm out.*"

Sven had turned often to monitor the progress of the overtaking boat. The big sport fisherman churned past a hundred yards off GULL's port side silhouetted against red sky and red water.

"Saturday night's party seems to still be going on." Leda observed, finally lowering the glasses and bracing herself for the wake rolling toward GULL. She continued to watch the big cruiser out of sight, trying to reverse the pat theory she had just accepted a short time before. Matt's right, she thought. We know too little and we jump to dangerous conclusions. She studied Sven's face, but he was busy settling the boat back on course after the wake had passed under her and she could read nothing there. She braced herself into the corner at the high end of the bridge deck and fell into deep thought.

Sven had been weighing the relative merits of being sighted and reported. On the one hand, they had been passed off as a yawl. He also knew MOTHER'S crew had seen three people in the cockpit, even though no mention was made of it.

This could mean that when GULL met the chasers coming south, they'd be given even less notice since the trawler would be expecting them and once identified, they'd be passed off quickly as a known quantity and the hunt would continue elsewhere.

Would the chasers wait at Chub for MOTHER to arrive, knowing that if GULL did not come in first, she must be hiding somewhere between there and the tear drop harbor?

Why did the trawler (was it the trawler?) use another boat's call letters? How did she know them? Boat name yes, but call letters only if she had monitored a call. If she had monitored a call then she knew that MOTHER was in the islands and would probably hear her call. Not much subterfuge in that. Why not use her own name? Would we, or someone else recognize it?

Who made the first call? There had been no trace of any accent, island or Cuban, in the caller's speech. Was it the trawler and was Fatso's superior aboard now?

Where had MOTHER started from today that she should have been on 'this track' all afternoon? At the speed she was making as she passed she could have started somewhere well south of Elbow and still made Chub before dark.

Why had the trawler used another name and call letters?

"Why'd they use another name and call letters?" Leda asked.

"They didn't want anyone listening to know who they were," Sven said automatically.

Neither wondered about the fact that the other was on the same mental excursion.

"When I was in college," she said, musing, "I'd go back to school after a weekend at home and I'd make a long distance person-to-person telephone call to myself. My mom would answer and say, 'Sorry Leda's not here,' but my folks would know I had gotten back safely."

Sven looked at her a long, grave minute, then nodded.

"If you're right, we fooled 'em. We passed inspection," he said.

"If I'm right, when MOTHER gets to Chub, the net will have closed and there will be no fish."

"On th' other hand, we ain't got much evidence ta hold MOTHER on. The D.C., Deltaville, canister connection is purty speculative. Have ta be careful about theories that ya like too well. Affection sometimes clouds yer thinking." Leda was not sure if the statement carried a double meaning. "One way or another, they'll have a plane in th' air by mornin'," he finished.

The sun crouched just a moment on the watery horizon, then purposefully slipped away leaving an already risen moon to tat together the night's lacy cloud cap. The sea and sky had melted together in the fire of the sunset, but then mellowed into soft shades of purple and lavender. The hard edged statements of the day gave way to the gentle suggestions of dusk. But, as with all things of beauty, the twilight was short-lived and the purple shadows deepened into black, and golden ripples were exchanged for silver ones.

Sven, almost automatically, aligned the compass card and when he was dead on course, looked up to see at which star the bowsprit pointed. And with this easier point of reference, he placed the whole mechanical operation of steering on a subconscious 'automatic pilot', freeing his mind to tussle with the parts of the puzzle which refused to bend to his reason.

Do I dare to take Leda out of this legal jurisdiction and risk the suspicion that that would cause? Can I leave her in the hands of the crooked cop? If she stays with us, do we go into Chub for a radio? We really need a radio. We ought to be able to sneak in in the dark. I'll contact the DM and one way or another get a radio and put back to sea tonight. That'll put us at Bimini just after one in the afternoon tomorrow.

He looked at his watch. It would be eleven when they got to Chub. An hour to anchor, dash over to the Club, run down the DM, dash back and up anchor. Underway again by midnight. The moon would set about 1 a.m. He wanted to clear the entrance buoy before the moon set.

The important unknown. Where would the DM be? How long would it take to find him? Would he have a calibrated radio that Sven could borrow or buy? He could not take a new one off the shelf, even if he somehow got access to the ship's store at Great Harbor, the nearby marina. It probably wouldn't be calibrated.

The tide would be low at 10:30, so he would enter the relatively shallow channel on a rising tide and leave with even more water under him. That suited him fine. He knew the tight confines of the harbor well. He mentally selected the best anchorage. It was not the best when it blew from the northwest as it was now. But the wind was not strong and it might even lay completely by then. It was not now so brisk as it had been when he had taken the helm.

His ruminations went on. He attempted to mentally walk through each aspect of the stopover. He ate the meal that Leda offered with hardly an acknowledgment and she seemed to know what he was about and left him to his careful process.

She wondered if he had decided to keep her on for the trip across the bank? Had he finally decided to stop at Chub?

At a little past 9:30 the wind shifted and softened so that Sven feared that his careful schedule would be disrupted. He had Leda call Matt and the sails were furled and the engine started. Matt ate a hasty supper and considerably refreshed, took his trick at the helm. Sven retired for a nap with instructions to wake him at first sight of the light on the entry buoy. He was pretty sure that they would make the entry about 11:00, he told Matt. They should have enough water in the channel, but he knew the deepest portions and wanted to be on the con as they made their approach.

One of Leda's questions was answered. GULL would stop at Chub. But, would she be on the cutter when it left?

She had cat-napped, cooked and cat-napped again. She had begun to throw off the fatigue that had plagued her at sunset but knowing the uncertainties ahead, she lay down again on the cockpit cushion and stretched a lean leg out to rub the top of her foot on the hairy back of Matt's calf. He responded with a thrown kiss but no answer to the question on her face. She decided to regard no news as good news—surely he would have told her if she were to be ready to depart on arrival—and she promptly fell asleep.

Sven had said nothing to Matt about her fate aboard GULL. Rested and with time to reflect, He had gained confidence in the masquerade and felt that if they kept going after the short stop at Chub, they might indeed elude their tormentors yet.

His nap had precluded a spin in FAST FUN as Sven had advised when he had laid out the battle plan in the early afternoon. So he went over the various elements, wondering if the hastily done preparations were complete. Did he have everything on FAST FUN he'd need? Were they stowed so that he could go pounding across the waves at high speed and still reach what he needed when he needed it?

The throb of the engine had dulled his senses somewhat and Matt only slowly became aware of the moving light off his starboard bow perhaps a mile ahead. Striding to the bridge deck he snatched the binoculars that Leda had left there and, behind the helm again, studied the oncoming boat. He could see the green running light and the white one on the short pennant staff just above the windshield. The white hull shone clearly in the moonlight. She was a traditional island trawler. He could hear her heavy diesel now and its growl increased as he suddenly saw both red and green running lights. She had turned and was coming straight toward GULL.

Chapter Six

Independent American men are often confused with the corps of development arrested 30 somethings who hell around on-road in their off-road pickup trucks. Such confusion was never a problem for Sven because the distinction became clear after only a short acquaintance. And since that independence was solidly based on a carefully conceived value system and a rational behavior pattern to maintain it, many less self disciplined types found it to be too much work to keep up more than a tangential relationship with him.

Many women who were initially attracted by his rough good looks and what they regarded as his romantic life style, were discouraged early on if he perceived a shallowness of character, or worse, empty headedness. His speech was a buffer that winnowed out many whom he would have rejected anyway.

But there was one.... And my interview with her gave a truer measure of the man than any yet garnered. But only a small part of her story impacts GULL's trial.

PLEASURE HOUSE

Leda stood bravely in the moonlit cockpit, her white shorts and halter-top hopefully proclaiming her gender. She grasped the helm and peered first at the guiding star then at the approaching boat. The red glow from the compass light tinted her bare stomach and revealed the pistol thrust once again into her waistband.

Matt stood on the bottom step of the companionway ladder, head and shoulders protruding above the combing. The Uzi lay on the hatch cover before him. He had plugged in the powerful hand-held searchlight but had not turned it on. In his left hand he held the binoculars.

The trawler came on.

Sven was at the forward hatch, the all-stainless steel .16 gauge shotgun resting on the combing. The trawler's running lights gleamed like the eyes of an evil dragon, one green, the other red as she bore down on GULL. Then the green one disappeared and a strong search light stabbed across the dark interval.

"She's gonna cross in front of us," bawled Sven. "Turn on your light and track her after she gets a first good look." With that he withdrew into the shadows behind the stock of the shotgun. He would remain low so that no good look at his face would be possible.

As soon as Matt thumbed the switch, he became invisible behind the blinding glare of the light. They would know someone was there, but as in the opposite situation the night before, they could not be sure who or how many or if the light bearer was armed.

The trawler powered past the bowsprit, perhaps fifty yards ahead, and turned to pass down GULL's port side. Their powerful light probed the length of the cutter again and again. Matt responded in kind. The other boat displayed no marks of registration. GULL surged through a cloud of the trawler's diesel exhaust as the island boat came abeam fifty feet away. The rumble of her great engine made the air in GULL's cockpit tremble in response. Then her throttle was advanced, the rumble increased, the searchlight's beam shrank to a small red glow and the crisis passed astern.

GULL's crew could still hear her long after the small white stern light had winked out in their wake. And she left one new piece of information for them. As it swept past, Matt had shown the light on the transom. And there was the *casa* that the fat man had called the previous night: PLEASURE HOUSE.

GIRL OF MIAMI had passed her second test. Their behavior was not the sort that would arouse suspicion, given the conditions in the boating world of the day. Any prudent skipper would have regarded a vessel approaching in such an obvious way with suspicion and would have taken similar precautions. Sven was pretty sure that the Uzi had not been seen at all and their visitors probably did not even notice that he was armed in the fore hatch.

"They was lookin' at her name on the quarters and generally tryin' ta recognize anything familiar about the boat. I doubt that they looked at us much at all."

"Yeah," Matt nodded in agreement, "they hardly slowed down."

"I thought my wave to them was a nice touch." Leda smiled, tongue-in-cheek. She was exhilarated. The enemy had been engaged and defeated again, and it didn't even know it. And she had played an important part.

They settled back into the routine.

Leda remained on the helm and at 10:30 Sven began to run over his plan for the Chub stop. He made no mention of putting her ashore. Matt did not bring it up. She seemed to have won her berth on the distressed cutter and she remained quiet and listened intently to the discussion.

Basically, Matt and she were to remain on GULL, anchored just across from the club. Sven would take FAST FUN to the gas dock and walk up to the clubhouse in search of the dock master and a radio. Every effort should be made to maintain a look of everyday calm.

Sven had awkwardly stressed that Matt and Leda should remain on the alert in the event it was necessary to take a hasty leave. Matt responded with a wounded look and Leda smiled in the darkness.

The con in through the entrance at Mama Rhoda Rock would probably be where most caution was required. Because the wind had lain,

Sven suggested the light 'lunch hook' anchor again since it was easier to handle and there would be a constant anchor watch. They were to look for his return and have the engine running and be ready to weigh anchor the moment his painter was secure. He mumbled an apology about losing the time by stopping for the radio, but felt that under the circumstances, the time and the risk was made up for by their ability to call for help if they needed to. Also, since the addition of the radio would be unknown to their adversaries who might do something careless, GULL could use the radio to sudden advantage.

The cockpit fell silent, its occupants each thinking of what had to be done. The diesel droned on.

Sven had tried not to think about the complications of his meeting with the DM. Each time he had had to mention the man he had forced himself to think of him only, and only in the context of getting the precious radio. Again he ignored the barnacles that clung to their relationship. Tonight's business was too important to allow himself to be distracted.

Leda called him from his contemplation to identify the light they were approaching and Matt took the helm when Sven verified the blinker code and explained the channel approach.

Although Sven had been in and out of Chub a dozen times, this was his first entrance at night, but the landmarks emerged one by one only a little less obvious in the moonlight than in the sun. Matt wondered if Sven would have attempted it had he not been so familiar with the channel. Once lined up on the range lights he told Matt to note his compass course.

The crew was a model of efficiency as they approached the chosen anchorage. Sven, already in FAST FUN signaled and Leda dropped the hook, Matt backed down and set it. All was secure with no shouted word nor any noise louder than the engine. Then it was quiet, too.

Sven cautioned Matt to watch FAST FUN until he docked, in case he had to go someplace other than the gas dock. And watch for his return.

He tried not to be too obvious in his emphasis. There would be no time to waste under the best of circumstances and even less should something go awry.

He punched the starter button and Matt cast off the painter. He was away, unhurried and relatively quiet.

Leda went below to make a pot of coffee; Matt climbed out on the bowsprit the better to see past the other boats in the anchorage. Sven had chosen to anchor just past the club and to the edge of the anchorage where there was plenty of room to maneuver should it be necessary. There were not many boats either at anchor or tied up at the club's slips. It was Tuesday night. Most of the long week-enders had left yesterday. Several large sport fishermen were tied stern-to near the club house. This was prime sport fishing country and there were always a few of the big, wealthy boats from Miami at the club or the marina a little farther in.

Sven was almost to the gas dock now and he slowed to study the situation. A large sport fisherman was tied up there. A late arrival, he surmised. Sometimes a boat which arrived after the attendant had quit for the day but which wanted an early departure, would tie to the gas dock in order to be first in line in the morning.

Some sounds of muffled merriment wafted out of the interior, but there seemed to be no movement on deck. There was space to tie FAST FUN in front of the cruiser, but the smaller, darker niche aft of the tall transom appealed to Sven in his present mood. He slipped the boat deftly into the space and then jumped to the dock and tied it off fore and aft. As he turned, he noticed the name of the fisherman for the first time.

It was MOTHER'S FUR COAT, and a movement on the sun deck prevented Sven from retreating. He did not look up; instead, he tugged his canvas hat a notch lower on his forehead and walked leisurely up the dock toward the club house.

"Damn!" he muttered to himself. What a foul up. Hell of a way to begin this leg of the operation, he thought. Well, MOTHER, as a suspect in the plot, had not been confirmed. Get your mind on the task at hand.

He paused in the shadows between the yellow lights strung along the dock to pat his pockets as if in search of a cigarette. The gesture of forgetfulness, followed by the moment of indecision about returning to the boat gave him an opportunity to check all around for anyone who might have seen him come this far. No one was in sight the length of the dock. Somewhere, from one of the big fishermen tied stern-to, a laugh escaped and then another. Then it was quiet again. Sven continued up the dock and entered the club. It was not crowded. A couple sat at one table looking rather morosely into their half empty glasses. Four large, sunburned men from one of the sports fisherman laughed loudly at every clever utterance made. Three other tables entertained solo audiences and that was the lot.

The bartender stood at the other end of the bar, like a bit player in a B movie, actually drying glasses and holding them up to the light for inspection. He put the towel on the bar and ambled toward Sven who had folded his tall frame onto the stool nearest the door.

"'Allo. Wattle it be?" The barkeep revealed no curiosity about this stranger in his club.

Sven called his beer brand, then when it was delivered, asked, "I need ta get a-hold of Nigel. I know he's long gone for the day, but would ya have a phone number where I can reach him?"

"Sorry about that. Against club rules. Can't give out home phone numbers." He paused a moment.

"It's pretty important that I speak with him," Sven urged.

"It's pretty late," the other countered.

Sven gazed at him steadily, then the man moved closer and lowered his voice. "But if you give me your name, I'll ring him and if he wants to talk to you, I'll call you to the phone." He looked at Sven for agreement.

Sven nodded, then said, "Tell him it's Sven from Boston, he'll know who it is." The bartender bobbed his head in response and walked to the phone at the far end of the bar. Sven swiveled around to survey the room again and saw that the despondent couple had taken their misery somewhere else, but two new men now occupied a table just inside the door. One seemed vaguely familiar, but before Sven could give it any thought, the Brit called and waved the receiver in his direction.

This was a stroke of luck—catching Nigel home—he was a recreational drinker and always sought company to share his pleasure.

"Hello, Nigel? I'm real sorry to bother ya this late…," he blurted only to be stopped by the feminine voice at the other end.

"Sven, it's Sybil. I'm sorry. Nigel's not here. He went to a party on the other side of the island and he's not back yet. I expect him any time." She paused, then with a new, lighter note in her voice said, "Can I have him call you?"

"Damn!….Oh, hi, Sybil. I hope I didn't wake ya."

"Oh, no. Jan is restless tonight. She may be coming down with a cold…. And I don't like to go to bed until Nigel's in anyway." There was the hopeful pause again. But it prompted no response so she went on. "He promised not to drink much tonight. The road's so bad from that side of the island." Pause. "But I'm expecting him any minute, really." Then: "Can you come up to the house and wait?"

To wait for Nigel to stop drinking and come home could be an all night wait. Unless he'd changed since the child had come along. But Sybil's voice had momentarily arrested time. In fact it had turned it back. It had also activated memories and feelings that had received no attention for a decade. Sven was shocked at how fresh they still were and how painful.

"Oh, no thanks. I'm sure you're tired and I don't have transportation. Listen, I'm at the Club and I'll wait here. Please have him call me when he comes in. And give me your number. I'll call you back with the number of the public phone on the dock so he can call me there if he comes in after the Club closes." He paused a moment. The rush of words had betrayed him. His heart was beating wildly. Then he said, "It's real important that I talk with him right away when he gets in."

"I understand. I'll be sure he does it right away." She gave him the number and then told him something he knew but had apparently chosen to forget. "The jeep should be there. You could just drive up and be here when he arrives." The pause lasted too long again and then she added. "Let me talk to the barkeep. I'll tell him to give you the key."

The jeep was an amazing piece of machinery of World War II vintage that Sammy Johnson, an island boy, kept running by some method that verged on voodoo. It was a courtesy vehicle for those transients who occasionally needed to make a short trip beyond the comforting confines of the club bar.

Sven was surprised that he did not immediately decline and more surprised to find that he had handed the receiver to the passing barman without a word to Sybil.

"Where....?" he began when he had the phone to his ear again.

"Out the gate, to the right at the first turn and left at the second after that. Three quarters of a mile on the right. Only one there. I'll have the lights on for you." The eagerness in her tone was evident.

Sven hung up in a mental fuzz. The fact that Sybil was here and that he might encounter her had not penetrated his conscious mind as he had struggled with the decision to stop here in GULL's flight. Now his sneaky subconscious had surprised him again. Had he really stopped here for the radio? How the hell had he agreed to see her? How the hell could he risk being in her house when a drunken husband would return in the wee hours of the morning? The thin excuse that being there when Nigel showed up would accelerate GULL's departure, showed some partial return to rationality.

His mind plodded dully as he turned to walk toward his unfinished beer. He glanced again at the two men at the table near the door, then sat down quickly, his back to them. His mind was instantly clear. One of the men was Diego!

Sven looked at the clock behind the bar. It was almost twenty-four hours ago that he had hit the skinny Cuban and sent him skittering, unconscious, across GULL's dinette table. It would take more than a single punch to dispatch his companion, Sven thought. The other man was about six one or two and hovered around 240 or 250 pounds. He did not look like a yachtsman on holiday.

Where the hell had they come from? he wondered. The trawler must have dropped them here as sentries. If GULL shows up, they're to keep it here and call PLEASURE HOUSE to come back, he reasoned, fuming.

Where were they when GULL arrived a few minutes ago? Sven had seen no one on the dock. There were a dozen places that could be used as a look-out to monitor the entrance channel. Was it dumb luck that they had grown tired and decided to take a break just when GULL arrived on the scene? Or was some one on watch while they took a break? Had the lookout dismissed the GIRL OF MIAMI? Surely they must have or the alarm would have sounded and these two would not be dawdling over a beer. How many were there? Where the hell is Nigel?

Sven dropped a five on the bar, snatched up the Jeep's key that had just been delivered and swiveled away—stepping off in a casual amble toward the door. He had not taken off his hat, so as he neared the table, he raised his right hand and tugged the brim down a little further, keeping the hand up until he was safely past. As soon as he cleared the door, he quickened his pace and without looking back, strode toward the nearly empty parking lot. Only after he had climbed onto the Jeep's tattered seat did he casually shift about so that he could see the club entrance. No one had followed. He toed the ancient starter button and the engine, as if being disturbed from a sound sleep, came grudgingly awake after a long, irritating grind.

It was a few minutes before midnight. There was no telling how long before Nigel would show up at home, Sven thought. He was a prodigious drinker and story teller. On the other hand, there was no telling how soon he might show up either.

Sven was not a man to fall in love easily. Nor had he had many opportunities. His environment in the early years of his manhood had been often harsh and demanding and such a climate offered few creature comforts and fewer female creatures willing to do without them. But, during the 60's and 70's a plethora of women, young and not so young, had descended on the cruising community, eager to capture their fair share of the adventure of the sport. As boat manufactures made it easier, desk-bound men abandoned their careers for the dream of being charter captains on their own craft. Some wives went along as cooks—some lasted—many didn't go at all. It made no difference. Their absence was filled by the women who were determined that no man would experience more of anything than they. Somewhere among this self sufficient and gutsy group there had probably been a mate for Sven, but the dynamics of the group was such that he had avoided it like a plague. Many thirty-something cooks/crew, their beauty beginning to wrinkle under their eternal tans, found that the bunk of one 'captain' was pretty much like that of another and perhaps the grand adventure was over. Sven had suspected that that was what had happened to Sybil.

Twelve years ago she had appeared at an anchorage in Eleuthera—peering over the toe rail of an old schooner that he had been sent to recover and deliver to a new owner. Pulling up alongside she had stood on the dinghy's thwarts peering at him as he had carefully brushed a tenth coat of varnish on the companionway hatch. She was looking for a new berth, she confided after he had granted her permission to come aboard and examine a 'genuine' schooner. She thought maybe the boat was his and that Sven might be planning a circumnavigation. She was looking for a berth on a boat that was going to go around the world and she didn't care how long it would take.

Sven's schedule had been more narrowly prescribed and the cruise to Miami would be considerably shorter, but that hadn't gotten in the way of her rather prompt return the next day with all her worldly belongings. She was tired of bleach bottles boats, she had announced.

"If God had wanted us to have a Fiberglas boat, he'd have made Fiberglas trees."

It was a cliché, but she had delivered it in such a way that Sven forgave her for it and set to work immediately to make her understand the truth behind her statement. The schooner's deck planking had opened up under the tropical sun and each seam had to be payed. The old caulk had to be scratched out by hand first.

In the ensuing weeks—as the schooner was brought to life—so was the relationship between them. Initially it had been pure lust. Sven and Sybil had explored every opportunity the schooner offered for a unique sexual experience—including an attempt at coitus in separate bos'n chairs while suspended from the foremast.

Later the relationship had become much more as she grew to appreciate the gentle, self-effacing man whose body she regularly tried to dismember during long moments of orgasm. His knowledge and skill with boats was no small part of the attraction. He taught her how to shoot a star and work out a position, how to tie a proper bowline and how to coil a heaving line so that it carried true on the first throw. He taught her to splice and whip a line. He taught her how to brush on a coat of varnish without a single bubble. He taught her how to feel the wind on her face, testing it for true or apparent. He taught her how to steer while standing forward of the helm, facing aft, when running with a fluky wind. And he had never let her near the galley.

All this lay in his memory somewhere but he had pretty well managed to suppress it. Now as he muscled the Jeep around the first corner, he briefly wondered how he had again allowed himself to fall under the spell of this woman, but the short ride did not permit him to think back much beyond their last parting.

"If you don't take this one," she had shouted, "I'll go without you." The 'one' was an offer to skipper a wealthy man's yacht on an around the world cruise. It was the third such offer he had turned down in the two years since they had delivered the schooner to her owner and had become lubbers.

She had eagerly accompanied him as he sorted out things at this or that maritime museum. She was a sponge for information about anything nautical. She had crewed on the several deliveries that had come his way. The longest had been from Panama to Boston. But each time he had turned down the circumnavigation on the basis of boat or owner or both.

He was too picky, she said. And stubborn too. On that last point they had easy agreement. Still, she had raised the ante against the odds and when he still refused after she had signed on for the cruise, she had no recourse but to sail when the big ketch had left the dock.

Stubbornness was contagious, she had blubbered through her tears as she had kissed him good-by.

As Sven had predicted, the voyage began to turn sour after the second leg ended at the Azores. All had been lovely as far as Bermuda. But the early tropical storm that had overtaken them mid-ocean had shaken the green crew's confidence. Nigel, who had been hired in Sven's stead, had only a shaky hold on command. The owner, as Sven had suspected that he would, constantly interfered with the running of the ship. And always at the most dangerous of times.

However, quantities of good wine and the lovely green Azores summer had papered over the differences and by the time that they arrived on Spain's sunny, southern shore it again appeared that things might work. The short hops and the charm of the Med, particularly the golden days along the azure coast of Turkey, had lulled them into thinking that they were blue water sailors again. But the Indian ocean held new surprises and by now Sybil's pregnancy had begun to show.

It had happened, she had told Sven later, after she had called him from Bodrum on the Turkish coast: Nigel was drinking too much. He was quarreling with the owner. Come to Turkey, she had pleaded to Sven. Nigel was perfectly happy to resign and stay in Cyprus for the winter, or for ever, and Sven could get them all out of a mess. He refused. Then she suggested that he come and meet her there. She would quit the boat and they would spend the winter in Spain on the

Costa del Sol. His schedule wouldn't permit it. He had two maritime museum contracts to fulfill. Besides she could come back anytime she wanted to. He had told her so at the dock when she had sailed.

None of that had suited Sybil, and that night, in anger and frustration, she had drunk too much and cried too long and Nigel had taken her to bed to cheer her up. The 'up' she had gotten, as she later reported, was not 'cheering'.

Nigel had a brother, a specialist serving spooky duty for western intelligence on an isle in the Seychelles, who managed to get him and Sybil passage out on an empty military supply plane bound for Cairo. In the ten ensuing years they had been land-bound as Nigel moved from one job to another on the periphery of the boating world, attempting to save the capital needed to build a blue water boat.

The house was ablaze with light. It was one of those wonderful tropical houses built many years ago by someone with enough money to do it right. The porch surrounded the house on three sides. Its overhang was sufficient not only to shade the wicker chairs but also the large screened windows that gave light and vistas in equal amounts.

The walls were of foot-thick coral and the ceilings were high. A row of short, screened windows, constantly open, topped the outside walls just below the overhang. The prevailing breeze thus carried away any warm air that dared to accumulate inside.

She was on the porch to meet him. The brightly lit window behind her made it impossible to see her face. He mounted the low porch slowly as she greeted him.

"Well, it's good to see you. Even if you didn't come to see me." There was a trace of irony mixed with the unmistakable light heartedness that he knew so well.

"Well, it's good to see you too. Even if you never got around to comin' to see me," he answered in like kind.

He was on the porch now, beside her, and as she turned and the light flooded her face his throat tightened. She had not aged in ten years. Her tan was intact and the firm body that he had known so well graced her short loose shirt and tan shorts. There was a maturity that the years had brought, but she wore it with grace. It was not a care-worn face. Sybil had an ability to make a triumph of what others might call 'making the best of a bad situation'. Some, given a lemon in life, might merely convert it into lemonade, but Sybil would not settle for less than a meringue pie and a few friends in for a party.

"Let's sit out here," she said, motioning toward the wicker chairs and chaise ranged near the large windows. "I'll turn off some of these lights. Can I fix you a drink?"

"Naw, thanks. I just had a beer at the club. I gotta

keep a pretty clear head tonight. But I'd give a small fortune fer a shower. I promise not to use much water." She complied, of course, laying a finger to her lips as they passed the room with the sleeping child.

When he had again donned his shorts and hat, he appeared on the porch and allowed the gentle breeze to dry the last wisps of wet hair on his chest.

Sybil snapped off all the lights and slipped back out onto a moon muted porch. In the moments in the bright light she had studied Sven. His beard was edged in wisps of gray as were the sideburns that crept from beneath the canvas hat. He appeared as robust as he had been ten years before. The common sense and strength of character that she had so much admired still shone in his blue eyes. Had she seen just a hint of the old desire in them?

"Can I ask what's going on?"

"Well, I wish I knew," he began. Then in as shorthand a manner as possible he laid out the events of the past 24 hours.

She sat quietly until he finished.

"So you need a radio," she said.

"Yeah. Preferably two—one a handheld. Has to already be calibrated. And I don't know how long before I can return 'em."

"Well, Nigel is pretty good at solving problems like these. But until he comes maybe you can help me solve one. And please pardon me if I miss a few of the courtesies along the way. I don't know when Nigel will be back, but I suspect soon and I need to tell you something before he gets here."

Sven had been standing, looking at the moon-clad island. Sybil motioned him to a chair, but he dropped his shirt on it and chose the chaise instead, stretching his long tired legs out along the cool wicker and finally removing his hat.

"I wanted to talk to you about this a year ago when you passed through, but I didn't know you were here until after you had gone. You seem to have had a very long talk with Nigel about practically everything but me."

"I found it a little difficult ta talk about an old flame with her husband. I thought he might be uncomfortable too. He didn't offer any information and I decided not ta ask." He paused, then, "Why didn't ya call or write? I answered yer letter after ya returned from Cairo."

The moon, now just above the western horizon, shown under the overhanging roof lighting her face as she sought words for her reply. "I did call several times. But you were off somewhere and I got no answer. And the subject matter is not what I wanted to discuss in a letter."

Sven began to think that the chaise had been the wrong choice. Sybil's tone told him that this was to be no casual chat. He sat up and straddled the lounge in an effort to appear more attentive and to be on her eye level.

"But maybe Cairo's the place to start." She took a deep breath and began. "When we finally got out of there to Cyprus, the pregnancy was obvious to the naked eye. Nigel, ever the gentleman, even when he's had too much to drink, agreed that we should tell his friends there that we were married. He had apologized immediately and repeatedly after the night in Bodrum for 'taking advantage of me', as he called it and of course, made no advances after that, drunk or sober. He promised me, when we got our finances straight, a wedding and a name for the child. All this very proper for the very proper Englishman that he is. I was too distraught with the recent hellish experience and the sudden reality of the pregnancy to respond to anything but the easiest solution to anything.

"Hasty decision—one of the pitfalls you always used to warn against.

"Finally, with access to his meager savings and a small loan from a friend, we made it to England where he was able to get work immediately and I could take advantage of the free medical care. With this little security we both began to relax and think more clearly. Soon, and by common, but unspoken consent, the marriage didn't happen, He's a very sweet man, but I wasn't in love with him and he wasn't in love with me. He was always the gentleman and stalwart in meeting his financial responsibilities. Our charade protected my 'good name', as he called it, and we avoided discussing the long term as we prepared for the immediate reality of the coming baby." She stopped, shifted back in her chair and seemed to be preparing her next sentences carefully.

Sven studied her face in the semi-darkness. He knew most of this already. Some had come by mail from her after they had reached England, some other from mutual friends that had heard from her. The lack of a marriage, however, was news. Did her pause herald other surprises?

"The mid-wife who had agreed to deliver Jan didn't care about whether we were married or not—she was preoccupied from the beginning about the size of the baby. She sent me to the hospital at one point. She thought I might be carrying twins. When only one was confirmed, she worried about a premature birth because the baby was too big for a short term pregnancy. As we got closer to delivery day she sent me to the hospital again for consultation about the conflict in what she was seeing. The doctor asked me again and again about the date of conception and said that I could not be so specific about it. When I insisted that I was positive about it, he said that, using that date, the baby shouldn't come for six or seven more weeks, yet the fetus appeared to be completely mature. He became concerned about an early delivery too."

Sven sat back in the chaise. Six weeks, plus or minus a few days, placed the magical moment during the last week of their argument and near the start of her ill-fated voyage. There had been a lot of tearful sex after tearful arguments, as each had stood unyielded ground. Sybil had always defiantly insisted that she would take responsibility for her own body, and contraception was part of that. But something must have slipped or as the powerful love between them appeared to be doomed by their stubborn intellects, their bodies had taken over and nature had prevailed.

"So, Jan's mine?!!" Sven blurted into the silence left by Sybil's pause.

CHAPTER SEVEN

Diego was hard to find and harder to draw out. In fact, the expense of time and money seemed completely wasted until I told him of Sven's bad luck in the last moments on the burning casino ship.

Then, as if partially avenged for his trials at the hands of the big Scandinavian, he grudgingly cooperated.

It's Just Like Old Times

Leda filled the coffee cups again. This time she drained the pot. She paused. The speed of developing events did not encourage her to make a new pot. She would do that when Sven finally returned. It would be fresh that way. She juggled the hot cups up the companionway ladder.

When Matt had reported Sven's departure in the Jeep, much of the urgency of the wait was dispelled. That and the relative safety of the harbor had allowed the tension of fear and flight to drain away for the first time since Leda had fallen into his arms those long hours ago this morning. The quiet of the harbor, the moonlight, stars and the freshness of each one's appeal for the other led to snuggled closeness, long kisses, small talk and drawn out tactile examination of one another's physical attributes. The results were a lengthy and leisure union with none of the hurried intensity of the morning or the pressure of time that had dominated the sandy tryst that afternoon. Leda found Matt to be a thoughtful and gentle lover, his hands magical in their touch and exploration. He kissed, nuzzled and nibbled with exquisite intuition in his selection of place, duration and caress. And she responded with less hunger and more attention to the details of his attempt to summon a gently increasing and extended intensity on her part. She had anticipated his movement from one part of her body to the next, moving slightly, rearranging, separating, making room for him and finally as he moved his tongue back up across the delta of mossy fuzz, the flat tummy, navel and around each nipple, his entry below was so easy yet so stimulating that her sharp intake of breath surprised them both. The gentle, long, slow strokes gradually increased in intensity and finally drew her spine into a bow. Watching, as she flung her head back, he carefully timed his climax to match hers and they clung together for a moment—transfixed in the cool light of the moon.

Each had gradually relaxed and they melted into a pool of cuddle and sighs, he clasping her close and she pressing herself to him in the simple delight of being there. Each had felt that something special had transpired—something that had not happened to either before.

Now, Matt put the binoculars down on the sleeping bag and rolled over on his side to receive the offered coffee.

"Still no sign of him?" Leda asked, sitting cross legged at his waist.

The unzipped bag had been their command post ever since Sven had departed. The bowsprit had been a better vantage point when he had left in FAST FUN, but when he had boarded the noisy Jeep and driven into the night, Matt had moved slightly aft to the foredeck. When it seemed that Sven would not come back soon, Leda had brought up the bag to make their vigil somewhat more comfortable.

Matt had gazed alternately at the ever-sinking moon and at the shadowy parking lot, reviewing in his mind's eye the transit of the entrance channel. They might have to exit in the blackness of a moonless night if things did not go faster.

Matt lowered the binoculars, sipped his coffee, and gazed at Leda, this new person in his life, and worried some more.

"A watched pot never boils, my grandmother always said." Leda looked at his shadowed face over the rim of her coffee cup. She leaned back against the overturned dinghy and waited. He didn't reply so she went on. "You said this afternoon that your academic life had been short. What did you do for money before that?" Then thinking he might mistake her interest as prying she added for levity: "Spy—gigolo—pimp?"

He laughed gently and shook his head. "Close. Same crowd. Whore. I had gone to a big university on a sports scholarship. I was on the tennis team. We were good and the coach tried to place those of us that he called 'real talent' with pro coaches looking for protégés. I was twenty-one, in top shape and aggressive as hell. I was majoring in philosophy and there were limited job opportunities outside academia and I wasn't ready for graduate school and that grind.

"This pro coach had a source for what he called "development money". The deal was that I train and play on the pro circuit at their expense until I began to win. When I did, they were to be reimbursed and of course, go on contract with me at a fat salary, plus a percentage, directing the rest of my career.

"At the end of three years, I was ready to challenge the big boys in pro tennis. I was also supporting four pimps. My coach, who did very little by then but keep me from picking up bad habits or becoming careless about my form. I had a trainer who kept me physically in shape, warmed me up before a match and rubbed me down after I played. And, big joke, my business manager, who 'invested' my winnings after 'expenses'. Then there was my public relations man who tried to keep me in the public eye by making sure there were photos of me in the newspapers regularly with whatever Hollywood personality was hot.

"I was a good whore and made lots of money for all of them for five years; then I became careless and didn't notice that the booze and the Hollywood personalities were bad for my game. The trainer became lackadaisical in my preparations. The business manager resigned because I was 'topping out' and he, like the coach, was committed to 'developing' new talent. That translates into I caught him stealing my money. The coach was more up-front. I *was* topping out. Most tennis players don't last more than seven or eight years. He was nearing fifty and there was only time for one, or two at best, new talents to develop before he got too old and had to hang up his jock strap.

"You can guess the rest. One day I came in hung over the same day the trainer was hung over. He didn't do his job and I pulled a muscle. He didn't follow up properly and I missed six tournaments. The rats abandoned the ship—no tournaments, no wins, no percentages above salary.

"My current Hollywood personality went into the Betty Ford Clinic; I went into the hospital for an operation to prevent permanent damage to my leg. Suddenly graduate school and intellectual pursuits took on a new appeal." He sat quietly and sipped his coffee.

A snatch of conversation broke the silence and Matt trained the glasses on the parking lot, but the talk came from two men who had just left the club. One was an above average size large man, the other a below average size small man. He followed their progress down the dock a few feet until they disappeared behind the docked boats.

Diego was in an ugly mood. He had had only two hours of sleep in the past 48 and those had come amid the almost constant party that went on on the big sports fisherman. MOTHER'S FUR COAT had met PLEASURE HOUSE early that morning and had taken him and the fat one on board where they were chewed out for their part in the loss of the prize. Diego had hoped that they would be put ashore when the fisherman had put in for fuel. But they had spent the day zig zagging across what was believed to be the course of the missing GULL.

Diego had not been surprised that he had had to take the brunt of the chewing. He would not be surprised if there were more and uglier punishment yet to come.

The fat one and the Yankee, Bubba (Why didn't he like it when I called him a Yankee? Diego wondered), had flown out on Bubba's plane as soon as the *CASA* had docked at Chub. Probably to make more trouble for me, he thought. Bubba was mad as hell when he had arrived at Chub and there was still no report of GULL.

Leo, the big American (Diego hated big people, but he hated big gringos doubly) had been sent with him on watch, as much, he suspected, to watch Diego as to watch for the boat. But Nick, their relief, who was due at midnight, had not shown up and now they would probably be chewed out again for leaving the channel unguarded. But it was Leo who had decided that it was a waste of time and had abandoned the watch after the last boat had arrived. He had told Diego that it was the one Bubba had reported and Bubba had not seen any other boats headed for Chub.

Diego had been surprised that Leo had offered to buy him a drink as they passed the club. He had been more surprised that he had bought a second and then a third. Most of these gringos had ignored him and he had not missed their company. The alcohol and the waning prospect of action had allowed the fatigue to creep over him and he longed for the comfort of his narrow bunk.

As they approached the big sport fisherman at the gas dock, the gringo spoke. "Let's fix Nick's ass. He's such a prick, anyway," Leo said. "We'll wake him up but we won't tell him we canceled the watch. He'll walk up there and be asleep again in ten minutes anyway. The only reason 'R' keeps him is because he's somebody's relative." Diego shrugged his approval.

They climbed the gang way to the sun deck of the fisherman where Nick lay snoring in a deck chair.

"Wake up, you lazy bastid," Diego growled, kicking the man's feet off the end of the chaise. "I'm dead on my feet and you laying here on your dead ass."

Nick yawned luxuriously, stood and stretched, then retucking his shirt, drawled: " Waal, ah take care a ma ass. You get yours chewed out one mo' time and you ain't gonna have no little Spick ass left."

Diego wheeled away, dragging furiously on his cigarette. The slur, capping twenty-four hours of fatigue and frustration at the hands of the arrogant, Yankee bastards brought him too close to doing something really stupid—like cutting one of them up.

Nick went ashore, leaving his .45 automatic on the table next to the chaise. Leo called his attention to it, but Nick allowed as how he wouldn't need it tonight. The other man shrugged and sought his bunk.

Diego stood at the transom rail finishing his cigarette and trying to calm the fury that had built up. He had little success. When he banished the thoughts about one of the incidents, another rushed in to fill his mind. He gingerly touched the corner of his left eye. The bluish bruise was tender. "The beeg son-of-a-bitch. I'll keel heem when we catch heem nex' time." He flipped the cigarette butt away, over the rail, and as it arced downward, he noticed the boat tied astern for the first time.

He was sure it hadn't been there when he went on watch. He liked those boats. He always took special notice of them. He wanted one. They were fast and could go into shallow water. He could go into some special places at home with one of those. Well, he had hoped to have one when this job was finished, but with the fuck-up last night there would be no bonus and without it he could not afford a boat—any boat. This one was like the one he had admired on the big boat they had jumped on Sunday. But this one had red stripes. He liked the red stripes better. The other one—what was its name? FAST FUN, yes, FAST FUN. It had blue....

He stopped mid-thought. This one was called FAST FUN too.

He paused a minute. What the hell. Americans are crazy. Anything could happen. He turned back to his careful examination of the boat. The engine. Diego liked big engines. It might be the only big thing that Diego liked. He liked big powerful boat engines. His friend did not have a big enough engine on his boat. When he towed Diego on the water skis, they never went fast enough. This engine looked plenty big.

His fatigue momentarily forgotten, Diego went down the gang way and walked over to take a closer look at the engine. The tide was high and FAST FUN presented her new colors rather proudly in the yellow glare of the gas dock lights.

This engine was exactly like the one on GAVIOTA, Diego marveled. He remembered the brand logo and the strange marks on the cowl. But the marks were not part of the decoration; they were like these, the result of some minor accident. Diego's brow furrowed. He walked back so that he could see the transom again and he studied the letters of the name. They were made of black vinyl and a wedge of the material was missing from the first F. It had been like that on the other boat too. He walked forward again and studied the registration numbers on the bow. Florida. Nothing strange about that. Then he noticed that the pretty red stripe was peeling off where it stopped at the numbers. And under the red tape there was a blue stripe. And the tape was not a thick vinyl like it should be, but a thin flimsy stuff which came away much too easily when he tugged at it. On impulse, he pulled the boat closer and leapt into it. He ran his hand over the console as he had done to the boat on GAVIOTA. The blemishes were the same. The chip in the throttle handle was in the same place.

"Thees damn boat came off GAVIOTA," he decided aloud. Some island scavenger had found her and stolen the boat and disguised it with tape until he could do a better job at it. "Damn, I weesh thees job was done," he thought aloud again, "I would steal hees stolen boat." He chuckled at his cleverness.

Diego reluctantly came ashore, but his gaze lingered longingly on the sleek craft and his mind toyed playfully with schemes to steal it. After all, he told himself as he climbed back aboard the fisherman, it would be no great loss to the thief. He had not had it long enough to get used to having it.

Someone was coming down the dock. Maybe this was the thief returning now. A flood of envy washed over Diego. To his peculiar turn of mind, the boat somehow should really be his. After all, he had seen it first. In an order among thieves, his lust for the booty should have taken precedence. He would have stolen it first had the circumstances allowed. In addition, he had participated in disabling GAVIOTA, thus making it possible for this vulture to come along after the dangerous work was done and pick the helpless bones. What other treasures had this scavenger come by as a result of Diego's risk and labor?

He decided to hold off his nagging fatigue. He would linger long enough to see this secret competitor and also enjoy the small pleasure of watching the boat raise its bow and skim away across the surface.

The man coming down the dock was tall, and he was carrying two radios. The big people in the world get everything, Diego fumed, and often two of everything. Were these expensive items the man carried booty from GAVIOTA too? Was he here trying to turn them into cash? What else had he sold? Maybe he had a roll of money that he had gotten as a result of Diego's effort.

He picked up Nick's gun from the table. The .45 was much heavier than the .32 to which he was accustomed. But he did not plan to shoot anyone, so the steadiness of his hand for accuracy was not a consideration. He wanted a weapon to compensate for his lack of size.

The big .45 made him feel much bigger.

There was a flurry of activity on GULL. Matt woke the dozing Leda and they scurried to clear the debris of their watch. Matt had seen Sven come out of the shadows of the parking lot swinging in his long gait toward the boat. He had confirmed that it was his friend, carrying two hand-held radios, before he put the binoculars down. But not having heard the start-up of the outboard, he picked the glasses up again and trained them on FAST FUN. Two men were silhouetted against the brightly lit dock. Sven was in the boat and another, slighter figure stood on the dock motioning with a gun for him to move forward to the console. As Matt muttered an oath and called Leda, he watched as the gunman lithely jumped into the stern of the boat and approached Sven from behind. He said something that Matt couldn't hear, of course, then brought the barrel of the gun down on the taller man's head.

"Come on," Matt hissed to Leda. "We've got to get the dink in the water. Some bastard just cold-cocked Sven." He was already pulling at the lashings that held the boat to its chocks.

But Leda had snatched up the binoculars and was studying the scene with care.

Sven's knees had buckled at the unexpected blow and one of the radios went skittering across the seat. He remained on his knees, the empty hand clinging to the steering console as he struggled to remain erect and clear his mind. His canvas hat, its high crown crushed by the blow, stayed on his head, but a warm trickle of blood ran from under the sweatband and down the back of his neck.

Diego was delighted. As he circled the kneeling figure, he was able to look him full in the face. The big man wasn't so big now. He was tempted to hit him again, but Sven spoke.

"So, we're even, pal. Now whatta ya gonna do? I just left the dock master at the club house. If he don't see me leave this dock and board my boat, he's gonna be down here to ask why. He knows how much of a hurry I'm in." Sven's head was clear and he knew the best thing he could do would be to get this lubber onto the water again. He had suckered him once and he could do it again. Without waiting for a reply he stood up and started to retrieve the precious radio.

"You fuckeen, smart bastid. You Yankee shit. You tink you so smart. Put the goddam radio down an' untie thees ting. We gonna go to your fuckeen boat and when we get there, it gonna be *my* boat. I got one hellava ass chewin' because of you smart bastids. Now, I gonna get a bonus." He stole a look over Sven's shoulder at the dark fisherman, then hissed. "An' be quiet. We got some pretty little asses on de boat an' they wants they beauty sleep."

Sven needed no urging on that score. He took his handkerchief, wadded it into a ball and all the while looking the little Cuban in the eye, purposefully removed his hat, pressed the ball of linen against the cut on his scalp and quickly clamped the hat back on to hold it there. Then he cast off the dock lines and pushed the bow out into the quiet waters of the harbor.

Trying to calculate drift, he reckoned that the tide was still rising and whatever current there was would take him generally in the direction of the anchored GULL. He pushed off of the sloop in the adjacent slip and deftly propelled the shallow boat out past the last piling with a final shove. Since the boat was steered by changing the direction of the outboard's thrust, he could do no more than allow it to drift with the tide. The boat, property of a typical power boater, Sven thought, had no oars aboard. He turned to the Cuban.

"Now what?"

Matt was retying the dinghy. Leda was giving a blow-by- blow account of the action which was now out in the channel itself.

"Start the engine," Matt ordered. "We'll power down on them and...."

"Wait a minute. Sven still hasn't started the motor. He's hand-paddling toward us. Get into the cockpit, quick." They raced to the cockpit and knelt on the bridge deck. Resting the glasses on the cabin top, she kept a running account at the same time she laid out her thoughts.

"I bet the guy either thinks Sven is alone or that whoever is aboard is asleep. If he's a common thief, he won't be too hard to deal with. If he's a professional pirate, we could be joined by a much larger group as soon as he's aboard." She paused a moment. "What do you think?"

"Where ees GULL," Diego asked and then squinted in the moonlight to make out the boat at which Sven motioned. "Start the motor, O. K? But when you get close, keel it and drift the rest of the way. I doan wan to wake your friend. Not yet, anyway." He smiled his satisfaction and watched with interest as Sven flicked the big motor to life and then, throttle at dead slow, pointed FAST FUN toward her new home. Diego, his feet apart, his wide smile intact, braced himself in the bow of the boat, his back to the looming boats in the anchorage.

It was a short trip even at idle speed and soon Sven cut the motor and they drifted toward the only boat with a bow sprit.

The deck was deserted. Sven fought the idea, but it pressed itself on him. Damn, is that all they can think of? Sven's sexual appetite was pretty healthy, he thought, but this would be three times today for them, as best he could count. Well, it's what happens when you got a woman aboard, he thought resignedly.

Diego had circled around to stand in the stern—the heavy .45 leveled at Sven for the entire circuit. Now he squinted again at the boat they were approaching. She looked different. She *was* different. They were ghosting up alongside and the red stripes glared out against the white hull.

"You bastid," he hissed. "Wat you tink I am? Dis iss not you boat." He raised the heavy pistol and leveled it at the back of Sven's head as the older man slowly turned around and quietly spoke.

"This is GULL, Diego," he said evenly and he hoped loudly enough to be heard on board. "We changed her look today so the boys on PLEASURE HOUSE wouldn't know who we were." He stood in the bow now facing the Cuban who was still aiming the gun squarely at his forehead. He reached out and grasped GULL's toe rail with his left hand to keep FAST FUN from marring the side of the larger boat. "Whatever it is you guys want is still aboard, but I don't think you'll find it. You'll have ta settle fer us as a prize, Diego. I hope it gets ya a bonus, if that's what yer workin' fer." With that he began to tie the painter to a nearby lifeline stanchion. Diego lowered the gun, shifted it to his left hand and grasped GULL's toe rail with the other. The stern of the smaller boat had eased away as Sven pulled the bow closer in. Diego's arm was fully extended.

Motioning with the gun he said, "You go first, and…."

"Welcome aboard, Diego!" Leda shouted, suddenly standing upright in the cockpit.

Matt erupted out of the black water between the boats and grabbed the skinny wrist with both hands. And for a second time in 24 hours someone bigger than Diego dunked him into a salty, tropical sea. The heavy gun fell from his hand as the salt water forced its way up his nostrils and the bigger someone kept hitting him and forcing him back down each time he surfaced. Finally, stealing a hasty gulp of air, he dived down under the big boat, deep into the black water, feeling along the boat bottom until he felt the curve that told him he had cleared it.

With bursting lungs, he kicked and pawed for the surface, but something held him back. His wind breaker, billowing away from his back, had caught fast on the propeller. Diego turned over to clear it and the snarl of cloth wound tighter, hooked on the two or three barnacles that had managed to make a home on the shaft.

"Start the engine!" Sven bellowed as he dragged the panting Matt into the runabout and then stuffed him unceremoniously under the lifeline onto GULL's deck. In the same moment, he hauled himself over the lifeline on a dead run for the cleat where the anchor rode was tied.

Leda, responding to the command, started the engine and kicked the shift lever. The big cutter eased forward as Sven's long arms, hand over hand, drew in the sagging nylon a fathom at a time. The small lunch hook broke out and was on deck as a dripping Matt took the helm and Leda ran forward to help stow the tangle of wet rode.

"Sail your reciprocal," Sven hissed as Matt pinched the big boat at hard left rudder until the compass read exactly opposite the course he had sailed when they had approached the anchorage. Then he pushed the throttle and GULL bore down on the narrow channel that would take her into the Alley at last.

Sven retied FAST FUN so that it followed astern. Then he went forward to con them out and past Mama Rhoda rock as the last silver disappeared from sea and sky. The moon had set. GULL was running for Bimini in the comforting cloak of total darkness. It was 1:30 a.m.

Out on the point overlooking the channel, Nick was awakened by the sound of a boat's motor. He stood up quickly only to see a boat leaving rather than arriving, so he checked his watch and lay down again.

Chapter Eight

The English ex-patriate drinks too much. I'm convinced that their genes were gin-pickled two hundred years ago when their great grand parents, herded off farms and into the smoky factories, made the Industrial Revolution happen.

I couldn't be sure whether it was the alcoholic fog through which Nigel navigated the evening in question or the same sort of one that surrounded us in his cockpit several years later, but my notes were near-victims of the same tool that had loosened his tongue.

Trees—1, Bleach bottles—0

"Didja see him surface anywhere?" Sven asked Leda. She was cleaning the dried blood from his neck and shoulder. She had already dressed the wound—a not-too-serious cut, thanks to the heavy canvas of the hat.

"No. I hope you didn't kill him," she said, shooting an accusing glance at Matt. "Why did you keep hitting him?"

"I thought he still had the gun. I didn't see his empty hand until he surfaced the second or third time."

Sven sat on the bridge deck immediately in front of the open companion way. Leda worked by the light of the cabin fixture below. It was the only light on GULL except for the red compass bulb. A few minutes later she stowed her first-aid kit and turned it off too.

GULL was running under power in the dark night with no lights to betray her presence. The big diesel was powerful, but not meant to push the displacement hull through the water at a high speed. The log indicated six knots.

Sven was thoughtful. "If sunrise is at 5:20 it'll start to get light about 4:30 or 4:45. That means we got 'bout three hours…18 miles into the Alley. The first twelve in very deep water—600 or so fathoms. The last six in a fathom and a half. I'd rather have daylight for them, but we don't dare wait. With or without Diego, they'll be lookin' fer us everywhere tomorrow. Probably have a plane in the air by then. If Diego survived, they'll be lookin' for GIRL OF MIAMI. If he didn't…waal it'll be a little easier fer us. With no interruptions and good luck, we oughta make Bimini about one or one-thirty tomorrow afternoon.

"Leda, can you stand watch with Matt for a couple of hours? I got a real whopper of a headache and I'm gonna hafta be a lot better than I am now when we get into that shoal water later on."

Leda nodded. They all sat around the helm, the red compass light casting ghoulish shadows across their faces.

"Th' first navigation light is about 12 miles along. It marks the beginnin' of the shallows. It's a flasher an you ought ta be able ta see it from eight miles away. Relax a while. Then in about an hour start lookin' for it with the glasses. As dark as it is, it oughta be pretty easy to spot.

"Matt, take it to starboard and pass purty close. It'll make our DR more accurate. And in this dark and that shallow water we gotta be as sure as we can be about where we are. We can get a new bearing on the second light then; it's a couple a hours farther on." Turning to Leda he said, "Wake me when we get ta the flasher. Don't turn on any white lights anywhere; it'll ruin yer night vision."

Reaching for one of the handheld radios, he placed it on the cockpit cushion near enough to the helm for Leda to reach. "Leave it on the channel I punched up. Nigel will talk to us directly on that one if there is need ta. If we get company from behind, wake me as soons ya see 'em. I'm gonna turn on the radar and put it on a 10 mile sweep. That'll give us about 20 minutes to get ready for 'em if they come in MOTHER. They ain't like to pick up this wooden hull on their radar that early. We'll know about them 'fore they know about us. That's the way I like it." With that, he rose and went below.

It was quiet in the cockpit for a long time.

Sven had gulped three aspirins before he lay down in the forward compartment. The ventilator scooped relatively cool air down upon his tired body. He lay on his back and the gentle breeze coursed through the hair on his chest bringing reminders of Sybil's fingers. They chased away images of Diego. Turning his head slightly to prevent pressure on the bandaged cut, he closed his eyes and wished for sleep. But Sybil's moonlit face danced on the backs of his eyelids. And images of the sleeping Jan too.

"When she was born any lingering doubt was gone," Sybil had said. "She has your eyes and she smiles crookedly as you do. She reminds me daily of you and that gave me a lot of pain the first few years." She paused again. "My first impulse was to tell you, but my stubborn streak surfaced when I remembered how you refused to prevent all this in that last phone call from Bodrum. That was the cause, I had thought for a long time, for all my recent chain of misfortunes.

"I started to work right away when we arrived in England. And after Jan came I always supported us. That's something Nigel and I agreed on very early. He and I had grown accustomed to our symbiotic relationship and decided to continue it. We were supportive of each other and I think he has come to genuinely love Jan. We live separate lives and respect each other's personal privacy. He has never understood why I did not tell you the whole story but he has gone along with my decision."

"Maybe you'll explain why ya *didn't* tell me all these years," Sven had said, finally settling back into the chaise.

"I tried and almost did several times. But each time I wrote I tore up the letter and the longer I put it off the harder it was. I tried calling you a couple of times thinking it might be easier telling you because I always seemed to bog down writing. When I couldn't get you on the phone, it was an excuse to put it off until I got up the nerve to do it again. As the years passed, the idiocy of the stubbornness and pride wore off and on one occasion, when she was ready to start school, I actually booked a flight to Boston. I was in Pennsylvania visiting my parents and on impulse I decided to go. But, of course, you weren't there. The people at Dorchester said you were in Japan and they didn't expect you back for months.

"When I got back, Nigel told me that you had been here, and the people in Boston were wrong. I was terribly depressed and we had a terrible row. I suddenly realized then that I still loved you very much. It showed in the terrible storm of emotion that I dumped on poor Nigel.

"Since that day, I've tried to become completely independent. In venting on Nigel I realized that the real problem all these years was that I was afraid that you would take me and Jan back only because you thought you had some financial obligation to us. I vowed that the moment that I could come to you and tell you the story without burdening you financially, I would do it.

"Well, that moment came about a week ago. I opened a marine canvas shop here seven years ago and made a bare living at it. Not a lot of money, but a living. However it was never a full time thing in the off season.

"I have always felt so sorry for these poor island women. A few years ago I found a way for them to make some money. I held craft classes for them and bought their products. I threw lots of their stuff away because it was crude and I couldn't sell them but there were many that I could sell as folk craft items in the states. As usual there were a few really nice pieces. Gradually I stopped buying the junk and bought only the stuff worth selling, But I encouraged all the women to improve so I could buy from everybody.

"Now I've built a ready market for their stuff in several outlets here in the islands and on the upscale tourist islands in Georgia and Florida. I have six artists whose things are now selling for several thousand dollars apiece. I market these with special care and last week I signed a contract with a chain of very posh gift shops to provide them with all that my people can produce.

"I love you Sven. I've been stubborn and foolish in my behavior and have lost ten years of what might have been a life together for us. This is a hell of a time to tell you all this, but your story has frightened me and added a new urgency."

Sybil in one fluid motion slipped from her chair, knelt next his chaise and grabbing his head with both hands, kissed him soundly on the lips.

There had been little for him to say. All the old passion and deep feeling for her that he had suppressed for a decade welled up in him like a spring crocus piercing lately frozen soil. Her hand moved to his chest and then across his flat stomach as she eagerly returned to what had been her playground in the past. Sven's momentary thought of Nigel's impending arrival had been swept away in the need to encourage her.

Images of her moonlit body bouncing up and down on him—her breasts afly—eased him into a contented sleep.

Diego embraced the mooring buoy, hugging it to him as if it were a long lost relative while he sucked in great gulps of air. The barnacles cut his hands and forearms each time they slipped on the slimy sides of the orange sphere. He wanted to scream for help, but there wasn't enough air yet, and it would have to be a loud scream and a frequent one if he were to be heard and located in the black night. When he did muster the breath, the pathetic result convinced him immediately that his waning strength would be better spent attempting to climb onto the boat tethered to the buoy. Hand over bloody hand, he pulled his pain racked body up the mooring line, and slithered aboard.

When Sven had left Nigel at the head of the dock he had asked the DM to watch for any boat that might make a hasty departure after GULL left. The flurry aboard MOTHER'S FUR COAT after Nick came running down the dock, had made him think that she might be Sven's chaser.

So he had set out to delay the departure of the big sport fisherman as long as possible. He watched with considerable mirth the comedy of errors surrounding Diego's location and rescue and then managed to remain hidden when attention was turned toward refueling the big gas-hungry boat.

Her crew had no qualms about breaking and entering his office in search of the key to the fuel pump. But he had anticipated that event and had taken the keys with him when he made it loudly known to the bartender that he was going back to the party on the other side of the island. It was a vain effort to hide however, because by the time the hapless Diego had been rescued, the club was closed. As he watched they resorted to a boat-to-boat interrogation which finally produced someone who knew where he lived. He arrived home minutes ahead of his visitors, with just time to warn Sybil, undress and arrange a look of drunken innocence on his face.

The professional Captain from MOTHER apologized, told his story of an unforeseen emergency that forced the immediate departure of his craft, and then paced impatiently as Nigel dressed and killed as much time as possible. Finally, the two large men who had accompanied the Captain made it plain that there was no longer any time to lose and, refusing to allow him to drive his own car, he was ushered into the club Jeep which had been commandeered for the purpose. Nigel had pulled the ignition wires on it before leaving the parking lot, but that had apparently slowed his pursuers for no more than the time it had taken him to disable it.

As they walked down the dock, Nigel nodded appropriately as the man called "R" approached and explained again the need for haste and made proposals for payment of the damage done to the Dock Master's office. His mind raced for a way to cause further delay.

When they arrived at the pumps, he laboriously unreeled the diesel hose, asked to be shown the fill pipe, apologized for his error, and cranked it back on the spool. The crew from the boat dragged the proper hose to the pipe while Nigel apologized again for his slowness—explaining that fueling was not one of his regular tasks. He finally faced the need to unlock the pump.

He patted the pockets of his shorts to locate the key. Earlier, he had removed it from the float attached to the ring and now he began to fish out the flat sliver of brass.

Nigel had spent all of his boating life admonishing anyone who trod a dock that a key was never to be removed from pocket or purse while on a pier. His inevitable experience had been that those who ignored this advice saw the dropped keys fall between the planks and plop into the water below.

At the moment the key cleared his pocket, he managed to fumble it. It fell, bounced once on its edge then lay gleaming dully in the yellow light.

The captain gasped. Nigel hiccoughed, excused himself, retrieved the key and unlocked the pump.

So much for luck.

The captain stopped the fueling before the tanks were full, payment was made with bills of large denomination and there was no urge to wait for change. MOTHER'S FUR COAT departed in haste, leaving the smiling dock master in a cloud of exhaust.

Nigel's watch dial glowed 3:33. It was the best he could have done, he thought, drunk or sober. He pushed open the broken door of his office, punched a two digit channel number into the VHF. Then thumbing the mike alive, he transmitted: "MFC departure oh, three, thirty-three." He repeated the message twice more then waited. A feminine voice replied. "Roger."

Nigel turned wearily toward the Jeep.

* * *

By some complement of current and tide GULL had made better than her six knots over the bottom and Sven, just roused from a dream-laden sleep, peered at the first flasher, now three miles astern. Then he began to scan the darkness ahead for the next one. He really didn't expect to see it yet.

The vagaries of wind and sea are the stock and trade of the sailor and always to be dealt with. At any other time the better speed would have been an unforeseen boon; now it endangered Sven's whole battle plan. It was the darkest part of the night, the time just before dawn. The success of his plan was completely dependent on darkness. If MOTHER didn't catch them soon they would lose the element of surprise and be victims again of the superior speed, maneuverability and possible firepower of the fisherman.

Bending over the transom he checked the two English outboard motors hanging from their mounts. Matt had rigged them carefully. They were ready.

He turned his binoculars astern again in search of the running lights that should announce the physical presence of the blip that had appeared some time ago on Matt's radar scope.

Leda completed the last of her preparations, laying the all-stainless steel, pump shotgun on the starboard cockpit cushion.

Matt kept GULL on course, thankful for the lack of wind and a calm sea for his task in the offing. And he worried.

"Ah, there she is," Sven sighed. "And she's comin' fast from the way her lights is bouncin' up and down." He was sure that it was the pursuers. Why else would anyone plunge along so fast in these shallows in this blackness. "Let's get this show on the road."

With that he stepped to take the helm. Matt went below to get the Uzi. Leda turned from the forward hatch, where she had just laid out the Winchester on the V-berth, and came to stand by him as he checked the ugly little weapon.

"I'm scared," she said as she handed him the portable VHF.

"Me, too," he replied, looking at her in the eerie red glow of the chart table light. "All the work today—all for nothing. Damn Diego and damn the rotten luck." He shrugged, then taking a deep breath and exhaling, he kissed her tenderly and turned toward the steps.

"Be careful," she called over the engine noise.

He paused at the bottom step, turned and studied her as best he could in the strange red glow. Then finding nothing better to say: "You, too."

"Reel FAST FUN in," Sven ordered when Matt had slung his weapon across his back. "When ya get in, double back on our track for five minutes at quarter throttle, then come back real slow until you can see me. When ya do, flash me with the light."

Matt did as instructed, but the blackness was almost liquid in its envelopment. He could not tell where air left off and water began. After a few minutes, he killed the outboard and listened for GULL's diesel noise. He flashed the light in that direction. Sven answered almost immediately.

"Yer real close, by the sound of it. Maybe 20 yards away, but off to starboard." Then his tone changed, "This is too dangerous. Come up along the starboard side and loaf along with me until she gets a lot closer."

When he looked again at the approaching cruiser she was a lot closer—and still running fast. He could see only the green running light now, an indication that she was a good way off on their port side.

"OK," he shouted to Leda. "Get that thing up."

Hand over hand, Leda hoisted the radar reflector up to the spreaders. It had an almost immediate effect. The cruiser's engines were backed down and she turned slightly toward GULL.

"OK, kill it," Sven ordered and moments later the reflector lay again on the cockpit sole. The cruiser came on, still too far off the port side for Sven's taste and closing too fast. He ordered the reflector up again. It stayed up longer this time and the cruiser was coaxed into a slower speed and a nearer track before it was again doused.

Now it was Matt's departure time and he pulled away in the ooze of darkness at low speed, not really thinking that his engine noise could be heard over the roar of the cruiser's twin V-8s, but not wanting to risk losing the surprise factor in this exercise. He could see the cruiser plainly; several of her portholes glowed with light. Instrument lights reflected off the windshield and the side windows of the control station. He punched 72 into the VHF keypad and said the code word. GULL's captain answered in a gruff one word reply.

Sven watched the cruiser's approach; she was perhaps fifty yards off to port and a quarter mile astern. This time Leda hoisted the reflector, tied it off, then plunged below and ran forward to the open hatch. She pushed the barrel of the Winchester out of the hatch, rested it on the combing and waited.

The cruiser's speed was further reduced and reduced again as Sven edged to port and closed the distance between them. The cruiser's Captain was sure of his radar fix. He was moving at dead slow now. A bright spotlight stabbed the darkness and found GULL. Sven barked into the VHF and spun the helm hard to port. Almost immediately he could hear gunfire from astern of the cruiser. GULL was now aimed at the cruiser's course just where Sven calculated she should be when GULL arrived. He turned, deftly lowered the two English outboards and snatched them to life with a single pull at each. "Best thing the Limey's has done since radar", he grudgingly praised.

Leda's second shot shattered the lens of the spotlight and Matt's first two Molotov cocktails crashed onto the cruiser's sun deck spilling runny fire everywhere. GULL pushed on, all three engines wide open, on a collision course with the cruiser.

GULL's bowsprit was the circumference of a medium sized telephone pole where it was built into the boat's bow and it tapered to eight inches across at the outboard end. It was braced by three chains, one on the bottom which stretched down and over a strut that protruded from the sprit and on to connect at the hull just at the water line. The other two went from the tip to port and starboard fittings just below the toe rail. The stainless cable forestay with a furling jib attached ran from the tip of the sprit up to the top of the mast.

The end of the sprit made contact with the cruiser's hull at one of the portholes, punching out the black aluminum fitting and allowing the sprit to stab deeply into the cabin beyond. The three chains and the stay, thanks to the different way in which the sea moved the two hulls, sawed a gigantic plus-shaped gouge into the cruisers side, tearing away slabs of fiberglass as they pushed ever farther in. The two feet of stainless wire connecting the furling spool to the end of the sprit sliced into the deck, and stopped all forward motion when the spool hit the cabin side. But that was far enough.

Sven, still partially blinded from the spot light, snatched up the shotgun and made two grapefruit size holes in the fiberglass below the side window of the control station before he found the range and hit the window with the third shot. The helmsman's hand fell from the throttle without moving it and the cruiser continued to try to drag GULL through the water sideways. A rattle of gunfire announced Matt's second assault on the cruiser's port quarter and new flames burst out in the main saloon.

Sven reversed the engines and as GULL disengaged, another great slab of Fiberglas caught on the chain and was torn away.

From her vantage point forward, Leda could see the two women occupants of the cabin cowering against the far bulkhead.

GULL backed away and Sven secured the two outboard motors, then called Matt to return. He would have no trouble finding GULL, for she was now plainly visible in the firelight coming from the cruiser.

"Is she going to sink?" Leda asked joining Sven in the cockpit.

Sven had no stomach for his handy work. He was somewhat surprised at how effective his effort had been. The cruiser's crew had been completely unprepared for any kind of attack and certainly at a total loss when confronted with such an aggressive one. Even the most experienced crew could not have coped with the suddenness of the blazes and the immediate extent of the cocktail coaxed fires. This group of Sunday sailors could do only one thing. They jumped into the black water.

"She'll burn ta the waterline first. I hope they all get off," he said ruefully.

"I hope it's MOTHER," Leda said tensely. "They didn't fire a single shot."

Chapter Nine

A uniform shadow crossed the face of each of the tellers of this part of the tale. Terrible things had been done by people unaccustomed to doing terrible things.

Those who were less sensitive to such excesses had slept through most of it, for it had all happened so quickly that they awoke just in time to abandon ship.

Be careful who you party with.

Leda's sentence reverberated in Sven's head like a scream in a cathedral. He was no less assured when Matt came aboard and asserted that the boat was indeed MOTHER'S FUR COAT, because when Sven pressed him, he had to confess that it had been too dark to read the name on the transom.

Had Sven jumped to a conclusion? Just because Diego and the boat were in the same place at the same time did not prove that the big cruiser was part of the aggressor fleet. Even Nigel's terse warning that the boat had hastily departed proved nothing.

The cold fear did not release its grip on him until he had pulled the bandaged Diego from the water in the breaking dawn. He thought earlier that he had recognized one of the other survivors as the man he had seen in the club bar with Diego, but the diminutive Cuban was the clincher.

And Leda was wrong. There were bullet holes in and about GULL's foredeck and cabin top.

The cruiser's entire crew, including the bandaged "R"—the right side of his face pock marked by half dozen spent skeet shot—sat huddled in her rubber dinghy and in FAST FUN. The two boats, tied one behind the other, were being towed toward Bimini while in GULL's sun filled cockpit her crew debated about the next step.

Diego had quickly told them that PLEASURE HOUSE had been alerted as soon as he was rescued at Chub and that she was now plowing in pursuit. "R" also verified that an SOS had been sent to PLEASURE HOUSE on a prearranged frequency when it had become obvious that the cruiser would sink.

"It's too dangerous to bring 'em aboard and we sure can't outrun the trawler even if we cut 'em loose. We need a delayin' tactic," Sven mused aloud.

They were abreast of the second flasher. It was a steel structure, its base members set into a block of concrete perched atop the coral a few feet below the surface of the water. At low tide the tiny coral islet on which the tower stood would be exposed. According to the chart, it was surrounded by sand spits that would make it unapproachable by a large boat. There was a steel service ladder running up one side of the tower to the light at the top.

Matt looked at the group huddled in the small boats. There was "R", the Captain, the two party girls, Diego, Mack and Nick, who still looked sleepy. Seven in all. Where had Bubba Winfrey gone? Had he flown away in a rage when the empty net closed? Flown ahead to lay a new trap? No time to think about that now.

He checked his watch, the tide was ebbing. It would be dead low at 11:30.

"Put them on the tower," he blurted. "That's the way to delay PLEASURE HOUSE. She'll have to stop to take them off and it will have to be done in a dinghy and it'll take at least two, maybe three trips." He looked at the amazed Sven for agreement.

"Hell, it's better than anythin' I can come up with. Let's do it."

GULL was soon anchored and then with Sven at the helm of the runabout and Matt standing guard, they ferried the prisoners to the tower. There was only about 18 inches of water and Sven tipped the big engine up and coasted the last few feet to the base of the ladder.

Then he turned to the miserable assembly and spoke plainly. "I don't know any a-you people. I didn't want to have anythin' ta do with ya. I don't know what ya want with GULL, but I know that I've got a contract to deliver her to Miami. I'm gonna do that. Ya got in my way. I'm sorry about yer boat, and I'm sorry about yer injuries. But, none of ya look like yer members of the church choir. In yer line of business ya make things unpleasant for people. Today it's your turn. I've half a mind to set you adrift an' be damned, but I'm not sure how deep some of ya are in all this an' how maybe some of ya don't even know what's goin' on.

"Cap'n, you lead off. Climb up that ladder as high as ya can go. Make plenty a room. All these others have to stand on it too. Only way to keep out of the water. Tide will go plum out in a while and ya can come down an' wait for PLEASURE HOUSE."

There were stormy protests from the men and tears from the younger woman, but a very tired Matt raised the gun and pointed it squarely at "R"'s head. The others had indicated in various ways that he was in charge.

"Tell them to move," he said menacingly, "or so help me I'll kill you. You've fucked up enough of my life and I'm really so tired that I could make a very bad decision right about now. MOVE!" he bellowed.

"Do what he says." "R" nodded toward the captain.

The man didn't argue. With a shrug he turned to the ladder and climbed. The other men followed one by one, each urging the captain to climb higher, to make room. But the mother sea eagle protested his nearness to her nest on top the light and squawked and beat her wings at every step he took.

The women, one tearful, pleaded to be taken on GULL. They knew nothing of what the men were doing, they said. They had just come along for the ride and the parties.

"Look out who ya party with from now on," Sven counseled as he firmly placed the smaller of the two on the bottom rung. The other one, somewhat older, looked him in the eye, shrugged, smiled and accepting his helping hand, stepped out of her own accord.

Sven pushed off, lowered the motor when he was sure of his water and headed for GULL still towing the inflatable.

"Now what?" the red-eyed Matt asked.

"We run like hell. Get as much distance between us and the 'casa' as possible."

"You think they'll still chase us after the beating we gave these guys?" Matt asked.

"I think somebody real important wants GULL and his options have run out. We've just ratcheted up th' level of violence. Th' one thing we can be sure is—they won't sink us in deep water." All the more reason not to stop at Bimini, he thought.

"This isn't deep water," Matt mused. "It's barely ten or twelve feet."

"Then I reckon we better find some soon's we can."

"Welcome back, guys," Leda chirped when they pulled along side. "I've got great news for you. We've got a leak. Cabin sole is under about three inches of water."

Sven bolted for the companionway as soon as he touched the deck. He snatched away the ladder and the housing covering the engine. The water was close, but had not reached the starter yet.

"Start the engine," he bellowed to Matt, who was hanging head down from the bridge deck. When the engine was running, Sven snapped the bilge pump switch and he heard the comforting whine from under his feet.

"Go ahead dead slow," he yelled when Matt had the anchor on deck. Then he began to pull up sections of the sole in the forward compartment, looking for the crack between planks that had opened. He knew that the ramming of the cruiser could open a seam but he felt at the time that the risk was worth it. Now he ran his hand the length of each seam, seeking the pressure of the incoming water. The pump had been pumping fifteen minutes and he could see no decrease in the level of the water, in fact, it had risen still further. The pump was not only not emptying the boat, it was not keeping up with the leak.

"Leda, take the helm. Matt come down here and help me."

When Matt scrambled down into the ankle deep water he was handed a plastic bucket. "Bail," Sven commanded. "Throw it out into the cockpit." At first Matt got only a quart or so in the two gallon bucket, but soon he forced it down and flattened the edge he was dragging along the cabin sole, and his aching back told him that he was nearly filling the bucket with each swipe.

Sven was now busily pulling drawers out and working to get behind other fixtures in the compartment. Again he felt along the seams and suddenly cursed an enlightened oath.

"I found the damned thing," he bellowed. "Bring me a towel out of the head." The damage was where all damage on a boat is: Where it's most difficult to deal with. When Matt arrived in the forward compartment with the towel, he found Sven stretched full length in the water, his arm outstretched into a housing for a drawer. The leak was barely within reach. But it flowed, fountain like from the seam of a plank just below the water line on the port side. The plank was secured to the vertical stem at just about where the eyebolt fastening the bob stay entered the stem. The bob stay—one of the chains that had so recently sawed its way through the cruiser's hull.

Sven's efforts at jamming the towel into the crack were wasted. All the tonnage of the boat pressed into the water around the crack, forcing the stream into the boat at terrific pressure.

"Stop her dead in the water. Keep the engine running," he yelled as he scrambled to get himself untangled. "Forward motion just increases the pressure. We got to get that seam up out of the water."

On deck he turned his face into the breeze that had returned with the sun. Turning his head from side to side he allowed it to flow past each ear. He thus judged its true direction and that allowed him to guess at the compass course he might be able to sail.

"Let's get up some sail. That's a beam wind. It won't heel us much, but it may freshen and it may back around to the west and that would be real good." It might veer all the way south-east, too, he thought. That would be bad. If it moved all the way into the northwest where it had come from yesterday, it would be devastating. He had to find another way to keep the seam out of the water in that eventuality and he had to find a faster way of pumping out what came in.

When the mainsail was hoisted and the big ginny and jib unreeled, the pressure of the wind against the tall sails heeled the boat somewhat, but not enough for the ruptured seam to clear the water.

Matt went back to bailing and Sven rigged a hand bilge pump which sent a gush of solid water into the cockpit. Temporarily relieved, the weary Matt climbed to the bridge deck where he soon took over the pump handle because Sven had another idea and went off to shift the port outboard motor to the starboard lifeline. Sven then wrestled GAVIOTA's jerry cans filled with water and gasoline from their fastenings astern and lashed them to the starboard lifeline stanchions as well. He had brought the extra water to fight fire if their exchange with the cruiser had caused it. Now the heavy stuff might save the cutter by merely sitting in the shade. But when he checked, the seam was still submerged.

Next he pulled the small bilge pump from its bracket in the dinghy and pumped the port fresh water tank dry. He could afford this waste under the circumstances. The fuel tank and one water tank on the starboard side worked in his favor. But the stubborn seam refused to rise to the surface.

A check below confirmed, however, that the water was not gaining on them. Sven sprawled again in the water of the forward compartment. He twisted and turned but could not get two hands near the leak.

Rummaging in the ditty bag, he unrolled a length of caulk and attempted to force it, one handed, into the seam, but the awkward position allowed him no leverage and even with the thinnest of the selection of caulking irons, he failed. Not even a steak knife would fit. After all, the planks had been fashioned to take caulk from the outside not the inside. But there was some good news: the two bilge pumps were keeping up with the inflow. But how long could the crew keep up with the exhausting task of manual pumping.

Sven took a turn on the pump handle. Matt, sensing a change in the wind, trimmed the sails differently and GULL heeled a little further. But not enough.

"How about this?" Leda offered when Matt sat down again. "If water is the heaviest thing we've got to work with, it's also the thing we've got most of. How about pulling that dinghy amidships on the starboard side, wedge it or lash it in position and fill it with what we're—you're—pumping out?"

Sven looked at her a long moment; then a smile, the first one in many hours, cracked his weary countenance. Matt looked at her in unabashed admiration. But his mooning was short-lived as Sven rousted him forward to help manhandle the dinghy into position.

Leda looked at her watch. Six or six and a half hours to Bimini. Where was PLEASURE HOUSE? How far away was she when she was called back? How soon would she arrive at the flasher tower and how long would it take her to catch up after that delay?

Leda shook her head in disgust. Not a single answer to the whole knot of questions. What would GULL's crew tell the authorities at Bimini? How would they explain their suspicions that led to the ramming and fire bombing of the cruiser? She had been wrong about not being shot at. They could show the row of nine bullet holes stitched across the deck and the half dozen others that seem to have been more randomly fired, but how would they explain not calling for aid or reporting the incident to the police by radio as soon as it happened? How much weight would her story about a suspect cop carry in explaining this reluctance to cooperate with the police? She had a growing misgiving about stopping at Bimini.

Could she coax these two very honest men into breaking another law and leaving the islands without clearing immigration? They might want to come back some day. It would be hard to ask for another favor.

She stopped thinking about it and concentrated on keeping the boat on course and pointing higher any time the wind allowed. For the higher she pointed, the more GULL heeled and the wider margin made Leda feel that she was contributing something in return for the favors granted her.

Soon, Matt, the pump repositioned below deck and its output hose led through a porthole, was filling the dinghy with a solid stream. Sven watched with interest as the water rose. Every gallon weighed roughly 60 pounds. How many gallons did the boat hold? Would it make a difference in levering the heavy keel? Yes. But would it make enough of a difference? He trooped again to the life line at the port bow and studied the seam. It occasionally cleared the surface, but Sven was sure that it did so only when the wind gusted and GULL heeled as a result.

While the dinghy filled, and between his turns on the pump handle, Sven checked the wind speed indicator. He didn't want to tell his tired crew yet, but he was sure that for all their effort, the wind would be the determining factor in keeping the leak under control. He clicked the VHF dial to the weather channel and listened carefully to the recorded loop twice.

A low pressure center was moving across the panhandle of Florida, dragging an arcing warm front to the south and southwest. Northwest winds becoming westerly would prevail over most of the southern Florida peninsula beginning midday and lasting all night. The winds would drag in moisture from the Gulf and drop rain as it passed over the peninsula, and winds would increase from an average 12-15 knots to as much as 50 knot gusts during the rain squalls.

It was the average 12-15 knots that interested Sven. It was blowing perhaps 10 now. If it freshened to 12 or 15 and didn't back into the south-west, it would be almost perfect. What bothered him was the fact that the weather forecasts were rarely perfect.

What also bothered him was that he was thinking of ways to avoid stopping at Bimini. He realized that he had little stomach for the questions that might be asked if the aggressors now decided that they might want to involve the police. What would he say if asked why he rammed a non-threatening pleasure boat making a night passage? The bullet holes in his deck and cabin top were little excuse. After all they were fired from directly in front of the boat. No ballistic expert was needed to determine that GULL was already on a collision course when she was fired upon.

Superficially—a case of self defense.

Down deeper was the logic of Leda's earlier question. Who were the good cops?

When the dinghy was full, the two men fell exhausted into the cockpit. Leda reminded them that no call had been made to PLEASURE HOUSE to tell them where to find the cruiser's survivors.

A suspicious voice answered Matt's call on Channel 16 and was eager to shift to a more private channel. He was equally eager to terminate the conversation once the location of the crew of MOTHER had been given. Matt had been careful to paint the picture of survivors clinging to the steel tower. He noted that the man called "R" was wounded and gave rise to additional anxiety he hoped by referring to the group as 'remaining' crew. He also hoped the haste with which they might be prompted to respond and the pressure of a wounded boss's wrath might cause some poor decision making aboard the trawler.

The breeze stiffened while Matt was making the call and careful trimming of the sails by Sven allowed an almost perfect compass course and brought the open seam out of the water for the first time.

After the men had prepared soup and sandwiches, Leda remained at the helm while they crashed for a few minutes of sleep.

The constant tension, from the time the cruiser's lights had appeared last night until the seam emerged from the water, had driven all thoughts of sleep from Leda's mind. She had slept an hour or so before they reached the first flasher last night, but that was a long, strained time ago. She began to feel the fatigue well up. Sven had been the last to sleep. He had had two full hours before Nigel's transmission had awakened him. So it was Sven that she woke when she could no longer keep the big cutter under control. He had had two more hours.

Sven scanned the horizon astern. There was no sign of a boat. He scanned the horizon ahead and there was no sign of the squalls. He looked again at the water level inside the boat and was sure that the single bilge pump was now keeping it in check. He looked at his compass and at his sails and found a better course that kept his necessary heel.

His down-east upbringing had taught him to be wary when things appeared too easy.

Could he reconstruct with any accuracy PLEASURE HOUSE's track? How much farther south had she gone after their encounter the previous night? How far away was she when she was called back? Would she have to stop and fuel up at Chub too? If the old trawler had gotten very far south, GULL might have a chance of sailing into darkness again before her arrival.

In the deep water of the stream, in the dark, did he dare to think that he had a chance to evade detection? Was PLEASURE HOUSE the only boat at their disposal? Would the dirty cop radio to Bimini and have them stopped on some excuse or another and delay them until the chasers could catch up?

He gave it up. The margin for error was enormous at every conjecture. He looked at his watch. Eleven-five. Four and a half hours to Bimini. This breeze he was sailing must be part of what was not to start until mid-day, he thought. If he could depend on the rest of the forecast, it would freshen and stay all night.

The wind. If he passed Bimini without stopping, it was 45 miles to Miami, eight or nine hours if the wind was steady.

The wind. Did he dare to pass a safe port when he had a damaged boat? What kind of captain did that? If he put in at Bimini he only gave PLEASURE HOUSE an opportunity to catch him.

The wind. The wind was the thing.

Minutes after he passed Bimini he would be on the edges of the Gulf Stream. It would want to carry him north. He had to sail a course south of Miami to compensate for that drift. If the wind shifted and he could not maintain his course, he would be drawn north and a landfall that created new problems of another sort. He could not douse the sails and power because he would lose his heel and drive new water in around the sprung plank. He trimmed his sails.

He prayed to the wind gods.

The first squall came up late in the day. Just about the time they were abreast of Browns Cay. Sven could see the island on his port beam perhaps five miles away. He had cheated south all afternoon in order to keep as much water under him as possible. Just past Browns the soundings dropped from two fathoms to 10 and a few minutes later to 400. He was a little south of Miami, so the drift of the Stream would help carry him toward home. He didn't really expect a police patrol boat to come in pursuit, but the distance was comforting. So was the poor visibility afforded by the coming rain.

He couldn't leave the helm so his shout woke both his crew and when the groggy Matt appeared, Leda was not far behind—full of questions.

"We got a squall coming an' we can't take down all the sail, or we'll lose our heel. But we gotta shorten down. We'll have some hefty gusts. Reel in that ginny all the way, reel in the jib about half—she'll bag probably, but we need somethin up there. And lets throw a reef in the main. Here, Leda take the helm a minute."

The crew complied and soon Matt was pulling a slab reef into the stiff Dacron mainsail. "You think we ought to pull it down to the second set of ties?" he asked. Matt didn't care much for squalls at sea. He always chose to err on the safe side.

"I don't know if she'll heel enough with so little up," Sven replied. "It'll be a few minutes yet before it gets here."

When they were in the cockpit again Sven said, "I hate to tell you this, but that squall will kick up waves and most of 'em will cover that seam momentarily. We're gonna have ta pump all during the storm. It won't last long—20 minutes or half-hour at most. They move through fast."

A few minutes before the squall hit, the wind fell almost completely, then came back with a vengeance. GULL heeled and with her teeth into the white caps, she plunged forward at almost hull speed. Sven stood at the helm gulping great lungfuls of the fresh salt air and experiencing, almost for the first time this trip, the pure joy of sailing. Then the rain came and soaked his tired body from canvas hat to canvas shoes. And the gusts came too; powerful knockdowns that heeled the boat so far that her lee toe rail was submerged. The water in the lashed dinghy poured back into the sea from where it had come, then as GULL righted herself, the rain filled the little red boat again. The process was repeated a dozen harrowing times in twenty minutes and each time Sven, bracing himself against the torrent of wind and rain, twisted the helm to port, bringing the bow further into the wind until the blast blew past and GULL righted herself. At one point between gusts, he loosed the main sheet and let the boom out in an effort to reduce the pressure on the rig. But a terrible gust heeled the boat so far that the end of the boom dragged in the water and at the next opportunity he sheeted it back in.

It was over as fast as it had begun. The wind fell, the rain fell and the boat sat upright and leaked profusely. A wild eyed Leda, bruised from being banged about trying to steady the pump for Matt, climbed into the cockpit.

"You better go down there and check on things," she blurted. "Matt's seasick and I don't think we moved much water." Then after a moment, "We're not going to have to do that again are we?"

Sven avoided replying by disappearing into the cabin where he quickly opened hatches and portholes hastily closed to keep the rain out. There was the faint smell of vomit. Matt, wedged between the table and the settee, doggedly pushed the pump handle back and forth with one hand while he steadied the base with the other. His knuckles were bleeding and a large lump was growing on his forehead.

Sven sent him topside and then bent his back to the pump. The water had not appeared above the cabin sole again, but he knew that with only the list provided by the weight he had shifted to starboard, the seam was submerged and the water was pouring in.

Matt sat in the cockpit, wet, sick and disheveled. Leda wanted to go to him, but couldn't and knew that he wouldn't want her to. He had brought a can of soda crackers up with him and he was eating as fast as his saliva would moisten them. The color had begun to return to his face and when the first faint stirrings of a breeze wafted aboard, he breathed deeply of the fresh air and seemed to strengthen immediately. He managed a faint smile around a mouthful and then frowned and touched the bump on his forehead gingerly. He was about to say something when Sven called him below again.

"Pump again for me, will ya?" he asked. "Somethin's funny."

With that he went forward and lying on his side again he reached into the drawer hole and felt along the hull. The seam had widened, the fountain was half again as large as the original.

"Waal, damn it," he said, returning to the main cabin. "I need wind to keep me afloat; then I get a little too much and it may sink me. That blowin' around we got up there, the strong wind and the waves, opened the seam wider. We'll never be able to keep up with it with both pumps unless she stays heeled and that seam stays outta the water."

At that moment the breeze did freshen and as it did GULL began to heel, ever so slightly at first, then more and the seam was finally out of the water and the two bilge pumps began to gain on the leak.

All hands came on deck to dry out in the late afternoon sun and none remarked on the fact that the water in which they sailed was deep blue. No one cared that they had not sought the questionable safety of Bimini. Every one sensed that for all their bedraggled appearance and numbing fatigue, they were on the last leg of the trip. Soon the enveloping darkness would hide them from their pursuers again and amid the shipping and the myriad navigation lights of the Stream, they would not be easy to find. If the wind held, they would make it. If the wind held they might even relax.

Leda's reverie was disturbed by the sound of the airplane. And all the old fear that had gripped her throughout the chase of the day and night before, rushed up to engulf her once more.

The two men who had been dozing and drying in the cockpit were immediately alert and shaded their eyes as they followed the plane's circuit in the now cloudless sky.

The plane was definitely interested in GULL. It circled several times at a modest altitude then made three low-level passes. Sven was seriously contemplating the risks in attempting to shoot it down when he stopped mid-thought and tore his hat from his head with a glad cry.

"It's Pete. He don't recognize our new paint job and all. And he don't know nothin' about Leda." He waved the hat energetically.

"How did he know where to look for us?" Matt wanted to know.

"I told Nigel to give him a call and explain as much as possible just using my name, not GULL's. I don't think the bad guys know our names. I wanted Pete to check on us to see if we survived the night in the Alley.

If we was being towed by the trawler when he found us, he was to go straight to the Coast Guard and report us missin' at the hands of pirates."

With that he hurried down to the VHF. He had left the channel indicator on the weather channel earlier, so had not been able to hear Pete's call. Rummaging under a settee seat he found one of the portable radios and began to call the pilot.

"Sorry I'm so late getting to you," Pete said. *"I wasn't sure what Nigel's double talk was all about this morning when he finally got hold of me, so I flew to Chub as soon as I could get away to try to get it all straight. Then, I was coming down the Alley when I see all these people stranded on this rock with a blinker light on it. I'm about ready to set down and see what I can do when I see this trawler steaming along. So I call him and ask if he can stop off long enough to pick them up. He talks like he knows all about it and thanks me, but says that he can take care of everything. He tells me to go about my business, in fact. Well, I hung around until he finally got them all aboard. Don't know how long they had been there."*

Sven didn't take time to enlighten him, but asked instead: "What time did he get them all aboard?"

"*Must have been about two or two-thirty. Why?*"

"It's a long story. I can't tell ya now. Did ya notice which direction he took after he got 'em all loaded?"

"No, I left when it looked like he was going to finish up OK"

"Look, Pete, I don't know how much Nigel told you, but they're the ones who boarded us the first night at Elbow. I haven't got time to go into it all and I don't know who's listening. The important thing right now is, I got a bad leak. Sprung a plank. I gotta keep heeled over to keep the seam up outa the water. When we got no wind and I'm upright, she leaks faster than the two bilge pumps can control. I need you to do something for me. Can you fly back and find that trawler? Tell me which direction she's travelin'? I gotta keep sailing, take advantage of this wind. If I can stop worrying about being chased, I think I can get this boat close enough to Miami for the Coast Guard to come out and give me a handy-billy pump. That'll move enough water to keep me afloat 'till I get home."

"Sure, I can do that. Why don't you call the Coast Guard now? They can come out to meet you," Pete suggested.

"I can't reach 'em on this hand-held. Antenna is too close to the water, I guess. The other rig with the mast antenna is without a mike. I can't transmit."

"Well, let me go check on the trawler. I'll call the Coast Guard and give them your position. You sit tight."

"No, no. Doan call the Guard until we know if the chase boat is still chasing. I doan want them to be able to pin point me. If they're still coming, I want to be able to hide in the dark as much as possible."

"You got it." Pete said. *"I'll check it out. If they're coming in this direction, I won't come back anywhere near you, I'll radio you the situation."*

He signed off and flew off in the direction of Bimini.

The breeze stiffened again to its former strength and Sven busied himself lengthening the hose on the engine water intake. Then he fashioned a strainer over the end and dropped it into the bilge water. When Leda started the engine again, it drew its cooling water out of the interior of the boat and pumped it over the side via the exhaust pipe. Now they had three bilge pumps. Since the engine had to run to keep the batteries charged for the other power pump, it pumped constantly also. Sven was beginning to run out of tricks. He hoped this would be the last one necessary.

In due time the VHF crackled with Pete's report. The trawler had put into Gun Cay. He was sure it was the same one. He had had a very good look at it while it loaded the survivors that afternoon. There was no way to tell if it would come on later. It was not tied to the fuel dock.

Pete had figured out a way to give the Guard their position, he told Sven. He would fly GULL's compass course, figure their speed and plot a course. Then he would radio the Miami tower on a frequency the trawler couldn't monitor and have them call the Guard on the telephone, telling them about where to intercept GULL. Sven agreed to the plan, thanked him and promised to buy him a drink when they got home. Maybe more than one.

Matt was at the helm now. The bilges were under control, the wind was strong and from the right direction. They had two hours of daylight and four hours of darkness to spend before they could get off this once pleasant boat. Somewhere ahead, just after dark probably, the Coast Guard would meet them and transfer the large gasoline pump. More than likely they would not tarry to escort them in, but they would check constantly on their progress. GULL's crew began to relax. If the chasers came on and if they found GULL in the dark, perhaps the proximity of the Guard boat would keep them at bay.

Sven began to believe that they were safe on the water. But GULL might still have to meet her appointment with the aggressors in Florida. He had no reason to believe that that group would give up merely because the boat was in Miami. But that was someone else's worry. By tomorrow night at this time he would be drinking beer with Fats Barlow on MOON SHOT at Dinner Key marina. These guys could find somebody else to shoot at.

It was his turn for a nap again and he lay down and went immediately to sleep.

The storm came up rapidly, Matt said later. The moon was high and the sky clear. Then out of the south, the cloud appeared almost upon them before Matt could sound the alarm. He furled the big ginny quickly, but without immediate help, there was no chance to reef the huge main before the first blast of wind and rain hit. GULL was heeled well over in an instant and stayed that way for the duration of the storm.

Leda, caught unaware down below, had been trying to heat some soup. Dishes and cutlery bounced about the cabin on wild trajectories. The heel was too severe for the gimbaled stove and Leda muscled the pot of hot soup into the sink at the last possible minute. It spilled out and was sucked down the drain by the water rushing past the hull outside. Sven rolled out of his berth and clambered topside to size up the situation. It was too late to reef. The gusts were stronger than this afternoon and oftener. He let the main sheet run as much as he dared. Then he went below to check the bilge. The storm had kicked up sizable waves and GULL was plunging into them with considerable force. Each time she did, the fountain gushed. Soon he and Leda were again at the hand pump, one steadying it, the other pumping. Then they traded places.

The storm lasted no longer that the one that afternoon, but the greater sail area had made it a much more punishing ride for both the boat and its occupants. Had the sail not been new it might have blown out. It was not the way Sven liked to sail a boat. She strained at every joint and seam. Her rig was punished unnecessarily. But she was a sturdy boat. Everywhere but where she leaked.

When the storm blew itself out, as before, the rain continued into the calm that followed. GULL stood upright in the sea and the seam was submerged. The three pumps struggled, but it was obvious that they could not keep up. The dinghy which had spilled its contents at the first knock down of the storm was filled again, but inside, the water rose above the cabin sole. Leda stroked the pump, Sven and Matt bailed, the power pump whined, the engine sucked its share and spat it out the exhaust. But the water didn't drop and the wind didn't rise.

Afraid to stay too long below with no watch in this busy shipping channel, Sven went topside to scan the horizon. There was a hint of a breeze. He called Leda to the helm. She set the course with the engine and waited for the wind. Sven returned to the cabin below. He had just one more trick. He had to try it. Maybe it would keep them afloat until the Coast Guard came.

With that he began to pull up sections of the cabin sole in the area of the companionway and worked forward toward the galley. Lying between each rib were lead ingots. Inside ballast. Weight placed low in the boat that offset the tremendous pressure of wind in the sails aloft. The hot lead had been poured into molds with bottom and side angles approximating that of the boat's planking. The tops were flat. Each weighed from sixty to eighty pounds depending on it's location.

The two men began the laborious task of moving the ingots one by one from the port side of the boat to the farthest point starboard. Sven hoped to create a list sufficient to keep the split seam above water without depending on the wind. If he was successful, they could motor the rest of the way in if they had to.

They began aft near where the companion-way ladder had been and they gradually worked forward where bulkheads, plumbing and other obstacles made the work slower and harder. The men were dead tired but the rising water prodded them on. After a time they stooped almost automatically, grappling in the shallow water, grasped the pig with both hands, straightened and, with a flowing motion, setting it down a few feet to starboard. Again and again they repeated the move, automatically, almost unthinking now. Or, more likely, purposely thinking of other things.

Then Matt removed a new section of cabin sole and an ingot floated to the top of the water!

The pig was not a pig at all. It was a zinc box fashioned in the shape of a pig and it was soldered closed.

It was a water-tight canister.

The two men looked at one another for a moment. Then Matt tossed the object responsible for all their pain onto the settee and they bent again to their task.

When all the pigs had been moved, Sven again checked the crack. The seam had stopped its hemorrhage. It was above the surface. They were all right again for a while. If the wind came back, they'd be even better. Where was the Coast Guard?

They collapsed into the cockpit again. Matt had never worked so hard in his life. He had never been so scared for so long either. He would make every effort never to repeat the experience.

GULL lounged in her list to starboard. It was as if she were a drunk, leaning upon nothing. As if she were falling over, but never completing the dynamic. Her sails hung limply aloft; her bowels were flung about the cabin below and her exhausted crew clung to the sides of the cockpit. But when Leda put the diesel in gear, GULL moved through the water firmly, lacking only her grace and style, which, she seemed to realize, was only temporarily missing.

Sven suddenly understood why he had not heard from the Coast Guard. He had turned off the hand-held VHF to conserve the batteries and he had left GAVIOTA's maimed unit set to the channel where he and Pete had talked earlier. Flicking the indicator back to 16, he was almost immediately rewarded with a call from an approaching cutter. Thumbing the hand-held alive he responded, reciting the litany of information that his rescuers most needed in order to do their job. It was part of one of the many lessons Matt had attempted to learn. The younger man was again amazed at his friend's ability. With all the distractions of the storm and the emergency, Sven had kept mental track of just how far along on the Dead Reckoning course he thought them to be. He supposed that the storm had blown them somewhat north of that position and he reckoned that they were farther north again as a result of lying dead in the current while the ballast was shifted.

The wind had begun to rise and when Sven appeared on deck, he gave Leda a new course to steer and instructed Matt to shine the spotlight on the vast expanse of the mainsail.

There was no conversation in the cockpit. Each clung to something or braced against something to offset the list. Each wondered if the arrival of the Coast Guard heralded the end of this nightmarish adventure. No one wanted to contemplate the legal or possibly criminal complexities that awaited them. Each decided privately that what was wanted most was a good night's sleep.

Chapter Ten

So far the sources had been few, but they had confirmed one another. Now, there were many and while some upheld a single version, others, mostly governmental, seemed regularly reluctant to confirm or even clarify events. On the contrary, those reports were often so vague as to be empty—-verbiage that did not report.

Party time

It was almost a good night's sleep. Matt was awakened by the patterned rapping on the hull. Forcing his eyes to focus, he found that it was almost nine-thirty. Florida sunlight blazed in through the porthole. Miami humidity made him wonder that he had slept so long.

On his way to the companionway, he paused to gaze at the still figure of Leda. She slept soundly. On deck, he quickly surveyed the surroundings which had been hidden in darkness on their arrival last night. The bustle of the Coast Guard station was everywhere to be seen. A new sense of security flowed over Matt as he noted the high fenced perimeter and the guarded gate. GULL was tied to a quarantine dock. A young guard slouched at the head of the pier.

Matt found Sven in MOTHER's inflatable. He had brought it around to the bow and, leaning over its rolled side, he was forcing a narrow strip of caulking cotton into the open seam with a flat caulking iron and a hammer. It was a tricky task because the iron was under the surface and the water resisted the hammer's every blow. Several other strips which had been dipped into a thick gooey mixture lay waiting their turn. He looked up when Matt's groggy head appeared over the toe rail.

"Sorry to wake ya," he said, not really sorry. "The owner is probably gonna want us ta take her to a yard so's this can be done right. It's gonna take a good wood-boat man ta do it.

"The Officer-of-the-Day tried ta reach Andrews about an hour ago ta report bringing us in. He ain't available. I finally talked to his secretary—Shirley, she knows me from before—and she says he's outa town but will be back for some big swa-ray he's hosting tonight. She's gonna talk to him about two this p.m. she sez and she'll try to get some instructions fer us.

"Meantime we leave her tied up here. Him or his lawyer has got to come down and sign something. The OD sez I can go ahead and move her after that, but I'm pretty sure the man is gonna want her to go directly to a yard fer repair an I ain't a gonna do that 'till I can talk ta him myself. This muck will plug her up enough sos we can put her back together down below and clean her up. I doan want him to see her like this." He paused a moment then went on, "She'll leak a little but the pump can handle it. We won't be movin' her very far."

"What do you want me to do?" Matt asked, almost afraid to hear the reply. His back still ached from moving the heavy pigs in the darkness the night before.

"Empty that dinghy, is first, I guess." He paused long enough to slither the end of another strip into position then went on. "I talked ta the OD and he sez there's a labor contractor they use when they need odd-job help here. I called 'em and they're sending four strong backs ta put all that lead back where it belongs. I told the guy not to send 'em 'till after noon. I won't be ready 'till then."

Matt turned away and then swung back. "You had any breakfast yet?"

"There's a fast food place a couple a blocks up from the end a th' causeway on th' Miami Beach side. It's OK ta go. I checked us in with immigration and customs. Eggs is terrible. Coffee's tolerable."

"Even terrible eggs would be tolerable today," a bright eyed Leda said from the companionway. A few minutes later she and Matt strolled out the gate and up the street.

Leda had gone to sleep almost immediately upon the fastening of the towing hawser the night before. The sight of the cutter and the friendly and knowledgeable skipper had allowed all the tension to drain from her and all of the fatigue to consume her. Now she was curious about the way the night had ended.

"The skipper was a sailor himself," Matt said, sipping coffee from the Styrofoam cup. "We got the big pump going right away. It ran all night. The skipper knew that we couldn't be towed faster than our hull speed, so we loafed along. He got us tied up at about one-thirty. I crashed right away. Sven was still fooling around when I dropped off."

"So what do we do now?" she asked, dread in her voice. Several times in the past twenty-four hours the ever deepening impact of her father's death had attempted to wedge its way into the preoccupation with threat and danger. Now it had begun to dominate her every thought. But Matt misunderstood.

"Sven and I talked about it on the way in last night. He thinks the best thing is to wait and talk to the owner. The guy is a lawyer. He ought to know how to handle both situations. Yours is, after all, connected to ours. Maybe after a talk, you can introduce him to your dad's friends who are 'fixers' in the islands."

"I don't think I can wait that long. If the marine police notified the Coast Guard yesterday like they said they would, these guys are going to wonder why I didn't come clean as soon as I got here. Goosing with the Bahamians is one thing, with the Coast Guard is something else." Sven had been right about the eggs. She pushed them aside and sugared the cooled coffee.

"Well, it's really up to you. Sven thinks you have to do what you think is best for you. There is nothing contradictory in our stories." When he did not make a recommendation, she changed the subject.

"What do you think is in the canister," she asked.

"Well, it isn't Spanish gold coins, that's for sure. It rattles slightly, but it sounds like mostly paper." He paused then went on. "I'm not sure I want to know. At this point, I want to turn the boat and all over to Andrews, make sure we're not going to get hung up with the Bahamian cops for ramming boats and leaving the jurisdiction and get back to my life as it was." He stopped and looked at her. "Well, almost as it was."

"Do you think it will be that easy? I don't even know where to start. Who do I report to about my dad and GAVIOTA?"

The discussion continued over the second cup of questionable coffee and the walk back to the boat. After checking with Sven, they decided to begin with the Coast Guard.

"Now, wait a minute," the young lieutenant said, stopping Leda after two or three breathless sentences. He went back slowly over the details of GAVIOTA's boarding, Eddie Malone's kidnapping, her stay in the gun closet, and her eventual release. At that point he stopped her and asked them to wait while he got some help. A few minutes later he led them upstairs to the Commanding Officer.

"I'm not even sure if I'm supposed to be bothering you with this," Leda said apologetically after the introductions were completed.

"Well," the smiling Captain said, "neither am I, but start again and I'll stop you when I know." With that Leda took a deep breath and began again. The Captain did not stop her until she came to the appearance of the man she called The 'Stache on the police patrol boat. Then he held up a report that a young yeoman had brought in earlier.

"This is the telex we got from the Bahamians late yesterday asking us to check on GAVIOTA's documentation," he said. "It came too late for us to do anything about and it came with no details.

"It may be our legal entry into this intrigue. We've been working with a special unit the Bahamian government set up a while back to investigate a spate of assaults on pleasure boats. It has some good people and backing from high up in the government. They can't afford to lose the American yachtsmen's tourist dollars in those islands. Because the head of this unit distrusts the laxity of lower echelon police, they are pretty exclusive in their operation. I'll try to channel all our information through that group." Then he turned to Sven who had recently arrived, still cleaning tenacious traces of goop from his hands.

"Now, Captain Olafson, I need your story. It falls into the same category and under the auspices of the same group."

And so it went. First one and then the other spoke, interleaving the events as they had happened. They stopped for lunch and Leda and a grousing Sven went back afterwards so the Captain could continue his questions. Matt stayed on GULL to supervise the four Mexican laborers in replacing the ballast, emptying the dinghy, storing the outboards and generally cleaning up the mess. They had just finished all that Matt felt they were necessary for when Sven came swinging down the dock. He signed the card each offered then asked what the agency paid them an hour. After their rather shamefaced reply, he took out his wallet and, calculating the time worked, he paid them as much again as their wage.

"Shirley, the boss's secretary, called. He's real upset about the boat. Wants ta see us but can't before tonight. He's throwin' a party for some bigwigs and he's tight fer time 'till about ten p.m. He's gonna send his car around fer us purdy soon. Wants us ta bring our glad rags, take a shower and a nap at his house this afternoon, eat dinner and rub some elbows at the party 'till he can talk ta us later on.

"The Coast Guard Captain wants GULL ta stay put fer a day or two 'till he can issue some kind of official result of the inquiry this morning."

"What's Leda doing?"

"Tryin' ta reach her dad's lawyer. The Captain thinks she's gonna need some legal help with an international flavor. She hopes this guy can recommend someone."

"She know about this party?" Matt asked.

"Yep. Like most women, she's stewin' about not havin' anythin' ta wear."

But much to the anguish of Andrews' chauffeur, Leda found something suitable to wear—just at the beginning of rush hour. The delayed arrival at the estate allowed for only a very short nap, but a long shower. The trio was well fed early in the evening by a clucking Mexican cook who came into their small informal dining room to be sure that they had enough to eat. Actually she wanted to be sure that they ate enough. Leda disappointed her, but Sven valiantly made up for it. She patted his forearm approvingly.

They all appeared in the walled garden of the compound promptly at 8:30. Too promptly, Leda scolded. No one who is anyone arrives on time. She went immediately to examine the *hors d'oeuvre* table.

Sven, in his newer pair of boating shoes, clean jeans, a maritime museum tee shirt and a gray tweed sport coat, strolled the paths. He looked quizzically at some of the exotic plants and generally tried to determine the plan of the garden. The paths, paved with multi-colored flag stones, swung graciously between flower beds and flowering trees, between mirror pools and water falls, past gazebos and arbor covered benches. The lighting was subtle and extravagant at the same time. And, the only thing that Sven really appreciated in this ostentatious display, the air was lightly scented with the aroma of the blooms. The garden was large and well kept.

At the rear boundary, a wrought iron gate interrupted the tall hedge that surrounded the entire garden. The gate was masked from view by a vine covered trellis that formed a short tunnel angling off the main walkway. Beyond the gate low buildings sheltered the large amounts of equipment necessary to keep the grounds cut, clipped, trimmed, fertilized and cultivated. Across the access road from them there appeared another cluster of buildings with a different color scheme. Obviously the rear of the neighbor's garden.

Sven was working his way back toward the house, up the side of the garden opposite of which he had taken on his journey down. A gentle breeze had found its way over the tall hedges and moved the still-warm air, promising a cooler evening.

He found Matt and Leda on a wooden swing suspended from a leafy arbor. Matt's blue blazer and khaki pants, clothes he had flown down in, had survived all of the rigors of GULL's torment and while not exactly evening clothes, they were sufficient for a young man whose self confidence had never been wanting, but which had in the last two days grown enormously. He could deal with being under-dressed.

A waiter wearing a white jacket approached with a tray

of assorted drinks. As the trio helped themselves he passed a message from Martin, the manor's major-domo. Mr. Andrews had arrived and inquired about their health and comfort. He was currently dressing and would indeed be able to see them for a short time in about an hour. As the waiter departed, they heard a tinkle of laughter announcing the arrival of the first guests. With that the dam seemed to burst and soon the garden was full of dinner jacketed men and over-dressed women. Sven remarked that their over-dressing often led to undressing. There was a considerable amount of bare skin in evidence. Leda's ankle length white sheath and bare shoulders allowed her to fit nicely into the company. The two men in sport coats stood out conspicuously.

Their early dinner had rendered the buffet uninteresting after the first exploratory nibbles, so the trio moved about and people watched. They commented on the expensive jewelry, the too-young ladies on some middle aged male arms, the subtle and not so subtle competitions waged between wealthy wives and the very hard look in the eyes of some of the obviously important men. Sven was sure that these men played for very high scores in a very hard hard-ball game.

Andrews had never appeared to Sven to be of that ilk. He was obviously successful, confident and a no-nonsense business man. But if these were his colleagues—could he be involved in intrigues as violent as they had experienced the past two days?

Sven wondered.

At last they were summoned into the library.

Arthur Andrews stood up from behind his desk and held out his hand to Sven. He was tall, six feet or so, with graying hair and horn rimmed glasses. He was a patrician of classic proportions. He nodded approvingly when Sven introduced Matt and he smiled carefully at Leda.

"Oh, yes, Ms. Malone. Shirley mentioned a female crew member. That's something new for you isn't it Sven? Isn't going to cost me any more is it?" He knew it wasn't and he laughed softly at his small joke. "This is Miles Connelly," he said, indicating the rather nondescript young man who stood a little apart. "He is one of my young trainees. Can he get you a drink before he leaves?"

Sven shook his head as he wondered what Miles was training to be.

Finding no takers the young man excused himself and left.

"Now," Andrews said, leaning forward on his elbows, "tell me what's happened to my boat."

Matt tensed. HIS boat? Yes, it was his boat and 24 hours earlier Matt would have gladly given it to him, or anyone, for that matter. But now the trials of the past two days seemed to be bonds difficult to sever. His boat. The boat that they had fought for, protected with their lives, patched and brought safely to port was theirs in spirit only.

Sven began to tell him about his boat.

But he interrupted after the first general statement that the boat had been attacked twice and was damaged.

"This is serious. Go back to the beginning. Tell me everything in sequence."

He was visibly upset when told about Ramirez's death. He was horrified as Sven described the boarding. The trio watched his face carefully as he was told what the boarders were looking for. No twitch, nor flicker of eyelid betrayed any prior knowledge of a canister. His face grew more puzzled as the story continued to unfold. When told about the attack on GAVIOTA, and that she was ransacked for a canister also, he stopped Sven mid-sentence. Snatching up the phone, he punched a single number and in a low voice told the hearer to find Jimmy. Then he asked Sven to wait. He looked in wonder at Leda as she sat before him in the very fashionably cut, long party dress. He struggled with the contrasting image of her in the cramped gun compartment.

James O'Hare was Andrew's lawyer. He wanted O'Hare to hear this story. It had to be done tonight, he apologized, for the two of them were to fly to D.C. early next morning. He poured martinis without asking and passed them around, all the while wondering at what lay behind it all. He asked Leda if she had a lawyer and asked his name when she only nodded because of the mouthful of olive.

Jimmy O'Hare was rotund, balding, red faced and carrying a drink which had probably contributed to his scarlet complexion. He was also a very affable man. He immediately set everyone at ease and asking for a brief rundown, listened intently as Andrews obliged. Both men then turned to Leda. O'Hare wanted her to describe again the boarding of GAVIOTA. When she finished they turned to Sven, but he nodded instead for Matt to take up the story of Leda's discovery. He then went on to describe the arrival of the patrol boat. O'Hare reacted overtly when Leda revealed that the mustached policeman had also been on the marauding boat that had captured GAVIOTA.

"Damn," he said. "This is serious. Christ."

The tale continued. Andrews' attitudes passed from wonder at the disguise of GULL to dismay at Sven's capture by Diego to horror at the ramming of MOTHER'S FUR COAT and its aftermath.

"Christ." Jimmy said for the fortieth time. Maybe it was the fiftieth, Sven thought. He must be a liability lawyer.

"And you've told all this to the Coast Guard already?" he asked.

"Christ," he said again when the three nodded in unison.

"That's when we sprung the plank," Sven said. "All th' twisting on that bobstay where it was secured at th' stem must have been just enough ta allow some old fasteners at the end of that plank ta pull loose. Then every time we got a knockdown in the squalls, the strain just loosened it more."

He was about to outline their struggles to make her list to starboard when a knock at the door interrupted and Miles Connelly slipped quietly into the room.

"Sorry to interrupt you, sir, but the Ambassador is arriving and Under Secretary Bell is getting nervous because he hasn't had a chance for a word with you yet." The young man lingered, nodded when Andrews held up five fingers, then left.

"I want you to stay the night," their host said. "Go up and take a rest if you must. This crowd will clear out of here around two and I want to hear the rest of it then. Jimmy and I'll decide what to do on the plane to D.C. in the morning and Miles will give you detailed instructions relative to the legal aspects of this thing. You know, of course, that here in the states I would be liable for all your actions—don't get me wrong, I appreciate every step you took. In the Islands, I'm not sure. They've retained a lot of British procedures."

Sven was momentarily concerned that they had not gotten to the climax of their story—the discovery of the canister, but on second thought he decided it would be a nice night-cap.

"Christ," Jimmy said to his boss, "If we have to prove in court what these people say without any witnesses to confirm a single statement.... Christ."

"On the other hand," Andrews said, checking his black tie in the mirror over the mantle, "the owner of MOTHER'S FUR COAT may not want any serious questions asked. He may find a way to pass it all off as piracy. Blame the Bahamians for it. We may never hear from him." He brushed a stray strand of gray hair from his lapel and walked briskly out of the room.

"Christ," Jimmy O'Hare said, brightening at the thought, "He may not even report it to the Bahamian police." And he left too, puffing in the wake of his boss.

"So, are we covered or not?" Matt asked. "Hey, we were the ones attacked. Every move we made was in self defense. What's this crap about him maybe not being responsible for it. It was his property we were protecting with our lives." Sven came to Andrews' defense, counseling that the man hadn't heard the whole story yet. He was about to go on, but the major domo's appearance at the door convinced him that they were not to wait in the room.

Outside again, they strolled with the other guests until they came to the arbor where Sven had found Matt and Leda earlier. It was a few feet off the path and offered as much privacy as they could expect to find.

"What did yer dad's lawyer have ta say today?" Sven asked Leda when they were seated.

"Well, first, he was really upset. He and dad go back a long way. He wants to talk to the Coast Guard Commander tomorrow."

"Did he recommend somebody in international law?"

"No, he said somebody in admiralty law might be better. All of this stuff has to do with piracy as it's legally defined. He said admiralty law is very clear and specific in British jurisprudence and he thinks that the Bahamians have adopted that body of law wholesale.

"He's not sure, but he thinks that we should file joint action with the Bahamian police. That is, I should file the same charges that you filed with the Captain of the patrol that day and against the same unknown assailants."

"Yeah, the thing is we know more now than we did then. There's no proof that PLEASURE HOUSE is the same boat that attacked GAVIOTA, but it meets the description and we know it was in pursuit of GULL."

"Yer fergettin' one thing boys and girls; we ain't got witness one ta anything. We got friends and people who helped us based on our say-so—Pete and Nigel—but we ain't got anybody who actually saw anything. Nigel was in his office when Diego jumped me. It ain't likely he saw anythin' that took place after we parted at the top of the dock. Sure, he saw MOTHER take off after we left and he figgered she was chasing us, but that doan prove that she was. The only reason he had to suspect her was my say-so."

"Next time, we keep the prisoners," Matt proclaimed. "The dock master at Walker could identify the giant and testify that he got very excited about seeing GAVIOTA. Some of that group on MOTHER didn't seem to be real committed to a life of crime either. They might have been a big help under police questioning. That Captain looked pretty unhappy to me."

"Waal," Sven drawled, "the Coast Guard C.O. said this afternoon that he thinks the FBI could take an interest in this case on th' basis that somebody tried ta secretly send contraband into the country. They would turn it over to Customs or Drug Enforcement after a preliminary look-see, but they might knock on Bubba's door and talk to his captain before they do. Those two would be easy enough ta find."

"What else is the C.O. going to do?" Matt asked as Leda whispered something into his ear and hurried off toward the house.

"He's a-goin' to try to get that special Island police unit ta find PLEASURE HOUSE. He's afraid that if that whole crew was Cuban, after yesterday's rout they might cut and run for Havana. If the cops can round 'em up and we could ID any of 'em they might have th' makin's of a case." He paused and nodded at the disappearing Leda. "Pump her bilge?" he asked.

"Powder her nose," Matt nodded. "She says martinis always go right through her."

"Me too," the older man nodded knowingly. "That's why I always drink bourbon."

The conversation drifted off on the subject of drinking and its after effects with a note of experienced wisdom marking Sven's utterances. Matt hadn't noticed how many drinks the older man had had before the martini inside and the short highball he had just finished, but there was the possibility that he was beginning to feel their effect however many there might have been. Matt had never seen Sven drunk. Usually when they were together they were on a job and Sven never would drink on the job. It might be amusing, he thought. Would he be the dignified sort who'd try to hide his diminishing control, or would he be a certified hell raiser and want to kiss all the women and fist-fight the men? The latter would be far from amusing in this venue.

"Speaking of drinking, Sven. I've never seen you in your cups. What kind of a drunk are you?"

"Whatta ya mean what kind? Drunk people are all pretty much alike. Wobbly at first and sloppy later."

"No," Matt persisted, "there's at least two kinds—the lovers and the fighters. The lovers tend to be the ones who think everything is funny and want to kiss all the women. The fighters think every glance their way is a provocation."

"Waal, I try pretty hard ta stop before it comes ta either a that. I stopped drinkin' too much thirty years ago. It became pretty obvious ta me that it takes no skill or talent to drink. All you have ta be able ta do is open your throat and let it run down. Ya don't even *need* to swallow. It's pretty much like makin' babies. Even the almost mindless slug can reproduce. Seems the thing that makes us humans supposed ta be different is the ability not ta do somethin' that nature made too easy." He paused and looked up the path. "Boy, I don't know if she got in or not. She's a comin' back faster than she went."

A breathless Leda grabbed his arm and pulled him toward the arbor where Matt sat in the swing. "Get out of sight for a minute. We've got to think of something fast. I just overheard somebody giving orders to find us and kill us."

Chapter Eleven

The author of one agency report gave Leda her fifteen minutes of fame. But, titled 'The Biscayne Incident', he spent more time describing the design of her dress than on the incident that had threatened her life. The narrative is so confused that it quickly reveals the depth of ignorance of the writer, so it contributes little.

The Coast Guard OD, not so generous with his space, referred to her in his report on the shooting only as a member of the crew, even though she had been the shooter. The Petty Officer sentry offered the theory that 'the girl's' short skirt and long legs had perhaps been an effort to distract the guard detail'.

Leda smiled indulgently at the reports' shortcomings when I presented them to her.

Things were only beginning to get bad.

"Open carefully—contents under pressure."

They stood behind the arbor now, its leafy back wall between them and the occasional passers-by on the path.

"Don't talk. Whisper," Leda hissed. "I just learned how little privacy this shrubbery gives."

"What in the hell are you talking about?" Matt asked, taking her by the forearms as if to calm her.

Her voice lowered and steadied. "I came out of the house just now and decided that my underwear needed more adjustment. I stepped behind a lattice that masks the caterers' prep area from the entrance to the house and rearranged things. I was about to come out when I realized that the snatches of conversation I was hearing through the lattice were about us. One guy was describing what you two were wearing and he spent some time detailing my dress. Then he said to get us out of here. Make it look like an accident. A hit-and-run would be good, he said. Take care of it right away. Then he said, 'He wants them out of here as soon as possible.'" She mimed the quotation marks in her usual way. "The men began to move and when they got out to where I could see them, there were four of them and they separated into two teams to start the search. The talker stood there a minute, then lit a cigarette and went back inside. I never got a look at anybody's face."

Sven had been listening intently. "Let's move. Matt ya gotta go first. That blazer makes you the most conspicuous man in the place. Ya need all the head start we can give ya." He lowered his voice. "There's a gate in the back wall of this place. It leads out ta an access road. Ta get ta it go left on the path and bear left at every opportunity. That'll keep ya on the perimeter. You'll know the path to the gate when ya see it 'cause it branches off a sharp left and disappears into a trellis. It hides the gate. Wait there. We'll come one by one." He started to push the hesitant Matt from behind the arbor, then pulled him back. "Take off that damn jacket. It won't help much, but if they're lookin for a blazer ta stand out in this sea of white, they might overlook ya. Now, git!" Matt moved out without a word. Sven rolled up the offending garment and pushed it down inside the branches of a nearby shrub.

"Good show," Leda said, fumbling at a flap of decorative material on her left hip. "But what are we going to do about you. You're so damn tall." Finally finding the tiny handle of the zipper, she pulled it diagonally across the front of the dress, around her right thigh and, changing hands, around and back to where she had begun. The lower portion of the dress fell away and she stood in a dramatically cut mini skirt. Practical girl that she was, she had kept them waiting that afternoon while she shopped for something that could do double duty in her limited wardrobe.

"Doan worry about me," Sven said, shaking his head in admiration at the transformation. "I'll do just fine. You git on outta here."

"Wait a minute. I've got an idea. Give me the biggest bill you've got in your wallet. Hurry up, I'll explain later. All right! I'll pay you back later!" She waited impatiently for him to comply, all the while muttering something about damn Yankees. "Stay here," she admonished as he started to follow her. She strolled slowly out into the path and turned toward the house. Sven took off his sport coat and emptied its pockets, then he hid it in the convenient shrub. He had just relocated the important contents of the garment when Leda returned with a white waiter's jacket and a tray.

"This kid was pretty big. It may not be a perfect fit, but you can hide in the crowd better in this. Wha-a-at??" She looked at Sven's puzzled face. "Hey, these are mostly college kids that work these parties for the caterers. He's glad to get the money. Besides it was a better deal than he's offered by most of the bored wives who proposition him. Here, take the tray and put your empties from the swing on it. You get started. I'll bring up the rear. I'm the most difficult of all to spot. He told them if they didn't find us together I'd be almost impossible to come up with. Now, it'll be harder." She rose up on tiptoe and kissed him lightly on the cheek. "Now, go on," she said softly. "I don't think we've got much time." Sven smiled and did as he was told.

Half an hour later he was trying the second time to pick the massive lock wrought into the iron gate. It hadn't been locked when he found it earlier. A bonnet of spiky ironwork arching over the top of the gate discouraged any attempt to climb over it. They had already found that a chain link fence backed the hedgerow, so there was no slipping between or crawling under.

The key hole in the lock was huge, suggesting that the key for it was suitably large and by logic, the mechanism it turned also large. But try as he might, Sven could not catch the bolt from inside with the spike of his rigging knife and drag it back. A momentary wave of panic swept over him. Had he led them into a trap? The entire length of the garden lay between them and the only other way out. And there were four determined men working their way methodically back and forth across the expanse.

He turned to the two white faces behind him and started to lay out a desperate last chance tactic when he heard a snatch of conversation from beyond the gate. Turning, he saw a man and woman emerging from one of the garden houses. They were in animated conversation. Spanish conversation. In the shaft of light from the open door, Sven recognized the cook who had fed them so well earlier. Between them, Matt and Leda figured from the Spanish that the man must be her husband and he had not done something to her liking. They were moving toward a junky pickup truck parked under a light pole.

"*Senora,*" Sven ventured. The two stopped and peered toward him. The single globe in the fixture above the gate gave only a little light. He spoke again and they came cautiously nearer.

"Can ya open the gate?" he asked. Then recognition brightened the woman's face and she rattled brisk instructions to the puzzled husband, Manuel.

"*Pronto, pronto,*" she urged as he hung back, wondering why anyone wanted to walk among these dismal surroundings. Finally, he returned to the shed, impatiently answering her shrill question. He had to get the key.

By the time he returned, Leda, her Spanish having more of Cuban than Mexican flavor, had communicated sufficiently to cap the fountain of questions the woman had unleashed. The cook still looked suspiciously at the waiter's jacket until Sven took it off and tossed it into a trash can.

The attempt now was to get a ride to the nearest place where they might get a taxi. Manuel indicated that they were welcome to ride in the truck. The cook concurred. Sven nodded. Manuel's eyes strayed regularly to Leda's exposed thighs and he urged her into the front seat. The cook, uttering something that Leda decided not to translate, pushed ahead of her and planted her ample body in the middle of the seat. Leda climbed in and slammed the rickety door. Manuel sighed, shrugged and climbed in behind the wheel. Sven and Matt were already perched across from one another on the sides of the pickup's bed. The longer Manuel fumbled with his keys and delayed their departure, the oftener they cast worried glances at the gate. Manuel had locked it again, but if they were seen, whatever advantage their initial escape had given them would be gobbled up by quick pursuit of the wheezing truck.

The access road was paved and the quarter mile ride to a feeder street was gentle and at a moderate speed. However, the increased traffic on the street seemed to agitate some inner competitive spirit of Manuel's and soon the two men were sitting down inside the dusty truck bed, leaning against the cab and holding tightly as he swerved in and out of the late evening traffic.

When he stopped for a traffic light Matt noticed that they were in front of a hotel where a line of taxis stood waiting. He banged on the top of the cab and the two men scrambled out. Leda, having also seen the opportunity, wrestled the door open and leapt into the street.

The startled lead cabby, stopped in the middle of an agitated conversation and ran around to climb behind the wheel of his already loaded car.

"Where to?" he asked expectantly. The trio looked at one another.

"The cops," Matt posited.

"Not 'till we've hadda chance ta talk," Sven objected.

Then in unison they sang out, "The boat."

As the cabby set out to follow Sven's detailed instructions on how to reach the Coast Guard Station, the three tried to decide if Andrews had been the one who set the thugs upon them.

"Goddammit," Matt cried in frustration. "Every time I relax a little, somebody tries to kill me again." Sven motioned him to be quiet, indicating that the driver's ears had gotten noticeably larger as a result of his outburst.

"I ain't ready ta point th' finger at him yet. I've done business with this guy for a lot of years. I've seen him on the boat and I've made one passage with him. It's just a gut feelin', sure, but I don't believe he's a killer."

"Who else knew we were going to be at his place? Did the guys off MOTHER phone someone here and have us followed from the Guard station?" Leda speculated.

"How would they get in to the party?" Matt countered. "It was a large group, but I got the impression from watching the major domo greet people that he knew everybody. Except maybe some of the little chippies the old guys were showing off. This was a crowd that had been to this place often."

"Now I think yer gettin' closer. I think what we got here is somebody close to Andrews usin' him. Somebody who knows about the comin's an' goin's of GULL. Somebody who knew when we got here that we shouldn't a got here. Somebody with enough horsepower ta move freely about in this combination headquarters and household. Somebody that can give orders." He turned to Leda and asked, "Can you remember, word fer word, what the guy givin' the instructions tonight said?"

Leda put her palms together in front of her, bowed her head, as if in prayer and thought for a long moment before answering.

"The first thing I heard him clearly say was, '…he's wearing a tan sport coat. The other one has got…' that's what he said. Not, 'wearing'. He said 'has got'. He said, 'The other one has got a blue blazer' Then he began to describe my dress in detail. He must have taken a good long look at me sometime, because he didn't miss a thing. That's when he told them that they had better find me with one of you two, because it would be hard to be sure about me if I was alone. He told them to work in twos. If either team found us, one guy was to go get the other two and all four were to approach us. Then he said this," and she made her quote signs again. "'He don't want any slip-ups on this. Get them and get them away from here fast. Take them somewhere and do a clean job of it. Make it look like an accident. A DUI or a hit and run would be good. Don't call me. I'll check with you in the morning for details.' That's all he said." She shuddered and then looked up at the driver. But he had apparently lost interest when the voices had become too soft to hear easily.

"There's something," Matt began. "Why did he want us caught and taken away fast? If this is an inside job he must have known that we were going to stay the night. We would be under their watchful eye. They could take their time. What's the rush? Why take all the risk of pulling us out amid a crowd of people?"

"Look at the schedule," Sven said with a note of triumph in his voice. "Andrews is too busy with the Ambassador now to finish hearing our story, but when the party's over, we're the next item. Didn't he say about two a.m.? We gotta be outta there long before then or someone will be roundin' us up to talk to Andrews again. If the Ambassador leaves early or somethin' else compresses the schedule, we could be called anytime." He paused to allow what he had said to be digested, then he added, "All the more reason fer me to believe Andrews ain't on the wrong side. Somebody doan want us to tell the rest of the story."

"But why," Leda asked. "What are we going to reveal?"

"The canister!" Matt blurted. "The canister. We would have told him that we found the canister. If they presume that we opened the damn thing after all the misery it caused us, we'd tell him what was in it!"

"But they donno if we found it or not." Sven countered.

"Yes, but they can't take a chance," Leda mused. "I think he's right Sven. They can't afford to risk our knowing what's in the damn thing. They think they can take care of the canister later if it's still on GULL. But if we did find it and there's a chance we're going to reveal the contents, to anybody, then we have to be taken care of now."

"Well, by God," Sven scowled, "if I'm a-gonna git killed over it, I'm a-gonna damn well know what I'm getting killed for. We're a-gonna open it soon's we get there."

But they didn't get there soon. It was a long ride and when they got to the gate the young guard knew nothing of GULL or that her crew was supposed to be allowed to enter and board her. They couldn't even prove that they were her crew. After lengthy delays that Matt sometimes wondered were not purposeful, so the guard could prolong his gazes at Leda's legs, they began to make progress. Initially the idea of calling the base C.O. was scoffed at, even by the OD who had been summoned to the gate. He shook his head and called their attention to the time. Finally Sven looked the young lieutenant in the eye and lied.

"At oh-nine-hundred tomorrow morning, ah'm a-goin' to set down in that office on the third floor across from your Commanding Officer and he is going to ask me for the report that ah'm supposed to have ready for a District Inquiry. Ah'm a-gonna look him in the eye and tell him that you," and he paused to squint at the officer's name tag, "Lieutenant j.g. Malcolm Thomas, prevented me from boardin' my command and preparin' said document. I will then have him roust yer ass up there to confirm what ah'm a-sayin'."

They were quickly escorted to the OD's desk where he dutifully dialed the Commander's home number. The Commander was not in, of course, but the OD was given a number where he could be reached and in due time the OD, more dutifully, ushered them down the dock to where GULL lay.

Then the canister itself became an obstacle. It had been well made and the soldered seams, the first point of Sven's attack, refused to give way. Considerable bending of the metal had occurred in their efforts so far and the concern about internal damage was growing. Finally speed was sacrificed for sense and the laborious job of melting the solder around the perimeter of the cap seam was begun.

Leda, fearful of missing the magic moment, remained in her party dress, her feet drawn up under her as she sat on the settee.

The two men, one wielding the solder gun, the other holding the slippery can, grunted and cursed their way along the long seam.

"This gun is no good for this," Sven muttered. "A good heavy iron and we'd a-had this thing done already." But their persistence, if not their patience, paid off finally and the top was bent back out of the way.

"Uh, uh!" Leda cried, unfolding herself and reaching out to prevent Matt from dumping the contents on the dirty table. "Wait a minute 'till I clean that mess. You two ought to wash your hands too, before you touch that stuff."

The two men, like naughty schoolboys whose treat was delayed, stood side by side at the galley sink scrubbing their grimy hands with dish detergent. They both looked over opposite shoulders in an effort to prevent Leda from brashly dumping the contents before they could be there for the event.

She had torn a section of six paper towels from the roll and after cleaning the table, spread the towels down. Then picking up the dirty canister with two oven mitts, she spilled the loose items out of the container onto the table.

One was a sheaf of papers sealed into a transparent plastic envelope. One was a bundle of hundred dollar bills.

Resting the canister on its side, she removed a mitt and reaching inside, dislodged six more bundles of bills, all fatter than the first. She put the dirty canister on the cabin sole.

No one touched anything.

Finally Sven broke the spell. "Waal, it doan look too impressive so far." He picked up a bundle of bills and tossed it to Leda. "Guess we oughta take inventory first." Then he passed the envelope to Matt and picked up another bundle of cash.

The cabin was silent while the two counted the money and Matt removed the waterproof tape from the flap of the envelope.

The sheaf of papers was divided into three groups. The first was an eight page essay typewritten in Spanish. It appeared as if it might be a preamble to the others. The second group, joined with a rusting paper clip, was a series of memos, directives and letters. The letterheads bore symbols and crests of the FBI, CIA, National Security Council, Naval Intelligence and two or three other groups less well known and hence less glamorous.

The third sheaf, its clip equally rusty, were official Cuban documents, their specific offices or ministries, Matt was unable to determine. He counted the pages. There were a total of eighty.

"Two thousand." Leda stated, tossing the packet of bills on the table. "Times six, makes twelve."

"Less in this one. Some's been spent outa it." Sven said, dropping it in the pile with the rest.

"Started out being, maybe, twelve thousand, then," Leda said. "Twelve thousand for what? Payment for services rendered? Bribe? What do the papers say?"

"Look at the dates on the bills," Matt countered.

Each took a packet and fanned them. Then they took another.

There were no dates later than 1963.

Matt told them briefly what the envelope contained. "All the dates that I can read and what references are not in bureaucratic gobble-de-goop speak to the period immediately after the Kennedy assassination. Most of the memos refer to other memos, phone conversations or code named operations. I guess they're code names, they're all typed in caps. I don't know what it means, but I'm afraid we're up to our butts in some interagency competition that's sufficiently shady to fall under the catch-all heading of 'National Security'. I do know what that means: we get in the way and anything they do to us is OK"

"Well, welcome to pitsville, guys. I couldn't go to the cops in the islands because I didn't know which was the good cops. Now you can't go the FBI, because those boys really stick together. They'll protect their rears at all cost." She was back in her perch in her corner of the settee. "Let me see that first thing. The one in Spanish. I can barely remember enough oral Spanish to buy groceries in Miami, and I haven't tried to read it in a long time. But, I used to be pretty good."

They were silent then, Sven flipping through the English documents, Matt looking again at the Official Cuban letters.

"I don't know, but this looks like it's some sort of explanation of the documents," Leda began, but she was cut short by a call from the dock.

"Ahoy, GULL. This is the O.D. Anybody awake?"

Sven climbed to the middle step and looked out the companionway.

"No problem, Lieutenant. What's on yer mind?"

"Well, this man," and he indicated his companion, "says he's also crew on GULL and he's got credentials to prove it. Under the circumstances I didn't want to cause you any further delay. He says he'll explain to you why he's come so late."

Sven climbed out onto the bridge deck and stepped over the lifeline to the dock. "Hi, Carlos. What ya doing keepin' honest folks awake?" He had completely forgotten about the Cuban boat keeper. He took the papers offered by the O.D. One was a very creased, and pocket-worn letter with a 'To whom it may concern' greeting stating that the bearer, Carlos Valdez, was a member of the crew of the yacht GULL owned by Andrews Enterprises Inc. The other was an Andrews Enterprises employee ID card complete with picture. Sven nodded to the O.D., folded the letter and handed them both back to Carlos.

"Yep, I know him. He keeps th' boat up. He's a good man."

"Tell me something Captain Olafson," the OD said, squinting in the yellow light. "Why don't you have credentials like those? Sure would make life a lot simpler."

Sven looked at the young man a long minute then replied. "Because I'm not an Andrews employee. I'm a delivery Captain. I brought this boat in from the Islands last night. Don't you guys ever talk ta one another? The boat's th' subject of an investigation. I'm instructed by the owner ta stand-by and move it ta a yard for repairs later. I think that's really all ya need t' know, Lieutenant. Good night." Turning to the boat keeper he said, "Com'on Carlos. Hate to tell ya, but I sure as hell messed up your nice neat boat."

Carlos stepped deftly aboard, his short legs barely straddling the lifeline. His short stature was made up for by broad shoulders and generally agile movements.

There was no sign of the canister or its contents when they arrived below. Sven introduced the middle aged Cuban, offered him a drink and asked what brought him to the boat so late.

"One of Mr. Andrews people called me about eleven-thirty. He said GULL was back and had had some trouble. Mr. Andrews wanted me to come out to his house to hear what happened. It was about twelve-thirty when I got there." Carlos' English was almost perfect.

"They told me Mr. Andrews wanted us in the Library about two a.m. unless the Ambassador left early. Martin told me that you were in the garden somewhere, so I started looking, but I couldn't find you. Then about one, they started looking for you too.... They said Mr. Andrews was waiting. Pretty soon, Martin said I could go home because they couldn't find you."

What had first appeared to Matt as a methodical pattern of delivery that one might expect from a foreign speaker of English, he later reinterpreted as a studied, almost calculated method of waiting to gauge the result of one sentence before composing another.

"Waal," Sven said, "somethin' came up. We'll finish with Mr. A. tomorrow."

"No, Mr. Andrews will be in Washington tomorrow." Carlos said evenly.

"Carlos," Sven said changing the subject, "isn't Ramirez, the guy who crews for Mr. A in the Islands, a relative of yours?"

"Yes, he is. He's my cousin."

"Waal, I think the reason Mr. A wanted you to come to the house tonight was to tell you that Ramirez had an accident."

"Captain, I know about my cousin's 'accident'. The police informed the family and the family called me."

"I'm sorry, Carlos." Sven looked at the small man who sat so utterly composed in front of him. "There is a hell of a mess that GULL has gotten involved in. I…we keep tryin' to find out what's goin' on. We ain't havin' much luck. We was boarded and almost killed the same day Ramirez was. They tried to get us two other times. I'm in the boat delivery business, Carlos. I don't know why they killed your cousin. I honest-to-God don't."

Carlos turned to Matt and Leda. "I know you don't, Captain." His gaze became cooler and more penetrating.

"I've heard you talk of Matt before, but why is a woman on such a troubled boat so late at night?"

Leda leaned forward to speak but, fearing what she would say, Sven answered the question. "She's a boatman..er person too. She lives here in Miami. She's, uh, a friend of Matt's."

"I hope she is a good friend of Matt's," Carlos said, looking even more penetratingly at the young woman. Then he turned to Sven.

"Captain I know what caused your trouble and who caused it."

It was so quiet on the boat that the clang of a channel bell-buoy was clearly heard.

"Captain, the reason you were boarded and the reason my cousin was killed is that a group of very important papers were hidden on GULL while she was is the islands. Very powerful men in both the U. S. and Cuba want those papers. You were boarded because my cousin refused to tell where they were hidden before he was killed. I think the killers thought you might know. I'm sorry that you were caught up in it. We had been so successful in the operation up to that point, but just at the last moment, our security was breached."

Sven studied the man carefully. This was the first time he had held a lengthy conversation with the Cuban. Before they had always spoken briefly about some aspect of GULL's maintenance and schedule and no exchange had amounted to more than a half-dozen sentences. Very little had been revealed of Carlos's personality and what had emerged, now appeared to have been a role—a carefully rehearsed role of the subservient immigrant laborer.

"Who is 'we', Carlos?" Sven asked.

"I'm sorry, I can't tell you that, Captain."

Sven had not left the companionway since he had followed Carlos down. Now he lounged against the steps, blocking the only exit, his left elbow resting on a step near the top.

"Waal, Carlos, I'm sorry too. But, if you're tellin' me that you're a Cuban spook and you refuse to tell me what's going on after the hell I've been through, your chances of gettin' off this boat alive ain't worth a damn." Bravado had paid off earlier in the evening, perhaps it would again.

"Captain, what I'm telling you is that all your grief has been caused by a package of papers that are of no worth to you. You have been accidentally caught between three forces, none of which you know anything about."

"Three?" Matt blurted.

"Yes, three. I am not an agent of communist Cuba as you suggest, Captain. I am an agent of Free Cuba. We are the third force in this dynamic. I am here for a simple reason. I know where the canister is hidden. I can go directly to it. I will remove it from the boat and the others will immediately lose interest in you and the boat. Your life can return to normal."

"Waal, now how are they a goin' ta know so immediately that this cross has been removed from our shoulders?"

"Part of our strength in having the papers is their knowing that we have them. They will be promptly informed. You have been here almost twenty-four hours, they can marshal formidable forces in twenty-four hours. I suggest that you allow me to get the papers and leave at once."

"The papers ain't here, Carlos. We discovered 'em accidentally last night in a storm. We figgered somethin' so important to cause all this trouble oughta be put someplace real safe," he lied. "Leda here has got some real good legal connections here in Miami. We put them papers away where they ain't likely to ever be found. Now we knew we was puttin' ourselves between the forces again. But we opened the canister and we got a pretty good idea what they're all about. We wrote several letters to prominent lawyers, the FBI and my senator from Mass. Fella named Kennedy. These letters all tell where a certain important package can be found in the event that somethin' bad happens ta us."

Leda nudged Matt under the table and he recovered his fallen jaw. Was Sven good at everything? The confidence and articulation of the gigantic lie was masterful. Almost as masterful as the poker face that Leda maintained throughout.

"I wish I had gotten to you sooner, Captain. It was foolish for you to take on this additional risk. What do you hope to gain from it?"

"Some answers. I wanna know what the hell happened to me for three days and three nights."

"Are you saying that you would be willing to surrender the documents if you were told the entire story?"

"It would go a long way toward salvin' some of my hurt feelin's, yes!"

"You realize that there are liabilities in that too. The story is very embarrassing to a lot of people. Politically embarrassing. Some, not my group, but some, might think you were safer dead if you know the whole story. Particularly since you brag about having certain political connections. Of course, even if you knew the story, no one would be apt to believe you without the documents to prove it. And we will have them, of course. How do we arrange the swap?"

"Let's keep it simple. You tell us the story, we'll tell you where ta pick up the papers."

"And if they aren't there?"

"Waal, I reckon your organization has got resources enough ta follow up."

"What? And shall we kill you? Then the papers will be found by your lawyers and released. They'll be of no good to us then. The power is in threatening to go public with the information, but keeping it secret.

"I have a better plan. I did not come here alone nor will I be alone when I leave the gate. I will tell you the whole story now, then we will leave together and pick up the papers. In the event of your betrayal, Ms. Malone will be our uncomfortable guest until the papers are provided. Do not doubt me, Captain. Terrible things happen on the streets of Miami in the wee hours of the morning."

"Don't insult me, Carlos," Sven bluffed. "If ya tell me the story, you'll get yer papers. I've done business all my life on a handshake. I ain't about ta change my ways at this late date."

Carlos' cool gaze circled the cabin, pausing a moment to look into each pair of eyes. Returning to Sven, he said, "May I have a tall glass of water?" Leda slipped out of the settee and opened the small refrigerator. She poured the water, replaced the bottle and slipped back into her place, the noise of each action reverberating in the depths of an almost audible silence.

Carlos took a small sip of the water and began.

"In the early sixties, the two charming Kennedy brothers had managed to marshal a terrible array of hatred against them. While the general public in America adored these white knights of the white house and cheered their social programs and their handling of the threat of the Russian Bear, these two were making enemies with organized crime, organized labor—also crime, if you will, the FBI and the Military Industrial Complex.

"But no one hated John Kennedy more than Fidel Castro. From the Bay of Pigs, to the Missile Crisis, Fidel fumed at the upstart patrician, epitome of a wealthy capitalist pig. And he was willing in those dark hours of the Missile Crisis to sacrifice our lovely island in his all consuming hate. He begged the Russians not to back down.

"When the security breach revealed that not one, but several assassination attempts had been made on Castro by the CIA, his fury reached a peak and suddenly realizing how much more vulnerable Kennedy was in the open American society of the '60's, he made it a top priority of his Secret Police to kill the President.

"Two could play the assassination game.

"In many respects, his people were crude oafs. They tipped their hand domestically and in the States. The CIA, admittedly weak in Cuba in those years, never-the-less, knew of the plot. The FBI knew about, and for a time infiltrated the Cuban group in the States, then wrote it off as a bunch of bunglers. Some still say J. Edgar Hoover purposely allowed the plans to mature. He had little love for the younger Kennedy. From Cuba it appeared that the CIA, unable to cross jurisdictional bounds and meddle on what was the FBI's turf, began to prod Navy Intelligence, the National Security Council and anyone else in the intelligence community who would listen, against Hoover's disclaimers. Unfortunately, none of the other agencies were willing to cross Hoover either, so they all clasped their hands and sat back while the Cubans muddled along toward Dallas. All the soap operas written about a grand conspiracy integrating arms industrialists, the Teamsters union, organized crime and the rest is all wool conveniently pulled over the public eyes after the event. It was, like so many disasters in history, simply a colossal screw-up by a lot of egotistical people.

"Cuba doesn't know anything about Lee Harvey Oswald. Some will say he and the events that swirled about the man that day and in ensuing days were orchestrated by Hoover again. Perhaps so. Organized crime's hold over him, blackmailing him because of his alleged homosexuality, may have made a puppet of him.

"Whatever, the Cubans were the shooters that day in Dallas. I know that to be a fact. There were three. One of them was my uncle. He was one of the most trusted operatives Castro had at the time.

"But, the aftermath is what's important to our story. While all America mourned, the agency heads, like facile magicians, kept the eyes of the audience on the right hand while it performed the trick with the left. Every agency had bulging files about the impending assassination of the President of the United States. Each had encouraged the other to take action. There were dozens of memos referencing files and conversations and meetings. They were the smoking guns of ineptitude. Everyone's hands were dirty. Suddenly some organized cleansing effort was necessary or the hue and cry from a sorrowing public would butcher sacred cow after sacred cow.

"Groups which earlier couldn't cooperate on setting a time for lunch, now provided one man each who was the epitome of co-operation. All the incriminating files that could show culpability had to be destroyed. Shredding was too slow and done in such huge amounts, would attract attention of lower echelon personnel who must not know. After a frantic three day meeting, three men knew where every file, memo and voucher was located.

"The key man in each agency used the list for his unit and in all-night sessions, the files were gathered and boxed and finally trucked to a warehouse in Maryland. From there they were to be taken in small amounts to one of several incinerators for classified material located in the greater D.C. area.

"Then the strangest thing of all happened.

"Security agencies, as you probably know, are often familiar with their opposites. In countries that maintain embassies, often intelligence officers of opposing forces will meet at a Chinese restaurant and discuss matters that the diplomats regard as being too messy, or too dirty, to be handled formally.

"My uncle, who had slipped out of the country immediately after the shooting, flew back in a few days later on a forged passport as an Argentine business man. He did not fool the FBI, who now had its net out for anything Cuban. The day after he arrived in D.C., he received a note in his hotel from a National Security Council operative with whom he had had earlier dealings.

"The operative had heard that the egg foo yong at the new Chinese restaurant on 'I' street was particularly good.

"When my uncle arrived at the Red Dragon that night, the American, had a companion at the table. My uncle immediately recognized the KGB man assigned to the Russian Embassy.

"The situation was simple, the NSC guy said. There was incontrovertible proof that the Cuban government was responsible for the assassination of the American president. It was cause for war. The American congress would declare war instantly if the documentation was presented to them. He produced a sample of that documentation revealing the names of the Cuban operatives, including my uncle, their suppliers, the clumsy Cuban network that had provided general overall support and a host of additional information that totally convinced my uncle of the completeness with which the operation had been revealed

"At that point the KGB man interceded. Just, as he said, his country had interceded to prevent war during the missile crisis. Obviously, he said, if Cuba is attacked, Russia will have to respond. Not to respond would injure its creditability everywhere in the communist world. On the other hand, he had to be frank, Cuba was not worth total war with the United States. And, the American added, so soon after the missile confrontation, neither nation wanted to play out another face saving war of nerves.

"The upshot of it all was that even now the Cuban representatives in Moscow were being screwed down with threats of reduced aid and general support if any breath of this operation were revealed. Moreover, the KGB man added, no Cuban operation with any international repercussions were *ever* to be implemented without express permission and approval from Moscow.

"No mention was made of the intelligence community's failure to prevent the assassination. But because feelings were running so high in the country, and because of the danger resulting from the revelation of these records to ambitious politicians, both Russia and Cuba were being promised that the entire body of documents had been gathered in a safe place. All agency heads privy to the affair were, under threat of prosecution under the National Security Act, sworn to secrecy.

"In closing, the NSC agent assured both men that the group being formed to investigate the incident, later called the Warren Commission, would bring in a benign report. There was no need to worry about embarrassment for either communist government."

Carlos finished the glass of water from which he had sipped throughout the extended monologue. His audience looked at one another with raised eyebrows and shifted in their seats. Then, to their surprise, he asked for a refill, adjusted his glasses and continued.

"The Fix was on. Everyone relaxed. Everyone, but Castro. He, David, had scored a devastating blow against Goliath, the giant that threatened his very life. Hadn't he had a right to strike back? And hadn't he a right now to stand on the chest of the fallen Titan and brag? The Russians were depriving him of that ego satisfaction and his frustration fermented into new clandestine action.

"The Americans had proof of his magnificent deed. The Russians might gag him now, but a time would come in the future when the truth could be told and he wanted the documentation to be on his side when the time came. He would not allow the big power players to brush off his claim as the boasting of a bit-player on the world stage.

"My uncle was given the dubious honor of protecting the prestige of Cuba—and Castro, of course. He was to steal the documents before they could be destroyed. The Americans had not rushed to the incinerators, holding back long enough to be sure that the deal was firm and that all the players were going to stick to the rules.

"Of course, as soon as this crisis was past and others pushed to the fore, there seemed less urgency to actually destroy the material. After all it was in a safe place.

"But, the task of stealing it was an impossible one for the fragmentary Cuban espionage organization that survived the FBI's onslaught after the assassination. There was a way however, if the Russians could be recruited to help. Castro reluctantly gave permission when my uncle told him of the approach.

"If this documentation was so damming and could create such havoc if it fell into the wrong hands wouldn't it be safer in Communist hands? Yes, the Americans said they would keep it from surfacing, but could they be trusted to do so in the future? Who knew what shifts in international or domestic politics were down the road. Besides, couldn't the KGB profit from a look at these documents? They would definitely reveal something about the inner workings of the American intelligence community.

"At times of crisis the Russians had agents who watched which windows in which bureaus shown their lights late into the night. They also had chasers who followed vehicles that left those buildings in the wee hours. Their records showed that trucks leaving the several intelligence agencies in the nights following the president's death all went to the same building in a warehouse complex just across the border in Maryland. It was not a depository for classified items. It had been purposely chosen so that no one would place unnecessary value on the cardboard cartons as they were stored. At the time the ruse worked, the

Russians paid no more attention, save to make a record of the event. Now that record proved valuable.

"The rest was easy. Security at the warehouse was lax, after all none of the stuff there was classified, right? The boxes were spirited out one at a time and each was replaced by a dummy. It was not until almost a year later when the burning finally began that the theft was discovered.

"Now, the balance had shifted. The documents were no longer a black mail lever held by the Americans, but a dirty secret that none of the three powers wanted revealed.

"At Castro's insistence, the files were shipped to Cuba when the KGB researchers had concluded that there was nothing that Castro shouldn't see. And after they had copied each one."

Carlos looked at his watch, leaned forward and gave the impression that he was going to shorten the dissertation.

"As the years passed my uncle became disenchanted with Castro and he fell from grace. He had never spent lavishly (he was a good Communist). The bonus he had received for his part in the Kennedy shooting lay largely unspent. When he did spend, it was for crying needs that Castro's policies were failing to meet in our home village. Finally, he became completely disillusioned with the movement and when the Soviet Union collapsed, he resolved to make a clean breast of it. He felt that the threat of war on Cuba for the assassination was long past and the Russians were no longer a factor of any sort. The American people also had a right to know. The few members of the intelligence community still alive were in retirement and would have to live the rest of their short lives with the truth.

"He spirited the boxes out of Cuba one at a time on an old Bahamian fishing trawler, first to a way station in the Islands, then on to a series of individual rental storage places in and around Miami. Only he knew where they were. When the shipment was complete, he prepared a sample of the documents, a cover letter explaining their importance and where to find them, and the last of the bloody bonus money. These were put into the canister and given to Ramirez to hide on GULL for transport here to me.

"At the very last minute, Uncle slipped. Somehow he was revealed to Castro's secret police and rather than face the sure torture after his arrest, he died in a shoot out when they came for him."

Carlos straightened in his seat, surveyed his audience and leaned forward, resting his elbows on the table.

"The people after you are Castro's agents and retired U.S. intelligence interests. Castro no longer wants to brag about his deeds. In fact he fears that he may yet live to stand trial before some world court for his crime. He had to have the documents back at all cost. But his people are no less bunglers now than they were all those years ago.

"The U.S. intelligence has-beens appear to be little better. They sent a boat to the islands, thinking that the Cubans would intercept the canister and turn the location information over to them. They supposed that all they'd have to do would be to pick up the boxes here and there when they got back to Miami.

"You really screwed them all up."

The silence hung heavy in the cabin again.

"Now, it's very late. We need to go and pick up the documents." He stood up in anticipation.

"And your group, is it going to release the documents to the press? Will it all come out now?" Matt wanted to know.

"No, not yet. We think they are good for one more blackmailing. Castro may initiate political reforms if he is threatened with exposure. It would be much better for him to do it than have the growing number of Cuban hotheads in Miami try to overthrow him by force." He turned from Matt and faced Sven again.

"Questions and answers were not a part of our bargain, Captain. I suggest we go for the papers."

"They're here," Sven said flatly and he nodded in the general direction of Leda. She slipped from the settee and went forward, returning a few minutes later with a black plastic garbage bag, the contents of which she dumped on the table.

Carlos stepped across the cabin, picked up the transparent plastic envelope which Matt had resealed, hefted it as if to check its weight then glanced disinterestedly at the cash. With a sweep of his hand he scooped everything into the bag and said, "Everything's here. I'm sure of your integrity." He held out his hand to Matt and Leda in turn and then crossed back to Sven.

Leda took the opportunity to duck quickly into the head. It had been a long story and martinis....

"I'm very sorry that your lives have been so affected by these events," Carlos said to Sven. He shook the big man's hand and turned to climb the ladder.

But he had taken only the first step when he was propelled back into the cabin by the feet of a black clad body swinging down the steps, suspended from the companionway combing.

"I'll keel the first man which moves," the intruder shouted.

Almost immediately the entire group were unbalanced by a great weight landing on GULL's toe rail.

A moment later the leering face of the Cuban giant appeared in the companionway opening.

Chapter Twelve

Documents obtained by the Freedom of Information act do not confirm Carlos' story. But they are so heavily censored that they do not refute it either. The gigantic size of the lie perpetrated at the time seems to guarantee its continued existence.

Retired operatives, fume their denials as wives remind them of their high blood pressure. Some who didn't retire are dead and others who are neither dead nor retired are very hard to find.

The fat lady begins to sing.

The head on GULL had been built in the aft end of the forward compartment. The stool and tiny sink occupied the same space on the port side that the chest-of-drawers and hanging locker took up to starboard.

The door to the forward compartment had been designed to be the same size as the doorway to the head so that when the door to the compartment was opened, it hinged back and closed off the head. When access was wanted to the head, the door was swung in the other direction and closed off the entire forward compartment from view.

But not from sound. Leda sat, stunned at what she had heard.

The man astride the fallen Carlos wore a complete wet suit. He also had a large mustache. He held a handgun of strange design that Matt immediately decided was meant to fire dependably no matter how wet it was or how long it had been that way. The menacing muzzle swept over the assembly and stopped at Sven. Then he stepped quickly the length of the cabin to allow the giant to let himself down onto the sole. Carlos scrambled quickly out of the way.

The giant's frightening face was topped by a diving mask perched on his forehead.

Damn, Sven swore to himself. Not again. He had beaten all the others, but the giant, one on one, was formidable. He watched as the other man, the one they had come to call The 'Stache, snatched the black bag from Carlos and spilled the contents on the sole. Ignoring the money, he picked up the plastic envelope and pitched it to the giant who tucked it into a waterproof pouch that had thoughtfully been brought along for the purpose.

The exchange in Spanish was apparently relative to escape plans. Obviously, the giant with his precious cargo was to go first. Sven wondered what was to be done with witnesses. But he couldn't understand what was being said.

Carlos asked a question, but was menaced with the gun and fell silent. The giant appeared to ask the same question and got a grudging reply. That prompted a lengthy exchange in which The 'Stash's name was revealed to be Pablo and in which the giant seemed to win a concession. With that he turned to go.

As he climbed the steps, he raised both hands in an effort to swing the strap of the pouch over his shoulder. It banged against the side of the combing on the first try and he had to climb another step before he could try it again. This time it was snatched from behind his back by Leda who lay on her stomach on the hatch cover. She didn't know what was in the pouch, but he had it, so she guessed at its contents.

The surprised giant, swearing in Spanish, took the remaining steps in a single stride and whirled when he made the bridge deck. Leda, standing now, sighted down the barrel of the little Beretta.

God, he's big, she thought. Would a .32 caliber bullet stop him? Would several bullets stop him? She wished hard for the Uzi, but it was under the settee with the other guns.

The giant did not seem eager to test her marksmanship. He obviously knew that he presented a huge target. She was wisely too far away for him to risk a lunge. He'd wait her out, she'd falter or give him some other opportunity.

Leda knew that she dared not falter and she didn't have much time. If the other man below had half a wit and knew anything about boats, he knew there was a forward hatch and she couldn't have someone popping up behind her. Without a wince, she dropped the end of the gun barrel and fired twice at the giant's right knee, then pausing only long enough to see him collapse into the lifeline and then into the black water, she whirled and ran for the bow of the boat.

The forward hatch hinged along its after edge. Earlier, so that her exit would be unencumbered, she had swung it back and rested it completely on the deck. Now, below, Pablo approached it slowly, stuck his gun out first and pivoted so that he would be facing aft when he emerged. His first look was obscured by the deck boxes at the base of the mast. He had to be higher to see over them. He lowered the gun momentarily and held to the combing as he sought a foot hold on the edge of the v-berth below. As he rose again, head and shoulders out of the opening, attention focused aft, still holding to the combing with one hand, Leda reached out from the darkness under the over-turned dinghy and pressed the Beretta against his spine.

It was all over.

Matt was on deck a minute later with the Uzi. The giant had to be fished out of the water. The O.D., who had worried all night about this boat and its strange crew, had come running at the first shot from Leda's pistol. Carlos quietly retrieved the satchel and excused himself with some quip that it was late and he had to be at work early in the morning. The trio denied knowing what the two pirates were after, save it was the mysterious canister that no one seemed to know the whereabouts of.

But the 'why' of their harassment at the party had not been answered by Carlos' tale. And would it cease, as he said, now that the papers were in other hands?

Since he had warned that the knowledge of them was a liability, the trio decided that since neither Pablo or the Giant revealed that the canister had been found and Carlos never showed up the next morning for work, perhaps admitting to Arthur Andrews that they knew anything might still be dangerous. After all, a direct threat to their lives came from his home.

On Saturday, the question was put to him. Who in his circle would have done such a thing?

"I'm terribly upset that something like this has happened," he said. "I am horrified to consider the possibility that one of my friends or associates could have been responsible for it. I've given Martin instructions to cooperate fully with the police investigation and Jimmy," he turned toward the chubby lawyer who sat listening intently, "put some of your special people on it."

"What kinda special people?" Sven wanted to know.

"Well, as you probably know, Mr. Andrews has a variety of business interests," Jimmy volunteered. "Sometimes situations demand legal council—that's my job—and sometimes, in order for me to do my job, I need information which isn't easily obtainable through regular channels. Because of that we keep a private investigation company on retainer. I'll have the owner come around and talk with you." He indicated all three with a wave of his hand.

"He'll need to do that this evening or tomorrow. I fly out Monday morning," Matt said.

"How about you, Sven?" Jimmy asked.

"Waal, depends.... Mr. A, ya want me to take GULL to a yard before I go north?"

"Yes, of course, if your schedule permits. I'd also like you to make recommendations about anything else that you think ought to be taken care of while she's there."

He paused a moment. "Strange about Carlos. He was always such a good worker. Never absent nor late. You say he hasn't shown up at the boat yesterday or today?" Responding to Sven's shaking head, he went on. "I always suspected that he worked for me for the love of the boat. He seemed too well educated to have taken this sort of job otherwise."

Sven decided that no response was the best response.

"And Ms. Malone," Andrews continued, "you will be easily available here in Miami, right?"

"Yes, I have to get back to work. What was meant to be a long weekend turned out to be a long week. But I have an understanding boss."

"Oh, who is he? Perhaps I know him." Andrews said.

"Oh, you do, sir," she replied. "It's me. I own a flower shop with a chain of lobby installations in the better tourist hotels in Miami Beach. It's an outgrowth of my father's business. He owns—owned—half dozen nurseries and garden supply centers."

"Please give your address and phone to Shirley," Jimmy broke in in his best lawyer fashion.

A short time later the meeting broke up with assurances from Andrews that he and his people would complete a thorough investigation and inform GULL's crew of the findings.

The trio adjourned to a popular restaurant for a dinner prearranged by Andrews major-domo, Martin, and languished in their relaxed circumstances. They avoided the subject until the coffee and brandy were served, then it came up again.

"Let's go back to Thursday night," Matt requested. "We decided in the cab that the reason they came after us at the party was because they wanted us out of the way before we had a chance to talk to Andrews.

They were assuming that we had found and opened the canister and knew its contents. Let's talk about that for a bit.

"Maybe I'm just an optimist, but, I don't think they're interested anymore. We've made it clear that the canister was not found. Or at least not to our knowledge. So we don't know its contents. Pablo and the giant know only that the canister was found. But they think only Carlos knew where it was and have no reason to believe he told us what it was about. Remember, I sealed the envelope again, even before Carlos saw it."

"Well," Leda began, "you may think your theory comforts me because they've lost interest, but I still think someone in Mr. A's ranks is a very dangerous person. And if that person could change his mind about us because of something we don't know, he could also change it back because of something we don't know."

"I think somethin' Carlos said is important. He said that if we didn't have no documentation to back our story, no one would believe it if we told it. Let's face it, everybody's got a assassination theory. This one has as many loose ends, by Carlos' admission, as any of the rest. I guess I hafta think that since Carlos' people have put out the word that they've got the boxes, everybody will zip lips. It's a stalemate again. Nobody's likely ta rock the boat."

"Well," Leda said, "I'd feel better if I knew who. Remember what you told the girl on MOTHER: be careful who you party with!"

"True, true," Sven nodded. "But after about Tuesday or Wednesday, I'm a goin' to do my partyin' in Boston and these crackers can do as they please, but without me."

With that their party broke up and Matt tooled the rent-a-car across town past the Coast Guard gate, around to the motel a couple of blocks from the Miami Beach end of the causeway. Sven got out and reminded Matt that he had promised to take him to Dinner Key marina Sunday evening for the long awaited beer with Fats Barlow. Matt and Leda drove on to her father's apartment where, Leda explained, they would be safe from her snooping landlady. Actually, they were quite safe far into the night.

Sven slept late the next morning and was just returning from a fast food breakfast and a slow read of the Sunday Herald when he noticed a car with three men parked near the motel office. He had walked on toward his own salmon colored door when the voice stopped him.

"You Sven Olafson?" the man said, without preamble.

"Most of th' time," Sven said, turning. "Who wants ta know?"

The man had stepped out of the car and he came as far as the front bumper and paused to lean there when Sven stopped. He held out a wallet ID in Sven's direction.

"Ward Sellars, P.I. Jimmy O'Hare says ya'all had a bad experience at Arthur Andrews party Thursday night. Wanna tell me 'bout it?"

"Not till I get a lot closer look at your I. D. Com'on inside." He turned and fished the key from his jumper pocket and opened the door. Sellars followed. He was not a big man, but he moved with confidence and a certain disdainful air, as though he disliked the people and places with which he had constantly to come in contact. Sven's motel room was one of those places.

He came inside, didn't bother to close the door and handed the I.D. to Sven.

"O'Hare says ya'all are from Boston and ya work for Andrews off and on." He slumped into the stuffed chair. His suit was expensive. He wore no tie and the collar of his white sport shirt was pulled out and splayed over the collar of the coat.

"Dorchester, just outa Boston. I'm a delivery captain. I contract with Andrews now and then ta move his boat. I work *with* a lot of people. I don't work *for* anybody." Sven pulled the desk chair out and sat straddle of its back. He tossed the I.D. wallet back to its owner.

"So what happened on Thursday night?"

Sven told the significant elements of the story.

"She see any faces?"

"No, only the backs of four big men."

"Okay," Sellars said, rising. "Look, I don't know how much I can do. I'll interview your lady friend and I'll have a talk with Martin to see if there was anybody there Thursday that he didn't know. Hey, I haven't got a lot to go on here. Do my best."

Sven was sure that wasn't going to be very good. The man had asked no questions about details. Sven had left the details out specifically to test him. Sellars had flunked.

Sven closed the door and crossed to the phone. He punched the number pad, the outside dial tone hummed and he tucked in Leda's sequence. There was no answer. He tried the number for her father's place. A very sleepy Matt mumbled a greeting. No, he said in an injured tone, Leda was not there.

"What's going on," he asked with a yawn.

"I just got a visit from O'Hare's shamus. He's a turkey."

"Meaning?"

"Meaning, if this guy makes a livin' as a P.I. it's by breakin' and enterin'. He didn't ask any questions. Didn't try ta find out anythin' that would start an investigation. I got a real feeling that he's not interested. I think I'll have a talk with Martin after I put you on the plane tomorrow mornin'. I can't move GULL until afternoon anyway."

"Did he ask anything about me? I told Shirley that I was staying with you at the motel."

"Naw. Like I say, he didn't seem to be real interested. Listen, I just tried to call Leda. She didn't answer. I'd like ta talk ta her before this creep pays her a visit, if he bothers. You know where she might be?"

"What time is it?"

"Eleven-fifteen."

"Did you leave a message on the answering machine?"

"Didn't get no machine. Just kept ringin'"

"Well, she might have unplugged the phone. It was pretty late when she left here this morning. I'll try her when we hang up, if she doesn't answer, I'll drive by. She drove her car over here yesterday evening before we went to Andrew's place so I wouldn't have to drop her off when we came in. If her car's gone, then she's probably out somewhere. Maybe checking on one of her shops. They open about noon on Sunday."

Matt hung up the phone and jumped into the shower. He wanted to be what he acted. An optimist. But there was a dark doubt nagging at the corner of his mind and he hastened through his shave, paused long enough to punch up Leda's number and somehow was not surprised when he got neither an answer nor the machine. He dressed quickly and was about to close the door behind him when a thought struck. He went back in and crossed to a utility closet. Sven had thought it wise to get Eddie Malone's arsenal off GULL before more questions were asked about it. The Coast Guard O.D. had accepted the story that Diego's Beretta belonged to the giant and he had confiscated it. The rest of the weapons had been put in a sail bag that now rested in the utility closet.

Matt fished out the .45 automatic. He was surprised at how big the weapon was. How much heavier than the Beretta had been. It became heavier still when he inserted the clip. As he debated whether to arm the gun he was overcome with doubt. This was crazy. What the hell was he doing? He had no permit. This wasn't the high seas, this was Miami. But a crawly feeling on the back of his neck caused him to arm the heavy pistol, jamb it into his waist band at the small of his back and cover it with a hastily selected windbreaker from the coat rack at the door.

A few minutes later he drew up in front of the Spanish style hacienda where Leda rented the entire top floor. It was one of the last of the lovely old homes in Coconut Grove to survive the spate of apartment and condo building. Matt understood again why Leda put up with the snoopy landlady who occupied the first floor. The house was beautiful, the setting magnificent and the neighborhood quiet. Leda's car was there.

She had shown him the rear entrance the day before, a spiral stairway appliquéd to the back of the house to meet the fire code for a second story apartment. It terminated at a wrought iron railed sun deck. There were French doors leading to the dining room. He knocked, softly at first, then hard when he got no answer. He knocked again, this time on the other door and it swung open. His heart in his mouth, he strode across the room to the hall, shouting her name again as he entered the bedroom.

There was no answer and the bed had not been slept in. He raced back into the living room. The phone wire had been torn from the tiny connector which was still in the receptacle. The answering machine was unplugged, but a battery back-up kept its pilot light blinking.

There were four calls from Linda at the Royal Palms Hotel. Her fax machine was down and she needed to confer with Leda on the emergency instructions covering such a problem. Her last call was made at five minutes to four on Saturday the machine's disembodied voice reported. Her shift apparently ended at four because she said she'd try to reach Leda again in the morning. The call between Linda's third and fourth message was from a man. He said he was investigating the incident at Mr. Andrews' place on Thursday night. He needed an appointment. He'd call back later.

Matt examined the door to the sun deck. It had been jimmied. He looked at the door to the front entrance. The chain of keys was still in the lock when he opened it. Half-dozen pieces of mail lay on the floor just inside the door. She had come up the front way, into the house, picked up her mail, climbed the stairs, opened the door and was taken as she entered. The key was left because the door was pushed shut immediately when she was grabbed and the mail fell from her hand. But there was little sign of the struggle. A small wicker waste basket lay on its side, nothing else. Matt sat down weakly.

It was mid afternoon by the time Matt got to Sven on GULL.

He had called the detective whom they had first reported the party incident to on Friday afternoon. One of the blue coats that had accompanied him found a man's handkerchief near the gate in the side yard. It smelled of chloroform.

"He said there was probably two of them. One grabbed her when she opened the door, the other shut it. Then both of them restrained her until the dope took effect. That's why so little sign of struggle."

He sat dejectedly on the bridge deck in the blue awning's shade. Sven had stripped GULL of all the red sail repair tape and had replace her carved stern board. The red hull of the dinghy was the only reminder of GIRL OF MIAMI.

There was little the two friends could do until and unless they could find a handle with which to grab this slippery ball.

For, they were sure that the ball was in their court.

"Why did they want her? Carlos said they would lose interest in us as soon as the canister's contents changed hands."

"It ain't that anymore," Sven said conclusively. "I gotta feelin' we embarrassed some hard asses that ain't used ta havin' little people get in their way. We was supposed to be easy, like Carlos said. Hell, lookin' at it from their side, we sunk their Navy. We've got personal enemies in that crowd from the puniest low level Diego-type to 'R' and on up the ladder ta the spooks who fucked up th' initial operation in 1963. They've all got some reputation to lose, sure, but I think the real thing is they're pissed and they're gonna show us that we ain't so damn smart…." He trailed off, imagining scenes that he preferred not to put into words. He changed the subject by asking Matt to tell him again everything from the time Leda and he had parted that morning.

"She left my place about three or three-fifteen. It takes about fifteen minutes to get to her place—in traffic. There should have been very little at three-fifteen." He proceeded through the account up to the playing of the answering machine tape. He was about to recount the interview with the cop when Sven suddenly stopped him.

"What time did ya say the last call came from the girl—what's her name?

"Linda? She said it was five to four. She must have quit work at four, because she said she'd try again to reach Leda this morning. And they open…."

"An' that call from O'Hare's shamus came before that?" Sven interrupted.

Matt nodded, puzzled. Then he saw where Sven was going with it. "We didn't even start our conversation with Andrews until last night. Andrews didn't know about the Thursday incident and he didn't tell O'Hare to investigate until way after that call was made."

"Right, which brings us ta the interestin' question: Is O'Hare the perfect employee who anticipates his boss's every command? Did he send his boys out before Andrews told him to? If he did, how did he know about it? Or is it someone else's caper? Usin' the incident as an excuse to call? Who else knows about the incident? Only the guys who done it."

"And they and O'Hare's bunch could be one and the same."

"Ayeah. Damn. That's why I wanted to get to Leda before Sellars did. I wanted her ta listen real close to his voice. Ta see if maybe he was the one that sent the goons after us Thursday night."

"Did he say anything about Leda when he talked to you this morning?"

"Only that he was goin' ta talk ta her."

"To her. But he didn't say anything about talking to me. Yet I told O'Hare yesterday that I was leaving tomorrow. You two are going to be here after I'm gone. Logically, I should have been the first on his list."

"True. But, he figgered you was at the motel with me."

"Yes, but isn't it a little strange that he would purposely mention speaking to her, yet fail to even inquire about my whereabouts? Shirley would have told him I was with you at the motel."

"Unless he knew *where* you were. But, it's like I told ya. He doan show me too much."

"Sven—they followed us from Andrews's place to the restaurant, to the motel, to Eddie Malone's apartment and were waiting for her at her place when she showed up at home this morning. Then he mentions to you, real offhand, that he'll talk to her later, but doesn't mention me at all, yet I'm the one leaving tomorrow? It stinks, Sven."

"Okay," Sven nodded, "let's say yer right. It's gotta be O'Hare's P.I. because we had to be followed yesterday sos they could snatch her like that. But, I got lots of questions—Why Sellars? What's his reason? Who's he workin' for? O'Hare? If it's O'Hare, who's O'Hare workin' for? Andrews? I don't think so. Could Sellars have been at Andrews' party? Yes, if he regularly works fer O'Hare and Andrews on investigations. Martin wouldn't think of him and his boys as strangers. Could Sellars be workin' for someone besides O'Hare? Possible. Unethical, but possible. If the money's right, very possible."

"He could have more than Andrews, as a client. Unethical only if he's using *entrée* to Andrews' party for the service of another client. But you think he's a sleaze bag and might do that?"

"I think he's likely ta be persuaded by money ta do that. But, it takes a whole lot of money, a whoppin' fear or a political commitment ta make a man commit murder. Do these goons work for him all the time? Is it part of their regular duty ta take people out, kill 'em and make it look like an accident? That's not regular P.I. work. That stinks of spooks an' 'national security' an' dirty tricks an' …an' it scares the hell out of me, because there's no bounds fer rational men ta work inside of."

"Or the cops."

"No, dammit. It makes me have to take all that responsibility on myself. It forces me ta act like they do ta protect myself without the protection they get from the law. Tell ya somethin'. I ain't gonna let no bastard kill me just because he's allowed ta."

"What are we going to do?

"What they least expect us ta do, I hope."

"And that is…?"

"Get Leda back! Com'on."

Chapter Thirteen

The desperation that Sven had spoken of had spread with deadly contagion. He was loath to talk of this episode and Sellars demurred on the basis of agent-client confidentiality.

The increasing violence of basically peaceful people and the ease with which they embraced it was still a worry to Matt years later.

"It ain't over 'till it's over." —Y. Berra

Sellars lay face down on the cabin sole. The gray duct tape wound about his mouth wrinkled as his jaw worked soundlessly.

"How are we going to get him in the water with all this chain on him?" Matt asked. "He'll be too heavy to lift."

"We'll put a halyard down through the hatch soons it gets dark. Then we'll hoist him up and over the side when the tide turns. I don't want any divers finding him alongside here when he shows up missin'"

"How much of this chain have you got here?"

"Oh, we got plenty. It won't take all that much to keep him down 'till th' fish get to him"

The terror in Sellars' wide eyes had long since replaced the surprise when he had backed down the companionway stairs a scant half-hour earlier.

"Oh, I'm not worried about not having enough. This is way too much. You got some way of cutting it?"

"Oh, yeah. Damn I hate ta waste that. Once ya cut it, what's left will be too short ta use fer anchorin' Oh, well, I'll have 'em put a new length aboard."

Matt continued to lace the heavy galvanized chain in and around the strands of nylon cord that he had earlier wound about the struggling Sellars' body from shoulders to ankles.

"Now ya go back with this small stuff and tie individual links ta the cord at several critical places sos it doan shift."

Sven continued his instructions in as off-hand manner as he could muster, glancing occasionally at the terror stricken face flattened against the polished mahogany. "Idea is, if ya keep zig-zaggin' the chain across his back, he'll turn face up an' settle that way."

"What's to keep him from going straight down beside the boat?"

"I got this truck inner tube. It won't keep him on th' surface but it won't let him sink all th' way either. I'll adjust the valve core sos it'll leak real slow. More air it loses the deeper he'll get, but the tide will drag him pretty far out in th' channel by th' time is goes completely flat. It's deep out there. He'll be on the bottom before the tide changes back."

"Yeah, and tomorrow everybody will wonder what the hell happened to Sellars." Matt said, getting into the spirit of the game. "The psychology will be great. He just vanishes." Sellars kicked violently, but it was of little use. The two men who sat astride him continued their slow work. "Then the next day the same thing happens to the mugs they send looking for him. Just vanish, no trace. They'll begin to wonder what the hell they're up against. Here, hold this, while I tie it. It's like those damn fools in the Islands, they thought we'd just lie down and die for them."

"Yeah, waal, I'm gettin' a little tired of th' killin'. It's still too new ta me not to bother me some," Sven said gravely.

"Well, it's all been in self-defense. I'm damn tired of being the sitting duck all the time, waiting for some ass like this to come along and waste me in bed or something."

Sellars again kicked and squirmed and tried to talk around his gag. The blood vessels stood out on his forehead and his eyes bulged, terror and pleading a pathetic mix in them. His body was suddenly wracked and vomit spewed out his nose. Matt, quickly pulled the tab end of the duct tape and the wad of cloth came out in the second convulsion. Wouldn't do to have him drown in his vomit, Matt thought.

"You're making a hell of a mess. But you're the one who has to lie in it." And he began to replace the gag.

"Jesus Christ, you guys. What are ya'all doing?" Sellars blurted. "O'Hare said to find who went after ya'all the other night. That's what I'm trying to do. Why are you trying to kill me?"

"Shut him up, Matt. I'm so damn tired of these lying bastards." Matt dutifully tried to replace the wad of cloth. Sellars twisted away in protest.

"You don't know what you're doing," he yelled. "This is murder and the spooks will still…." Matt had forced the gag back into his mouth. He looked at Sven but Sven shook his head so he pulled the tape closed again.

"Lookie here, rectum. Doan talk ta me about murder. There's been an even dozen people tryin' ta kill me fer almost a week now. I'm pissed. It's my turn. I'm a goin' to kill everyone that even frowns in my direction. Somebody snatched a lady friend a mine this morning. I think it was you. I ain't got much hope a gettin' her back alive. But, I ain't a waitin' for the law to take a hold here. You ain't worth enough ta them ta swap fer the girl, so yer just a pawn ta me. My killin' you sends a message. They ain't just after me any longer. I'm after them."

Matt winked at Sven. "He said something about spooks."

"Ayeah. Next he'll be trying to tell us about 'national security'." But Sellars kicked and tried to bellow. Then he shook his head violently. Sven nodded and Matt pulled the tape loose and removed the gag.

"You guys are crazy. Ya'all don't know what you're involved in here. This is deep shit."

"What'd I tell ya?"

"I think you got it backwards. You are in deep shit. And in a while you'll be in deep water." With that Matt attempted to stuff the gag back in.

"No, dammit. Listen. Ya'all can't fight these guys. They're government spooks. They don't answer to anybody. They tell you to do something, you do it."

"An' what did they tell ya ta do?" Sven asked.

"He said ya'all were security risks. He said that ya'all were double agents and they were close to making an arrest."

"And who is he?" Matt asked.

"The CIA guy. O'Hare introduced me to him the day before the party. He said this guy wanted me to get some security people into Andrews party."

"What was this guy's name?" Matt pressed.

"O'Hare just called him 'R'.

"Sonnafabitch," Sven swore. "I shouda set that bastard adrift when I had the chance. So those guys were R's boys you sicced on us at the party?"

"Then why were you giving them instructions? Didn't they know what they were supposed to do?"

"All I was told was that they would arrive at the door, I was to tell Martin that they were extra security that I had ordered. When I got them into the garden, I was to describe ya-all and leave."

"That sounds like a whole lotta shit ta me, Sellars. I can see ya gettin' 'em in ta the party. I can see ya fingerin' us, but why would they arrive not knowin' what they was supposed ta do an' you havin' ta tell 'em?"

"I didn't tell them anything. I left them at the edge of the patio and went back inside. I don't know what they did after that."

"How many of them were there?" Matt asked.

"There was five. One guy did all the talking. Or all the listening. I told him what ya'all were wearing. He was smaller than the rest. The other four just looked like muscle."

"So you didn't actually tell them to kill us?"

"Hell no, that wasn't part of the deal. R said all he wanted me to do was to get them into the party and identify ya-all. He made it sound like they were going to arrest you. Hey, he's CIA. What do I know. I did what I was told."

"But ya'll submit a bill for services, a' course?"

"No, he paid in cash. In advance."

"So that's why ya wasn't very interested in th' details of this case when we talked this mornin'. Ya knew all about it already."

"Yeah, and I just figured it was a matter of time before they sent another squad after ya-all. That's why I was so surprised when you called and said you knew who was behind the whole thing. Because if you really knew and you were really what they said you were, you sure wouldn't have bothered to call me."

Both listeners moved away from the bound captive as he rolled himself over onto his back.

"O'Hare toss you jobs of this kind often?" Matt asked.

"Not this kind. I do a lot of work for him, but it's pretty routine corporate stuff."

"How well did he seem to know this R guy?"

"I don't know. He told me he was CIA doing some local security for the Secretary of Commerce who was attending Andrews' party. Didn't really figure, but hell I ain't in government work. All I had to go by was his ID. And it looked legit."

"Did R seem ta be a friend of Andrews or a friend of O'Hare?" Sven wanted to know.

More confident now that he was making progress, Sellars squirmed into a sitting position.

"I don't really know."

"Did you tell O'Hare what R asked you to do?"

"No, because I left the party immediately when I sent them after you. That's what R told me to do. I didn't see or hear from O'Hare, because he was in D.C. all day yesterday, until he called me about six last night and told me he wanted me to look into this incident. He was in a big hurry and I didn't want to discuss it on the phone anyway. I thought I'd get to him sometime today and explain it, but I hadn't been able to reach him before you called. Then, things started to smell funny when you said what you said. Look, I'm an honest gumshoe. I'm trying to make a living. I've never been involved in this kind of thing before. I don't know anything about somebody snatching your lady friend. But, if you'll untie me, I'll do my damnedest to help you find her."

"What exactly did O'Hare tell ya when he phoned ya last night?"

"Well, it's like I said, he was in a big hurry. He said three of Mr. Andrew's guests had overheard a plot to kill them at the party on Thursday night. He had already spoken with Martin about it and that I should get all the details from him."

"Did he give any hint that he knew anything about this, other than what he had learned from Andrews and Martin?

"If you're trying to figure out if O'Hare's clean, I think he is. R is pretty convincing. He had all the right credentials. If he showed O'Hare what he showed me, Jimmie had no reason to doubt the guy."

"This R guy. What did he look like?" Matt wanted to know.

But the answer just created another question added to the long list, because the description was nothing like the R from MOTHER that had been left on the navigation light.

"Just what happened to you guys? What's this about people trying to kill you for a week?" Sellars had begun to relax. He might be able to talk his way out of this completely with a little more patience, he thought.

Sven looked at him skeptically but finally began to retell what had become a tiresome story. When he finished, a thoughtful Sellars whistled his apparent awe. But before he could speak Sven shifted quickly back to the current situation.

"You got any reason to doubt the integrity of Andrews?" Sven asked.

"Hey, he's a lobbyist. He's no Sunday school teacher, but I've never seen anything to indicate that he'd be involved in murder and the kind of mayhem you've been through the past week. Look, I'm serious. I think you're a citizen whose gotten kicked around and you're mad as hell. But you have already committed a crime. This is kidnapping. You should stop while you're ahead and let me and some professionals help you out."

"Sellars, I'm a goin' ta untie you. But if you think for a minute you're a goin' to press charges agin' me, ferget it. It would be your word agin' ours and we'd accuse you of terrible things that ya wouldn't want to waste time defendin' yerself agin'. I gotta find a woman, who may be dead by now. I'd appreciate yer help, but doan get in my way. I also think that you're liable to lose a lot of business from Andrews if I tell him ya fell in with R on his shitty little deal. And he'll be even more pissed to think that ya brought them right into his house ta pull it off."

He nodded and Matt began to dismantle the elaborate bonds. When the detective was free, the two looked at him carefully as he rubbed circulation back into his hands. He studied them with equal care.

"Do ya'all know anybody in Miami that you haven't visited since you arrived?" he asked finally.

"Yeah. Why?"

"They know anything about this whole deal?" When Sven shook his head, he went on. "I want you to shake any tails," he paused "and you'd better be damn sure you do. Ya'all want ta play cops and robbers, this'll be your first test. Then get to your friend's house and phone me from there. Tell my secretary his name and phone...."

"He lives on a boat," Sven broke in.

"Better yet. Where's the boat?"

"Dinner Key Marina."

"Well, damn. Maybe we got a little of Lady Luck's lipstick rubbing' off on this deal after all. What's this guy's name?"

"Fats Barlow," Sven replied too quickly and was immediately sorry for. "I'd sure like ta keep him outta this. What you got in mind?"

"Nothing. I just need to leave a message with him for you. I'll call the Marina and the Harbor Master can deliver it. It won't reveal anything and if they've got me bugged, I can make the call from a booth somewhere. I'll do everything to protect him but you better be sure *you* don't lead anybody to him.

"Now, we can't be seen together. They're not like to think too much about my coming here today but likely they'll come to me if you disappear. That's what I need so that I can get done what has to be done. Don't do anything until you hear from me. It's almost six now. I'll have one of my boys on the dock at the marina as soon as I can. His name will be Mikey. He'll find a way to let you know who he is. Don't approach him unless you need him. He's ya'all's protection. I'll bill Andrews. If you should happen to see me at the marina, don't approach me either."

"I just got the feeling that we've been side-tracked," Matt muttered.

"Well, that's pretty accurate. Andrews would have my ass if he knew that I didn't help ya'all out. Now, I know a lot more than you do about how to get the information you need. You'll have plenty of time to be heroes again later. I'm pretty sure that I can have something for you before midnight—mornin' for sure. After that it's your ballgame again."

He gazed at the two for a few minutes then climbed to the bridge deck where he turned and parted with, "And for Christ's sake, don't shoot anybody with thing!" indicating the .45 that Matt finally laid on the mahogany table.

Chapter Fourteen

MOON SHOT

The neon sign, its electric eye responding to the darkening sky, flashed to life as Matt hefted Sven's faded duffel bag into the back seat of the rental car, started to get into the front, then returned to the door of the motel and paused in a listening attitude.

"OK", he shouted inside. "But we gotta stop at my place first." Then he returned to the car, started the engine and turned on the lights. Leaping out again, he left the car door open and went again into the room. Sven's long legs were just disappearing out of the rear window. "I left my damn shaving kit at the apartment," Matt said, a trifle too loud. Then he crawled after his friend—out into the narrow alley.

Sven, his few belongings stuffed into a pillow case, was making his way between trash cans, crates and other obstructions in the gloomy confines of the narrow space between the motel wall and that of an apartment house. Pausing, for only a moment, he replaced his broad brimmed, soft canvas hat with a small, black, Greek fisherman's cap. Matt shed Eddie Malone's oversize windbreaker, wrapped the .45 in it and tucked it under his arm.

Fifty or so feet along, a rear door to the apartment house was propped open and an elderly Cuban sat just inside hunched over his rosary. Sven swept past, through the short narrow hall and into the foyer at the front of the building. Matt stopped and dropped ten dollars into the old man's open palm, pressed a finger to his lips, winked and followed Sven out the front door. The Swede's long strides had taken him across the street and he was disappearing into an alley between two T-shirt shops. Emerging into the bustle of the boulevard beyond, they joined the throng at a crosswalk then ducked into an arcade of shops. Mingling with the crowd, they paused to look for pursuers.

"I think we made it," Sven muttered. "I figgered that if they had watchers on the rear, they'd call 'em around front when they saw us fixin' ta drive away. But, if they planted microphones and they don't hear us talkin' no more, that runnin' car won't delay 'em long. Let's keep movin'."

Emerging from the arcade into the next street, and having three bustling blocks between them and the motel, they paused a moment to study the possibilities. To their left, half a block away a busy one-way street funneled traffic up from the direction in which they had come. To their right, the one-way traffic went in the opposite direction. Beyond that street a large hotel occupied most of the block. They turned toward it and Matt crossed the street so they would not be seen together if they had failed to shake their watchers. When Sven arrived at the taxi stand near the hotel, Matt crossed back and leapt into the cab from the other side.

"Dinner Key Marina," Sven barked.

"You think we can trust Sellars?" Matt asked when the cab had moved into the flow of traffic.

"Too late ta think about that now. He knows where we're gonna be. Wish now I hadn't given him Fat's name, but I guess we gotta trust somebody." His voice trailed off. "Ya think he was pissed?"

"He was pissed. But I think he makes too much money off Andrews to be too pissed. He'll send Mr. A fine fat bill to salve his injured dignity."

They rode in silence a while then Matt asked, "What exactly is he finding out for us?"

"I donno," Sven said. "But he seemed to have somethin' in mind."

"What if it turns out to be nothing? What do we do then? He said it might be morning before he had anything." He paused, then went on. "Do you think they'll keep her alive as bait hoping they can reel us in?"

"Yeah, I'm sure they will," Sven said almost too quickly. They had had her almost sixteen hours now, he thought. An uncomfortable sixteen hours to be sure. The silence fell again on the taxi and hung there until they were dropped across from the marina gate.

The street lights glowed dully in the gathering darkness and both men looked furtively about as they crossed the street. The guard punched up Fat's number on the phone and the duo were immediately sent down the main pier. Their return to the world of boats was like donning a comfortable sweater, insulating them from what had become an ongoing threat from the outside. There was an unconscious but definite relaxation in their demeanor as they ambled down the dock.

"I hope he's got a cold beer," Matt mumbled.

"He's got a cold beer," Sven mumbled in return.

The marina lay before them, a trunk of the tree of life with smaller piers branching to the right and left and each of those branching with smaller mammary finger piers where the many yachts nursed. The main dock was well lit by lampposts on alternate sides occasionally interspersed with low boxes of fire extinguishers or telephone and electrical substations. Beyond, at the end, near the entrance channel, and more brilliantly lit was the fuel dock.

They turned right and Sven began to count slips. The dock was narrower and half as well lit as the main pier. Twilight cocktail parties had given away to fewer, quieter conversational gatherings on the mostly expensive yachts that sucked power, water and communications via cable and hose from both sides of the dock. Further along the activity lessened and near the end, the boats rocked relative silence.

MOONSHOT lay in her berth fifty or so yards from the intersection of the main pier. She was a schooner rigged replica of a late 19th century pilot boat. She was tied stern-to to the dock, near enough for the nimble boatman and the wary lubber to easily board. Her owner entertained one of the latter with a nasal rendition of an adventure during the heyday of NASA.

"That damn story gets wilder every time ya tell it," Sven called, tossing his pillowcase *comme* sea bag into the cockpit and waiting for the expected invitation to board.

"Listen to 'wild', coming from a Swede who thinks he's a Viking," Fats jabbed back, drink in hand. "Come aboard, you swab jockey. About time you got here. This is Mikey," he said waving the other hand at the large man in a casual suit who had stood up immediately on hearing Sven's voice.

Sven had begun to lean into a leap and pulled back upon hearing the guest's name.

Mikey, in typical lubberly fashion, stepped up onto the canvas cushion that topped the seating of the spacious u-shaped cockpit. Then placing the other foot on the wide varnished stern rail, he extended his long arm to shake hands with the startled Sven who still stood on the dock.

"I guess you weren't expecting me so soon," Mikey said, taking his hand. Sven was crouched in order to step down onto the boat and at the same time to duck under the after edge of the canopy when Mikey gave a sudden jerk pulling him off balance. Just as suddenly Mikey stopped pulling and Sven fell between boat and dock into the tepid water.

"Damn, I'm sorry," the big man said, straightening over the rail. Matt jumped aboard as Fats urged the bobbing Sven to come around to the starboard quarter where the freeboard was lower. Matt joined Fats, bending in anticipation of the swimmer's hands when Mikey clumsily joined them, managing to tumble Matt into the water in the process.

Then he suddenly became very well coordinated. He gathered the right hand of one and the left of the other, pulling them close to the hull with a powerful tug. Then, with a sardonic smile just visible in the reflected dock lights said: "Sellars sends his greetings. Wanted you to know that I'm on the job for you." With that he pulled the men up high enough for them to get a footing and scramble aboard.

Fats went below for towels and as the two bedraggled men waited for him to come back, Mikey continued.

"Sellars is off on a little trip for your benefit. He says that you are to stay here where he can easily reach you. He's trying to get something for you before midnight. He said to tell you he doesn't want any of your, quote—fuckin' heroics—putting him in danger. So dry off and stay put. I'll be nearby." He started to turn, then: "I wouldn't drink too much of Fat's booze. You might be able to move tonight if Sellars gets back in time and you'll need clear heads." With that he put his huge, shiny, wing tipped shoe on the varnished rail again and stepped easily to the dock.

"Thank you, Mommy," Matt spat mockingly. Sven glared from beneath dripping shaggy brows.

"Hey, no hard feeling, OK?" Not waiting for an answer, Mikey strolled toward the main pier.

"What the hell's that all about?" Fats wanted to know, arriving with the towels.

"Your Viking friend here got carried away earlier today and we just got a little payback. It could have been worse. Hi, Fats, I'm Matt. I'm Sven's foredeck hand. Sorry to bomb in on you like this."

"Welcome aboard. Here, dry off and shuck the wet duds. We'll throw 'em in the washer at the launderette. I'll rustle up something for you to wear."

Fats Barlow was a thin, wiry, little man with a nasal twang. He had been an engineer in the heyday of the race to the moon and had invested his generous salary well. When the first questions arose in the minds of some Congressmen about the space program budget, Fats took his stock options and retired. From that time on he had had only two interests—carving wood and fishing. The runabout, a production cousin to FAST FUN, occupying the oversize, adjacent berth attested to the latter. Fats faced regular hostility from boat owners docked further out who complained that this more convenient slip was wasted on such a small boat. But Fats had been a tenant since the misty past of the fifties and that seniority had bought special consideration from the management. Besides, he paid rent on the slip as if the runabout were twice its length.

Later, both visitors sat in the cockpit. Sven had donned his spare pair of wrinkled denims and cotton shirt from the pillowcase, but Matt sat uncomfortably in Fats' old sweat suit, the only article of clothing large enough to accommodate the younger man's bulk.

"Said he got his name from the old TV commercial where the big kids made 'Mikey' try the new cereal first. Seems his co-workers always give him the tough jobs—usually because of his size," Fats was explaining. It was his small contribution and a culmination of an hour of exposition that brought everyone up to date. Sven apologized again for involving Fats in the affair, assuring him that Sellars had been asked not to.

Fats and Sven had begun to ask about mutual acquaintances not seen recently and a nodding Matt was about to ask to be excused in order to catch a nap when these peaceful pursuits were interrupted by Mikey's return.

He carried what looked like a briefcase.

"Permission to come aboard," he asked, to the surprise of his now wary host.

"Sure," Fats nodded. "What's on your mind?"

"A little update," the big man said, settling onto the cockpit cushion. He stood the briefcase on its hinged edge on the table and released two legs that allowed it to lean at an angle sufficient to prevent its toppling over. Then with a press of a button, what appeared to be a rivet attaching the handle extended into a surprisingly tall antenna. Another telescoped out of the opposite rivet, was detached, and Mikey added it to the top of the first.

A second button released the top half of the front of the case which was hinged horizontally and as it swung down, a tape deck was revealed.

"This is a field unit like the permanent one we got in our offices. All conversations with clients or interrogations of anyone during an investigation, are transmitted to a bigger rig like this in the vault of Sellars' lawyer's office. This one is used in the field as a booster station to retransmit to that central recorder." He paused as he made some minor adjustments.

"We had you guys on the boat this afternoon until all the chain began to fuck up transmission. If we hadn't been delayed by traffic on the causeway and the pissy assed Coast Guard O.D. at the gate, you guys would be in jail right now and I'd be at the Heat game." A stab with a stubby finger brought the twin spools of the oversize cassette to life.

Sven's scowl deepened and Matt shivered in spite of the warmth of the sweat suit.

"This is a conversation recorded about an hour ago in our office. Sellars went there right after he left you two on the boat. He figured if you guys gave them the slip at the motel they'd turn up at our office to see if Sellars might know where you were going."

The tape had been running and Sellars was speaking: *"Hey, I was talking to these guys because Andrews hired me to look into their complaint that you and your boys leaned on them at the party Thursday night. Threatened to kill them, they charge. You told me you were going to arrest them."*

Sellars visitor was obviously the R who had requested his help to gain entry to the party. Sven and Matt leaned forward with growing interest.

"Look, this is too big for you to be poking around in," the other voice said. *"If you got any information about how I can find these guys, you better spill it. And,"* he added as an after thought, *"tell Andrews that this is all a national security matter and he should stay the hell out of it."*

"I'll tell him. I'm sure he'll want to check that out with some of his contacts in DC. In the meantime I need to deal with the current assignment. I don't like being made an accessory before the fact to an attempted murder

that you claim to be in 'national security' interests. So if you don't mind, I'll stay on this for a while yet."

A cigarette lighter's fizz filled the pause before he continued. "*I don't know what the two 'fugitives', as you call them, plans are. They obviously want the woman back. She apparently didn't figure in this thing that the men are wanted for. They say she was picked up off a sinking boat and was just an unknowing passenger. They asked me to find out what I could about it and they're gonna contact me on Tuesday at noon to see what I know. They want me to talk to your superiors to find out what kind of deal they could make to get her back.*" He paused a moment and then added for emphasis, "*She really didn't figure in this thing.*"

"*Bullshit,*" R spat. "*They're not in any position to deal.*"

"*Fine. I'll tell them that when they call Tuesday. And I'll make my report as you suggest to Andrews. Now if you'll excuse me I have an irate wife and kid who are expecting me at home.*"

The reels turned but there were no voices. Sounds of chair legs scraping on floors and footsteps of several people were heard.

"*Oh, one more thing.*" Sellars was saying to R, " *Maybe just the two of us could talk for a minute.*" A door was heard to open and shut and one pair of feet closed the distance between the two men now alone in the office.

"*I always hesitate to criticize another man's work because I've been in this business long enough to know how many variables can affect the success or failure of a job. But I also know that, in my case, clients and in ya-all's, superiors, don't always recognize those difficulties or sufficiently appreciate their influence.*" There was a short silence, then Sellars went on. "*Your boys fucked up Thursday night. Now, today, you were supposed to gather these two guys, figuring they would get together as soon as they discovered the girl missing and they'd be easy pickin's. But they weren't. Now that's double egg on your face. The fact is these guys—according to their side of the story—have been able to give a group of pros a hell of a egg smearing on several encounters.*" The reels were silent again. "*I think someone who has a claim on a sizable portion of your ass, is getting pretty impatient to end this little fuck-up festival. Now, if you ignore the possibility that my relationship with these guys could be turned to your benefit, it might be interpreted by your boss as another bad decision.*" The reels turned. "*I always like to let my clients make the bad decisions. Maybe you ought to let your boss make this one.*"

Matt imagined Sellars and R looking into one another's eyes as the reels again turned in silence. Then someone moved and then someone else moved. "*Dial 9 for an outside line,*" Sellars said. And the anemic winking bleats of the Touch-tone filtered through.

The ringing on the other end could be clearly heard. Sellars had a bug in the phone as well.

"*2230,*" a voice answered.

"*2203. Yeah. Let me talk to the Chief.*"

"*What's the report?*" came a growl a minute later.

"*The sailors have a P.I. to negotiate for them. Andrews hired him to look into the disagreeable incident on Thursday night. They gave him the slip but said they'd get back in touch on Tuesday. He doesn't know where they are. He wants to talk to you.*" R was speaking in a hushed tone, in an apparent attempt to prevent Sellars overhearing him.

"*So, what? They didn't go back to the motel? I thought you were going to pick them up at the motel.*"

"*Uh, well, Sellars, the P.I., must have spooked them when he talked to them this morning. They skipped.*" R rushed on, hoping to prevent further inquiry into the missed opportunity. "*The PI says they want to make a deal. He wants to talk to you about it.*"

"*Tuesday, noon is too long. This damn thing is taking too long.*" the gruff voice replied.

"*The PI says he's got no idea where they are. They gotta contact him. Besides, that'll give us—uh—me time to find them again.*"

The long pause was followed by a grunt and then the command: "*Bring him out.*" And the line fell silent.

R said something to Sellars but it was interrupted by a subtle beeping and a flashing yellow light emitting from the still covered lower half of the unit in MOONSHOT's cockpit.

"Ah, incoming mail," Mikey said, releasing the cowl that covered the transceiver. "That'll be the boss," he said, smoothly replacing the cassette with a fresh one and moving the switch from 'play' to 'record'. Then he rotated the entire unit until an orange bubble on a panel moved between two vertical lines and turned red. The crackling transmission followed suit—growing clear as the bubble ripened.

"Sorry, you're going to have to move your briefcase off the console here. You're doing weird things to my compass," a youthful voice was saying.

"Oh, right. Sorry. It's probably the battery in my cellular phone. It ought to be OK over here next to your VHF, huh?" Sellars asked.

"Good thinking, boss," Mikey chuckled. "His transmission will jump onto the VHF's antenna cable and he'll broadcast from the boat's antenna."

"God, she's a….

…beautiful boat. How long is she?" Sellars asked the helmsman, as he leaned out of the little cruiser's side window in order to examine the large yacht they were approaching in the moon light.

"Ninety-five feet," the helmsman said rather proudly. "Thirty-foot beam amidships," he continued.

"Damn. Something like that must run up into a lotta dollars."

"Well, it is if you try to build it in America or Europe these days. Or even in the Orient," he added as an afterthought.

Sellars didn't ask. He was sure that the youth's eagerness would supply the answer without the question.

"The owner was very smart."

Sellars noticed that R leaned forward to hear the conversation.

"He had it built in Turkey."

"Turkey? That's interesting. I didn't know the Turks had a reputation for designing yachts,"Sellars prompted.

"Oh, she was designed by an Italian guy, but they had her built in Istanbul because the labor is so much cheaper there and the workmanship is good. That is, the steel work. They took her to Italy for the interiors and the decoration."

"The Italians are good at that, I guess?" Sellars saw R relax back into his deck chair, apparently having decided the conversation was frivolous boating chatter that did not threaten to reveal anything damaging.

"Yeah, that's where the liner SS UNITED STATES wound up."

"In Italy?" Sellars asked.

"No, no, in Turkey. Istanbul. Several promoters had tried to refit her but they always went to the Germans or the Koreans or Taiwan. It was always too expensive. Some guy finally bought her to put her back into the Caribbean trade. She was in a hellava mess. It was a shame. She set the record for an Atlantic crossing in the fifties then almost immediately she was retired and sat around rusting to pieces for thirty years before some one rescued her."

Sellars prodded the youth to keep talking while he busied himself attempting to find landmarks ashore that would later help pinpoint the looming craft's position. "You seem to be very knowledgeable about this sort of thing. What's your job?"

"I'm the first mate on INSHALLA." He rushed on without urging, "I've had my ticket for a while, but I stayed on with her just as a deck hand hoping for a chance at the mate's job. Finally got my break last month. The mate got drunk and didn't make it back aboard when we stopped off in Freeport and the owner fired him." The young man looked lovingly at the looming hull. "She's such a good boat to work on."

"INSHALLA," Sellars repeated, looking at the gilded letters on the curving stern. "That the owner's wife's name?"

The young man laughed. “Naw. That’s an Arabic word I think. It’s supposed to mean ‘God willing’. The owner thought that was a good name for a casino.”

“She’s a casino?” Sellars said with some surprise. He noted the boat’s home port as Dover Delaware. It was a common ploy. Boats documented and home ported in Delaware could be found the world over. Some were corporate owned others merely escaping a local state sales tax or personal property tax.

“Well, only when the owner isn’t using her. We take private parties out on week-end gambling cruises. There’s a brochure on the end of the dash. Shows some pictures of the cabins and the casino.” He waved a careless hand toward a stack of colorful folders. Sellars took one, noticed the carefully drawn plan of the two decks and quickly tucked it into an inside pocket.

“Sounds like fun. Maybe I’ll join you some week-end. I noticed that there are several cabins for the crew. How many men does it take to run a boat this size?”

“Well, there’s a captain, of course, a first mate, and an engineer. That’s the officers. Then we have four deck hands.”

“That’s a lot of guys to have sitting around when you’re at anchor like this, isn’t it?”

“Oh, the Captain goes ashore as soon as the anchor is down and doesn’t come back ‘till we sail again. The engineer does the same. We only have the generators running when were hanging on the hook. I’m in charge at times like these and I keep just one deckhand aboard to fuel the generators. We pretty much sit around in the wheel house and watch TV.”

The mate was lining up for his run at the landing stage. It was suspended off the ship’s starboard quarter at water level by a connecting run of steps.

“Well, I guess you could draft the stewards if you needed an extra hand. Or the cook.”

"Oh, the cook and the steward come out in the morning and leave after they serve dinner. I just took them ashore. They're provided by a catering company." He backed the engine and tossed a stern line to the waiting deck hand.

"No stewards? I'd think a wealthy man like that would want to have servants around all the time."

The mate killed the engine and in the sudden silence R sat forward in his chair again and one of the two quiet, but ever present enforcers nudged the other awake and they prepared to disembark.

"Oh, he's a very independent kind of a man. He always makes his own drinks, or his daughter does. He doesn't throw his wealth around like some do."

The bow line was now secure and the little cruiser rubbed her quarters teasingly against the phallic fenders that kept her smooth skin from being marred by the landing platform.

R was the first to the top of the steps with Sellars close behind and the muscle bringing up the rear. The Mate stood in conversation with the deck hand on the landing platform below. Suddenly he called up: "Sir, you left your brief case. I'll bring it up to you."

"No!" Sellars shouted, dashing to the rail and looking down on the hand who had started to board the little cruiser. "No, thank you. I really don't need it up here. And I won't be long. It'll be all right there." The Mate shrugged and redirected the hand to some adjustment of the fenders.

INSHALLA'S commodious after deck was planked in narrow strakes of teak with white caulked seams. A dozen deck chairs were ranged in two arcing rows facing the stern rail. The rows were divided in the center by an aisle leading to the double mahogany doors of the grand saloon.

Inside, comfortable and stylish couches lined the

port and starboard sides of a room that grew in width from twenty to thirty feet as it stretched forward to half the length of the boat. Indirect lighting rimmed the overhead in a wash of warm light. Table lamps spilled intimate pools between the couches and smaller ones lit the sprinkle of small tables spotted about the room. The very center surrendered space for a tiny dance floor. The forward bulkhead was pierced in the center by a wide archway. A bar crouched in the dimmer light on the starboard side of the arch and a large screen TV balanced it to port.

Two women sat watching the TV, their backs to the

rest of the room. Two men sat at a table just aft of the dance floor. The one on the left stood up when R bounded through the door.

"This is Sellars," R said by way of introduction, moving past the two hosts to stand a few feet behind them. The muscle settled onto convenient couches flanking the door.

"Hi. I'm Ward Sellars." he said extending his hand toward the tall, chubby, red-faced man who had stood up. His grip was returned by the firm squeeze of a soft hand that had known no physical work. The man nodded his acknowledgment of the greeting but did not speak.

The much larger man remained sitting and made no gesture of greeting. The small table lamp lit his face from below, casting strange shadows and lighting a pair of hard blue eyes in deep set sockets. There was a hint of gray mustache on his upper lip and touches of black still at the temples of an almost totally white head.

The chubby man indicated a chair opposite, but remained standing himself. The hard blue gaze did not falter as Sellars pulled the chair back from the table, unbuttoned his linen jacket and sat, crossing one leg over the other as he did so.

The silent tension spread as far as MOONSHOT's cockpit.

"What the hell are they doing?" Matt fumed.

"Sizing one another up," hissed Mikey, with a gesture to be quiet.

Sellars gauged the man to be in his late seventies. His huge torso hunched forward over the small table threatening it with imminent collapse. Large hands, still powerful-looking even at that age, toyed with a pen knife and a large cigar.

"Andrews put you onto this, uh?" The voice was the product of years of careful, regular basting with fiery drink and tobacco smoke. Sellars imagined him gargling with *salsa.*

"Yeah, he wasn't happy about what happened at his party Thursday night."

"Weren't you told then that this is a NS matter?"

"Oh,right. By the way, I'd like to see some identification if this conversation is to continue on that basis."

"You were shown proper ID on Thursday night."

"Yes, but that was his," Sellars nodded toward R, "not yours."

"I don't carry that kind of thing around on a pleasure trip. It can be dangerous if it's lost or stolen and falls into the wrong hands. Mine are locked in a safe in my office ashore." The voice was as even as the gaze.

"Pleasure trip. My mistake. I thought I was here on business." Sellars stood up. "Get hold of me when you go back to work."

The big man did not look up.

"Ah got mine in ma cabin. Ah'll get it." The chubby man pivoted away toward the archway. Sellars sat down again.

"Like a drink while we wait?" the host asked.

"No, I never drink on the job. Hard enough to explain fuck-ups when you're sober."

"Never fuck-up. Never explain. And *never* explain a fuck-up."

"I don't work for the government."

What might have become a smile, had he allowed it, flickered at the corner of one side of the grim set of lips.

"Mind if I have one?"

"Hey, why not? You're on vacation." R, needing neither instruction nor prompting, crossed to the bar ahead of the returning credentials.

Sellars examined the laminated cards, removed them from their transparent pockets and under the light of the lamp carefully studied the reverse side, the photo and the signature. Then without replacing them he left the lot in the center of the table and leaned back.

"Believe what you were told?" he was asked.

"Oh, yeah. I was also told on Thursday that the 'suspects' were to be arrested."

"So what's changed?"

"Well, I find now that they were to be 'eliminated' instead of arrested."

"Disinformation. But even then, what's it to you?"

"Aiding and abetting. Accessory before the fact."

The lack of response spoke louder than anything the large man could have said.

Sellars went on. "Now these legal niceties may mean little to ya-all, but some of us have to live with them,"

"So, how does this little dance you're doing figure in?"

"Well, the suspects' story has created a 'reasonable doubt' in my mind about their criminal involvement and I'm completely convinced that the woman you hold is a victim of circumstance. They feel strongly enough that she is an innocent in this that they are willing to put their necks back in the noose to free her. And since that is a voluntary effort on their part, however dumb, I'm glad to help."

"That what they're offering? A trade?"

"Simple trade—two for one. They claim that they have nothing that ya-all want anyway. A Cuban who worked for Andrews took a canister off the boat and has since disappeared." Parrish accelerated his presentation without taking a breath. He was sure that nothing he was saying was new to his audience. "They know nothing about what was in it or where to find him. If you waste them it will be a meaningless gesture of overkill based on your simple ability to abuse your power." He paused. "But if you must have them, turn the girl over to me in exchange for them."

The pause in the transmission gave Sven an opportunity to break the tension in MOONSHOT's cockpit. "Damn free with my life, ain't he?" he grumbled. Matt was silenced before he could speak.

"Whai should we screw aroun' with ya-all?" the chubby man broke his silence. "We'll find 'em ahselves," he said, jabbing a thumb over his shoulder toward R as he scooped his ID from the table.

Sellars smiled in the soft light and leaned forward over the small table, ignoring the servant and speaking to the master. "I don't think so. They're amateurs, yes, but they've given you guys back as good as they've gotten so far. Now they've learned how to play your game. The older guy especially. He's mean as hell. They made a believer outta me today." He broke off with only a glance at the squirming R.

On MOONSHOT Sven could not suppress a smile. Matt just shook his head. He was busy trying to place the third voice.

"It's faster, safer, surer their way," Sellars continued. He and the older man now sat gazing into one another's eyes across the small table.

"And how does this cure all of that boy scout idealism of yours?"

"Well, two ways," Sellars answered promptly. "One, I get the girl out of danger. Two, the men are asking to confront you, not being kidnapped—it's voluntary. Besides I don't think you'll waste them now. I think ya-all' are smarter than that. I think that they'll convince you that they are no threat to you."

"Sombitch sank ma boat!"

"BUBBA WINFREY!" Matt sang into the Dinner Key darkness.

"What the hell," Sellars exploded. "Is this some personal vendetta shit? You said this was NS. What's this about somebody sinkin' a boat?" He was standing now, both hands on the table, leaning toward the older man who had sat back in his chair.

But Bubba answered. "None-a-ya goddam business. Ah think ya-all made ya point heah. We'll take it unda advisement. Ya'all get along now an' we'll call...."

The big man had held up his hand. The hand motioned Sellars back into his chair.

"We got reason to think that the Cuban who took the canister revealed some sensitive NS data. We need to clarify that by having a long talk with these guys."

"No bullshit here? That's the real reason you want them? They claim absolute ignorance of any reason for you to want them. That's why they're so pissed and why they are so dangerous. They are ready to lash out in any direction at the slightest provocation and they are deadly, like most amateurs are when threatened. I also think that if they heard something classified, that they would be too ignorant or politically naive to recognize it."

"We'll get the details of the swap to you tomorrow.," came the unmoved reply.

"Make it early, because if I don't like 'em—if I'm not assured of the woman's safety—it's no deal."

"For someone who's so fa' outa his league, ya sho
got some big balls," Bubba smirked.

"I been in this business thirty years. Either the balls get bigger or ya lose 'em along the way. Now, before I go, I wanna know that she's alive and well."

"What makes you think she's here?"

Sellars had stood up and the older man had leaned forward again.

"Because you can keep an eye on her here. Besides if she's bait in a trap—to lure the men into a stupid rescue attempt—you'd want her where you could see them coming from a long way off."

"Let him see her." Bubba was instructed. "Have Fran take him. I need to talk to you for a minute," he added and Bubba moved away. "My guests and crew think she is my alcoholic sister who's here under medication to dry out. She's sedated, naturally, but can respond to your questions. She eats well and is taken for a walk once every four hours. Hal," he identified R with a nod, "will go along to see that you behave yourself."

"Hal? I thought he was 'R'.

"A little custom we have in the Company. At the close of briefings on a new assignment, the designated leader of the task ceremonially asks who's to command. The reply is 'You R'"

Sellars started to comment, thought better of it and shifted his attention back to Bubba's errand. Bubba had interrupted a young blonde woman's TV show, but she waved him off and the brunette followed him back to the table instead.

"Fran's had it with her today," Bubba explained. "Madeline said she'd take a turn."

"Madeline," the older man picked up without looking, "this is Dr. Sellars. I've brought him out for a consultation on my sister's case. Please take him forward. Make sure she's dressed, then let him in to talk to her for a few minutes."

"Glad ta meecha ya, Doc" Madeline said and moved toward the archway forward. She was mid-to late thirties, Sellars judged, with too much mascara and too red lips. Her short dress clung to a well preserved athletic figure. She blew a kiss to Bubba as she passed.

Through the arch, wide steps led to the lower deck. Short halls on either side arced forward to the center leading to a single companionway beyond. A lone door on each side just inside the passage suggested to Sellars that these were owner and special guest cabins. Further in, near the end of the short hall, two additional doors indicated a smaller cabin on each side. A glimpse at the flyer he had picked up on the way over, indicated that the casino was below the saloon in which they had stood and the remainder of the guest cabins were down on that deck also.

A sign on the door in the bulkhead at the end of the passage identified the companionway beyond as crew quarters. Madeline opened the door and held it for Sellars' and Hal's entry. There were three more doors to port and four opposite. A narrow spiral staircase punctured both the overhead and the deck at the far end.

Sellars guessed that the larger Captain's quarters was the first one on his left. That's where his guide stopped.

Madeline stood on tiptoe under a glass wall sconce, reached up and fished a key from the bowl shading the single bulb. Then looking up through mascara clotted lashes she unlocked the door and said by way of explanation: "She gets sorta wild sometimes and Land's afraid she'll jump overboard or somethin' dumb, so he wants her locked in. Let me go in first so I can be sure she's decent."

In MOONSHOT's cockpit Mikey was punching up digits on a cellular phone. "OK we got names for all but the muscle. Three first names, women first: Fran and Madeline. Then Hal. Then, Bubba Winfrey," and he looked at Matt for help.

"He had a documented sport fisherman home ported at Deltaville, Virginia named MOTHER'S FUR COAT."

"You get that?" Mikey asked his listener. "OK, now this last one could be a first or last name. All we got is Land. Enter 'em in an' see what comes out. Later."

"If she's sleeping, I'd appreciate if you'd wake her," Sellars said before the door closed behind Madeline.

But it opened again almost immediately and he was beckoned in. Hal lingered at the open door. The cabin was a 10 by 15 feet snug rectangle. A double-size berth was built in under the large porthole opposite the entrance. A navigation table and desk with a gooseneck lamp occupied the bulkhead to the left of the door. A sofa faced a TV on the aft wall and a wire-glass fronted bookcase spanned the forward bulkhead. In the middle of the room a round coffee table was flanked by two comfortable chairs.

In one of them Leda Malone sat in glassy eyed stupor.

"The doctor is here to see you, honey," Madeline said, watching Leda's face intently.

Sellars sat in the other chair and leaned forward to look carefully for signs of physical abuse. None were obvious. "Can you hear me?" he asked.

Leda turned a bleary gaze on him and first nodded, then replied with a thick, "Yeth."

"Don't be afraid, I won't hurt you." She studied him with all the mental capability she could muster. "Are you Leda Malone?" he asked.

Madeline, who had knelt down beside Leda's chair, swung her gaze sharply toward the detective. Hal cleared his throat from the doorway. Sellars waited for the response. It finally came in the form of a tentative nod.

"What's the name of your father's boat?"

Hal interrupted: "Madeline, maybe you should wait outside 'till the doctor is finished." Madeline stood up but did not move toward the door. Leda struggled to maintain eye contact, lost it and then got it back again.

"GAVIOTA." Her head fell forward on a palsied neck and she struggled to look up again.

"May I take your pulse?" he asked. She nodded a careful, shaky nod. Reaching for her nearest hand he found it cool and clammy to his touch. He felt her pulse. It was slow, but steady and he replaced the hand in her lap.

"Can you stand up for me," he said, rising himself.

Madeline put a hand on her shoulder. "She don't do too good by herself this soon after her shot." But there was communication in the older woman's eyes and eyebrows that spoke of things other than Leda's ability to walk. Puzzled, Sellars studied her face until she broke contact, then in a very light voice said, "But, you don't need to worry, she'll walk all by herself in a couple of hours." Then she crossed to the door indicating that the interview was finished.

A wicker wastebasket caught Sellars' eye and a step toward it revealed an empty medicine vial. Scooping it up he recognized it as a common, but powerful sedative.

"Is this her medication?" he asked.

Madeline nodded, then added, "Yeah. She's due for another shot about four a.m. I'll probably hafta give it to her again. Fran's not so good with her—and she's her own kin."

Hal had given way and she turned at the door to again look knowingly into Sellars inquisitive face. Then in a voice much lighter than the expression she conveyed she said, "She's doin' real good. She hasn't even asked for a drink since she woke up this morning."

Hal started aft, Sellars paused while the door was locked, and Madeline stepped out in front of him. She paused to look pointedly at him again as she dropped the key into the bowl of the lamp, then hurried on past Hal. By the time Sellars cleared the arch she was in her chair before the TV, inserting the remote earphone and appearing to be totally involved in the silent machinations on the screen. The young blonde didn't seem to notice her return.

"She seems OK," Sellars said, pausing at the table where Land and Bubba sat hunched in collaborative silence. "I'm on my way unless you have something else," he said buttoning his linen jacket. "I'll expect to hear from you tomorrow morning. Early." And he strode toward the doors to the after deck. The muscle stood up to bar the way, but someone waved them away.

Outside, Sellars paused a moment, apparently to enjoy the evening, and studied the shores to port and starboard attempting to reconfirm a recognizable landmark. Hal broke away from the huddle at the table and followed him down the steps to the little cruiser. The muscle followed dutifully. The deckhand, who had been on station on the afterdeck well out of earshot of the conversations within, spoke to the mate via his walkie-talkie and followed the quartet to the landing stage where he took up the bow dock line. Sellars had quickly looked at the compass heading and then sighted across the gently bobbing compass card toward the landmark on the starboard shore. He muttered the bearing numbers and Mikey wrote them down at Sven's urging.

Hal stopped the muscle from boarding, then stepping down into the boat he took the PI by the arm and led him forward.

"You're reminded that you are participating in an operation involving national security and are accordingly subject to the security regulations that govern all such activity. These discussions are confidential and not to be repeated on penalty of law." It was a carefully memorized speech and he was most officious in its delivery.

"You're to be escorted to shore. You will be contacted in due time. You are to notify us by leaving a message at this number immediately upon contact by the suspects. You will be given explicit instructions on how you are to proceed." He handed Sellars a card with a hand-written phone number and turned to mount the stage.

The mate had come aboard and was stirring the engine to life.

Sellars followed Hal to the rail muttering the phone number aloud, then he shouted to Hal over the engine noise. Handing the card back, he said, "Tell Land to stick it in his ass. He knows my conditions." He turned away and the muscle tumbled aboard as the stern line was released and the small cruiser angled off.

Twenty minutes later Sellars and his escort came ashore at a municipal landing and the mate waved a friendly hand in departure.

"You guys need a ride somewhere?" Sellars asked.

"Naw," one of them replied. "We'll take a cab."

They walked toward the parking lot in silence. When Sellars paused at his car he asked: "You get much work from Hal?" The same one who had answered before immediately shook his head. The other blurted: "National security. Not allowed to talk about it." And he scowled at his companion who just shrugged and they walked on toward a cab lurking at the curb.

Sellars eased the big Chrysler into the traffic and noted that the cab pulled into the stream a couple of cars behind. Accordingly he decided against the drive to Dinner Key marina and began his oral report as he threaded his way through the near midnight Miami traffic.

"OK. I think all this NS stuff is bullshit. I'm betting that this is a private excursion by these guys using their official capacity to throw weight around. The two stooges that just got off the boat with me are nothing but small time hoods looking for an easy buck. They're not trained operatives. That's why ya-all got away clean from the motel.

"I don't quite know what to make of the woman, Madeline. It looked like she was trying to tell me something but couldn't because Hal was too close.

"Land is obviously the brains. I suspect that he's a retired spook—that's why he could show no ID. The chubby guy, Buford Winfrey, who is obviously pissed about his boat, is still active, maybe involved in the caper out of some loyalty to Land, who may have been his superior at one time.

"Hal is a low level field operative who might be effective in a legit operation, but is operating too close to supervision for comfort and without the backup of the organization.

"There was a younger woman who refused to escort me to visit Leda. I can only guess that she may be the daughter of Land that the mate referred to as his bartender. Madeline seems to be Winfrey's girlfriend.

"Summary. There are three competent men aboard. Two women who are probably not participants. The two crewmen appear to be outside the loop as well, but they would probably do what they were told if ordered to by Land.

"Now, listen carefully, here's the layout of the boat."

"Hold it a minute, Boss," Mikey broke in. "I think that's the boat that Joey Todd bounced on a couple of years ago. He's at the head of the dock. Why don't I get him over here and he can draw us a damn picture of it? I'll take the watch up there and he can come down here."

Sellars thought a moment, then concurred. "Call him first to make sure it's the same boat."

Mikey dutifully complied, got an affirmative answer and departed, stepping again on MOONSHOT's varnished rail.

Fats had been scrounging in his less than organized chart locker for the one that would give the largest scale look at where INSHALLA lay. Now he spread it on the cockpit table and turned on the light above it.

Sven busied himself with a piloting protractor. When Joey Todd arrived, he and Matt bent over the evolving sketch of INSHALLA's layout. As Sellars' transmission continued, he pointed out where he thought each of the boat's occupants would be at 3:00 a.m.

It was 1:30 when Joey left the trio in MOONSHOT's cockpit, their plans laid. It took another half hour to gather their meager armament and bundle into the freshly fueled runabout. As quietly as possible they threaded their way out to the channel where the gaunt figure of Fats Barlow, standing at the console, pushed the throttle full forward.

Matt shivered inside Eddie Malone's oversize wind breaker and had great trouble expelling a mental image of a print on his college dorm room wall—Don Quixote and Sancho Panza with a large windmill looming in the background.

Chapter Fifteen

ROSINANTE

The almost 45 minute ride to INSHALLA's anchorage gave Matt time to think about their latest march into danger. He had dealt well with the sudden confrontations aboard GULL and had for the most part accepted the deliberate counter actions that had been necessary. However this Sunday, from the time he discovered Leda missing until the end of the planning session to rescue her, the confrontations of this day had been sobering. He had been introduced to professional conduct that was in stark contrast to their own dangerous fumbling of the afternoon. The basically defensive actions taken within the small world of GULL was very different from the frontal attack they had mounted on the dark forces of the much larger universe beyond her narrow confines. The careful legal counsel that Sellars offered throughout the planning of their assault on INSHALLA was in sharp contrast to the buccaneering quality of their early efforts.

"I can't go any farther in this until I consult my client," he had explained. "Legally, with or without his consent, I got to report to the police my evidence that a crime has been committed—a kidnapping. I should do that immediately, but it would be understandable if I waited until morning. Now, ignoring the fact that I'm fracturing my client relationship by allowing you to "overhear" information that the client is paying to have protected as private—you might be wise to move on the information before these other parties have time to make decisions. I, of course, can't advise you to do anything illegal, but it has been my experience that local police are reluctant to buck any claim staked out by the feds, so they might turn a deaf ear at the first mention of NS.

"However, if you can rescue the kidnap victim, our combined testimony might get the FBI to investigate after the fact—they hate the spooks anyway.

"I can't risk losing my agency by taking part in what should be a police action, so you guys will have to do this thing yourself, tonight, with the only hope of help, if you get caught, to come tomorrow—if the police and FBI choose to move fast. Even then, if you blow it, you could all very quickly become fish food and all hands on INSHALLA could profess ignorance, or better yet, be in international waters."

The word fish food kept ringing in Matt's ears in the same way that the image of Quixote seared the backs of his eyelids each time he blinked.

Deep in the pockets of the oversize windbreaker, he grasped his only defense. On the right side he clutched the stub-nosed flare gun and on the left, two spare phosphorus flares. Sven had speculated that a phosphors flare fired at close range would perhaps not kill, but would burn hell out of the target and prevent his advance. Sven, as a result of his assignment, now had custody of Malone's heavy .45. Fats, peaceable soul that he was, had no weapons aboard except a CO-2 spear gun—which the desperate trio brought along because of the relative silence of its discharge. Each also carried that indispensable adjunct to every sailor's toolbox, the ubiquitous roll of duct tape.

This paucity of fire power was to be balanced by the element of surprise that the confident Sellars had emphasized. He had been sure that the enemy would be caught completely unaware, asleep, separated and disorganized. He was equally sure that no watch would be set. The two crew members were not going to burden themselves without specific orders to the contrary. And Land, he thought, was very confident that tonight was too soon to be wary. Sven, nevertheless, had modified the plan to deal with the eventuality of a watch.

Matt was concerned about the older man's heightened aggressiveness after the anchor chain episode aboard GULL that afternoon. Could he be over-extending them again on this mission? Matt had never had cause to doubt his friend, but they had never faced these kinds of situations before. And Sven had woefully underestimated Sellars. After this, a gale at sea would be a piece of cake.

He was suddenly aware that Fats had eased the throttle and that he and Sven were in whispered confab at the console.

Ahead in the moonless dark the port lights of a large yacht glowed in wrinkled reflection on the dark water. As they drew near he saw the little cruiser which tirelessly rubbed her flanks on the fenders edging the landing stage.

It was impossible to see if a watch stood on the broad afterdeck of the larger craft.

They would approach from astern at dead slow until a quarter-mile away, then kill the motor and running lights and paddle the rest of the way.

At fifty yards off, GULL's crew lay down in the bottom of the runabout and covered themselves with a shred of old spinnaker that Fats used for a fishing sunshade, leaving him to paddle the now clumsy craft alone.

After what seemed an over-long time, Matt felt the gentle bump as the runabout nudged the little cruiser's shiny side. The cruiser's higher profile and greater length allowed the smaller boat to crouch along her starboard rail, out of sight of the yacht's afterdeck.

At a hiss from Fats, Matt rolled from beneath the nylon and, hand-over-hand, pulled the boat far enough forward to tie its painter to a life line stanchion on the larger boat. Fats then pulled her back to align her console with the boarding break in the little cruiser's varnished rail.

The canvas flaps attached to the cruiser's overhead which earlier had been rolled up to allow access, were now securely zipped down fore and aft. Fats stepped back as each of his friends began to ease amazingly loud zippers up sufficiently to allow them to wallow under the flap and onto the cruiser's deck. The transparent plastic window in the flap on the port side was not clear enough to see anything except that the stage was empty.

Fats, who had followed them aboard, urged them on and out under the partially unzipped port flap, then busied himself with completing the unzipping of both flaps as the boarders crept up the flight of steps. The port flap was secured down with a length of duct tape for easy, silent opening on the trio's return. He rolled up and snapped the starboard flap into place. Then he crawled forward along the narrow side deck and adding a length from his locker to the port bow line, tied it in a new knot, leaving the long bitter end trailing back to the runabout's console. A vigorous tug would untie the knot and quickly free the bow of the boat.

He then began the most difficult part of his task—he sat in the stern of the cruiser's afterdeck peering through the unzipped crack in the port flap and ...waited.

Near the top of the ladder, Matt found himself in the familiar position behind Sven. The two, over the years, had arrived at this relative positioning and Matt had never questioned it. The older man's expertise afloat made the relationship obvious. However, his series of decisions, beginning with the sinking of MOTHER'S FUR COAT had revealed a destructive facet to Sven's nature that had never been apparent before. The rigorous response to the threat to their lives aboard GULL had seemed necessary and right at the time. Now Matt wondered if the sinking of the big sport fisherman had been overkill. Were they now again forced to risk their lives and had they risked Leda's, because they had overreacted in the darkness of the Alley? Was Sellars, vindictive because of his humiliation at Sven's extreme actions on Sunday afternoon, leading them into a trap? Purposely urging them into a situation that he knew they were too inexperienced to handle?

Sven's signal precluded any further speculation. It was no time to break faith.

Light from the saloon tumbled onto the afterdeck from the glass half of the mahogany doors, now closed against the humid night air. As they scrambled over the closed gate in the railing, Matt paused to examine the catch. Could he manipulate it with an armload of drugged Leda? Would it make a noise as it was being opened? Could he get her over the rail without opening the gate? Why hadn't he told Fats to see to it that it was open in preparation for their return?

The brightly lit saloon was cheap insurance against collision in a narrow anchorage and it conveniently prevented the necessity of the duo feeling their way among the scattered tables and chairs in the dark. Their naked exposure was the down side. They deftly moved chairs away from the stationary tables, opening as wide an escape route as possible. At the arch there were no light switches to be found on the bulkhead, but behind the bar a small box of circuit breakers allowed Sven to darken the saloon and the passage beyond. Only the spill from a large brightly lit clock face on the bar side of the arch reflected off the wall and produced a flash of the illuminated Matt as he hurried on his errand.

Inadvertently Sven flicked a breaker that set a mirror ball turning, reflecting the narrow shafts of four pin spotlights. It provided a murky half-light streaked by the spiraling individual colored squares. He left it on. It would provide enough light to negotiate the tables on their return, yet not illuminate the interlopers so fully.

It was dark past Land's door on the port side. Bubba and Madeline were probably in the first starboard cabin and perhaps Fran and Hal, separately, further down opposite one another.

Past the door to the crew quarters the passage was also dark except for a dull glow from red bulbs at either end. Their gleam lent an unreal quality to the grim countenances of the rescuers. Matt raised a hand, paused in front of the door Sellars had designated as Leda's cell, listening. Sven did likewise at the others—two of which should have held the mate and the deck hand behind them. No snores betrayed occupancy. He shrugged his lack of information to Matt, who then checked the first two dark sconces to no avail and found the key in the third.

Sven had moved on to the spiral staircase which led up to the pilot house and down to the engine room. His deck shoes made no sound on the perforated steel steps as he mounted enough to confirm an empty wheel station. Below, it took him longer to prowl the huge, well-lit engine room behind the sound-proof door at the bottom of the steps.

Caged work lights glowed brightly. A primary diesel generator and its standby were easily identified relatively near the door to the right. Then there were air conditioning compressors, tool racks, work benches, large fuel tanks and spare parts lockers. Finally, completing the U-shaped perimeter surrounding the two huge engines, there were Halon fire suppression tanks. Their attendant piping and nozzles formed a necklace around the entire room. Alternate portholes were opened around the semi-circle to allow for cross ventilation.

There was no one there.

Sven returned to the crimson companionway where Matt stood with key in hand before Leda's cell. He nodded and passed on to the door that separated the two communities aboard ship. Opening it a crack so that he could watch the passage on the other side, he turned, nodded again to the scarlet figure at Leda's door and then drew Eddie Malone's heavy .45.

The key, of course, sounded overloud in the lock and the click as the lever handle turned, assured Matt that it would awaken Leda and frighten her. But he need not have feared, for when he let himself into the soft darkness its occupants were awake and waiting.

"It's about time," the woman hissed, as she snapped on the light over the navigation table. Straightening, Madeline adjusted the negligee which had gaped open when she stooped over the desk. In the semi-darkness, Fran steadied Leda, who clung weakly to the back of one of the stuffed chairs. Two faltering steps brought her into the surprised Matt's arms.

"Matt!" she cried. " Twice," she mumbled in his ear.

"What?" he said.

"Matt??" Fran said in an incredulous voice. Stepping into the light, she caused the still startled rescuer to turn so she could see his face.

"Flash!?" he exclaimed in wonder and disbelief. "What the hell are you doing here? What are you mixed up in now?" Immediately he had another pair of arms about him and a second worried countenance thrust next to Leda's.

"My dad…" she began in a strained whisper.

"Land…? he croaked.

"Oh, God, I'm glad to see you. You always know what to do." She kissed him, squeezing all three heads together in a massive hug.

"No time for mushy love stuff," Madeline said, parting them unceremoniously and pushing Fran completely out of reach. "She's too woozy to make it down that ladder to the stage," she continued, nodding toward Leda. "Do you know how to do a fireman's carry?" she asked the still stunned Matt. He nodded dumbly as Madeline turned him around and struck him lightly on the shoulder. He dutifully crouched and she draped Leda over his back, leading both her arms over his shoulders. "Keep hold of both of them," she ordered, clasping the girl's hands together. Matt, whose brain had begun to work again, produced his trusty roll of duct tape and Madeline deftly wound a two foot strand around the girl's crossed wrists, firmly attaching Leda to him and freeing at least one of his hands to fend or fight. Madeline placed herself in front of Matt, her back to the door.

"The crew will sleep through or ignore noise around this cabin. Fran's is the first cabin on your left in the other passage. She'll go back to it first so if anybody has heard you they'll see her and won't pay any attention. The guy opposite is a newcomer, I don't know about him. *Be quiet.* Bubba, in the last cabin on your left, can sleep through a hurricane—and did. The guy across the hall is the boss and a light sleeper. He may just figure it's me, but he is just as likely to check to be sure. *Be quiet!*" She repeated. Then opening the door she urged the protesting Fran out with repeated hushes. A surprised Sven held the door for her as she approached, finger to her lips.

Madeline waited until she was sure Fran's door was closed, then she ushered the burdened Matt into the glow of the corridor. Sven, holding his door open as Matt crept through, gaped in surprise again at the satin clad figure in his wake. Pausing in the light of the red globe, she looked at him knowingly and whispered: "Be careful who you party with." Then with a wink she turned on slippered feet and re-entered the cabin she had just come from, closing the door behind her.

The phrase rattled around in Sven's head, but he was too busy watching the progress of his partner to be able to place it. When Matt cleared the arch into the saloon and no doors opened in wonder, he strode to the arch himself, paused to see that he had stirred no curiosity in passing, crossed the dance floor, then wove his way between the tables to the afterdeck.

Matt was halfway down the run of steps, walking backwards to keep Leda's feet from dragging on the steep flight. Sven watched until Fats flung open the canvas flap, and rescuer and rescued disappeared onto the little cruiser. Then whirling, he danced back into the salon, almost pirouetting among the tables, his deck shoes silent on the shiny mahogany.

Past the arch and then the door, he lunged for the spiral steps and flung himself down them. Wedging the engine room door open with a wooden shim that had been used for the purpose many times before, he strode to the first rack of tools, didn't find what he had seen before and went to the next. Then snatching what he needed, he opened a metal bin and removed a handful of oily shop towels.

Back near the door Sven looked at the gauge on the elevated diesel fuel tank next to the generator. It read at half tank—about 25 gallons he estimated. The copper tube that fed the generator engine came out of a large fitting on the top of the tank. The other end fed the row of fuel jets at the engine. When disconnected that end was lower than the bottom of the tank. He knelt and sucked on the brass fitting until the oil burned his tongue. He unbent the tube slightly and a solid stream coursed out, pouring through the steel grating that served as a walk way around the room. Lifting a short section of the grate, Sven saw that the rapidly forming pool would soon overflow the compartment formed by the structural members of the hull and eventually flow into the shallow sump amidships that served as a bilge.

Straightening, Sven strode to the bank of Halon tanks and rapidly twisted their valves shut. Then returning to the widening pool of diesel oil he dumped the handful of shop towels in. Nice thing about diesel, he thought, it doesn't flash like gas. Picking up the propane torch he had brought from the rack, he scraped its lighter in front of the nozzle and the blue flame leapt out, seeming in search of something to burn. It found it in the mound of rags in the middle of the pool. Dropping the tank, Sven turned and fled up the steps.

Pausing a moment outside the cabin where Leda had
been kept, he opened the door slightly and said evenly,
"Fire! Abandon ship! Hurry!"

Inside he interrupted a glaring Madeline, duct tape wound around her mouth, as she had just finished binding her ankles and was preparing to twist the sticky stuff around her wrists. Sven didn't see this, of course, and he ran on, through the door, which closed behind him, and on to the arch where he turned, and with pistol drawn shouted, "FIRE, FIRE! ABANDON SHIP!"

Hal was the first into the dark corridor. He stood in his shorts blinking in the shaft of white light that tumbled through his open door. He looked dumbly at the figure standing silhouetted in the faint glow of the clock.

"You'd better move yer ass," Sven prodded. "The engine room is afire."

At that moment the door to the crew's quarters burst open and a wide eyed Madeline hopped forth on taped together feet tearing at the gag. Smoke poured after her through the open door.

"FIRE," she screamed when she finally fought the tape off her face. This brought Fran into the dark hall and shouts from the crew's quarters beyond. Land was next into the corridor, his pants on and a 9mm. pistol in his hand.

Sven bolted across the tiny dance floor and turned in the greater safety of the semi-darkness, the .45 extended, as the entire ship's company, including the tardy Bubba, surged into the swirling light of the mirror ball. The deck hand had wisely shut the door to the forward part of the ship and cut off the gathering pall of smoke in the passageway.

"I've got the girl," Sven exulted. "I ought to let all of you fry, but I think some of you are ignorant." At that moment he remembered who Madeline was. But there was no time to dwell on it.

Land stood in front of the rest, as they, all clad in underwear or night clothes, formed a semicircle to his right and left, the forward points of which being Hal and the awakening Bubba. Madeline sat in the light stripping the last of the tape from her ankles.

"Your shore boat is gone," Sven lied. "You'd best get your butts overboard." Sighting down the barrel, he hoped that Land could not see the .45 waver in his hand. He also hoped that he made a poor target in his dark jeans and Fat's black sweat shirt.

As for Land, he held his weapon waist high,

its muzzle seeming to automatically seek out its target.

"So who the hell are you? John Wayne?" the big man asked. He stood, broad shoulders only slightly stooped, a hulking silhouette against the slightly brighter, clock-lit arch.

"I'm what used to be known as a citizen." Sven spat. "And I'm pissed at being treated like a piece of shit by out-of-control assholes like you. Believe me, if it wasn't for the crew and the women, you would be a dead man now." A bright square of light traveled across Land's face momentarily revealing the intensity of the watery blue gaze.

"Ya'all are the sombitch that sunk ma boat, aintcha?" Bubba interrupted taking a step forward.

"I'm the 'sombitch' that is gonna kill you if you

move anything on your body again," Sven replied. Bubba stood still, his hands doubled into fists resting where his shiny bare hips emerged from his pajama bottoms.

Sven went on. "Th' fire in th' engine room has a good head start, th' suppression system is disabled. It may just burn for a long time or it may find somethin' it particularly likes down there and cause an explosion. In any case this ship is going to burn and burn fast." As if in punctuation, a puff of black smoke rose up the staircase from the casino deck and wafted out into the saloon.

Sven began to back away and Land's 9 mm rose higher with each step he took. Suddenly with a shriek, Madeline grabbed Fran's hand and bolted through the tables on Sven's right, dragging the startled girl with her.

"We're all agonna die! We're all agonna be burned to death!" she wailed.

Taking advantage of the momentary distraction, Sven turned, ducked and ran. Land raised the gun to fire, but both Hal and Bubba were between him and his target, either in pursuit of Sven or in haste toward the rail. Sven arrived at the afterdeck, crossed it in a stride, leapt to the top of a lifejacket locker, paused a moment and dove over the stern just as the repeated crack of the 9mm reached his ears.

Matt, standing on the stage with the stern dock line in his hand, was surprised to see the two women at the head of the steps instead of Sven and then was dismayed to hear gun shots and splashes. Fat's engineering background had been applied to the little cruiser's ignition system and its motor now sprung to life.

Madeline dragged the panicked Fran onto the stage, whirled and grasping her shoulders, said something that shocked her. Then the older woman pushed her unceremoniously onto the boat, which only Matt's curiosity continued to hold to the stage.

"Sven?" he blurted after Madeline.

"In the water," she said without turning and she too scrambled aboard the cruiser.

As she spoke other splashes were heard behind him and Matt tossed the line aboard and leapt after it. Fats, unable to hear over the noise of the idling motor, and assuming the latest arrival to be Sven, pushed the throttle forward and the tandem boats moved off into the night.

Sven had been in the water a half hour when they finally heard his hoarse cry. The ebbing tide had carried him almost a quarter mile aft of INSHALLA and if he had not come upon one of the life jackets the mate had had the presence of mind to throw overboard, he might not have been able to stay afloat.

The limp left arm insisted on bleeding even with the clumsy tourniquet he had rigged. The slug, the shock and the fatigue had pushed him near to passing out by the time half dozen hands finally dragged him over the transom of Fat's fishing runabout. Only then did he notice its name: ROSINANTE. His mind smiled, even if his tired body could not, at Fat's sense of humor.

But, his subconscious only saw irony as he became vaguely aware of trussed bodies lying on the afterdeck of the little cruiser to which the runabout was still tied. For, as he slipped into the black void of unconsciousness someone was intoning the mantra: "You have the right to remain silent. Anything that you say…."

Chapter Sixteen

The Thin Lady Sings.

Sven's arm ached. The slug had splintered the bone in his upper arm and, while now healed, he had been told that it would ache on occasion. This was one of those occasions. He, Matt, Leda, Fats and Fran Harrington sat on the hard seats in the Federal court house in Miami listening to the drone of the lawyerese fall like a pall of smog around them.

They had completed their testimony earlier but had sat, patiently waiting for what was to be the hearing's star witness. Now at almost 11:30 and without a lunch break, she had just been called. As the woman they all knew as Madeline entered from a special waiting room and approached the witness stand, they straightened in their seats to appraise her. This was the first time they had seen her since the dark night six weeks before. She had been very busy.

As she stepped up on the platform which supported the stand, her tanned calf appeared in the split of the tailored white skirt. The navy blue jacket, tucked about her narrow waist flared into wide lapels trimmed in white piping. The collar of a white satin blouse splayed atop the lapels. Her sun-bleached hair had been trimmed and it framed a face now demurely made up. The lashes, no longer mascara clotted, rimmed steady brown eyes that seemed very different than the blue, contact-tinted ones they all remembered.

"Identify yourself, please," the clerk instructed.

"I am Mary Lee Fredrick, Special Agent in the Counter Intelligence Division, Federal Bureau of Investigation, Headquarters, Washington, DC. Temporarily attached to Miami District."

Matt looked across at the defendants table. Hal sat stoically, turned half away from Bubba. The latter gazed with a mixture of hurt and hate at this woman he had spent so much time with and whom he had thought so little of.

The judge leaned forward holding an open file folder, "In an earlier deposition you identified the defendants as active operatives of the CIA, Covert Operations Unit whom you observed and gathered evidence against in the act of abrogating certain sections of the Federal Criminal Code. Is that correct, Agent Fredrick?"

"That is correct, your honor."

"These activities apparently went beyond the specific charges of kidnapping on which they are currently here arraigned?

"That's accurate, although that act was in some respect the culmination of a series of desperate efforts to cover earlier irregularities in their behavior and that of others stretching back as much as 35 years."

Her voice betrayed none of the poor English that had characterized her as Matt had first listened from MOONSHOT's cockpit or as Fran had come to know her in their tangential relationship.

"For the record," the Judge asked in proper tones, then in a more conversational mode: "You have observed the testimony of a series of witnesses earlier today. To what degree are you able to corroborate the testimony of any of these participants?"

"All of that which Ms. Frances Harrington spoke of while in my company. She indicated the several occasions when I was a guest aboard her father's yacht. In earlier depositions I detailed my observations and noted recorded evidence gathered at those times which verifies her testimony."

"Is it your conviction that Ms. Harrington was not an accessory to the kidnapping which is the central issue of this hearing?"

"I am convinced that Ms. Harrington was not aware of the planning of the crime, nor was she a party to its commission and when she became aware of it after the fact, she argued vehemently with her father about it and threatened to expose the crime."

"And why didn't she inform the proper authorities?"

"She had no real opportunity to do so because in some respects we were all prisoners aboard the yacht. That is, Mr. Harrington controlled the limited access to shore. In addition, I believe that Ms. Harrington had constantly to struggle with the misinformation her father gave her about his activities. She had been taught since childhood that she was not to question his actions. They were all a part of his mysterious job and, according to him, always justified—and legal—no matter how questionable."

"Do you have any direct evidence of this?"

"Yes, several times I heard them in intense quarrels about 'ends justifying means'; 'greatest good for the greatest number' and other quasi-philosophical subjects. On the Sunday in question she had unburdened herself to me at length on her doubts about the veracity of her father's explanation of the victim's presence. The story he told her was different from what he had told me and the crew earlier—that the victim was his sister. Ms. Harrington was pretty sure that the one explanation was as bogus as the other."

"Can you corroborate any other testimony?"

"Yes. Those portions of Mr. Blair's and Mr. Olafson's statements concerning the actual rescue of the victim from the yacht. I only suspected Mr. Olafson's setting fire to the engine room. All the statements of Ms. Harrington and Ms. Malone are accurate according to my observations on the day in question. I was not privy to Ms. Harrington's confrontation with her father nor the interview between Mr. Harrington and the victim before she was sedated."

The Judge nodded. And paging through items clamped to the back of one of several folders at his elbow, he paused, adjusted his glasses and asked: "How is it that you were able to record such intimate conversations among the accused when you were brought along to these meetings as, in your own words, a 'party girl'?"

"I and other women were brought along on various trips aboard both Mr. Winfrey's and Mr. Harrington's yachts as much for cover as for the parties. They were very interested in making their movements look as much like lavish holiday activities as possible. At the times when we were left alone while the men parleyed, there was always a large screen TV for our amusement. My remote earphone which appeared to be plugged into the TV's audio track, was in reality a high fidelity eavesdropping system which allowed me to hear and record many of their sessions held on deck or in the saloon of the yachts."

Seeming to be satisfied with the answer, the judge closed the prominent folder and shuffled for another. Scanning its brief, he nodded, turned and removing his glasses, asked:

"Why were you on hand to assist the 'rescuers'?"

"When Mr. Sellars visited the victim, I told him when she was due for her next sedative in an attempt to let him know when she would be most able to help herself. I could not be sure why he was there, but I hoped he would be sharp enough to indicate to the authorities that any rescue attempt would be best planned around that time. I also attempted to prompt his speculation that I was not what I seemed and that there was significance in what I was saying."

"That you could be counted on to assist?"

"Not necessarily. It was more that I could be trusted."

Donning his glasses, the judge glanced at the folder, then closed it, removed them again in an almost comic sequence and turning again, he asked what appeared to be a troubling question.

"All of the witnesses on the small boat that night have testified that after abandoning the yacht, every effort was made to locate Mr. Harrington, the defendant charged as the prime mover in this case. Are you confident that such effort was indeed made?"

"Yes, your Honor. I believe…."

"The search was not called off hastily because of the wounding and collapse of Mr. Olafson?" the judge interjected.

"No, your Honor. We had been systematically searching the area for half an hour prior to picking Mr. Olafson out of the water. According to others who abandoned the yacht after Mr. Olafson, Mr. Harrington was the last to jump. Since Mr. Olafson was first he had been carried the farthest away by the tide. It was the consensus of the group of experienced—what I might call 'water-wise'—people among us that logically Mr. Harrington should have been nearer the yacht and nearer to our rescue efforts. I think it is significant that we searched near the yacht for the better part of the half hour before finding Mr. Olafson and found no trace of Mr. Harrington, even though the yacht's crewman believed that the defendant had one of the life jackets. Since we rescued Mr. Olafson primarily because we were able to see the emergency light attached to his life jacket and no other light nor any shouts answered our calls during the following fifteen or twenty minutes, I feel sure that we did all we could."

"Is it possible that Mr. Harrington did not want to be rescued?"

"In circumstances like these that is always a possibility. But, Mr. Harrington is over 70 years old and it would take a man of consummate self-confidence to make that choice. Either way."

"Either way?"

"Yes. Either to take his chances on escaping or to decide to die rather than being picked up and face prosecution."

"In your estimation, then, did the man survive?"

"I would have to turn to Mr. Olafson's testimony for support. He was in the water longer than anyone else. He is the most experienced of any of us relative to matters of the sea. This morning he estimated the speed of the tide race to be such that only the strongest of swimmers, without the encumbrance of a life jacket, could have made it to either shore before being swept by that tide into the bay."

"And, of course, neither a body nor that last life jacket has been found," the judged finished.

With that, the judge appeared to lose interest in the proceedings and they lumbered in a humdrum of routine legal technicalities and on to a final gavel which mercifully released them all into the merciless midday Miami heat.

"I'm starved," Matt blurted.

"I need a beer," Fats offered.

"Best testimony all day," Sven agreed.

Leda looked at Fran. The two had gotten acquainted in the past few weeks. Most of the time Matt had been between them, in mind or in flesh. Leda, at 34, had felt older lately. There was only four years difference in the women's ages, but she was definitely in competition with a younger woman. Damn thing about it she could detect no real effort being made by Fran. Her presence seemed threat enough. Leda was mature, Fran was young. Leda thought about things; Fran did things.

"I've got to fly out tonight," Matt said in response to Fats query. "The red-eye to Apple city then the commuter to Beantown in the morning," finally looking Leda in the eye. "I'm about to lose a big contract. I've got to be there for the final negotiations."

"What happened to Smoky Joe, the miracle manager?" she asked. They had had this argument last night—she knew the answer.

He smiled weakly. "One of my first clients. She—er—they expect a little personal attention. I'll call you later," he quickly followed up.

"I won't be home 'til late." And she walked into the simmering mirage of the macadam parking lot.

"I'm not hungry," Fran said. "But, I've got a hell of a headache and I can't face that hotel room. Mind if I tag along with you guys? Maybe I can pick up an aspirin along the way."

When Matt did not respond immediately, Sven spoke up.

"Sure. I donno this area, but maybe we can find
a drug store along here somewhere."

The four turned and ambled aimlessly toward the first opportunity for food, each locked in thoughts—memories refreshed by the morning's proceedings.

Matt unconsciously shook his head to dislodge the images of the aftermath of the attack on INSHALLA. A dozen times in the past six weeks he had awakened from the dream. It was always the same—dragging the bodies out of the black water, the flashing firelight of the doomed casino painting each in red and tricking his tired eyes with the prospect of blood streaked corpses—each a death chalked up against his conscience. Each time he woke up he had to remember that there had been only the near fatality of Sven and the apparent one of Harrington. But these had been enough. They had affected him deeply. And that impact had caused sharp confrontations after Sven had begun to recover. Matt found it hard to accept his friend's simple explanation that he could not risk letting these men who had threatened their lives, slip away to threaten them again. And the only way to deal safely with them, he had argued, was one at a time on his terms for a change—as they needed to be plucked out of the water—to save their own lives. *Ergo* INSHALLA had to be destroyed so they would abandon ship. The end justified the means.

But Matt had a growing conviction that the endangerment of four innocents— only one of whom was trained to deal with such situations—made him and his allies as reckless and as irresponsible as the criminals.

A restaurant door with a large sign offering air conditioning beckoned them to enter.

"Do you think he's dead?" Fats asked as he slipped into the semi-circle of the vinyl-clad booth.

"Dead or damn lucky," Sven said with conviction. A conviction that was part of the total stance taken in his arguments with Matt. And it was the part that had not been shaken. Internally, his young friend's ethics had gotten to him and he had traced his own progression from the reluctant ambusher of MOTHER'S FUR COAT to the hostile belligerent firing INSHALLA's engine room. Yet, outwardly he clung to his position for some obstinate, Yankee reason. Lately, he had been careful to avoid the subject with Matt. Both hoped their friendship could overcome the difference.

All of that aside, he was confident that Land was dead.

"Sorry, Fran. Didn't mean ta be callous."

"No offense taken," she replied, scooting around the arc next to Fats, then craning immediately to spot a waitress.

"What prompts a man like that to go bad?" Fats wondered.

"Power corrupts, my educated friend tells me," Sven answered nodding toward Matt, who, almost reluctantly, moved in to sit beside Fran.

Deciding it was not a challenge, Matt finished the quote, "And absolute power corrupts absolutely."

"But your father came from family, money, position," Fats said to the pained girl beside him. "Guys like that are born with power."

"Being a little powerful isn't like being a little pregnant," Fran counseled. Sven, squinting at the glossy menu, peered over the top of it as she finished. "A little bit is not enough to do the job."

"Care for a drink while ya'all decide?" the waitress asked, smiling her tip-provoking grin.

"Draft here," Fats said raising his hand.

"Two," said Sven, missing the offered smile as he continued to study the menu.

"Three," nodded Matt.

"Have you got an aspirin, by any chance?" Fran's countenance underscored her need.

"No, Hon. But I got a seltzer tablet. Will that do?" Fran's smile and nod sent her on her errand of mercy.

Matt continued his thought. "Well, in some ways power is like being pregnant. Once the seed is planted it tends to grow. The first conquest is the birth of a series of bigger and better opportunities."

"You'd think the family's reputation would be a check," Fats offered again.

"Black sheep are rarely concerned about the family's good name," Fran corrected.

"Damn shame too," Sven said looking up. "I remember yer granddaddy gave a lot of money to open up a bunch of orphanages."

"Well, he was busy creating that good name Fats was talking about. His dad was one of the robber barons of the last century and charity had not been one of great-granddad's chief interest. But granddad's was the generation with the first Ivy League liberal education and the first to decide that public service was a duty to his less fortunate countrymen."

"Yeah, it was sort of a game of dividin' up the world if I remember right. One son ran fer governor, 'nother fer the Congress, yet another was a ambassador."

"Yeah," Fran agreed, "But they always kept one in the kitchen, of course, stirring the family business interests so everyone could continue to eat very high on the hog. I guess if Land had kept up the tradition, I'd have been the cook, except I only like making enough money for myself. I don't think I'd want to spend the time necessary to keep all the rest of them fat."

Sven closed the menu. "Kennedys may be the last of that kind."

"The family was traditionally Republican," Fran countered, "but no one in my generation wants to run with the current crowd of that name."

"There's another factor with Land," Matt said, returning to the initial point." He was the last of the brood, you said. Your uncles are all dead now?"

"Yes. They were all much older than he was. By the time he came along they had all the good jobs. He was spoiled, according to my mother. Wild and rebelling against pretty much all that the family stood for. Then suddenly when he was 25 he was recruited by the spooks and he seemed to find his place in the world.

"Ten years later he had pushed his way into and through some pretty tough assignments and could begin to choose his jobs. In another ten, he seemed to be calling some very big shots. I was only five when I remember he was suddenly home a lot more and we began to spend a lot of time on vacations in the Bahamas and the Caribbean. He seemed happier, my mom said. He told her that now he could keep an eye on what he called an old enemy."

"Here's your seltzer, hon. The barkeep's tapping a new keg, guys. It'll be a minute for the beer. You ready to order?

Orders were given and taken and attention turned again to Fran's story. "At first the boats were modest ones, so as not to attract undue attention, but by the time I was 10 something had changed and the boats had become large and were tactical command centers. Of course I didn't know that then. But that's when my mom's health started to go and she was left behind with greater and greater regularity. I was in school, of course, but always taken along on any break. It was about then that Mom told me about his job and that I was not to be surprised at anything I saw or heard, but that I was never to repeat any of it. And most important, he was never to be questioned about it. We were always to pretend that we were wealthy people doing what wealthy people do. Which to a large degree we were.

"After Mom died, there were always several men and two or three 'party girls' aboard. Once when I was in college the first time, I'd brought a boy along to spend the spring break. We had found a little privacy in a small dark compartment of the yacht, but I knew by then that I wasn't supposed to be hearing what we overheard through the bulkhead. The day before I returned to school, Land and I had a long talk, one of many that would span the years. Talks about right and wrong, patriotism, democracy, ethics…."

Fran had gulped the seltzer, but her face showed no signs of relief. Matt studied this woman he had once loved. Now almost thirty, she was perhaps at the peak of her adult beauty and sophistication. No physical aspect betrayed any hint of age except the eyes which in unguarded moments held hints of fear and a knowledge of life beyond her years.

Salads were served and Fats' query about the beer was met with that large smile and a promise of a prompt return.

"I left college after my sophomore year because I wanted to interfere in what Land was doing and I could only do that by being free to move about at will. I had come into my inheritance at 18 and was at first intrigued by the financial advisor, whose first year's salary was a part of it. He taught me to do some clever investing and I continued to do that. The money and free time made it possible to dog Land's movements.

"After a couple of years I had to have more and better arguments and I went back to school where I met Matt. I tried to use him in my project, but he foiled me because he was always working. Often when it was most critical—a time when we could have confronted Land, Matt was too busy. And because of the nature of the whole spook business I could never bring myself to level with Matt.

"Then two years ago Land retired. Actually he had officially retired earlier, but had stayed active in order to, in his words, 'clean up a few details'. Things went from bad to worse. His actions became more brazen. He seemed to focus on only one operation. There were mad races around the Caribbean. Strange people began to appear on the scene. Only occasionally did the activity resemble what had gone on before. And it had often been weird before.

"My own life was going down the tubes. I lost Matt because I was incommunicado most of the time and I also hesitated to involve him in what was becoming more and more legally questionable.

"Before long, I realized that Land was working outside the Company. He appeared to be obsessed with the project and so secretive that methods I had used for years to monitor the operations failed to reveal anything. Former fellow operatives who would occasionally drop by, fell into two groups. Some who subtly cautioned him about something and others who seemed to be urging something onto him. I didn't know what it was until you guys told me what Carlos revealed. But in the meantime, I had grown frightened and tried to reach him. His reactions would border on violence. Finally I felt that maybe all I could do was try to prevent some ultimately stupid act." She paused, looked longingly at the beer being served, then finished.

"But, finally, I couldn't do that either."

They ate in silence.

"When are you going north?" she asked, changing the subject.

"Tonight," Sven answered between bites. "Only thing that's been keepin' me here is this damn hearin' today. The yard had GULL ready two weeks ago."

"Yeah, but that wing of yours wasn't ready two weeks ago," Fats admonished. "I wish you'd wait a week so I could go with you. My grand kids are coming to visit," he shared with Fran. "And I don't get to see them that often anyway. You damn stubborn Yankee!"

"Yeah, and single-handing her is really nuts," Matt chimed in. "You know that arm's not back to full strength yet. If you'd just wait a week, I can wrap up things and be back here to help."

"Waal, I'll meet ya in Bermuda."

"Or at least coast hop," Fats pushed. "Non-stop to Bermuda would make sense if you had a crew, but you got a thousand miles by yourself."

"Twelve Hundred," Sven corrected.

"Yeah," Matt reasoned, "why go to Bermuda at all? You can coast hop all the way, except Hatteras."

"Waal, 'cause I reckon, I want ta sail the damn boat. I need ta clean out a lotta stuff that's all stuck inside me. Left over from this last job."

"I think he's getting senile," Matt baited. "I don't think he'd have done a damn-fool thing like that ten years ago."

"Lissen," Sven retorted, almost spilling his beer in his haste to set it down and reply. "Ten years ago I was single-handing boats all over the damn place!"

"Yeah, and ten years ago you were nearing 50, not 60," Fats posited.

"Waal, I can do more at 59 than most can do at 49!"

And so it went.

In the preceeding days, the FBI revealed that they had questioned Bubba Winfrey soon after GULL's arrival in Miami, but had released him when Madeline's larger investigation was threatened.

The Bahamian authorities were never able to apprehend a boat called PLEASURE HOUSE, but they did find Eddie Malone's body in a warehouse in Nassau. Pablo and the giant didn't talk much but the Coast Guard were satisfied, based on Leda's identification, that Pablo was involved in GAVIOTA's demise. So he was turned over to the Island police to prosecute for piracy and abetting in the murder of Malone. The giant was held until his wound healed, then returned to the Islands for prosecution in the boarding of GULL and the death of Ramirez.

GULL's crew never revealed to anyone but Fran that the mysterious canister had been found.

Carlos never showed up for work again.

"Don't th' idea of having th' money and th' time tempt ya ta do some cruisin'?" Sven prodded. He had watched Matt's careful walk of the tight rope between Fran and Leda over the past several weeks.

Matt was taking in the fenders, the last of several tasks he had helped with in Sven's race to clear the entrance channel before the twilight settled into darkness.

"Yes, but not much. Flash—Fran—tempted me that way long ago and I was able to turn a deaf ear to that siren song then. It's easier now. It was an immature romance. There is a very different thing going on between Leda and me. It has a breadth and depth—even in this short time—that I never had with Flash." He threw the last fender into the lazarette.

"Ya better take care a that situation. She didn't look none too happy when she left us at noon t'day."

"Taken care of," he answered, smiling in remembrance of the vision of Leda astride him an hour earlier in Eddie Malone's dusty apartment, the slanting rays of the late afternoon sun reddening her freckled breasts.

Sven had removed the mainsail cover and all but two stops so that he could hoist it quickly. Now he came back to the cockpit, surveyed the deck, glanced at the winch rigged halyard and turned the key to ignite the rumble of power.

Matt turned to his old chum and took his extended hand in both of his own. "Listen, you damn, hard headed, dear friend.... I wish to hell you would wait until I could go along on this hayride. I've never made an outside transit to New England. I'd dearly love to make my first one with you. And I don't think it's the best idea for you to single-hand it. But if you must—for Christ sake, practice what you preach. Don't fail the boat. She's well-found. She won't fail you." It was the only way he could say it: "Catch the tide. The Blue Peter is struck."

Matt stepped ashore, strode forward and releasing the bow line, he pushed the newly painted prow away from the dock. The stern line was similarly loosed and GULL moved, freed of her tether, free of the land.

Sven did not look back. The evening breeze held promise. Perhaps he could sail soon.

Out of the channel he felt the first surge of the sea under him. That movement rippled up his legs, rang some primeval bell in his genitalia and radiated out to the rest of his too-long land-bound body. The breeze was fresher. He swung the bow to his compass course. The zephyr blew from behind—past first one ear and then the other. A little fluky perhaps, but a following wind. Following wind and following sea. Good omens for a fast comfortable passage.

He coiled and stowed the dock lines. Looking for shipping on the darkening sea, he leaned in and flipped on his running lights. Then turning into the wind, he killed the engine, pulled the stops from the main and holding them in his teeth, he cranked the flapping main to the truck. Its sheet tackle clanked and jangled until he fell off the wind, the huge sail filled and the taut sheet quieted the noise.

He payed out the sheet gradually as he fell off and the wind moved astern. Finally the great sail flew well outboard to port. Deciding not to set a preventer yet—the fluky wanton might just be teasing—he carefully set the ginny on the starboard side. The jib was useless in this configuration

GULL settled a little uneasily to her wing-and-wing rig, but Sven soon came to gauge the rhythm of the following sea and subtle adjustments of the helm anticipated the minor yaw that might dump either sail. Once the wind veered suddenly and the long main sheet sagged, the tackle at the boom's end jangled loosely until Sven corrected and the sail filled again. He thought again of a preventer, but that could wait until he became bored. Now he wanted to sail the boat, to feel her every whim.

At first he did it consciously; then the sheer joy of being at sea and skillfully sailing a tricky wind, gave way to a feeling of simple subconscious contentment.

The dusk turned to dark and the light of the waning moon reflected dimly off the freshly varnished cockpit. Sven scanned the horizon for shipping, sat down behind the helm, looked at the red tinted compass card, then at the sails. Then for the first time in years, wished for a smoke. This had always been a time for a pipe—when the sails were set and the routine was established. He looked again at the card, a stronger puff pushed the bow past the lubber line and the next one pushed it back. The second time he looked quickly into the night sky between the two sails and tried to isolate a star on which to guide. It was easier than staring at the red light of the compass. But the slot between the forestay and the mast was narrow and he gave it up after a while and in some minutes fell into a mechanical series of helm adjustments freeing his mind to wander.

He rejected the first thoughts. He had poured over the events of the last couple of months too much. He had self-examined and Monday-morning-quarter-backed to an extreme.

He turned his thoughts to Sybil. Nigel had followed up, of course, to see that they had made Miami all right and she had found reason to make a trip too, but at the worst time. She came again when she had read in the papers that he had been wounded. He remembered her touch in the hospital. He remembered her touch on that night at Chub. He had to think about this woman. That's why he had to single-hand GULL at least as far as Bermuda. He had to think again and again about this woman…and the child.

After this trip to Block Island, he and Matt had to go back to Nassau to return the repaired GAVIOTA for Leda. He had to think about this woman now.

Uninterrupted.

He did not see Land's head emerge from the blackness of the cabin because he was mesmerized by Sybil's face super-imposed on the compass card. The big man was almost at the top of the ladder before Sven was aware of the movement and sprang to his feet.

Land, amazingly agile for his years, leapt from the bridge deck to the port cockpit seat. Sven's only thought, as the red oval faded from his after-sight and he looked clearly at the man standing in the puny moonlight, was the absurd fact that the man hadn't even dropped his damn 9mm when he leapt over INSHALLA's side. Its one eye stared unerringly into Sven's surprised face.

"Goddam, you're hard to kill," the big man said.

"I might say the same fer you," Sven growled in return.

"Yeah, but I've had more experience than you."

"Waal, if practice is any factor, I've had plenty a' that lately too."

"Un-huh. But as you can see," he waved the gun, "the old saying that 'practice makes perfect' is just an old saying."

The surprise was wearing off. Sven was thinking. He had to stall for time.

"Will ya hunt down the rest an' kill them too?" He didn't wait for an answer. "It'll be easy for ya now. Everybody pretty much thinks yer dead."

"In time. All in good time."

Neither man had been able to gauge the other in the semi-darkness of INSHALLA's saloon on their first confrontation. Now both gazed steadily into the opposing countenance—measuring, judging.

Land's already hulking figure seemed monstrously huge as he stood on the cockpit seat looking down on his trapped quarry. Tonight it was Sven's face that looked ghoulish in the red glare of the compass. Shining up from below, it cast strange shadows, but penetrated beneath his shaggy brows. Land could clearly see his opponent's eyes. There was no fear in them.

Suddenly the ginny began to flap. Sven, preoccupied, had temporarily abandoned his careful balancing act with the fluky breeze. Looking down at the card, he measured the distance to the lubber line and turned the helm accordingly, watched it begin to correct and as the ginny filled he countered to keep from spilling the main. Land had stopped talking.

"Why, Land? How in the hell can we harm ya in any way?"

The laugh that escaped from the big man's twisted mouth was a cross between a snarl and a sob. "No, it's not what you can do. No, no. Now, it's what you did."

"Now?"

"Oh, yes. You see your stupid meddling began as nothing more than an inconvenience, but it grew into encumbrance and finally to the destruction of years of careful work."

"Waal, at what point on that scale did our lives become so cheap? Please don't say 'inconvenience', ya arrogant bastard."

"No, it was 'encumbrance'. When Carlos decided it was worth trading the secret for the canister."

"What?" Sven looked down at the card regularly now. "Is yer stupid vanity so great that ya kill just to cover the possibility that someone would have believed our story about the CIA fuckin' up in 1963? Hell, half the population probably thinks that—in one version or another.

Besides, what's new? The Company's—isn't that what you hot shots call it—the Company's reputation is shit now anyway."

"Oh, yeah. Evaluation by a lot of ignorant bastards like you. But that's another sore. The real rub was Carlos spilling the New Cuba deal. He shouldn't have done that. That's when everybody's ass got very cheap. It was too early to have that blabbed about. By some amateurs like you—we could have lived with that—but we couldn't have Andrews and the crowd in Foggy Bottom dabbling about in it. We tried hard to get to you before you could report to Andrews. The Cubans fucked up and let the woman queer the rescue of canister. They were supposed to dispose of you that night, too."

Sven steered the boat, feeling the wind on the back of first this ear and then the other. "You spooks are so full of shit. So paranoid. Why should anybody be surprised that a buncha has-beens would have been willing to throw in with the 'enemy' to save yer precious reputations and egos? After all, as Carlos said, it was in both country's interest not to have that paper floatin' around."

"Oh, that was secondary as soon as he told you the other thing."

"What other thing? What the hell are you talking about?"

"The New Cuba thing. What? Were you too stupid to under-stand what he was saying?"

"Look, Land, Carlos said you and Castro's misfits had linked up in desperation to prevent th' documents surrounding th' assassination from becoming public. He said his Uncle was the prime mover in th' deal and that the man was already dead. He talked only vaguely about his group being one of several looking to overthrow Castro. I never heard the words 'New Cuba' 'till you stick you head up outta my damn boat wavin' yer surrogate dick around." He stopped and looked again at the crimson card. "By the way, where the hell were you? You're awful big to hide on a boat this size."

Land was studying the scarlet streaked face and he answered almost absently, "'Way up forward. Under the sail bags."

"Figures. Only compartment I had no reason to open today. How long you been in there?"

"Cut the bull shit. Carlos told you about everything the night Pablo and Big Foot boarded you at the CG station. They told us that he had been there an hour talking to you before they got organized enough to make the hit. We know what he said. They listened and later he verified what he had told you when he informed us that he had the papers."

Sven's mind raced. Had Carlos said more than they had understood that night? If not, had he lied to Land—and if so, why? Had he lied so that Land's people would do dirty work that he was too fastidious to do?

The sheet block at the end of the boom rattled as the strain was released. Sven had allowed the main to dump. He was brought back to attention as much by the automatic fall of his stomach as by the noise. He quickly prevented the jibe.

He had finally confirmed what GULL's trio had always feared was true. They were being hunted because of something they did not know rather than for something they did. There was little use trying to convince Land of that ignorance now, but if he could be made to talk about it, maybe Sven could buy time to organize his head. Accordingly he chose what he thought would get the biggest reaction.

"The only thing that Carlos hinted at was that you had cozied up to Castro. He didn't come right out an say ya was a traitor though."

He looked down at the card again.

"Traitor! What the fuck do you know about 'traitor'? You big mouth bastard. And your half-assed notion of putting things right. *A pissed citizen tired of being pushed around!* You dumb prick. Some of us spent almost fifty years trying to save you middle class bastards from yourselves. Or haven't you noticed that the 'New World Order' is a sack of shit that the rampant capitalists have permanently strapped around your neck?"

Land's vehemence jolted Sven. Was the man demented?

"We had one more chance to save you from yourselves—a small controlled experiment that would prove that there could be a Communism free of dictatorship. And you have screwed it up! Years of work!"

"Wait a minute!" Sven shouted in shocked amazement. "Is this Landon Winthrop Harrison th' second—or was it th' third? Whelp of th' original wolves of Wall Street tellin' me that he's a Red? Fifty years! Jesus, Land. Ya tellin' me ya've been a mole in the Company ever since ya wuz recruited? Right through to retirement?"

"That's right. That's what I'm telling you. Right through to retirement and after. Angleton didn't even get close to me. He could smell the smoke, but he could never find the fire."

"Now yer braggin'. So the end of all that lying' and treachery was some grandiose plan ta establish a reformed Communism in the West? In Cuba?"

"Yes. We had been playing ball with Castro for years and we knew that Cuba was the best place for it. We had finally convinced Fidel to trust us. Damn thing about it is it all could have been done in the fifties when he kicked the Mafia out—if it hadn't been for Nixon's political ambitions. He and his coterie convinced Ike that here was Stalin on his doorstep. All Fidel wanted to do was to stop the exploitation of his people. If the US had not been so stupid as to force him into the other camp, if they had helped him, instead of isolating him…." He was warming to his subject.

"How can *you* be a red, Land?" Sven's curiosity was more than tactical now.

"In 1946 the whole world knew that what Stalin called Communism was shit. By 1950 we knew the same disease had infected the Chinese brand. Neither of those was Communism. They were raw examples of tyranny that used the gullible, starving workers' need for change as a ladder to climb upon their backs and suppress them. The West cut them off and deprived them of everything that a successful economy,

Communist or Capitalist required. Capitalism did not triumph over Communism. Ronald Regan bankrupted it—just before he did us."

"So you and Castro was going ta give it a fresh start? Th' time is right. Th' world don't look too kindly now at the States continuin' pressure on him. He could look forward ta a more natural commerce with other countries?"

"So there we could see a progressive, pure Communism experiment on a small enough scale that it could be shaped and tweaked into the vision that Marx saw." Land was bordering on rapture.

"So that's what Carlos meant when he said his group was tryin' to control the hotheads. Th' exiles in Miami had ta be kept at bay. They couldn't be allowed ta topple Castro 'fore the mushrooms sprouted in this here dark, rarefied atmosphere where the experiment has ta be planted."

"And it had to be kept in the dark long enough to take root. Both political parties in the States are desperately looking for a diversion from their own problems. A Cuban boogie man would be perfect."

"So how many people did ya make suckers of, Land? Did Bubba really know what he was involved in? Did he think he was helpin' t' perfect the 'reputation' of the Company? Did Hal? What about poor Diego, that I almost killed twice? Was they all to be used as ya saw fit in this grand scheme ta keep afloat a dyin' dream?"

"They were expendable. Minor players, small time crooks. Useful for the short term in their petty roles for the greater good that the experiment would prove."

"Don't sound too much different from th' tripe Stalin and Mao preached. And I guess that was th' philosophy of the Company, too. Wasn't it? Any means ta the end?

"Ya complain that there was no difference between the tyranny of Capitalism and that of the examples we had of Communism. But ya practiced th' same bad behavior in the name of something as puny as efficiency.

"That's really it ain't it, Land? Finally, it takes just too much precious time ta convince people of your 'truth'. Takes too much patience ta answer their questions—ta overcome their doubts. Force is required ta save 'em from themselves. An' that means enforcers—apostles or dupes, volunteers or draftees, militants or military. All—what did ya call 'em—expendable? Ain't that a four-bit word for 'waste', Land. And who gets wasted in the end. This 'expendable' humanity or *your* humanity?"

And, Sven wondered momentarily, if Matt had been right. Had his own humanity been expended, too.

"You, of all people, oughta know better."

"Don't be a simple shit. People don't think. They don't want to think. That takes too much effort. They want somebody to fix it if it's broke. And it's certainly broke."

"Waal, I hate to tell ya, Land. Ya been wasting yer time and energy. We didn't know any of this. We sure as hell didn't tell Andrews about it. We didn't even tell him we found the canister."

"No, but you finally fucked it up. Your interference, your delays, your attracting attention to us." His voice rose in pitch.

Sven studied Land's face between glances at the card. Were Matt and Leda yet to be the targets of this old man's revenge for a failed plot? A plot that he and his own blind power plays had bungled?

"Waal, I think that the real problem with your operation was somewhere else. Ya had the FBI drinkin' yer booze and fuckin' yer help for several years before we stumbled onta the scene. The fact is, we're the easiest ta blame, ain't we, Land. An' the most defenseless."

"Defenseless? You took out a twenty million dollar yacht with at least that much command and communications gear. You think there was nothing but roulette wheels and black jack tables on INSHALLA? You threatened the lives of my team. You destroyed the yacht of another operative and crippled his effort, further limiting our abilities. You can't keep out of other people's business."

"Ya mean, we didn't lay down and die so ya could get on with your game. How many other people did you 'waste'—that's the popular term now, ain't it Land—waste? 'God's will'—isn't that what *inshalla* means? Obviously your game was not His will."

"Do you naive people think that what has allowed you to live your fat lives of comfort and inattention for a half-century has been bought with Christian kindness?"

The 9mm had long since been lowered as Land's passion for his subject had warmed, but he raised it again on this note. Sven pretended to pay no attention.

Two years ago the cleat on the jiffy reefing downhaul, which was screwed to the side of the wooden boom, had pulled out and Sven had replaced it with one a little larger.

"Land, I think yer a bitter old man whose wants has always been got by brute force. Now, through no fault a' mine, them dreams has been dashed and I just happen ta be handy and easy ta blame. I'm th' one that had th' balls to tell ya that yer a criminal. Yer one of th' animals that is no better than th' corrupt bastards in suits who you attack. They rape us quietly and subtly and legally. Yer just cruder. Ya hide behind a ideology and defend yer action just like the suits do. The important difference here, Land, is that for just a moment ya've crawled from under the rock of like-minded protectors and someone has told ya what a slimy thing ya are." He paused again, then without looking up from the compass, he went on.

"I'm sure that ya've got this last act all worked out. Ya shoot me an' dump me over the side. Then ya drive the boat some where and scuttle her near enough for you to get ashore in the dink."

"Close enough," Land confirmed. But his quarry could not suppress the chuckle.

Sven had put the larger cleat on the boom because it had larger holes to accommodate larger screws.

"Yer outa yer head and outa yer league, Land. You can't handle this boat as she's rigged. All ya know about, if ya know anything, is how to drive a stink pot. And ya think by wavin' your hand-gun courage around that I'll douse the sails so you can conveniently shoot me and ya can drive this thing away under power."

The prongs of the larger cleat also protruded further from the boom, making it easier to fasten the line in the haste of shortening sail in a rising wind.

"Don't underestimate me. You didn't think I could get to shore when you fired INSHALLA, either. I didn't know about Madeline's little game, but it wasn't the first time I'd had to think on my feet to save my ass. Look at me, I'm almost 80 and I'm still better than most men I know that are half my age."

Sven chuckled again and sat down. Never taking his eyes off the compass, he turned the helm three or four spokes, and heard the clank of the block at the boom end as the main sheet suddenly slacked.

"Waal, ya see, Land. That's yer trouble, ya don't know many 'better' men."

The prominent prongs of the larger downhaul cleat caught under the hook of Land's jaw just as the boom slammed into his temple. He may have been dead before he was dragged across the opposite cockpit cushion, over the lifeline and then brought to the jolting stop as the sheet finally arrested the mad jibe of the boom.

He hung, limp, suspended by his jawbone for a few moments, then the cartilage parted under the weight of the huge body. As the sail filled and the boat heeled, the end of the boom dipped and Land was deposited, almost tenderly, into the warm water of a sea that he had regularly traversed, but about which he really knew...nothing.

Sven had not looked up from the glowing card. Reaching behind, he lifted the horseshoe life ring out of its rack and tossed it overboard. He continued to round up into the wind—automatically executing a maneuver he had practiced a hundred times before. He hauled in the slack main sheet as the boom came amidships and cleated it, then he strode forward and released the main halyard. The main cascaded down along the starboard side deck as he rolled in the ginny and fired off the diesel. In less than five minutes he was up wind from the place where he judged Land to be.

The sickly moon was little help. He dutifully criss-crossed his earlier track in a methodical search. Frequently turning off the engine, he called into the silent night and received no answer.

After an hour of repositioning, searching ever farther down wind and down current, Sven snagged the bobbing life ring with his boathook. He set sails again, found his previous course and went about his business. GULL was due in Block Island.

Sven had a contract to honor—and Sybil to think about.

THE END

About the Author

The author is a retired Professor and a sailor of some fifty years experience. He has lately abandoned living aboard his sloop for a new home in Hawaii's Manoa valley where he resides with his wife, author, Shirley Tong Parola.

0-595-20653-0